What Lies Beneath

What Lies Beneath

Sarah Rayne

FELONY & MAYHEM PRESS • NEW YORK

All the characters and events portrayed in this work are fictitious.

WHAT LIES BENEATH

A Felony & Mayhem Mystery

PRINTING HISTORY
First UK edition (Simon & Schuster): 2011
Felony & Mayhem edition: 2013

Copyright © 2011 by Sarah Rayne

ISBN: 978-1-937384-67-8

Manufactured in the United States of America

Library of Congress Cataloging-in-Publication Data

Rayne, Sarah.
  What lies beneath / Sarah Rayne.
   pages cm
  ISBN 978-1-937384-67-8
  1. Chemical weapons--Fiction. I. Title.
  PR6118.A55W43 2013
  823'.92--dc23
                    2013008080

For my brother, Tony Duggan,
who provided the concept
of the 'Poisoned Village'
for this book.

ACKNOWLEDGEMENTS

Grateful thanks are due to Philip and Keith Cartwright, Organ Builders and Tuners of Slindon, Staffordshire, for their excellent help and practical demonstrations of the mechanics of church organs in the beautiful St Andrew's Church, Weston; also to Rob Robinson, who supplied invaluable technical details about light aircraft and their capabilities.

The icon above says you're holding a copy of a book in the Felony & Mayhem "Wild Card" category. We can't promise these will press particular buttons, but we do guarantee they will be unusual, well written, and worth a reader's time. If you enjoy this book, you may well like other "Wild Card" titles from Felony & Mayhem Press.

For more about these books, and other Felony & Mayhem titles, or to place an order, please visit our website at:

www.FelonyAndMayhem.com

Other "Wild Card" titles from

FELONY&MAYHEM

What Lies Beneath

CHAPTER ONE

ELLA HAYWOOD WAS IN the delicatessen counter queue at the supermarket when she heard the news that ripped open her life and brought her childhood nightmares gibbering back.

She had not been expecting those particular ghosts to come boiling out of the past while she was waiting for her farmhouse Cheddar to be cut and weighed, but a gossipy shopper just ahead of her was telling anyone who cared to listen that Priors Bramley was to be reopened—imagine that, after all these years they were going to let people back into the Poisoned Village.

'The Poisoned Village'. The words fell on Ella's mind like hammer-blows and for several minutes everything else was blotted out. Priors Bramley, the tiny village abandoned fifty years earlier when a government department had planned to route a motorway through it, and had peremptorily rehoused all the residents elsewhere. The motorway had never been built, though, because another department had seized on the deserted village for an experimental site. Priors Bramley had been drenched in an ill-judged and macabre cocktail of chemicals, which meant the village had had to be sealed off. And no one had been there since.

The gossipy shopper knew all the facts. That long-planned motorway was finally going to be built, she said,

1

very self-important, and in a few days, Priors Bramley would be decontaminated. People would be able to walk down the village street again, right up to the gates of Cadence Manor, if they wanted.

'Always providing they aren't worried about breathing in whatever's still lingering on the air,' said a sepulchral voice from the end of the queue.

'Oh, nothing's lingered there for years,' said the gossipy one cheerfully. 'The authorities simply forgot to take down the barbed wire and the notices, that's all. It's a piece of the past being reclaimed,' she added romantically.

'Reclaimed and then bulldozed and covered with concrete,' said the pragmatist, to which the shopper tossed her head, said some people had no soul, and went off with her veal and ham pie.

Back at home, panic clutched at Ella's stomach. She pictured in her mind's eye Cadence Manor—huge rusting iron gates, the sunshine glinting on them...Ivy-covered walls, crumbling brickwork and an air of brooding desolation...The images rose up sharply, and with them came the memory of her mother declaring the Cadence family had been a bunch of villains, never mind they were supposed to be respected city bankers, rich and influential. 'Not to be trusted,' she always said. 'Not a one of them.'

Still, what had lain behind those festoons of barbed wire all this time surely could not damage Ella—not now. There was nothing she need do about it. Derek would certainly have agreed with that if he knew what was beyond those spiky defences, which he did not. But one of Derek's philosophies was that you never troubled trouble until trouble troubled you.

Amy, their granddaughter, had once asked Ella how she had put up with Gramps's little sayings for so long, but Amy's generation did not understand about marriage— not the permanent kind, such as Ella had entered into. Amy thought that because Gran was young in the 1960s she must have had a permissive, flower-power time, but flower power and the permissive society had never actually reached Bramley, and Derek was then, as now, an auditor at the County Council, and a rising star in the local Operatic Society as well, so flower power and permissiveness had never really been an option.

Amy was coming to stay in a couple of weeks' time, at the start of the Easter holidays. It would be nice to see her and hear about her life at university; Ella always listened round-eyed to Amy's tales. None of the things Amy described would have been remotely thinkable in Ella's own life. But then some of the things in Ella's life would not be remotely thinkable to Amy—it was important to remember that.

By that evening, Ella felt better. Probably all that talk about opening up the village and finally building the motorway was just a rumour, or an item on a vague council agenda and unlikely actually to happen. There could be protest groups at the destruction of green belt— all kinds of things that would prevent the whole thing.

But the next morning a council leaflet slapped through the letterbox, horridly explicit. Government approval had been given for the revival of the 1950s motorway scheme, said the leaflet, and added firmly that this was very good news for everyone. The motorway would not actually go through Priors Bramley, but a link road would, which meant the demolition of the major part of the village. Preliminary plans could be inspected at the council's offices between 9 a.m. and 5 p.m. any weekday. Local residents could be assured there was no longer any danger from the chemical trials carried out in the 1950s, but to be on the safe side a team of decontamination experts would go in on the tenth of this month. The information about there being no danger was repeated so many times Ella thought most people reading it would keep their windows and doors closed for the next six months.

She did not take in much of the scientific information about decontamination or the original chemical experiment—she had never been very good at science at school. A boys' subject, her mother used to say. Concentrate on the cookery classes: that's what will get you a husband. In those days getting a husband had been the prime goal for girls. Ella sometimes wondered what her mother would have thought of Amy, currently rioting through three years at Durham University, studying archaeology and anthropology.

She threw the council's leaflet in the bin, but when even Derek began to talk about the Poisoned Village being opened for the new motorway, Ella knew the past was surging forward, and it was a dark and dangerous past. She would have to do something.

Entries from an Undated Journal

The time has come when I will have to do something...

Because in seven days I'm going to die.

There! I've written it at last. I am going to die. And now I see it set down on the page, it's suddenly and dreadfully real.

I'm afraid of dying but I'm equally afraid of going mad while waiting for death—and by mad I don't mean those spells of darkness that sometimes close down over me like a stifling curtain...They never lasted long, those darknesses—no, I'll amend that—they never *seemed* to last long, and in any case it's important to remember I always managed to fight my way back up into the light.

By going mad, I mean the real thing. The tumble all the way down into an endless, unforgiving blackness—the blackness you see staring out of the empty eyes of the poor creatures locked away in Bedlam: drained, husked-out fragments of humanity who were once people. So let's make it very clear at the outset that I was never mad in that way.

I'm hoping that writing everything down will stop me speculating what's ahead. (Will it be quick? Will I struggle?) And although I don't suppose anyone will ever read this journal, you never know, so I'll write it as well as possible. I used to have the way of turning a good phrase at one time—it's vanity to say it, but I don't care—although I never had any romantic dreams about writing books. But I've had my romantic moments, that's something else I'd like understood.

I'll count the seven days ahead of me, of course, although I'll try not to count the hours. But there's a clock in here and I can hear it ticking the seconds away. I suspect I might have to find a way to muffle that clock before the end.

I don't think it will be a very comfortable death and if I had any courage I'd find a way of putting a swift and clean end to myself beforehand. But there are no sharp knives here, no cut-throat razors, no pills that could be downed in huge quantities. No gas ovens to turn on or lengths of rope to fashion into a noose. And there's just a chance I'll escape, and although I was never a gambler in the accepted sense, I'm certainly going to gamble on that tiny chance.

I think I'll be reasonably comfortable in the time that's left. It's knowing what's ahead that might tip me over the edge. That and the ticking clock. I could simply not wind it, but then I might lose all track of the days and I don't think I can do that.

Perhaps I can pretend the ticking is something else— something small and unthreatening and friendly? A small mouse behind the wall, or an energetic house martin building its new home under the eaves somewhere. Yes, I'll create a pretence that it's a house martin, flying to and fro.

Actually, when I look back I can see I was always very clever at pretence. I certainly fooled all the Cadences—the entire smug, self-satisfied clan. Or did I? I'd have to say there were times when I wondered if Crispian sensed what I was thinking. He had a way of looking at people, a sort of speculative appraisal.

I knew from quite an early age I was going to kill Crispian Cadence, and I suppose if you're intent on killing someone, it's possible your victim might sense danger, even without realizing the exact nature of the danger.

Danger. It was remarkable how anything I ever had to do with Crispian always spelled danger.

The Present

Ella's mother used to say anything to do with the Cadences, no matter how remote, always spelled danger.

Faced with the unsealing of Priors Bramley, Ella was forced to admit her mother had been right. This was a danger she wanted to ignore, but other people were involved—two other people to be exact, and both were still here, living in Upper Bramley. She invited them to her house that evening, confident they would accept; they had always looked to her for guidance and leadership, right from childhood. Derek would be safely out of the way because he had a rehearsal with the Operatic Society. They were doing *The Mikado* this year, and Derek was playing Nanki-Poo, the hero. He was a bit stout for the part, but Ella would make sure he slimmed down in time. Some people said he was a bit old as well, but there was nothing anyone could do about his age.

She tidied and polished her sitting room, which Derek still called 'the lounge' despite all her reminders, opened a bottle of wine, and set out a few canapés. They were actually bought frozen from the supermarket, but no one would know that. Arranged on good china plates they looked home-made and quite classy.

Clement Poulter was the first to arrive, and although he was not exactly nervous, he was certainly not very comfortable. Ella noticed a faint sheen of sweat on his forehead and the top of his head where the hair was thinning.

'I suppose this is about the reopening of Priors Bramley,' he said.

'It is,' said Ella, firmly. 'I thought we should have a little meeting about it. Just the three of us. In case of any... awkwardness that might be ahead. They really are going to bring it out of quarantine, aren't they?' She had tried out several acceptable phrases before lighting on this one, which seemed to reduce the whole thing to nothing worse than a dose of chickenpox.

'They are,' said Clem, nodding. 'They're going to fumigate it, sterilize it, disinfect it—however you want to word it. But I'm seeing it as the village being brought out of purdah.'

'Whatever you call it, it's being done on the tenth,' said Ella, before Clem could become carried away with one of his annoying fantasies.

'I know. We were sent a poster to display in the library. I'm going to arrange one of my little exhibitions— the village before they poisoned it.' Clem liked arranging little exhibitions at his library; he always had one for the Operatic Society's productions, with photographs of the cast and notes about the plot. 'I shan't call it that, of course,' he said. 'Just "Old Bramley", or something like that. And it'd be a shame not to make some kind of written record of Priors Bramley before they demolish it. There's masses of material lying around. Remember that local ghost story about people hearing organ music from within the old church on some nights? I do love that tale, don't you?'

'That's just people's imagination,' said Ella. It was typical of Clem to miss the threat in all this—to focus on unimportant details: the stupid ghost tales that had grown up about the village, and his diaries, which he was always telling people about.

'Yes, but people like a ghost story,' Clem was saying. "Specially something about a really old church like St Anselm's.'

St Anselm's church. Despite the warm April evening, Ella shivered.

'If you walk to the highest point of Mordwich Bank you can see the sun glinting on the stained-glass windows,' said Clem. 'It looks sort of remote and unreal. The lost church in the Poisoned Village.' He contemplated this phrase approvingly for a moment. 'It's absolutely classic English ghost stuff.'

'Derek says the only people who hear anything are the ones walking home from the Red Lion late at night,' said Ella tartly. She had never told Derek or anyone else that she sometimes dreamed she could hear the organ chords, menacing and achingly lonely.

'Yes, but it's still a good story,' said Clem. 'Is Veronica coming?'

'Yes, of course. She should be here by now.'

'Oh, she'll be late. She always is—she likes to make an entrance.'

But Veronica was not particularly late, although Ella was sorry to see that as usual she was overdressed for the occasion.

'I see you've got some of those frozen canapés,' said Veronica, having ostentatiously arranged her unsuitably short skirt over her thighs. 'They're good, aren't they? I bought some last week for a—a friend who was coming to supper.'

There was no call for Veronica to bat her eyelashes in that simpering fashion: it was clear she meant a man. Nor was there any need for Veronica to say the canapés had been on special offer. 'Two for the price of one; they're very cheap, aren't they?'

Ella handed Veronica a glass of wine, and said, 'We need to talk about Priors Bramley.'

'I thought that was why you phoned,' said Veronica. 'It's a bit worrying, I suppose. It's good about the motorway, but opening up the village made me feel quite shivery. Didn't you feel shivery, Clem?'

'Well, personally I seldom shiver over anything these days.'

'Did either of you ever tell anyone what happened that morning?' said Ella.

'Oh God, no.' But Clem poured himself another glass of wine with a hand that shook.

Without even being asked, thought Ella, annoyed, but she only said, 'Veronica?'

'I've never told a soul,' said Veronica at once. 'Not a soul. We said we'd take it to the grave with us, and I shall do so. We made a pact, don't you remember? We swore on all we held sacred never to tell.'

'I don't think we did that exactly,' said Ella. 'There's no need to be so dramatic. What we did was to promise each other we would never tell anyone.'

❄ ❄ ❄

The promise had been made over fifty years earlier, when the three of them were children. It had started with a dare, although afterwards none of them could remember whose idea that had been.

A plane was going to fly over Priors Bramley that Saturday in order to drop a small explosive device. But it was not a bomb, people said firmly. It was the planned and precise dispersing of chemical substances; a geological and botanical experiment. Whatever it was called, it was quite a big event for the area; people talked about it avidly. It helped balance the shock the Priors Bramley residents had received when they were told they had to leave their homes.

Clem's great-aunt Rose had lived in a cottage in Priors Bramley all her life. 'She had to move out, though,' he said, as they walked out of Upper Bramley that Saturday morning. 'She said she doesn't mind giving way to progress, but she doesn't hold with folk careering along roads at fifty miles an hour. And the money they gave her wouldn't buy a dog kennel, never mind a decent house for folk who had to put up with six years of fighting Hitler.' He put on a voice like a cross old lady when he said this, and Veronica giggled nervously.

'The lady in the wool shop told my mum she'd spent all those years dodging German bombs and now they're going to drop one right on her own village,' put in Ella.

'It isn't a real bomb, though, is it?' said Veronica worriedly. 'It's only to spray chemical stuff into the village to see what happens to the plants and things. Then they'll build the road. We had a letter through the door telling us about it.'

'So did we,' said Clem. 'But my father says they aren't telling us the truth. He reckons it'll be ages before they get round to making the motorway, and he says they're experimenting with nerve agents, like that place near Boscombe Down. They've got laboratories and whatnot there, and it's all really secret.'

'What's a nerve agent?'

'I think it's stuff they might want to use if there's a war. My father doesn't think it's a good idea at all; he says those things make people really ill or grow two heads. He's pretty worried about the Russians, though. Well, he's pretty worried about a lot of people in the world.'

'I don't want an atom bomb to be dropped on Bramley,' said Veronica. 'Atom bombs burn your bones. I heard my parents talk about it.'

'They aren't dropping an atom bomb,' said Clem in exasperation.

'Whatever they're dropping, they aren't doing it until midday, anyway,' said Ella. 'So we could walk through the village one last time, couldn't we? I'd like to do that.'

'I would too,' said Clem eagerly. 'I could write about it in my diary. Did I tell you I was given a diary for Christmas?'

'Yes, about a million times.'

'It'd be a pretty good thing to write. "The Last Day of a Doomed Village", that's what I'd call it. And it could be an adventure for Ella's birthday.'

Ella's tenth birthday was the day before, which was important because of being double figures. Veronica's mother had said it was a landmark, and added it was a pity Ella's mother had not let her have a party.

'She's got too much to do to be having parties,' Ella told her friends. 'But she'll make sandwiches and we can have a picnic on Mordwich Bank. After the dare, I mean.'

Veronica was still not sure about the bomb, but they generally did what Ella said on account of her being the eldest, so she said it would be a good thing to walk down the village street on its last day.

They set off at half-past ten, which Clem thought would give them masses of time for the dare.

'I had to tell my mother a lie about where we're going,' said Veronica, as they went over the old railway bridge, which was called the Crinoline Bridge, and from there into Sparrowfeld Lane, which was fringed with big horse chestnut trees, and where they came to collect conkers every autumn. 'And I had to promise we weren't going anywhere near Priors Bramley, on account of the plane and the bomb.'

'It *isn't a* bomb—'

'Well, whatever it is, how long will we be doing this dare?'

'Not long. It's twenty to eleven now,' said Ella, who had been given a watch for her birthday. 'We could do the walk in half an hour and we'd be in Mordwich Meadow for half-past eleven easily. We'll see the plane go over while we eat our sandwiches.'

They went down Mordwich Bank towards the village in its saucer-shaped piece of land. For several weeks the area around Priors Bramley had buzzed with all kinds of activity—people moving out of their shops and houses, like Clem's great-aunt Rose, and men unwinding immense rolls of barbed wire to fence the village in and keep people out, and nailing up notices that said 'Danger!' and 'Keep Out!'.

'It's very quiet,' said Veronica nervously as they went round the curve in the lane.

'That means we'll hear the plane coming.'

'Good, because I don't want to be sprayed with poison or grow two heads.'

'It's just for the plants, I *told* you. And you'd better take that red hair ribbon off,' said Ella suddenly. 'It'll show up on the hillside, and we don't want to be seen.'

CHAPTER TWO

Even without Veronica's red hair ribbon to advertise their presence they had to be careful, but as they approached the lane that wound straight into Priors Bramley, the only two people they saw were a workman knocking nails into a big notice board, and a policeman talking to him.

They pressed back into the hedge and Clem said, in a whisper, that they could squeeze through it. 'Then we can scurry along until we find a break in the wire. I bet there'll be a bit where we can wriggle through.'

'I don't want to wriggle on the grass. I've got my pink frock on,' objected Veronica.

'That's your silly fault.'

They squeezed through the hedge and ran along the sides of the spiky wire, keeping as low as they could. Ella's heart was racing and she expected to hear the policeman shout to them at any minute. But nothing happened and everywhere was silent.

It was Clem who found a place where they could edge through the sharp coils of wire. 'But keep flat to the ground,' he said. 'I don't think that policeman can see us from where he is, but you never know.'

Tacked to the fence was another warning sign. This one was in scarlet lettering.

Government Notice.
DANGER—KEEP OUT!
This village is the subject of important trials for the testing of the compound Geranos. Unauthorized persons must not enter beyond this point.

Veronica faltered at the sight of this, but Ella grabbed her hand and hurried her along the road because if they were going to do this they didn't have time to waste. From within the village came the chime of St Anselm's church clock. Eleven chimes.

'That might be the last time we ever hear that clock chime,' said Veronica. 'That's sad, isn't it?'

'They aren't going to poison the clock,' said Ella. 'It'll go on for ages. Anyway, we'll hear it chime the quarters. A single bong for the quarter and two bongs for the half-hour.'

'It's still sad, however many bongs it is.'

'And anyway,' said Clement, 'St Anselm's hasn't been used for years and years. I'm surprised they've still got the clock going at all. The church has got deathwatch beetle or something. That's why everyone goes to St Michael's on Sundays.'

But it *is* used, thought Ella. None of you knows it, but when no one is around somebody goes inside the church and fills it with music. I've heard it.

'Where now?' said Veronica, as they reached the village street.

'Cadence Manor,' said Ella. 'That's what we said. It isn't far.'

'We'd better keep as close to the buildings as we can so we won't be seen.' Veronica kept looking nervously over her shoulder.

'That's my great-aunt Rose's house, just along there,' said Clem, stopping to point down a winding little lane near the bakery. 'I used to go there for Saturday tea every week. We had fresh currant bread from the bakery.'

The village street was silent and still, and Veronica whispered that it was like a ghost town.

'Maybe we'll become the ghosts,' said Clem.

'Oh, *no!*'

'It'd be good.' Clem was well away on a new story. 'We'd be the three children who haunt the deserted village. And when they build the motorway, sometimes drivers will see us, wandering down the road at midnight.'

'It's eleven o'clock in the morning,' said Ella repressively.

'I know, but you only get ghosts at midnight.'

They all knew the village quite well, which Ella thought should have made their walk ordinary, but somehow it did not. Priors Bramley seemed to have changed: it felt as if eyes watched from the deserted shops, and invisible people peered out from behind the shuttered windows. It's waiting to die, she thought. It knows what's going to happen.

Here was the little shop that sold bull's-eyes and sherbet dab with liquorice sticks, and next to it was the wool shop where Ella's mother bought knitting yarn and patterns.

With a show of bravado Clem pushed open the door of the sweet shop, and the little bell over the door clanged tinnily. It made them all jump, and Clem, who had been going to make a joke about asking for a quarter of fudge, backed away.

'What'll happen to the sweets and wool and everything?' asked Veronica, in a half-whisper as they walked along the street. 'They won't be poisoned, will they?'

'My great-aunt Rose said all the shop people packed everything away in wooden boxes and some vans came and took the boxes away. Buck up, Veronica, think how brave you'll feel when we're up in Mordwich Meadow, scoffing our sandwiches.'

'We'll sing "Happy Birthday to Ella",' said Veronica, trying not to let her voice wobble.

St Anselm's was ahead of them, and Ella's heart was starting to beat very fast. The lich-gate leading to the ancient, disused church was surrounded by trees—old cedars and English oaks. In the morning sunlight the leaves cast dappled shadows on the ground, and Clem paused to stare along the rutted driveway leading to the church itself.

'My father says *lich* means corpse,' he said. 'Dead body. They used to carry the bodies up to the church and rest them on the lich-gate for the first bit of the funeral.'

'That's really creepy,' said Veronica, shuddering. 'Your father tells you horrid things.'

'They used to ring a lich bell too, sometimes. Death bell,' said Clem.

'Well, whatever they used to ring, let's get on,' said Ella, who was hating being so near to the shadowy church.

'It's a nice old church, isn't it?' said Veronica, not moving.

'My father says it's tragic the way it's been left to rot,' said Clem. 'Can you see the coloured windows? There look, through the trees.'

'One of the windows is broken,' said Veronica. 'And—' She broke off, her eyes widening, and grabbed Clem's arm. 'Did you hear that?'

'What? I can't hear anything,' said Ella, but her heart was starting to race.

'*Listen*,' said Veronica urgently. 'Someone's in there.' From within the abandoned church came the sound of footsteps.

An icy hand closed round Ella's heart, and her skin prickled with fear.

'Veronica's right,' said Clem, still looking back at the church. 'There is someone in there.'

'Yes, but whoever it is, is only doing what we're doing,' said Veronica. 'Saying goodbye to the church.'

'Probably the vicar,' said Ella, walking towards the manor, hoping the others would follow.

'Shouldn't we go in there and tell whoever it is to come out?' said Veronica, starting back towards the lich-gate.

Ella turned and ran after her, grabbing her arm. 'Veronica, we can't, we're not supposed to be here.' She risked a glance along the path. There was the low door, black with age, slightly open, and it was possible to see the shadows lying thickly across the stone floor just inside. Pulling Veronica away, she said, 'We mustn't go in there, we really mustn't.'

'Anyway, whoever it is, he'll know about the plane coming over at twelve o'clock and the bomb. Everyone knows,' said Clem.

'It's a bit creepy, though, isn't it?'

'No. Let's keep walking to Cadence Manor, like we said. Just up to the gates. Whoever's in there won't see us—the road goes round to the left after those houses.'

'I thought this would be an adventure, but it isn't,' said Veronica, as they went on, leaving the church behind. 'I don't like it,' she said, but she walked between the other two, around the left-hand curve of the street and across the cobblestones that had once been part of an old coaching inn.

'The church clock's striking again—one chime. Is that for the quarter-hour?' she asked.

'Yes. Quarter-past eleven. We've got masses of time yet,' said Ella.

'How much further is it?'

'Not far. There are the gates. They're huge, aren't they?'

The gates to Cadence Manor were tall and tipped here and there with gold, but there were patches of rust on the black scrollwork. The manor itself was hidden by a high wall and trees.

'My father said they used to be really rich, those Cadences, only they were moneylenders and you shouldn't trust people like that,' said Clem.

'My mother says they were Italian bankers,' said Veronica. 'She said they used to have grand parties here, years and years ago, before the war. They went on for a whole weekend, sometimes, the parties. But they gave a lot of money to the children's home at Bramley Gate.'

'Well, *my* mother said the Cadences were a bunch of villains,' said Ella. 'She said you couldn't trust a one of them, never mind they were rich and all the rest.'

'That's the old lodge house,' said Clem, pointing to the square grey building on the left of the gates.

'It's a bit crumbly, isn't it? And the gardens are all overgrown.'

'If the Cadences really were a bunch of villains, like my mother says, I think it serves them right if their house crumbles.'

'Let's just go in through the gates, so we can say we've been to Cadence Manor before it was poisoned by the Geranos stuff and crunched up for the motorway,' said Clem. 'Then we'll go home.'

'We'd better go along Meadow Lane,' said Ella. 'We can climb the wall and get over the stile to Mordwich Bank. We can't go near the house itself anyway.'

'Why not?'

'We haven't got time.'

'What if there's another policeman there?'

'There won't be—they won't think anyone would climb over the wall.'

The gates were stiff and almost rusted into place, but when Clem pushed hard, one of them swung inwards, the hinges squealing like an animal. The sound tore across the quiet morning, and Ella jumped and glanced behind her in case anyone had heard and was coming to catch them.

Stepping through the massive black and gilt gates felt like entering another world. They all looked nervously towards the windows of the lodge. Curtains still hung at several of the windows. Ella thought one of them moved, but before she could be sure they heard a shout from the street—outside the gates.

'Someone's coming,' said Clem. 'Let's get out before we're caught.' He grabbed the girls' hands.

'Where?'

'Towards the house,' said Clem. 'Come on. We can climb over the wall and be back in the lane, like Ella said.'

'It'll be the policeman,' gasped Veronica. 'Or that workman banging up the notices.'

'Or whoever was creeping around in the church.'

'Oh, *no...*'

'Never mind who it is, we mustn't be caught!' said Ella. 'Come *on!*'

They were halfway along the tree-lined drive, still holding hands and running as hard as they could towards the manor itself, when there was a movement within the trees, and the figure of a man stepped out and stood in front of them. The sunlight was behind him, silhouetting him against the brightness.

They had been running at full pelt, but they skidded to a sudden stop, and stood uncertainly. The man did not speak, and Ella felt Veronica's hand tighten around hers. She shuddered, staring at the man, trying to think of something to say.

It was Clem who finally spoke. He said, quite politely, 'I'm very sorry if we shouldn't be here. We just wanted to—um—take one last walk through the village. But we'll go now, we really will.'

The worst part was that the man did not reply. He took a step or two nearer—he doesn't walk, he sort of shambles, thought Ella, horror sweeping over her—and they could all see there was something wrong about his face. He did not come any closer, but he peered at them intently as if he was trying to decide what to do. Clem tightened his hold on both girls' hands, and ran towards the trees, pulling them along with him.

They ran as hard as they could, until they were deep in the undergrowth that had grown up around the deserted manor.

'Oh, please stop,' gasped Veronica. 'I've got a stitch—I can't run any more...' She bent over to touch her toes.

'Has he gone?' said Clem, panting and looking back through the trees.

'I think so. I can't see him.'

'Who was he? He wasn't the policeman, was he? Was he the workman?'

'I don't know,' said Ella.

'There was something wrong with his face,' said Veronica, straightening up. 'And did you see the way he stared and stared at us, as if he wanted to do something very bad to us? My mother says you have to be careful of men in case they try to—you know—*touch* you.'

'We'd better go round the side of the house,' said Ella. 'We'll climb over the wall like Clem said.'

They forced their way through the thick rank grass, sending thistle-heads flying, trampling down the rose-bay willowherb, no longer caring if the man heard them, intent only on getting to the wall that backed onto Meadow Lane. Once Veronica stumbled and half-turned her ankle on a stone, but Clem hauled her up again and they went on and came out onto a rutted and cracked terrace. There, before them, were the rearing stones of Cadence Manor. Ella stared at it in fear.

Then two things happened almost at exactly the same time. The first was that they heard the man coming through the trees towards them.

The second was the sound of St Anselm's church clock, chiming the half-hour before midday.

❀ ❀ ❀

There was no time to think or plan. They ran straight towards the house and half fell through the main doors. Ella's heart was racing and she thought she might be sick from fear, but they had to get away from the man, they absolutely had to…As they went into the great ruined hall, the smell of damp and dirt and loneliness reared up like a wall. Veronica flinched, but Clem dragged her inside.

No sunlight came into the hall and there was a bad moment when none of them could see anything. But as their eyes adjusted they saw there were doors opening off and a wide stairway directly ahead. The banisters were sagging and some of the stairs were missing.

'In there?' gasped Clem, pointing to a room with a half-open door.

'No!' said Ella at once.

'Why not?'

Ella stared at him. Because that's where the ghosts are, she thought. Terrible ghosts. It's the place where I mustn't go, not ever. But she managed to say, 'Because we'd be trapped. Let's go up the stairs. We can hide on the landing and if he comes in to look for us, we'll wait until he goes into one of the rooms—'

'But the plane,' said Veronica in a frightened voice. 'How long is it until the plane comes?'

'Half an hour,' said Clem. 'We've got plenty of time. Once he's gone we'll run back downstairs and outside. We'll be on Mordwich Bank ages before the plane comes.'

They went cautiously up the stairs; they were rickety and the wood had rotted completely away in places so it was necessary to tread carefully. Veronica was crying, a snuffly whining cry, that made Ella say sharply, 'Do shut up or he'll hear you.'

They reached the landing, which had tall narrow windows with seats set into them, and crouched down behind the banisters.

'He's coming,' whispered Ella suddenly. 'I can hear his footsteps.'

The footsteps came nearer and a figure stood in the doorway below. It was too dim to see him very clearly, but Ella knew they were all remembering his face—it had been somehow misshapen as if a hand had wiped over it before it had quite set and smeared some of the features. She shuddered and pressed back into the shadows, her heart thudding. Clem was gripping the banisters, staring down at the man, and Veronica's face was tear-stained. If Veronica did not start crying again they would probably be all right—the man would think they had run off into the grounds and he would go away.

But he did not. He stood very still for a moment— as if he's sniffing the air like an animal, thought Ella in horror—and then, very deliberately, as if he knew exactly where they were, he crossed the hall towards the stairs.

CHAPTER THREE

For a DREADFUL MOMENT none of them knew what to do, but as the man stepped on the first stair a shaft of sunlight from one of the narrow windows fell across him and they saw again the frightening stare in his eyes and the dreadful *wrongness* of his face. Ella could not bear it. She looked back at the wide passage behind them. There were five or six doors, some half-open, others hanging crookedly on their hinges, but one near the far end was firmly closed. She touched Veronica's hand, then Clem's, and pointed to it.

They tiptoed towards the closed door. The man was coming quite slowly up the stairs. Sunshine poured in through the windows so it was just possible he could not see them through its glare. Praying the door would not squeak, Ella opened it. It did squeak, but only faintly, and they tumbled inside, closing it. The room was empty. There was a deep bay window and a massive chimney breast, which had half fallen away from the wall; there were piles of bricks and bits of timber, and a gaping blackness where the hearth would have been.

'Will he come in after us?' whispered Veronica, cramming her fist into her mouth.

'He might, but we'll hide behind that crumbly brickwork by the chimney,' said Clem. 'Have you still got that red hair ribbon, Vron? Put it in that far corner so he'll think we're over there. Then we'll dodge out while he's looking, and run for our lives. All right?'

'But will we get out before the plane comes?' whispered Veronica, doing as Clem said.

'Yes, there's masses of time.' Ella said this confidently, but she had glanced at her watch and seen with horror it was already twenty to twelve. Her heart thumped with panic. What would happen to them if they did not get out before the plane sent its dreadful bomb onto the village?

Grabbing Veronica's hand, she pulled her into the small space behind the chimney breast. They had to squeeze to get in. A sooty stench came up from the hole in the floor and Veronica shuddered. Clem tried to squash in with them, but there was no room, and he looked frantically about him, then ran across to a tall bookcase and crammed in behind it.

'He's coming down the passageway,' whispered Ella, urgently.

They waited in terrified silence, their hearts pounding, hardly daring to breathe. The footsteps paused at each door and then moved on. Ella stared at the dull surface of the closed door, willing the man to walk past it, to decide it would just be another empty room. But empty rooms had things in them, things that must never be seen...

Next to her, Veronica was trembling and Ella put an arm round her. As she did so, a faint sound came to them from the village, and fear swept over her again. It was St Anselm's clock chiming the quarter-hour. There were only fifteen minutes left before the plane came with its dreadful cargo. What would happen if they were still here then? Was Clem's father right, and did the plane really have all that stuff that could give people dreadful diseases? The notice board had said it was called Geranos. If they breathed in the Geranos would they die? If they ran out now they would have plenty of time to scramble over the wall of Cadence Manor and be up the hillside and far enough away to be safe. But they could not run out because of the man. Perhaps he might not mean them any harm: he might be trying to find them to warn them to run out before the plane flew over. But then why hadn't he simply called out?

He was outside the door now—the handle was being turned. The door swung inwards and he was there, staring into the room, and of course he was not here to warn them at all. His eyes glared with madness, and a smile—a truly dreadful smile—widened his face. Ella pressed down into the tiny corner, but he knew where she was, of course—he knew where they all were. There was a movement over her head, and when she looked up, the nightmare face was looking over the top of the broken brickwork. The smile came again, and one hand reached down.

Veronica let out a scared whimper and tried to cower back, but Ella was suddenly angry. A fierce burning anger scalded through her entire body and made her feel ten feet high and as strong as a giant. She sprang up and flew at the man, pushing him as hard as she could, screaming at him to leave them alone. His eyes widened with shock and, caught off balance, he stumbled back, missing his footing and half falling against the bricks of the collapsed chimney breast. The anger gave way to triumph and Ella ran straight at him, her hands clenched into fists, shouting to Veronica and Clem to help her, yelling that they had only ten minutes left to get out.

Veronica hung back, but Clem, his eyes huge with panic and excitement, ran from behind the bookcase and kicked the man, sending him slithering a little way across the floor.

'Harder!' shouted Ella, and Veronica came out from the hiding place.

This time, in the panic and confusion, one of them must have kicked a bit harder because the man rolled all the way across the floor to where the floorboards had collapsed over the old hearth, right onto the edge of the black jagged hole. He made a scrabbling movement at the ground with his hands to stop himself from toppling into the yawning blackness. Ella heard Clem and Veronica both gasp in horror and she thought Clem started forward as if to help the man. But the anger was still filling Ella up, and before either Clem or Veronica could do anything, she bent down and pushed the man as hard as she could. With a dreadful kind of grunting scream, he fell down, down into the bad-smelling blackness of the chimney shaft. There was a whoosh of sound as he fell, and clouds of soot and dust and fragments of bird skeletons flew upwards. Ella and the other two flinched, coughing and gasping, then Clem scrambled to the edge of the hole and peered down.

'Can you see him?' said Veronica, fearfully.

'Um, yes, I think so. He's lying all sort of broken,' said Clem. 'He's right at the bottom.' When he looked back at them his face was white and he seemed as if he might be about to be sick.

'We'd better go down to see,' said Ella.

'We haven't got time,' said Clem, sounding frightened. 'It's nearly twelve o'clock.'

'We'll run for all we're worth,' said Ella. 'But we need to know if he's dead.'

They ran down the stairs, their footsteps echoing loudly in the empty old house, leaving prints behind them.

'Which is the room underneath?' gasped Clem.

'In here.'

'How do you know? Mightn't it be that one?'

'No,' said Ella quickly. 'No, it's this one, I'm sure.' Before Clem could argue she pushed open a door on the ground floor and peered in. 'Yes,' she said. 'That's the room.'

'Is he there?'

'Supposing the man wasn't dead when we left him? And don't say you never thought about that,' said Clem, 'because I bet we all did.'

'I didn't,' said Veronica at once.

'Of course he was dead,' said Ella. 'We knew he was.'

'Did we? You were ten—Vron and I were nine.'

'Excuse me, I was only eight,' said Veronica, who was not having anybody add even one year to her age.

'Well, none of us was old enough to tell if somebody was dead,' said Clem, ignoring the interruption. 'We didn't even go up to him to check his heart or anything.'

'We didn't have time! The church clock was chiming twelve and the plane was coming!' said Ella.

'You don't really think he was alive, do you?' said Veronica nervously, because this really was the grisliest idea to put in a person's mind. It was to be hoped it was not going to spoil her anticipation of the evening planned for later. She had bought new silk underwear and everything.

'But what if he was alive?' said Clem. 'I used to have nightmares about that, you know. About how he might have come round just as the bomb went off. How he might have lain there, with all that poisonous stuff choking him.'

They looked at each other, then Ella said very firmly, 'That's nonsense. His neck was broken.'

There was a rather awkward silence, then Clem gave another of the nervous giggles. 'This is starting to be like a film about three middle-aged people meeting in a teashop to discuss covering up a murder they committed.'

'It's not a matter for silly jokes,' said Ella sharply.

'I know, but on the other hand there's no need to get it out of proportion,' said Clem. 'Or to lose our sense of humour. Or have you mislaid yours?'

'I think that's very unkind of you, Clem. I have a very good sense of humour,' said Ella. 'Derek and I often have a good laugh over all kinds of things.'

'I'm sorry. I was only thinking if anyone filmed this, my part could be played by Anthony Hopkins,' said Clem.

'And I'll be Meryl Streep or Helen Mirren,' put in Veronica eagerly, because this was a much more interesting turn of the conversation, and anything that would push away the really horrid memories was welcome. 'Somebody with cheekbones.' In case anyone was still adding anything to her age, she finished by saying that, of course, she was a good deal younger than Helen Mirren.

Ella banged down the canapé plate with irritable vigour and said, 'I wish you'd take this seriously. They'll find the body—because of course he was dead—and when they do they might find something to link it to us.'

'Like what? Ella, it's over fifty years!'

'You're just being silly,' said Veronica.

Ella said, 'But there is something that might link us.'

'Oh God, what?'

Veronica saw that Ella was looking really ill, almost as if the flesh of her face had fallen away from the bones. This was so dreadful she drank some more wine while she tried to think what to say. Perhaps Clem would think of something. Veronica looked at him hopefully, but Clem was simply staring at Ella in goggle-eyed silence.

In a tight, dry little voice Ella said, 'My wristwatch. I'd been given it the day before for a birthday present. Don't you remember—we checked the time on it?'

'Vaguely. What about it?'

'When we got back to Mordwich Bank,' said Ella, 'I hadn't got it on.'

This time the silence lasted much longer, but in the end Clem said, 'You mean you lost it while we were in Cadence Manor?'

'I must have done.'

'You never said.'

'There was no need to worry about it while Priors Bramley was sealed off.'

'But...it's only a watch,' said Veronica. 'It won't have survived all those years, and even if it did, nobody will know it was yours.'

'It had my initials engraved on it, and the date,' said Ella.

'Well, I suppose a date might be traced back, but initials aren't very recognizable.'

'Mine were,' said Ella. 'ELF—don't you remember? I was Ella Lilian Ford in those days. Have you forgotten how I used to be teased at school about being an elf? And as for the watch not surviving—it was gold. Gold survives everything.'

'Yes, but are you sure it was gold? I don't mean to be rude or anything, but gold's frightfully expensive.' Veronica did not want to say it was unlikely that Ella's mother could have afforded gold, but everybody knew the family had been really hard up.

'Yes, I am sure,' said Ella, her mouth set in the stubborn line Veronica recognized only too well. 'My mother saved up for it for ages because it was a special birthday—double figures—and she wanted to mark it. She did double shifts in the Railwayman's Arms for months beforehand.' She broke off, compressing her lips, and Veronica knew Ella must be very upset indeed, because she hardly ever admitted her mother had worked as a barmaid in an adjoining village. Genteel poverty was the usual pitch, generally on the lines of, 'My family lost their money in the First World War'. Clem's father had once said that far from losing their money in any war, the Fords had never had any money at all, and had been reduced to all kinds of straits to make ends meet. In fact, in certain quarters Ella's mother had been known as Barrack Room Brenda. Veronica had never given any of this much credence, because Clem's father liked to make up dramatic stories.

'My mother wanted me to have something I'd keep for years and years,' said Ella, and added rather waspishly that this being so, it was a pity she had had to lose the watch the day after being given it. 'Gold's indestructible,' she said. 'So if they find the watch near the man's body, they'll trace it back to me.' She looked at the other two. 'And that means to the two of you, as well,' she said. 'So you've both got to promise me that you'll keep to the vow we made all those years ago.'

'I promise,' said Clem after a moment, and Veronica, who wished Ella would not be so intense, because, for goodness' sake, nothing was very likely to happen to any of them, shrugged and said, 'I promise as well.' Then she finished her wine and hoped that her exciting evening could now proceed without any more interruptions.

❀ ❀ ❀

In the event, Veronica's evening was very good indeed. The scented candles burned alluringly and the chilled wine and neat little snacks went down well. Veronica smiled to herself, remembering Ella's pretentious frozen canapés. She thought she was so great, that Ella. It was a pity she could not see Veronica now, serving this elegant little supper, embarking on the first exciting steps in a new love affair.

There was nothing quite like the start of a romance— Veronica liked the word 'romance'; she always used it in preference to anything earthier—when you were both finding out about one another. You planned what you would wear for each meeting, and you devised sexy romantic games to play. It was an adventure, and if Ella wanted to look down her nose and consider Veronica a slut, Veronica did not care.

When the food had been removed and the glasses topped up, there was nothing slutty about permitting a civilized embrace. It was a testing of the water, as it were, the first steps in establishing how far things could go.

After a while, the embrace became fevered, and after a longer while it became insistent. Veronica giggled suddenly, and he drew back at once.

'Is something wrong?'

Giggling at such a moment had been a very bad move. It was partly nerves, of course, but men did not like being laughed at, especially when they were revving up to be amorous. He looked angry, and Veronica sought frantically for a way to retrieve the situation and his dignity, and found it.

'Nothing's wrong at all. I was just thinking you have unsuspected depths.'

'Oh, you'd be surprised,' he said.

It was all right; he sounded mollified. She said, 'No, but really. You almost seem like a different person.'

'Well, let's explore those depths and that different person, shall we? Do you want to do that?'

'Now? Tonight?'

'Isn't that what this is about?'

And even though one was still not a slut, this was the twenty-first century and Veronica was a modern woman, quite capable of giving those pert twenty- and thirty-year-olds a run for their money. She had kept her figure and looked after her skin, and in a dim light she could pass for a lot younger than she actually was.

In any case, she had spring-cleaned the bedroom that morning and put lavender-scented sheets on the bed, and it would be a pity to waste all that effort.

Entries from an Undated Journal

I had to expend a good deal of effort hiding what I came to call 'the darknesses'. I think I managed it very well, though. I don't think even Crispian, with his perceptive mind, knew about that side of my nature. I often thought Serena knew, but she never referred to it. She was a cold-hearted bitch, Serena Cadence. I didn't hate her, but I didn't much care for her.

I hated Crispian, though. It was partly because he stood in the way of things I wanted, but also because he had all the attributes I longed to possess. I used to look at him, and think: how does he exert that charm over everyone he meets? He was not especially good-looking, you understand, in fact you'd have said no one would afford him a second glance. Brown hair, the colour of clear honey, and eyes to match, and the characteristic slanting cheekbones of so many of the Cadence men. But people did give him that second glance and they usually gave him a third, as well.

The curious thing was that my decision to murder him never shocked me. It didn't even frighten me, and it certainly never worried me in...in any moral sense, I mean. I believed then and I believe now that I had logical and sane reasons for it. I really was, and still am, entirely sane. Although as the hours tick away in here, I'm not sure if I'll remain sane.

Sane...

I wonder if anyone who reads this will be familiar with the novel by Robert Louis Stevenson—*The Strange Case of Dr Jekyll and Mr Hyde*? It was fashionable in the closing years of the nineteenth century and it's a chilling tale. I've sometimes had the eerie feeling that Stevenson was able to look ahead over the years and see straight into my own mind. His tortured misguided Henry Jekyll went through the agonies I go through, and as for the evil-intentioned Hyde...

To those who encounter him, Edward Hyde gives the impression of repulsive deformity, but without having any actual malformation. He speaks in a husky whisper, but with a murderous tone of timidity and boldness (Stevenson certainly knew how to put opposites together to good purpose!), and lives a callous and cruel life, but does so in the shadows.

The ill-starred Dr Jekyll unleashed his dark *alter ego* by means of a powerful drug, which he compounded in his own workshop—a drug intended to separate good from evil in a personality. But, drinking its smoky potency, he caused his dreadful inner self to come alive. The change happened in me in much the same way, although of its own accord. A deep apprehension would stir in the dimmest recesses of my mind, and moments later it was as if greedy ogre-hands reached down and took hold of my mind, wrenching it mercilessly, *deforming* it, until it lay bleeding and panting in a wholly different shape; altering the essence of what I really was. And if I looked in the mirror—

I can't bring myself to write a description of what my mirror showed me during those darknesses and, after the first time, I never looked voluntarily in the glass. *It was not me* who looked back out of the silvered depths. And while the darkness was on me, I was not safe and no one was safe from me...

I make no apologies for the melodramatic nature of those last two paragraphs. A man facing death is allowed a few extravagances in his journal.

CHAPTER FIVE

London, June 1912

CRISPIAN CADENCE DID NOT indulge in many extravagances, but on the night he left university for good he reached London and his parents' house slightly drunk. He had intended to arrive at a civilized hour, but the goodbyes in Oxford had taken longer than he had expected, and then the train had been delayed, so it was midnight before he let himself in. By most people's standards this was not particularly late, but by the standards of Crispian's mother, Serena, it was outright dissipation.

He stood in the big shadowy hall with its black and white tiled floor and considered the stairway. It was in near-darkness, his bedroom was on the second floor, and he was by no means sure he could get up to it in seemly silence. He was perfectly entitled to make as much noise in his own home as he liked, but he baulked at being seen in this condition by his mother, or—God forbid—his father.

'Your father's jealous of you, of course,' Crispian's cousin, Jamie, had once said.

'Why would he be jealous?'

'Do you really not know? Crispian, your father's an ageing roué no longer able to indulge in the pleasures of his youth,' Jamie said. 'He sees you indulging in them, and it makes him jealous.'

'Come up to Oxford sometime and join me in a few,' said Crispian, who had been in his second year at the time. But Jamie, who was serious-minded and rather quiet, had merely said politely that he would think about it.

He was crossing the hall, when Flagg, the butler and general factotum, came out, pulling a dressing gown round him, a look of anxiety on his face, which cleared when he saw Crispian.

'Beg pardon, Mr Crispian, I didn't realize it was you. I heard a noise—'

'And I was trying to be so quiet, Flagg.' Crispian grinned at him, and lifted his hand in the gesture implying drink.

'Ah, yes, I see. Black coffee, sir?'

'Better not. I don't want to wake anyone. Is my father at home?'

'Not at the moment.'

'Thanks. You get off to bed, Flagg. I'll make my own way upstairs.'

He waited until Flagg had gone back to his own quarters, then grasped the balustrade and started up the stairs, hoping he could manage to be quiet. The stairs swung sharply back on themselves in a hairpin bend, then went on up again to the second and attic floors. Crispian and Jamie used to play games on these stairs when they were small, making faces at one another through the banisters, one on the higher flight, the other on the lower. Jamie had made up splendid games for them and, remembering this, Crispian smiled. Jamie had not been so serious in those days.

There was a wide half-landing at the top of the main stairs, with a long deep window. The curtains were only partly drawn across it, and shadows slanted in and lay across the stairs. Crispian had almost reached this landing when a faint movement from above made him look up.

Standing in the half-curtained window was the figure of a man. A burglar! thought Crispian, and fear scudded across him. The man pressed back into the shadows, putting up a hand as if to keep his face in shadow, but Crispian had already started up the remaining stairs, shouting loudly to rouse the household. At once the man darted out of his hiding place and hared up the smaller stairway to the top floor, vanishing into the shadows. Crispian followed him, missing his footing on the last few stairs, cursing, then regaining his balance. But the man had vanished, and Crispian stood on the upper landing, looking about him. Had the man gone into one of the bedrooms? Up the tiny stairs at the far end into the attics?

Crispian heard Flagg calling from below, wanting to know what was happening.

'There's an intruder!' called Crispian, coming back down the stairs. 'I've just seen him—he ran up to this floor. God knows where he is now—hiding in one of the rooms most likely. Tell everyone to stay in their room and barricade the door. You stay here to make sure he doesn't get out. I'll fetch the constable—there's always one on duty in the square.'

'Mr Crispian—' began Flagg, but Crispian was already crossing the hall and opening the front door. He gasped as the cold night air met him and cursed the wine he had drunk earlier, then managed to half-run to the far end of the square.

By the time he and the portly constable got back to the house, Flagg was hovering agitatedly in the hall.

'I'm *that* sorry, Mr Crispian, but it seems the ruffian's escaped us after all.'

'He can't have done,' said Crispian incredulously. 'He was on the stairs and he went up to the top of the house—I saw him. He couldn't have got out.'

'I'm sorry, but he did,' said Flagg. 'And I know you said not to, but I've looked in all the rooms. I took the fire tongs from the drawing room, and Dora and Hetty came along as well, for they wouldn't stay in their room alone, not for you, me, nor King George. Dora had the rolling pin and Hetty had the meat mallet. Mrs Flagg barricaded herself in our room with the frying pan.'

Despite the severity of the situation, Crispian was aware of a stab of amusement at the image of the stately Flagg prancing round the house in his dressing gown and slippers, brandishing the fire tongs, while the two maids tiptoed along in his footsteps, glancing nervously over their shoulders every few seconds.

He said, 'Did you go up to the attics?'

'We did,' said Flagg. 'But not hide nor hair nor whisker did we find.'

'It looks as if our man's got clean away,' said Crispian, turning to the policeman. 'But you'll make a report to Bow Street, will you? In case of any other break-ins hereabouts?'

'Yes, sir, you can be sure I'll do that.' The constable sketched a half-salute and went out into the square again.

'Flagg, one of the girls had better tell my mother what's happened—reassure her there's no cause for alarm.'

'I'll see to it, sir. And now, if you'd care for that black coffee after all...?'

'That's a very good idea, Flagg. Make about a gallon of it, would you?'

❧ ❧ ❧

Serena Cadence had gone to bed at her usual time.

Crispian had said he would be home this evening but that he might be quite late, so please not to wait up for him. He would see everyone in the morning.

Serena was glad he would be home for good. He was such a very presentable son, and so far he did not seem to be inheriting his father's tendency to portliness, which was a great mercy. He was slim and spare, and clothes always looked very nice on him, although he wore his hair slightly too long, as so many young men did. She had thought at Christmas, when the family assembled at Cadence Manor, that Oxford had smoothed away any youthful awkwardness, not that Crispian had ever been gauche, which was something else for which to be grateful. He was not as good-looking as his cousin, Jamie, who had been more or less brought up with Crispian since his mother died. Jamie was a dear good boy, hard-working and reliable, but Serena thought for all his good looks he had not a tenth of Crispian's quiet charm.

Unless there were guests Serena liked to retire by ten o'clock. There were not often guests now, although in the early years Julius had often entertained friends and business associates, and Serena had dutifully arranged dinners and luncheons. It had been rather novel at first and she had been an excellent hostess, everyone said so. But choosing the right gowns and jewellery so one looked prosperous but not vulgarly overdressed had been dreadfully tiring. Talking to people one hardly knew had been tiring as well. Even now it made her head ache to remember those interminable evenings.

Also—and this was not something she cared to dwell on—those dinner parties had invariably excited Julius in a very particular way. He nearly always came to her bedroom after the guests had gone, his eyes bright with the stimulation of the company and the talk, his face flushed from all the wine and brandy. He would compliment her on the gown she had worn or the way her hair had been dressed, then there would be one of the messy, fumbling, *painful* acts Serena had always hated but which she knew had to be endured from time to time in any marriage.

Still, all that was at an end. She finished the chapter of the book she was reading, and switched off the bedside light. Julius had had electricity installed two years earlier; it had meant a great deal of hammering and crashing and workmen everywhere, but it was certainly easier and more efficient than gaslight.

It was shortly after midnight that she was woken by the sounds of running feet and Crispian's voice calling out something about an intruder. Serena sat up in bed and considered whether to go out of her room, but Flagg was equal to anything, and if Crispian was with him, it would be all right. She waited until the sounds had died down, and presently heard Flagg call a good night to Crispian. She could relax. Whatever had happened had been dealt with.

She lay down again and tried to go back to sleep, but sleep, so abruptly interrupted, would not return; the images pouring through her mind were too vivid. She reminded herself that Flagg could be entirely trusted. But as the chimes of St Peter's church clock came faintly to her—1 a.m.—she knew she would not be able to sleep until she had made sure that everything was as it should be. It was not that she did not trust Flagg, simply that she needed to know for herself. Moving stealthily so as not to alert anyone, she got out of bed, slid her feet into slippers, donned a thin silk robe, and took a key from her bedside drawer, which she put in the robe's pocket.

The house was quiet and still, but Flagg had left a low light burning on the central landing. Serena stole along to the narrow stairs at the far end—the stairs leading up to the third floor. It was, of course, the height of folly to go up there on her own at such an hour, but there were certain responsibilities. A light summer rain had started to patter against the windows; she could hear it gurgling down the drainpipes. It sounded exactly like a throaty whispery voice. *Come closer, Serena…*

The house did not have attics in the conventional sense, but it had three rooms directly under the roof, either made by the original builder or created by some past occupant who wanted extra storage space. The rooms were small, with tiny windows overlooking the narrow walled garden. The first two were used for lumber— odds and ends of discarded furniture, and the trunks the family used when going away, or when removing to Cadence Manor for the holidays. But the third one...As Serena reached the head of the narrow stairway she could see the thick lock on the third door.

It was six months since Flagg had called in an incurious workman to fit the big new lock; Serena had been given one of the keys at the time. She walked down the passage and stood in front of the door. Then, her heart beating fast, she pressed her ear to the oak surface. Was there the faintest movement from the other side? She suddenly had the impression of someone standing up against the door in the room. *Come inside, Serena...*

One could take a sense of duty a bit too far, of course. But, thought Serena, there was some sort of disturbance earlier and I do need to make sure everything's all right. She glanced back to the stairs leading down to the main landing. The light was still glowing down there, and people were in earshot—Flagg and the two maids. And Crispian would be in his room by now. She slid the key from her pocket, and into the lock. Turning the lock, she cautiously pushed the door a little way open.

Bars of moonlight lay across the bare wooden floor, and there was a faintly sour smell in the room. But it was empty. Serena frowned, still standing in the doorway, unwilling to enter the room. Then a scrape of sound came from her left and a hand came round the edge of the door, reaching for her. Serena leaped back at once, her heart thudding, then slammed the door closed and fumbled frantically for the key to lock it. He had been there all the time! He had been standing behind the door.

But she was shaking so badly she dropped the key and, when she turned to run down the stairs, she caught her foot in the hem of her robe and half fell. To her horror, the handle of the door moved and it opened. A hunched-over figure came scuttling out of the room, and before Serena could call for help he was on her. One hand came over her mouth, and with the other he half dragged her back into the attic room. Once there, he threw her onto the narrow bed by the window, then bounded back to the door and locked it. At some deep level of her mind, Serena remembered the key she had used must still be on the landing outside. That meant he had his own key! He was able to go in and out—to roam around the house at will—even to roam around the streets! As he came back to the bed she opened her mouth to scream, but only a terrified gasp came out.

He pushed her down on the pillows. Serena beat against him with her fists, but he was too strong for her. Hammer-blows of terror beat frantically against her mind, and she fought as hard as she could, trying to cry out for help again. This time she managed a half-scream, but she knew with despair that no one could possibly have heard it.

He forced her back on the bed, his breath, dry and sour, gusting into her face, and Serena shuddered, turning her head to one side so that her face was half buried in the pillow. The bed creaked as he climbed onto it, and she felt his free hand pushing aside her robe and nightgown beneath, then fumbling with his own clothes. Serena sobbed and fought to get free. This was dreadful. *Dreadful.* The hammer-blows were beating a horrid tattoo inside her mind by this time. You-know-what's-going-to-happen, said these insistent beatings. You-know-what-he's-going-to-do...

He jerked her legs wide apart with one knee and, as he thrust against her, she felt the brutal masculine arousal. Serena squirmed and fought, but she already knew it was no use. He pushed himself hurtingly into her and the grunting heaving act began—the act that in marriage she had always found so repulsive.

'Please stop, *please...*' she gasped.

He seemed not to hear her; he went on, sweating and gasping. Once she thought he faltered and the feeling of hard intrusive masculinity lessened slightly, but then he gave a bellow of triumph and jerked convulsively. Pain tore through Serena and the shadowy room spun dizzily around her, then she was aware of him lumbering off the bed. She half sat up, pulling the robe around her. Her assailant was crouching in a corner of the room; in the dimness she could see him turning his head from side to side, as if bewildered, shrinking from the thin moonlight and covering his face with his hands.

Something akin to pity sliced through Serena, but moving slowly so as not to alarm him into making another move, she got off the bed, and went to the door. He flinched like a child expecting a blow, but he did not move and she reached shakily for the key, which was still in the lock. It turned, and Serena opened the door and almost fell onto the narrow landing beyond. She pulled the door shut, managed to lock it, and leaned back against it, gasping and trembling. But it's all right, said her mind. He's locked in again and I've got the key he had. Oh God, how did he get that key? I'll have to find out about that. But I don't need to do that tonight. I don't need to raise the alarm. I can go back to my room.

She went shakily down the narrow stairs and she was almost at the bottom when footsteps came up the main stairway, and Crispian appeared, a mug of something in one hand. He saw her at once, and stopped, clearly puzzled as to why his mother should be coming down from the attics at this hour. As Serena moved forward, Crispian's eyes widened in horror and she realized, too late, that her robe was torn and her hair was probably in wild disarray.

'Dear God, what on earth's happened?' he said, setting down the mug on the floor and coming towards her. He took her arms. 'You're hurt—it's the intruder come back, isn't it?'

'No—'

'Then what's happened?' His eyes went past her to the stair. 'What's up there?' he said. 'What are you hiding?'

'Nothing. Crispian, please don't...' But he was already ascending the stairs, taking them two at a time, and it was then that Serena realized her own key was still on the floor where she had dropped it. Would he see it? Yes, of course he would. She went up the stairs after him but it was already too late. Crispian had indeed seen the key and he had seen the thick, new-looking lock on the door. He had picked up the key and unlocked the door before Serena could stop him.

She cried out, 'Crispian—no! Don't!' But he was already stepping into the room. Serena saw him pause and peer through the shadowy dimness, and then grope, almost automatically, to find the light switch.

Light flooded the room, and fell cruelly and revealingly across the face of the man who was still huddled in the corner, his face turned away. Crispian gave a start of horror and, as he stood staring, Julius Cadence, his father, gave a cry of anguish and cowered back, covering his face with his hands.

❀ ❀ ❀

Crispian thought he would be ashamed for the rest of his life of the instinct that sent him stumbling out of the dreadful room. But he had been unprepared for what the sudden light revealed, and such sick horror swept over him that he had to get out at once.

For several moments he was afraid he was actually going to be sick—all that wine at the party!—but he filled the bathroom basin with cold water and thrust his head into it. As he emerged, dripping wet and gasping, he was dimly aware of Flagg's voice calling from downstairs, and of his mother saying that nothing was wrong, please to go back to bed. He dried his face and hair, his mind still seeing the nightmare thing cowering in the corner of the bedroom, the thing that was unmistakably his father despite...

His face, thought Crispian, horrified. Oh God, what did that to his face?

He took a deep breath, and went along to his mother's bedroom. She was sitting in the chair by the window, and, although there were marks of strain around her eyes, she seemed perfectly composed. She had put on another robe and was examining her reflection in a small hand-mirror, tucking a stray lock of hair inside a hairpin, as if the only thing that mattered at the moment was her appearance. Crispian saw she was doing what she always did: pretending everything was all right, presenting a determinedly unruffled appearance.

He asked a bit awkwardly, 'Are you all right?'

'I'm quite all right. But I'm sorry you had to see that, Crispian.'

'So am I.' He sat on the edge of the windowsill. 'What's wrong with him?' he said flatly.

'He has these spells from time to time,' said Serena defensively. 'For most of the time he's perfectly all right. I dare say he works too hard. Cadences doesn't run itself; you've all said that more than once.'

Crispian thought: but Cadences didn't do that to him. It didn't turn him into that cringing, hunched-over thing I saw. And his face...

He said carefully, 'Why does he have to be locked up?'

'He gets confused,' said Serena. 'He's not a young man any longer. He was over thirty when we married, you know. I was just seventeen—a child bride. People said it was a very romantic match.' She was watching him from the corners of her eyes to see how he was taking this.

'He attacked you,' said Crispian.

'Not exactly. When he's confused he mistakes people he knows for enemies.'

'He's not only confused, he's dangerous.'

'Oh, no,' she said at once, but Crispian knew she was lying.

'He must be dangerous or you'd never have made that arrangement about the attic room.'

'Dr Martlet thought it was best at the times when he's unwell,' said Serena. 'I shouldn't have gone up there at such a late hour, that's all. I startled him.'

'I thought there was an intruder earlier,' said Crispian slowly. 'Flagg pretended to search. But it was my father I saw, wasn't it? How did he get out?'

'I don't know. He must have got hold of a key. Perhaps Flagg was careless sometime.'

'I didn't recognize him,' said Crispian. 'It was dark and he was trying to hide...' Trying to hide, said his mind. Because his face...Oh God, yes, of course he was trying to hide from the light. He said, 'How long has he been like this?'

'I really can't remember,' said Serena. It was the dismissive tone she always used if anyone made reference to something she considered indelicate; Crispian knew that tone and he knew there was no arguing against it. But she seemed unharmed and she did not appear especially worried. Was that because she was accustomed to this kind of behaviour? To the fact that her husband had apparently to be locked away for fear he might attack people? It was purest Gothic; the mad relative in the attic. But if he really was mad, what was the alternative? Some bleak asylum? And what if it got out that the head of Cadences Bank was locked away, insane and dangerous? Crispian was not sure if he could cope with this.

He said, 'Would you mind if I talked to Dr Martlet about him?'

'Must you?' Alarm showed in Serena's eyes.

'I think I must.'

'Very well, if you feel it's necessary.' She got up. 'And now, I think I would like to go back to bed. We can talk again tomorrow.'

'Yes, of course.'

As he crossed the room to the door, she said suddenly, 'Crispian.'

'Yes?'

'I'm glad you're home.'

CHAPTER SIX

Entries from an Undated Journal

Everyone was glad Crispian was home. They all danced and fussed round him—you would have thought it was the Second Coming or a State visit at the very least.

I let them get on with it, but actually I was as glad as anyone that he was home. It's not impossible to murder someone who's living miles away in an Oxford college, but it's difficult.

Murder's a strange thing. There's no way of learning how to commit it. You can read accounts of famous murderers—even their own accounts, in some cases—but those are the ones who got caught. The successful ones don't write about it. So you learn as you go along, quietly and unobtrusively. But one of the things the books don't tell you is how overwhelmingly exciting it is. To hide in the dark and wait for your victim, knowing all the while you're going to kill him, is an extraordinary feeling. It's better than being in bed with a woman—and let's be honest here, I've been with enough women that I'm qualified to say that. Each murder attempt I made on Crispian—and there were several—caused that throbbing excitement.

The first serious attempt was during a big Christmas house party at Cadence Manor. I've always hated the place, although that's not something I've ever said, because the family love going there. They're quite clannish, the Cadences—that's the Italian ancestry, I suppose—and they've always liked to gather there: all the men from Cadences Bank with their beautifully dressed wives and daughters, and all the glossy young men with their complacent smiles and clever eyes, discussing their investments and decrying the foreign money markets. Local people generally came in to help cook and clean and wait at table; there would be dinners for thirty and forty people, elaborate shooting parties for nearly as many. I always thought it practically feudal, but Crispian shone at all those events. He could light up an entire room simply by walking into it, and he talked so easily with the guests, even the most distinguished: joining in the masculine laughter, but somehow keeping an edge of deference; flirting gently with elderly aunts, never once stepping over the line of what was acceptable. Crispian always knew to a hair's breadth where the line was, and he never once got it wrong.

'It's a trick easily acquired,' he said once when I mentioned it, just casually.

It was a trick I knew I could never acquire, not if I lived to be a hundred. Which, of course, I won't, not now. (There are six days left to me. That accursed ticking clock counts the seconds away all the time.)

On that Christmas night I got Crispian drunk, hoping it would fuddle his wits. It didn't. All that happened was that his eyes became brilliant, and his hair was slightly dishevelled. In the end, I was the one who crept away to be sick because I had tried to match him glass for glass and my stomach gave way before my head. No one noticed I left the party. No one noticed either when, much later, I crept along the corridor and went into Crispian's room.

I had worked it all out beforehand, when I was sober, and being drunk made no difference to the details. In any case, being sick got rid of most of the alcohol in my body and cleared my mind.

My plan was very simple—that's always best with murder. I was going to tell him I had heard an intruder downstairs and get him to creep along the upstairs landing with me to see if we could catch the burglar in the act. Then I was going to push him down the stairs. Cadence Manor has a wide stairway at its centre, lined with marble and alabaster. It's a touch pretentious, but people usually admired it. Pretentious or not, a tumble all the way down that stairway onto the unforgiving marble floor below and Crispian would never light up any room again.

He was asleep, but he came fully awake when I touched his shoulder—infuriatingly there was no befuddlement or bewilderment on waking. He opened his eyes, stared at me for a moment.

'What on earth's wrong?'

'I think someone's broken in downstairs—I heard a window being smashed. I don't want to rouse the house in case I'm wrong, but I think we should take a look. Would you come down there with me?'

'Oh Lord, you do pick your time,' he said, glancing at the clock, which showed it to be just before 1 a.m. 'But we'd better see what's happening.' He reached for a dark blue silk robe lying at the foot of his bed. He tied the cord, slid his feet into leather moccasins, and led the way onto the wide landing outside his room.

That was when the excitement began for me. It coursed through my body like a flame and, as we went stealthily towards the main landing, I felt as if I was on fire with the power. We stole along the dark landings and I let him get a little ahead. Once I stopped, because I had the strong impression that someone was watching, but of course no one was there. Even so, as we went towards the big gallery at the centre of the house, I felt as if the shadows shivered and flinched from me as if I was already marked as a killer. The mark of Cain. All nerves, of course.

My heart was pounding and my hands kept clenching and unclenching. In just a few minutes he would be dead.

But he was not. I fumbled it, as anyone reading this will realize. As we stood at the head of the stairs, listening for the non-existent burglar, Crispian still a little in front of me, I made a lunge towards him—intending to push him in the small of the back, then stand away as he fell to his death. But at the very last second he spun round, startled at the sudden movement, and my hands missed him entirely. In fact I had to grab the banister to stop myself going headlong down the stairs.

I covered it up quite well—I can think quickly when I have to. I said, 'He's there!' pointing into the deep dark blackness of the hall, making it seem that I had been bounding forward to catch the intruder. We went downstairs and searched, but found nothing, of course. And after half an hour, Crispian went back to bed, making some joke about me hearing things.

I didn't dare try again that night, but I knew I would in the future. It might be a long time before a suitable opportunity presented itself, but I knew it would do so one day. Every time I thought about it, that fiery excitement burned up and I found my fingers curling into claws again.

❊ ❊ ❊

Almost as soon as he returned to London from Oxford, Crispian spent a long time closeted with that old fool Dr. Martlet. He thought I was unaware what he was doing, but I knew, all right. I didn't need to listen at doors or open letters to know what was afoot. And more than once I laughed at his deviousness and the machinations.

But I'd still like it understood that I'm not and never was mad. What I did was nothing to do with madness. It was because of the decision Crispian made in the summer of 1912.

London, 1912

Crispian hated the decision he had made, but he could not see any other course of action.

'My father is dangerous,' he said, facing Gillespie Martlet in the small downstairs room that had always been regarded as Julius Cadence's study. It was lined with books Crispian did not think anyone had ever read, and there was a musty, unused smell about it. 'He somehow got hold of a key to that hellish room you've put him in, and attacked my mother last night.'

'Is she all right?' asked Martlet quickly.

'I think so. She's doing what she nearly always does with any unpleasantness—pretending nothing happened,' said Crispian caustically.

'How did he get a key?'

'I've questioned Flagg, but his own key never leaves his key-ring,' said Crispian. 'It's my guess that my father got an extra one from the locksmith when the work was being done.'

'Yes, that's possible. He could have gone up there and engaged the workmen in conversation,' said Martlet. 'They wouldn't have seen anything wrong. For long stretches he's been perfectly all right, you know. Completely lucid and normal. He might simply have asked for an extra key and they'd have given it to him.' He paused, then said, 'But I have to say, these spells of... confusion are becoming more frequent. And they're lasting for much longer.'

He's avoiding the words 'insanity' or 'madness', thought Crispian.

'Who else knows about this apart from my mother and Flagg?' he asked.

'No one. Flagg and his wife can be trusted, you know.'

'I know that. I'm thinking of Cadences,' said Crispian. 'If any of the investors were to know...' He paused, looking even more anxious. 'It could be the end of the bank.'

'Could it? Yes, I can see that's a possibility.'

'I'm also thinking of my mother's safety.'

'Oh God, so am I,' said Martlet angrily. 'Why d'you think I suggested that grisly little room? Your mother and Flagg have learned to recognize the signs now. They call for me at once, I sedate him and we get him into that room until it passes.'

'But that can't go on,' said Crispian, appalled. 'Not after last night.'

'No. Oh, no. But until we can think of an alternative...'

'I've thought of one,' said Crispian. 'I'll take him away from London. Somewhere where he can be kept safe. Somewhere where no one knows him.'

'What about Cadence Manor? That cousin of Sir Julius lives there, doesn't he? Colm, is it?'

'Yes, Colm. He's Jamie's father,' said Crispian. 'He's lived quietly at the manor since Jamie's mother died. You remember her, I dare say?'

'Oh, yes,' said Martlet sadly. 'A beautiful creature.'

'But the manor is the first place people would think to look,' said Crispian. 'Also, my father could escape too easily. So,' he said determinedly, 'I think we'll have to go out of England altogether. A sea voyage—a long one. Down to the Mediterranean and then round the coast of Greece, perhaps. We needn't go as far as the Turkish coastline, of course, certainly not with that trouble in the Balkans last year, although Thomas Cook say it's all died down.'

'Crispian, you can't do that on your own.'

'I know. I'm going to ask Jamie to come with us. I think he'll agree.'

'That's a good idea.' Martlet thought for a moment. 'But even with two of you, there might be times when it won't be easy to control your father. I wonder—would you consider taking a second companion?'

'Who?'

'Gil.'

Gil. Oh God, thought Crispian, and his mind went back to the last time he had seen Dr Martlet's son. Gil had been escorting two ladies along a London street, the three of them apparently bound for Gil's rooms where the two ladies, who proclaimed themselves artistes from the music hall, were going to demonstrate their performance to Gil in private. 'Would you like to join us, Crispian?' Gil had said.

He was smiling and Crispian had no idea if he was being serious. He said, as cordially as possible, that he preferred his pleasures in private.

'Pity. Fair enough, though. Good night.' The trio went boozily on their way singing cheerfully, and hailed a cab at the end of the street.

Crispian pulled his mind away from this scrappy memory. Martlet was saying that he would provide sufficient funds for Gil. 'That must be clearly understood. And I know he's a little wild at times, a little frivolous,' he said, 'but he's actually very trustworthy when it comes to things that matter.'

Crispian hesitated. He did believe Gil could be trusted over this; the trouble was that Gil could not be trusted in other directions. If he accompanied them Crispian and Jamie would spend half the time keeping him away from women and the other half dragging him out of gaming halls.

He said, 'But would Gil want to come? Would he want to leave London? I thought—' He broke off, trying to frame his next question tactfully. 'I thought he was studying medicine at Guy's. Fourth year, wasn't it?'

'It was,' said Martlet drily. 'But at present he's not likely to be reaching the fifth year, let alone the final one.'

Clearly there had been some new scandal, and if Gil had not actually been thrown permanently out of Guy's, he had obviously been rusticated. Crispian did not want to enquire too closely into the circumstances, and Dr Martlet was watching him with such entreaty that he said, 'Yes, all right. He can come with us.'

'I'm more grateful than I can say,' said Martlet, and Crispian nodded and hoped the old boy was not going to become maudlin. But he merely said, with a touch of awkwardness, 'You should be warned about Gil's particular weaknesses, I think.'

'I know Gil's particular weaknesses,' said Crispian rather caustically. 'And I'll hide the brandy and the cheque books.' As Martlet winced, he said, 'I'm sorry, that was unnecessary. And in the situation we're facing, things like that aren't very important. I'll be glad of Gil's company.'

And I *will* be glad of it, he thought determinedly. Jamie's a bit of dry stick these days and I'll probably be ready to scream at him before we get as far as Calais. At least Gil's good company and he'll balance out Jamie's earnestness.

Martlet said, very seriously, 'Crispian, you do realize that this journey could last much longer than you envisage? The four of you might not see England again for a very long time.'

'We might never see a great many things again,' said Crispian grimly.

❧ ❧ ❧

There was one thing Crispian was determined to see before leaving, and that was Cadence Manor. He was not sure he liked the place much. It was a vast echoing mansion, built by his great-grandfather, who could remember the decadent grandeur of his childhood in Florence, and consequently had a taste for ornate black marble and palladian pillars. But it was Crispian's family's place, and if, as Martlet said, he might not see England again for a long time, he would like one last sight of it.

He caught a train to the small halt at Bramley. A trap generally met the London train, so that travellers and their luggage could be taken to their destinations, but Crispian, intending to return to London by the eight fifteen train that same evening, had no luggage.

In any case, he liked the walk along the lanes, from where he could look across to the nearby villages, and he liked walking along Sparrowfeld Lane and Mordwich Bank, whose names evoked a much older English countryside. After the stuffy railway carriage, the air was fresh and clean, the hedgerows were frothy and the fields splashed with buttercups. In a distant copse he could see a hazy shimmer of bluebells. I'll miss this, he thought. Oh God, I'll miss England so much.

Jamie's father, Colm Cadence, met Crispian in the big echoing hall of Cadence Manor. Colm was a mild-mannered man, who found London in general and the world of banking in particular bewildering. He had not wanted to join Cadences Bank, so Crispian's father, with careless generosity, allowed him to live in a suite of rooms at the manor in return for acting as caretaker. Colm occupied three rooms, wandering around his well-stocked library, sometimes venturing into Priors Bramley, occasionally travelling to Oxford to potter happily among the groves of academe. Someone from the village went in to clean and cook meals for him, and the odd, hermit-like existence seemed to suit him.

Crispian explained that he was going out of England on a long journey and wanted to take a last memory of Cadence Manor with him.

'Jamie's coming with us,' he said. 'I think he's written to tell you about it.'

'The post is quite erratic down here,' said Colm, apologetically.

'We want to study foreign methods of banking and foreign finance laws,' said Crispian, hating the need to lie to the unworldly and trusting Colm.

'Ah. Foreign methods. I see. That will be very helpful to Jamie's career, I dare say. Paris and Rome, will it be?'

'We thought we'd go further afield if we can,' said Crispian. 'Greece, perhaps.' He watched Colm carefully to see if he accepted this.

Colm said, 'How interesting. The Greeks are remarkable people when it comes to finance—I might have some notes about that somewhere; I'm sure you'd find them helpful. Come into the study, my dear boy.'

It's all right, thought Crispian, following Colm's stoop-shouldered figure across the main hall, into the suite of rooms in which he lived. He believes me. He doesn't see anything odd in Jamie and I mad-rabbiting across the world.

'I dare say the notes will be somewhere in this cupboard,' said Colm, peering round. There was a large photograph of Jamie's mother on a desk—Crispian had been five when she died, Jamie a year or two younger. He could remember her only very dimly, and he did not think Jamie remembered her at all. But he had always liked the photograph, which showed her as dark-haired and attractive, and he liked her name, which was Fay. As a child he had thought it a name for a princess or a fairy creature from one of the old legends. His own mother had never seemed to like Fay very much; she had once said Fay was fanciful and impractical and a bit of a dreamer. 'An unsuitable wife for any man,' she had said dismissively, 'and especially for Colm.' Crispian did not think Fay's death had inflicted a particularly deep wound either on Colm or on Jamie.

'I was looking into the origins of banking quite recently, as it happens,' Colm was explaining, 'with particular emphasis on the Italians, of course. Cadenza, that was our family name generations back. Well, you'll know that. But I believe I've found a link to the Medicis—both families were Florentine bankers, of course, so it wouldn't be so very unexpected. There was a marriage in the fifteenth century; isn't that interesting? But we were talking about the Greeks, weren't we? Perhaps we should have a glass of Madeira while I try to find it all for you...Nonsense, it's no trouble at all, and I'm sure it would be of interest. If I could find my spectacles...

He's Dickensian, thought Crispian, watching Colm peer about him for the truant spectacles. Or he's even out of Restoration comedy. Not for the first time, he wondered if Colm minded missing out on his place in the Cadence financial empire, and its rewards. But he appeared perfectly happy buried down here in Priors Bramley, writing monographs and little essays, which occasionally appeared in scholarly periodicals. He reported scrupulously to Julius on the manor's maintenance, sending an account each quarter day. The accounts were as detailed and as precise as those of an Elizabethan household, and Julius usually snorted in semi-derision, paid what had to be paid, then consigned the accounts to the back of a cupboard, never to be looked at again.

CHAPTER SEVEN

The Present

For OVER FIFTY YEARS Ella had been able to push the memories to the back of her mind, but now they came pouring back.

The fact that Geranos was so harmful had been played down by the government.

'But everyone knew it was absolutely lethal,' said Clem, that night at Ella's house. 'Geranos had sulphur mustard in it, only nobody said so at the time. That's why Priors Bramley was called the Poisoned Village at one stage. Didn't somebody go in there and get horrible chemical burns or something?'

'I heard that as well,' said Veronica. 'And I remember hearing about the sulphur mustard being dangerous. I used to be worried about my mother putting mustard on ham. Listen, I was only eight,' she said defensively.

'Sulphur mustard was used in both World Wars, I think,' said Clem. 'But then the government stopped it. I can remember my father saying it had some useful qualities, only I can't remember what they were.'

'A lot of harmful things do have good properties if they're used correctly,' said Veronica, rather unexpectedly. 'Arsenic does. I remember reading that.'

'I suppose,' said Clem, 'that everything's got its dark side, hasn't it?'

Everything's got its dark side…

❀ ❀ ❀

Although the three of them had not talked much about what had happened in Cadence Manor that morning, Ella knew they all remembered it.

She had not really taken any notice of the stuff called Geranos in the beginning; it was just a word, something a plane had dropped on the village, a complicated science thing that the grown-ups probably understood. It was the man who lay at the core of all her nightmares: the man whose face was not quite right, and who had poured out the music in St Anselm's church and sobbed in that dreadful fashion. Afterwards she dreamed about him lying in the deserted manor house, staring upwards with sightless eyes because nobody had closed them. But she had tried not to think about it, because she would never see him again. She would never go back to Priors Bramley or Cadence Manor.

But she had. One week later she had gone back to Priors Bramley. And afterwards she understood why it came to be called the Poisoned Village.

❀ ❀ ❀

It had been Saturday afternoon, and Ella had been helping her mother make cakes. As they were putting away the mixing bowls, her mother suddenly said, 'Ella, where's your watch? Did you take it off to wash up? Where did you put it?'

Ella stared at her and felt a sickening jolt of panic. The watch, the gold watch that had marked her tenth birthday and that Mum had worked all those extra hours to buy. For a moment she was no longer in the bright kitchen, but in Priors Bramley just seven days ago. She had looked at her watch several times that morning to make sure they would leave before the plane came at midday, and also because she was proud of having such a grown-up birthday present. And then later, seated on Mordwich Bank, watching the plane come over, the watch had no longer been on her wrist. She had not noticed at the time, but standing in the kitchen with the warm scent of cakes baking, she saw her bare wrist as she, Clem and Veronica fed their unwanted sandwiches to the birds.

'Ella, what's the matter?'

'I think,' said Ella, starting to cry, 'that I've lost it.'

'Oh, you careless girl. That was a very expensive watch.'

'I know,' said Ella, crying harder.

'Well, try to think when you last had it. We might be able to track it down. There's no point in crying.'

But Ella could not stop sobbing, and the story of what had happened in Cadence Manor was tumbling out. It was a bit like being sick—you tried to keep it in but it came out of you anyway. The story of how they had gone into Priors Bramley came out like being very sick. She had not meant to tell the part about the man, but she could not help it. Mum did not speak; she simply sat there at the kitchen table, listening.

'...And when we got up to Mordwich Bank, my watch wasn't on my wrist any more.' Ella stopped speaking and she managed to stop crying. She felt empty but oddly better, as if she really had been sick, but she had no idea what was going to happen now. Mum was frowning, not an angry frown, but as if she was trying to think. Ella waited, and after a moment Mum squared her shoulders in the way she did when she was about to do something important.

She said, 'There's only one thing for it, Ella. We'll have to go out there and find your watch. No one need know—we can be there and back without anyone seeing us.'

'But we can't,' said Ella, horrified. 'It's all closed up. No one's allowed in.'

'I can't help that. That watch had your initials on it, and the date of your birthday. If that man's body is found and your watch is with him—'

'They'd think I killed him?'

'Well,' said Ella's mother, looking at her very directly, 'did you?'

Ella stared at her, then gave another sob and ran out of the kitchen.

❀ ❀ ❀

Her mother did not ask the question again. They finished the baking and set out the cakes to cool, then she told Ella to put on her coat because they were going to Priors Bramley. She said it in her firmest voice and Ella knew there was no arguing.

The sun was setting as they walked across Mordwich Meadow. Ella normally liked sunsets, but this one was an angry brownish orange, as if something had clawed at the sky and made it bleed. As they went down the bank the primroses that grew in the clay soil were dull and sad-looking, and when they came in sight of the manor in its dip of land, it was splashed with the same sulky light. Even the crouching outline of the lodge, set apart from it, looked as if it had dried blood on its grey walls. As they got closer there was a too-sweet scent on the air, and Ella shuddered.

'It'll be quite safe,' said her mother, seeing this. 'I'll go through the side door in the wall and across the old kitchen gardens. You can wait by the stile.'

'Everywhere smells horrid,' said Ella, wrinkling her nose.

'That's probably the Geranos. It's like geranium scent, isn't it?'

Ella did not say it was making her feel sick.

As they reached the lane with the high wall, in a very small voice, she said, 'He'll still be there, won't he? That man?'

'If he was dead he will. But you can't be sure he was dead, you know. It's very likely he was only knocked out and he got up and walked home.'

No, he didn't, thought Ella. I know he didn't. You know it, as well.

'But don't worry about it—I'll find the watch, then no one can ever prove you were here that morning.'

'Clem and Veronica know I was here.'

'If it ever comes out I shall say you were with me all day last Saturday,' said Ella's mother. 'I'll say Clem and Veronica are telling silly lies.'

Ella wanted to find this comforting, but the trouble was that Mum kept saying it. 'Silly lies, that's what we'll say,' she repeated. 'All silly lies.' The third time she said it the words came out sloppily, and Ella saw her eyes had the blurry look that meant she had taken what she called her 'special medicine' before coming out. She sometimes took a dose of it if she had to do something difficult or unpleasant; she said it gave her extra strength. Ella thought the medicine might have brandy in it, because it smelled like Christmas pudding.

The side door into the manor grounds was closed. There was a tangle of barbed wire over it—Ella thought that had not been there last week—and a notice saying to keep out.

'We can't get in,' she said in panic.

'Yes, we can. It won't be locked, and I've brought my gardening gloves to put on so I can unwind the barbed wire.'

'Are you sure about the—um—Geranos stuff being all right? I mean, really absolutely sure?' Ella was hating the geranium scent, and now they were closer to the manor a queer brownish haze seemed to hang over everything.

'Yes, I told you. It's just a test they're doing on the plants and wildlife. And they're only doing it because there's a delay about the motorway. It'll be months and months before they start building it, so they don't want anyone saying the Priors Bramley people were pushed out of their houses too soon. That's why they're pretending they need the empty village for an experiment. Only it isn't important at all, it's just to fool everyone...' The words trailed off vaguely and Ella looked at her worriedly. 'They think they're fooling everyone, those stupid government people, but they aren't fooling me. Not a bit, they aren't. You have to get up very early to do that. Geranos, ha! I'd give them Geranos.'

'Clem's father said Geranos was something to do with stopping the Russians from dropping bombs on us,' said Ella, hoping this would make Mum talk normally again. It was awful when she was all slurry and sloppy like this.

'Oh, the Russians won't drop any bombs. Certainly not on us. Clem's father is a stupid old fool anyway.'

Ella's mother tugged the barbed wire aside and opened the garden door. The hinges creaked gratingly and, as it swung inwards, Ella had the sudden feeling that a nightmare was opening up. But she could see into the manor grounds and everywhere looked exactly as it had done one week ago, except for the coppery haze that lay everywhere—like a diseased fog, thought Ella. That must be what had tainted the sunset.

Her mother did not seem worried by the copper mist. She went through the gate and across the tangled grass as Ella and the other two had done last Saturday, and then across the cracked pavings surrounding the house. The dust swirled a bit as she disturbed it; Ella saw that in places it lay on the ground in tiny glistening lumps like the top of a rice pudding when the skin got burned. She sat down on the grass to wait. It shouldn't take Mum long to find the watch. She had only to go up the stairs and into the room where the three of them had hidden, and then, if the watch was not there, to come downstairs and go into the room off the hall. That was where *he* was. What would he look like after being dead for a week? Ella had no idea what happened to dead bodies. Would his eyes be open and staring?

The garden door was still partly open, and Ella could see the house—the big doors and the marble pillars on each side. She could see part of the gardens, as well. In autumn there were gentians here, a patch of lovely blue mistiness under a big oak tree, but today the oak looked sick and dusty as if something had shaken masses of pepper over its leaves. The pepperiness was getting into Ella's throat a bit; it made her cough.

It was very quiet. Usually at this time the evening birdsong was everywhere, but now it was as if even the birds had been smothered. Ella began to feel uneasy; she looked across at the house again, hoping to see her mother come out, hoping against hope the watch would have been found.

And then into this thick tainted silence came a trickle of sound. At first it puzzled Ella, but with dawning horror she realized it was music: threads and curls of sounds, as faint as grey cobwebs that would dissolve if you blew on them.

She sprang to her feet, looking round, her heart starting to pitter-pat with nervousness, because no matter how faint the music was, she recognized it. It was *his* music, the music he had played and sobbed over inside St Anselm's church that afternoon. She stood very still, listening intently, wanting to run away as fast as she could, but not daring to move, listening to the music seeping into the sick-smelling gardens. It sounded as if it was being played on a gramophone, but whatever was playing it, there was no mistaking it. Was it coming from inside the house? Or was it from the lodge, a little way along the drive? Did it mean he was still here, that he wasn't dead?

When her mother appeared between the marble pillars, Ella gave a sob of relief and got to her feet. Mum would know what had happened and what they should do. Here she came, walking quite fast as if she wanted to get away from Cadence Manor and the sad sick village. As she crossed the terrace she stumbled on the uneven surface and Ella started forward, thinking she was going to fall, but Mum waved to her to stay where she was. Ella sat down again on the bit of grass, hugging her knees with her arms. The music had stopped. Ella knew the exact moment it had done so—she had felt the faint thrumming on the air fade into silence.

When her mother reached the gate, she was shaking her head. 'I couldn't find it,' she said. 'But that's all right, Ella, because I looked everywhere very thoroughly and if I couldn't find it, no one else will. We'll look for it as we go along the lane, though.'

She sounded all right but she looked all wrong. Her face was flushed and she was breathing quickly as if she had been running for a long time or was starting a cold. Ella said, 'Are you all right?' and her mother said at once that she was perfectly all right.

'It was just a bit warm in there. And it's a bit warm now—don't you think there's a lot of heat still in the day?'

Ella had had to wind her scarf tightly round her neck and dig her hands deep into her pockets because she had felt cold while she'd waited. But she said, yes, it was quite warm.

They walked home across Mordwich Bank and along to Upper Bramley, looking on the ground for the glint of gold from the wristwatch, but not seeing it. Once her mother paused and said she would have a little rest, she was becoming so out of breath, and once she stopped and unscrewed the top of the medicine bottle she kept in her handbag, and drank from it. The sun had almost set by this time, but Ella thought her mother's face looked as if she had been lying in hot sunshine for hours and hours. She was not sure if she should be worried about this.

It was not until they turned into the lane leading down to their cottage that Ella finally managed to say, 'Did you see him? The man?'

Mum took a few minutes to reply, then she said, 'Yes, he was there. He must have died at once. Clean and quick and painless. You don't need to worry about it.'

'Did anyone seem to be around?'

'No. The house was deserted.'

'Yes, I see,' said Ella. As they went into the house, she thought: but then who was playing his music?

❋ ❋ ❋

After supper Ella's mother complained of the heat again. 'It's really uncomfortable in here,' she said, taking off the woollen jacket she had been wearing. 'It's making my skin itchy. I wonder if we're due for a thunderstorm.'

Just before Ella's bedtime she was gasping with pain and her eyes were bloodshot. She asked Ella to switch on the light and Ella, feeling a bit scared, said, 'It's already on.'

'The bulb must be going. Or I might have a touch of that eye infection—conjunctivitis. I'll get some ointment from the chemist's.'

But by Ella's bedtime her mother was shivering and moaning, rocking back and forth in the chair. When the light from the standard lamp fell on her face, her eyelids were swollen, and large blisters had formed on her neck and on the side of her face. Once she rubbed at them and to Ella's horror the blister burst and thick yellow fluid ran out of it.

She said, 'Mum, you're ill, really ill. Should I get someone?' She had no clear idea who she should get, but her mother said, in a hoarse crackly voice, 'I think you'd better just go along next door and ask them to phone the doctor's surgery from the call box. Can you do that? Tell them to ask the doctor to come out.'

'Yes, of course.' Ella was off like a shot, trying not to shiver with fear, trying not to remember the coppery dust that had been everywhere in Priors Bramley.

'Chemical burns, by the look of it,' said the doctor when he arrived an hour later. 'Very unpleasant. I can't think how you'd get such a thing in an ordinary domestic environment, though, unless...Have you been near to Priors Bramley in the past twenty-four hours? Ah, that might explain it, then. They're starting to say that Geranos stuff might be harmful, although nobody's admitting it outright, not yet at any rate. Still, I'll report it to the Medical Officer for the county. He might be able to get some details about what it actually contains. That way we'd know what we were treating. I'm afraid we'll have to take you to hospital, Mrs Ford. But don't worry, you'll be all right.'

❀ ❀ ❀

Ella's mother was in hospital for three weeks, which everyone said was a long time, but Ella was not to worry, the doctors were marvellous these days and her mother would be fine.

Ella stayed with Veronica for the three weeks. She did not visit her mother; the hospital was twelve miles away anyway, which would have meant two bus journeys.

Veronica's father offered to drive her there, but Ella did not want anyone talking to the doctors or nurses in case it came out about actually being in Priors Bramley and the reason for it. So she said visitors were not allowed, and made up a story about a pan of hot oil, meant for frying fish, tipping over and burning her mother's neck.

When her mother was finally allowed out of hospital, everyone said how wonderful, and how pleased Ella would be to go back home. Ella did not say she was not particularly pleased. She had liked living in Veronica's house because it was big and there was a beautiful garden where they had tea on the lawn on Sunday afternoons. Several times, looking around her, Ella thought how much she would like to have a house like this.

Her mother was allowed home on a Monday morning, and Ella was given the day off school to meet her. Veronica's mother took her shopping first so they could get some nice food as a welcome home. She paid for all the food, buying things Ella's mother would have said were expensive and extravagant, and rounding it all off with grapes and peaches and a bunch of flowers. Ella could put them in a vase and it would be lovely for her mother to see them when she came in.

The cottage smelled sour and a bit damp, and there were newspapers and letters on the doormat. Ella threw these away and opened the windows to let in some fresh air. Veronica's mother helped put the food away, and hunted out polish and dusters so they could make the cottage spick and span. Ella began to think it would be nice, after all, to be in her own bedroom again, and she looked forward to seeing her mother's pleasure at the nice fresh cottage and the food.

But her mother did not seem particularly pleased at anything. She was wearing a thick sweater with a scarf wound round her neck, and her hair was combed forward over her face, which was a new thing. She did not say anything about the flowers or the nicely polished furniture, and she said the food was messy foreign stuff and she was surprised at Ella buying such expensive rubbish. When Ella explained that Veronica's mother had got the food, her mother said, very sharply, 'I hope she kept a note of everything so I can pay her back.'

'I don't think she meant you to. I think it was a sort of present.'

'I'm not having charity,' said Mum, even more sharply. 'I shall post the money to her, or you must give it to Veronica.'

She ate the food Veronica's mother had left, picking at it suspiciously and turning it over on her fork. Ella had been looking forward to having this meal with Mum after a whole three weeks, but it was all going wrong.

After they had finished eating, her mother's hair fell back into its usual place, tucked behind her ears. Ella stared at her in horror. Down the whole of one side of her face were dark lumpy scars, ugly and puckered. When she took off the sweater and scarf, there were more of the same scars down her neck.

Ella tried to look away, but could not, and her mother said, very angrily, 'Yes, Ella, that's what the Geranos did to me. It burned my skin and the scars won't ever fade. You killed that man in Cadence Manor—I know you did— and because of what you did I'm scarred and deformed forever.'

❈ ❈ ❈

They never talked about it again. Ella did not dare and her mother did not give her chance.

After she came home from hospital she was different. The doctor told Ella that her mother would have to take things easy for several weeks. He offered to organize visits by people who would help with cooking and shopping, but Ella's mother said they did not want that, and they would manage. After he had gone, she told Ella she did not want people poking and prying.

Even after the doctor said she was better, she did not bother about keeping the cottage clean or tidy. Dust and grime collected on surfaces and mould grew around the windowpanes in the scullery. Ella, hating the sour, wet smell of the mould, tried to clean things herself while her mother sat bonelessly in the chair, taking surreptitious swigs from the brandy bottle, telling Ella there was no point, everything would get dirty again, and anyway, nobody ever came to the house.

Nobody came to the house because Ella never asked anyone. She had never been ashamed of her home or of her mother, but she began to be now. Several times at school she heard whispers about her mother, and once one of the older girls asked her outright if it was true that her mother had caught a disease from going to bed with men.

Ella had no idea what the girl meant but she was still being very careful not to let anyone know about being in Priors Bramley that day to find her watch. So she tossed her head and said it was a lie, and people who told lies ended in being punished.

After a while she stopped trying to get her mother to go out. If there were school concerts or prizegivings, she no longer brought the details or the dates home. She could not bear anyone to see the unkempt wreck her mother had become, and as well as that she was frightened her mother would talk about that afternoon inside Cadence Manor.

She had no idea what she would do if Priors Bramley were to be opened up again and the body found, nor whether the man's death could be traced back to her. But as the weeks and then the months went by, the village stayed behind the black barbed wire and the thing that lay inside Cadence Manor remained in its secret tomb.

From time to time Ella thought about the cobwebby music that had drifted so eerily across the gardens, but she never heard it again and after a time she managed to push the memory of it into the deepest recesses of her mind. It was part of a nightmare, and as the years passed the nightmare gradually faded.

CHAPTER EIGHT

The Present

THE MAN'S BODY HAD not been found. Ella knew
that for sure, because news of such a discovery would have
caused a considerable stir in Upper Bramley. But the body
would certainly be found when the decontamination teams
went into Priors Bramley. Would the police be able to identify it after so long? Probably they would; you only needed to
watch a television crime programme to know about DNA and
dental records. But even if the man's identity were discovered
it would not matter, although it would feel strange to know
his name. What would matter was if Clem or Veronica lost
their nerve and talked about what had happened all those
years ago. How likely was that?

Ella could easily imagine Clem spinning one of his
stupid stories, telling everyone how the three of them had
walked through Priors Bramley on its last day. He would
probably not refer to the man's death because he was not
that stupid, but he might get carried away and embroider his
story with ridiculous little fantasies, never seeing the harm
he was doing. He was exactly like his name: he was like a
clucking old hen in a poultry coop, strutting round the little
local library where he had worked almost his entire life,
exchanging tittle-tattle with everyone who came in.

Derek, who had Scottish grandparents, said Clem was a bletherskite, but Derek had never liked Clem since he saw him smoking scented cigarettes. Affected, that was Derek's opinion. He never refused an invitation to one of Clem's elaborate little dinner parties, though, because Clem was a very good cook and Derek enjoyed his food. What he did refuse were invitations to evenings Clem called 'musical soirees', but everyone else called listening to records at Clem's house. Derek had once gone with Ella to one of these, but said afterwards she was never to drag him out to listen to such a load of boring rubbish again because he would rather watch television. This had surprised Ella, what with Derek being a member of the Operatic Society; music was music, surely. But Derek said there was a difference between Gilbert and Sullivan and the pretentious bilge Clem played. Ella had said, oh yes, of *course*, she had not seen it like that.

It was starting to seem as if Clem would have to be watched. He often sent articles to local magazines and county newspapers about events in this area. None of them was ever published, but the point was that he wrote about things that happened in Bramley—things that might provide clues to the past.

When Ella thought about it a bit more, she saw Veronica would have to be watched as well. She had been married twice, and had had a number of gentlemen friends since, although Ella did not ask questions and tried not to listen when Veronica talked about that side of her life. Bragging, that was all it was. But Veronica had been hinting that there was a new man in her life, and Ella thought she might spill the entire story to him while they were in bed. Pillow talk, they called that, although Ella had never really understood how it worked, because Derek had always fallen instantly asleep after that kind of activity.

The decontamination of Priors Bramley took place on schedule. A shocking disruption it would be, said people, torn between annoyance at having huge vehicles rumbling through the lanes, and subdued excitement at the reopening of the village. There was not a great deal of excitement in the town as a rule; the last time anything of any real note had happened was when a soldier, deserting from the Royal Fusiliers during the war, attacked a couple of village girls, and everyone thought he was a German spy.

People who liked to appear knowledgeable talked about neutralization and oxidation, which would be used in the spraying of all the buildings, and the *Bramley Advertiser* printed an article about a decontamination solution called DS2, which hardly anybody understood and which the senior science master at one of the schools said was full of inaccuracies.

Both the local schools took the opportunity to step up chemistry lessons, introducing sessions on the early pioneer chemists and formulae for organic compounds. The sixth formers were subjected to the complexities of synthesis, while one of the more progressive teachers tried to instil some recent history into his classes by drawing a parallel between the opening of the village and the fall of the Berlin Wall in 1989, although as somebody caustically pointed out, unwinding a few yards of barbed wire was not on the same scale as demolishing the Iron Curtain, and Sparrowfeld Lane was hardly Checkpoint Charlie.

No one was allowed into the village itself, but most of Upper Bramley went along to watch the start of things, and the mayor cut the barbed wire with special cutters and made a speech. The decontamination team walked dumpily along the lane into Priors Bramley, clad in white disposable suits and boots, carrying huge pressure jets and followed by a chugging generator on the back of a lorry.

There were parties of students from both the local schools, because it was a piece of local history and the teachers supposed a school project might as well be set up. The students were agreeable to the outing. It gave the girls a chance to wear jeans and high heels, neither of which were allowed in the classroom. Watching a bit of barbed wire being torn down and listening to some droning old fart make a long-winded speech was pretty boring, but it was better than sitting at a desk. Some of the older ones sneaked off to Mordwich Copse for various forbidden activities ranging from smoking to snogging, and were resignedly hauled back by their teachers.

The Red Lion, never slow to seize its own opportunity, made up batches of sandwiches and baguettes, and went along to sell them to the watchers, with bottles of cider and Coke.

Clem Poulter was there as well, telling the decontamination team please to ignore him, because his mission today was to take notes, like William Russell writing up the Charge of the Light Brigade for *The Times* in 1854.

One of the teenagers who had worn killer heels sprained her ankle falling down Mordwich Bank; two people were sick in the bushes from what they afterwards insisted was a rogue prawn in the baguettes but which everyone else said was overindulgence of cider, and Clem Poulter fell into a bed of nettles and had to be hauled out.

Ella had not wanted to go, but in the end she had done so because a lot of people were going and it might look odd if she were not there. But standing on the Crinoline Bridge along with a handful of neighbours, including Veronica, who was wearing a totally unsuitable outfit, she felt the past claw at her mind and for a really bad moment she was a child again, in the shadowy old church, listening to the sombre music pouring out, and hearing the agonized sobbing of the musician. But then she blinked and looked about her, and of course she was in the present-day, and the only sound she could hear was the phut-phut of machinery and the chatter of the local people. After a while she drove home, where she felt slightly better, but when Derek suggested strolling along to the Red Lion, Ella said irritably he had better go on his own because she had a headache and was going to bed early.

The air around Priors Bramley was filled with thrumming machinery for the next few days and a mist rose up from the high-pressure jets, causing romantically minded people to say the old village would reappear from out of the fog like the ghost village of Brigadoon in the old film. Less fanciful souls said that it was all a lot of fuss about nothing, and had anyone noticed how extremely low the water pressure was as a result of the Water Board allowing the decontamination team to connect their equipment to the mains?

Two days after the start of the decontamination, Ella went to meet her granddaughter Amy at Bramley railway station. Going down Market Street, driving slowly because of all the untidily parked cars and unwary pedestrians, she saw Veronica in absorbed discussion with a strange man. He could surely not be the one Veronica had hinted and smirked about, but if he was, he was certainly not her usual fare. In fact, Ella did not think he would be anybody's fare. He might be any age, from twenty-eight to forty-eight, he was wearing an aged herringbone coat that trailed on the ground, and he looked as if he should be queuing up for a hand-out at a Salvation Army hostel. She slowed down and leaned over to wave, but Veronica did not see her so Ella drove on. But pausing at the traffic lights at the end of Market Street, she glanced in the driving mirror and saw the man nod to Veronica, then go into the Red Lion as if he was familiar with the place. This was unexpected, because the Red Lion liked to think it attracted quite an elite clientele and would not be best pleased to have someone who looked like a tramp wandering in.

Parking in front of the station entrance, Ella was glad to think she had managed to veto Amy's plan to work as a barmaid at the Red Lion for the holiday, or to volunteer to help at the Bramley Gate hostel with the children taken into care. When Ella had been in her teens the only kind of part-time jobs available had been newspaper delivery rounds or Saturday morning work in shops, neither of which her mother would allow.

But when Amy's father, Andrew, was growing up, people thought it was useful and admirable for young-sters to take holiday jobs, and he had done what was called work experience, trying out different things for a few weeks at a time. He had finally gone into engineering, studying at a polytechnic ten miles away, catching a bus and later using a little moped, which Derek bought him. He had done well; Ella was very proud of him, although she did not really understand him. She did not really understand Amy either, or why she had decided to read such peculiar subjects as archaeology and anthropology at Durham University. In Ella's day girls had learned short-hand and typing, or book-keeping, and gone into offices. She could not imagine the kind of job Amy would finally get, but Derek only laughed and said Amy was headed for a very interesting career, and they would be as proud of her as they were of Andrew.

Ella was proud of Amy now; it was simply that she did not understand her any more than she understood Andrew. Still, she was pleased she had talked Amy out of the Red Lion idea. She had persuaded Clem to create a little part-time job at the library, which would be much more suitable and which Amy would enjoy.

❊ ❊ ❊

Amy Haywood, arriving in a tumble of untidily packed bags and flying hair at Bramley station, thought the next three weeks would be pretty boring. Gran would be stuck in the genteel 1950s, and Gramps would be stuck in his balance sheets by day and Gilbert and Sullivan by night. But it had been nice of them to ask her to stay for the Easter vacation, what with Mum and Dad being in Africa, where Dad was building a bridge or designing it, or something, and taking six months to do it so that Mum had gone with him.

And she would see if she could jazz up Gran's wardrobe while she was in Bramley, which would be fun, and maybe go along to some of Gramps's rehearsals and help slosh paint on scenery. She had intended to try working at the Red Lion for a couple of nights a week—it got quite lively there sometimes—but Gran had gone up in smoke at the idea and said they could not have their granddaughter working as a barmaid, whatever would people think?

It would be as well for dear, respectable Gran not to be told that Amy had recently been entangled with a very unsuitable person indeed or there would be a big row and boring lectures about correct behaviour and breaking the rules. It would all be devastating and Amy was devastated enough as it was, and screwing a tutor was only breaking the rules a very little bit. But Gran would be shocked to her toes and, even worse, Gramps might say he would have a word with Amy's College, because tutors were not supposed to have—h'rrm—*relationships* with students. That would be utterly mortifying, because Amy had so far managed to keep everything quiet, not wanting anyone to know she had been taken in by the tutor of English, the biggest screwer-around in college. It was utterly shameful to find you had been lured into bed with velvet-voiced quotations from John Donne and Shelley. Thirty years ago he would have been called a wolf and a rat, that tutor. He was a rat, anyway. He was not even a very good English tutor, and he had probably looked up the Donne and Shelley lines in a dictionary of quotations.

❀ ❀ ❀

Veronica had seen Ella driving through the village, but had not waved to her because of being in discussion with a very interesting new acquaintance. She had first encountered him at the Red Lion, when some neighbours had taken her there for a meal. She did not particularly like the neighbours, but she had gone because she had a rather elegant new jacket and it was a pity not to give it an airing.

The man had been at an adjoining table, eating the Red Lion's lasagne, apparently absorbed in reading a book propped up against his wine glass. Veronica had glanced at him indifferently, vaguely thinking him rather scruffy, and wondering that the Red Lion had deigned to serve him, because they were generally quite particular. But later, going up to the bar to order some drinks for the neighbours who had brought her, she had heard the man asking for the key to his room at reception. She had instantly revised her opinion, because he had the most beautiful voice she had ever heard—pure BBC, it was— and the landlord had called him Doctor somebody—the surname had sounded vaguely foreign. And, of course, circumstances altered cases, and you heard of absent-minded professors and research people who went about looking positively tattered. Considered again, in the light of this new knowledge, whoever he was, whatever kind of doctor he was, he had the kind of face you saw in old portraits—Henry VIII and people—well, not Henry himself, of course, but those people whose heads he had chopped off. Martyrs and suchlike. Paul Schofield had played one of them in a film.

Seeing the man again in Market Street, Veronica made a point of pausing to say good morning, and that she hoped he was enjoying his stay in Upper Bramley. This was not being forward, and anyway Veronica was entirely caught up with the new man in her life, but you had to be polite to visitors to your home place. Seen at closer quarters, the doctor with the foreign name was a bit younger than she had first thought, although it was still difficult to be sure. He might be mid-thirties. Asked, he said he was in Bramley for perhaps two or three weeks for local research; Veronica would like to have asked more, but he nodded a polite dismissal and went back to the Red Lion. Still, she thought he had looked at her quite fixedly and she was glad she had put on a particularly smart outfit, even though she was only shopping for a rather intimate little supper party. She went into the delicatessen to buy smoked oysters, pâté and French bread. No need for wine, that would be provided by her guest. In Boots she bought two packs of condoms so people would know she was still what nurses at clinics called sexually active. To emphasize the point, she added to her wire basket a pair of expensive black stockings with lace tops.

After this, she looked in at the library, to ask Clem if he knew who the visitor at the Red Lion might be. If he was really here for local research, the library would be his first port of call. But Clem was not much help. He had developed a cold since going to the decontamination of Priors Bramley and it was as much as he could do to sit at his desk, which he said was very annoying because he wanted to write an account of the day. Pressed about the man at the Red Lion, he admitted he had seen him, but he did not know anything about him.

'Well, that's other than the fact that he dresses like a dropout and looks like the Holbein portrait of Sir Thomas More,' said Clem, sneezing four times into a large handkerchief.

Veronica supposed, crossly, that she might have expected Clem to be absolutely useless.

CHAPTER NINE

CLEM POULTER HAD NOT really wanted to have Ella's granddaughter working in the library because she might disrupt his orderly routine. Also, he wanted to nurse his cold and sip mugs of hot blackcurrant tea and be given sympathy.

But Ella could be a bit of a steamroller at times and it had been difficult to get out of it, so in the end he had agreed.

And in fact he found he rather liked Amy being there. He had forgotten how unusual-looking she was—dark-haired and dark-eyed, with an odd cast of features that, in some lights, were very nearly simian and in others, nearly catlike. It was something to do with the length of the upper lip, which was unusually long, and the jawline. A lot of men would find her unattractive to the point of ugliness, but other men would see her as beautiful in a very singular way and consider her a one-off. But it would take a very particular kind of man to appreciate her. Clem thought about this, until some inner demon said, in the language of today's youth: Yeah, like you'd know about those things. Nobody's perfect, said Clem crossly to the urchin-voiced demon, and set about drafting plans for his Old Bramley exhibition.

Amy was full of energy and intelligence. She mixed Clem's cold remedies cheerfully, smuggled in a miniature bottle of rum for his sore throat, and entered into the exhibition project with enthusiasm. She helped Clem drag several boxes of archive stuff out of the cellars, dusted off display screens, and went off to the stationery store to dig out Blu-Tack, drawing pins and green baize. After this, she designed posters on the computer: bright jazzily worded advertisements with requests for people to loan any photos they had for the duration of the exhibition.

'We'll ask the Red Lion and the shops to display the posters,' she said to Clem. 'Oh, and I thought I'd see if the local newspaper has any archive stuff we can use.'

Clem felt a bit as if a whirlwind had dashed in and turned his orderly world upside down, but he was pleased. Meeting Ella in the greengrocer's two days later, he said Amy was turning out to be a great help.

'Derek says it sounds as if she's having a pretty wild time of it at that university,' said Ella, who seemed displeased with life in general and with the greengrocer's display of mushrooms in particular. 'I feel responsible for her, you know, with Andrew being in Africa. Why he ever wanted to go out there to build a bridge I can't think, because he could just as well build a bridge in this country I should have thought.'

Clem heard a faint note of envy in her voice. Poor old Ella, who had been born and lived in Upper Bramley all her life. Clem, with his three years of emancipation at Warwick University, from which he had emerged with a modest degree and a wish to do nothing other than come home to the familiar security of his home, felt quite sorry for her at times.

❋ ❋ ❋

Amy had not expected to get so absorbed in Clem Poulter's exhibition, but it turned out to be rather fun. She unearthed packets of ancient sepia photographs of

St Anselm's church, which looked utterly Gothic and gloomy, and several of the village street of Priors Bramley with the kind of shops you never saw nowadays: ironmongers offering paraffin for lamps, and flypapers, and sweet shops with bull's-eyes, and blocks of toffee you smashed up for yourself, and drapers who sold interlock vests and liberty bodices. What had a liberty bodice been, for goodness' sake, and when did you wear it?

There were photos of Cadence Manor, which looked as if it had been hugely grand and decadent. Amy was not in an anti-Establishment mood at the moment, so it was OK to admire Cadence Manor, with its stone scrolls and porticoes and its air of having been teleported from seventeenth-century Italy. It was very OK indeed to admire some of the men in the photographs. Some of them were pretty sexy: there was one guy of about twenty, who had dark hair and amazing eyes, and who you would certainly look at twice, if not three times. He was in several of the shots. There was a really cool one of a bunch of people at a party. Somebody had written 'Cadence Manor, Christmas 1910' on the back, and the man with the come-hither eyes was at the centre, wearing evening dress and drinking from a champagne glass. We'll have you in the exhibition for sure, said Amy to him.

Clem Poulter fussed and flapped around, wanting to see everything Amy found, exclaiming in delight over some of the stuff, trotting off to talk to the vicar and the choir-master about the church, so that Amy began to feel as if she had fallen backwards into Trollope or even Jane Austen. But it was all restful after the stomach-churning roller-coaster ride with the faithless English tutor. (Will he phone/will he turn up/will he ignore me…) She enjoyed pottering round the library, which was in an ugly Victorian building with a tiny art gallery on the first floor, and a meeting room for book clubs and craft groups and music societies.

Clem asked if she would mind helping out with a talk one evening, handing out coffee at half-time and things like that. He would normally do it himself, he said, but his cold had progressed to laryngitis and he had hardly any voice. Amy was agreeable to helping out, particularly since the evening happened to be a rehearsal night for Gramps's operatic gang, and Gran was taking the opportunity to give one of her polite sherry parties. Amy would rather help with a library talk—she would rather *listen* to a library talk, for heaven's sake!—than hand round Bristol Cream and defrosted savouries.

At first the talk did not seem particularly interesting. It was about the early church music that had been played at St Anselm's in its heyday, and Amy thought she would sit at the back with a book. In the event, however, she got quite interested. The choirmaster from St Michael's church was giving the talk. He was thin and bespectacled and earnest, and he said Ambrosian plainchant was less well known than Gregorian chant, but just as interesting and beautiful. He demonstrated a few bars of the Ambrosian stuff on a recorder. Amy thought it was not music you would want to hear when you were glammed up for a night out with a crowd of friends, but you might want to hear it when you were on your own and feeling a bit introspective and dreamy.

She handed out the coffee, collected the cups afterwards, and tidied up the leaflets the choirmaster had given out. She talked to some of the people who had come along, and thought it was a pity the faithless English tutor was not here to see how unconcerned she was about him and how well she was doing on her own. People were smiling at her quite approvingly, which put paid to the English tutor's last hurtful jibe about her having the face of a cat and a personality to match. A man did not want to wake up and find a scraggy alley-cat on his pillow, he said, and Amy had only just managed to get out of the bedroom before crying. She knew she was not especially pretty, but she had hoped she was interesting-looking. She did not think she had the personality of a cat, and she hoped the English tutor ended up with some vapid empty-headed chocolate-box.

Quite a lot of people were at the talk, some of whom Amy vaguely recognized as library users, others who came to Gran's house or to see Gramps about his opera rehearsals. But there was one she had not seen before: a shabbily dressed man who sat by himself, studying some notes with absorption. At first Amy thought he was a tramp who had wandered in to avoid the rain and drink the free coffee. One or two vagrant-type people came into the library sometimes during the day, pretending to read the newspapers, falling asleep and emitting meths and stale sweat. Clem always tried to get them out, but Amy thought they were as entitled as anyone to a read of the newspaper and a comfortable sit-down in a public library, and anyway, it was in the good old English tradition of coffee houses, if it was not in the even older one of soup kitchens.

The man tonight was not emitting meths or stale sweat, and he was making notes in the margins of the hand-out from the talk. Amy collected his cup and he looked up and said, 'Thank you.'

'Did you enjoy the talk?'

'I did,' he said. 'I'm tracing the usage of Ambrosian plainchant, along with one or two other threads of obscure music and poetry.'

'What kind of obscure?'

'Connections between music and poetry and their surroundings,' he said. 'Tracking down links—trying to establish if a local legend has brought about the use or even the composition of a particular piece of music or a sonnet.'

His voice did not match his ragamuffin appearance, and he looked a bit like a Pre-Raphaelite painter or even a consumptive poet from the days when romance had a capital R. Oh God, not Shelley again. And he had talked about sonnets, as well.

But he said, 'You've got an abandoned village here, haven't you?'

'Yes. Priors Bramley.'

'I'm hoping to go out there when they finish disinfecting it,' he said. 'Oliver Goldsmith wrote a poem called *The Deserted Village*. It's *a bit* idealized, but it's full of thumbnail sketches of people going about ordinary lives in the eighteenth century, then having to leave because the land was "usurped".'

He paused as if unsure whether to go on, and Amy said, '"Usurped"? Enclosure? Some feudal overlord yomping arrogantly across the fields, snaffling people's cottages to build a palladian folly or something?'

He smiled, but he said, 'Yes, something like that.'

'With Priors Bramley it was a government who did the yomping in order to build a motorway,' said Amy. 'Only then they sloshed a load of corrosive stuff everywhere and poisoned the place for years. Some people still call it the Poisoned Village.'

'That's what interested me. Goldsmith has a line about poisoned fields in his poem. That's why I thought I'd stay for a few days—I'd like to see if anything about Priors Bramley mirrors Goldsmith's fictional Auburn.'

'Art imitating nature,' said Amy. 'Or the other way round.' And then, because it was Priors Bramley they were talking about and she had spent the last few days buried in the place's history, she said, 'Did you find any other echoes?'

'As a matter of fact there is another one,' he said. 'An old, virtually vanished opera called *The Deserted Village*. It's by an Irish composer from the mid-to-late 1800s— John William Glover, he's called—and he based it on the Goldsmith poem. But the curious thing is that there's a recording of that music here in this library. It's old and very scratchy, and it's not the whole opera, of course—just a kind of potted version. Maybe even only the overture. But whatever it is, it's full of harmonies that chime with the cadences of the poem and it's really surprising to find it in any library...Sorry, I'm getting carried away, and it looks as if they're waiting to lock up. Do you work here?'

'Holiday job,' said Amy.

'Student?'

'Second year at Durham.'

He nodded as if this was an acceptable explanation, thanked her again, and went out.

'He's been into the library once or twice,' said Clem, when questioned about the man next morning. 'He's staying at the Red Lion, I think. Some sort of music researcher, somebody said. Unusual chap, isn't he?'

'I didn't notice,' said Amy, burrowing into her photographs.

It was an odd feeling to see the faces of people who had lived in the village—the deserted village, thought Amy, remembering the conversation about the poem. Some of the wartime photos were interesting as well. Amy liked seeing the hairstyles of the females, and the clumpy shoes, and she liked the paragraphs snipped from the *Bramley Advertiser* as well. They told how you could rub gravy browning on your legs to make it look as if you were wearing stockings, and what to do if the moths got into your woollen frock. There were reports of how the Spitfire Fund was getting on, grisly 'Beware' warnings to look out for German spies who might still be roaming the countryside, and what to do if people thought they had identified one. But to balance that were reports of the celebrations for D-Day and VE Day—street parties and victory marches. It looked pretty good fun. The Red Lion had provided most of the food for the celebrations, although Amy supposed it would have been fairly spartan, what with people's cupboards being bare after six years of war. Spam and eggless cakes.

As she went back to Gran's house for lunch, the air was misty from the spraying that was still going on down in Priors Bramley. People were finding it a bit irritating—

it got in your hair and made everything damp. But there were only another few days left before the village would be ready to be reopened.

Entries from an Undated Journal

There are only another five days left.

I've tried every way I can to escape, but it's impossible and I've run out of ideas. It looks as if I must acquiesce—sit here with my hands meekly folded and allow death to come to me. But it's a nightmare prospect, and then there's the matter of what comes after death—that's even worse. Or is it? I've been a good member of the Protestant Church—none of your papist rubbish for *me*, thank you very much—and I attended church service on Sundays, well, most Sundays.

When I pace the length of this small room, and when I see how swiftly the clock ticks its way round to yet another midnight, I'm filled with such despair and fury I can scarcely contain it. Who would have thought it would end here? Who would have thought that hell-inspired journey in 1912 would lead to this?

I didn't know the entire truth about that journey, not at the beginning. That was Crispian again. Devious, you see. I promise you, Machiavelli had nothing on Crispian Cadence. But if I'm honest—and since I'm staring death in the face it's probably the time to be completely honest—long before we set off it had occurred to me that the journey could present a whole range of opportunities to get rid of him. Travel's hazardous. People fall under railway trains or off ships. In foreign countries they're poisoned by peculiar food, or they contract malaria or jungle fever. They're bitten by venomous snakes or knifed by people with grudges against the British Empire. The list seemed endless. But whatever I did would have to be carefully planned and I still needed to be wary of the periods of darkness. I suspected I was not entirely in control at those times, and it would be no good doing something dramatic and unplanned during one of those spells. For one thing, it might fail. More to the point, I might get caught.

I wondered how many people would mourn Crispian if I managed to kill him. Quite a lot, most likely. He was so memorable, so noticeable. In any group of people he was always the one people looked at or turned to. I did myself, I couldn't help it. And I suspect that in fifty or even a hundred years' time, if people find photographs of him, he's the one they'll look at.

And so we set off for Marseilles. Crispian was being his usual charming efficient self with railway porters and carriage attendants. The porters were occasionally a bit surly, but I think money changed hands to smooth the way. There's nothing like the chink of a couple of sovereigns to solve difficulties.

Halfway to Marseilles somebody quoted the famous Flecker verse:

We travel not for trafficking alone;
By hotter winds our fiery hearts are fanned:
For lust of knowing what should not be known,
We take the Golden Road to Samarkand.

Very appropriate, of course, but within the first two days of the journey I saw that this bizarre, macabre voyage would be much closer to travelling the road to hell than to Flecker's visionary Golden Road.

I was wrong. The journey was far worse than any hell we could have imagined.

1912

Crispian had known the journey would be difficult. What he had not realized was that it would be hellish.

He had thought his father would create the difficulties, but Dr Martlet had administered some sort of bromide and

Julius Cadence went meekly into the cab that was waiting for them, the luggage and a big cabin trunk already strapped to the roof. Crispian felt a knife twist in his guts when he saw how obediently and unsuspectingly his father got inside.

The difficulties came mostly from Gil Martlet. Crispian supposed he should have known Gil would cause disruptions, but he had not expected any to occur quite so early in the journey. But heading south across France, in the first-class private carriage, Jamie suddenly said, 'Where's Gil?'

Crispian had been immersed in a *Times* article about the Balkans War. A 'Balkan League' had apparently been formed, with the idea of liberating Macedonia from the Turkish yoke. The aim seemed to be the ultimate ejection of the Turks from Europe, largely because the Turkish government had not carried out promised reforms. Crispian thought it sounded complicated and potentially dangerous. It was slightly worrying to read about Greece's involvement. Crispian hoped the decision to sail round the Greek coast would not turn out to be a bad one. Thomas Cook had said as long as they did not go near the Turkish coastline they would be perfectly safe, but *The Times* had provided a helpful map explaining where the areas of aggression were, and Turkey was worryingly close to Greece.

He looked up at Jamie's question and said, 'Gil went to the washroom, didn't he?'

'Well, either he's having the longest wash in living memory or he's been taken ill,' said Jamie. 'Because it's over an hour since he went out.'

'Oh Lord,' said Crispian resignedly and, putting the Balkan worries aside, went out to address a worry nearer home.

Gil was discovered in a carriage near the luggage compartment with the waitress who had served their lunch earlier. They had pulled down the blind, but behind it Crispian discovered they were tangled sweatily on a threadbare banquette, the waitress's skirts pushed round her waist, her bodice unfastened, revealing her breasts. He had time to reflect that this particular act looked extraordinarily ungainly to an onlooker, then embarrassment and annoyance took over.

Gil lifted his head and looked straight at Crispian. A grin lifted his lips. 'Be with you in a while, dear boy,' he said. 'Unless you'd care to join me...?'

'Good God, no!' said Crispian instantly.

'Pity. But I'll come back to the carriage fairly soon,' said Gil, as the waitress wound her legs round him again.

Crispian got himself out of the carriage, but he did not go back to his compartment. He stood in the corridor, staring through the window at the passing countryside, beating down the spike of sexual desire that had sliced through him at Gil's words. *Unless you'd care to join me*—the words throbbed in Crispian's mind.

When Gil came out into the corridor Crispian found he could not look directly at him. This was absurd. He ought to be feeling furious; Gil was supposed to be helping with this difficult, dangerous journey but at the first opportunity he had vanished in order to have sex with the nearest available female.

Gil appeared entirely untroubled. 'Have we reached Marseilles yet?' he enquired. 'I didn't think we were due there for another hour at least.'

In a low, furious voice, Crispian said, 'You're supposed to be here to help me with my father! Gil, how could you go off like that?'

'All too easily,' said Gil, lounging against the window, and looking out. 'It didn't matter, did it? Your father's all right, isn't he?'

'Yes, but he might not have been. Have you no self-control?' said Crispian, realizing too late what he had said.

'As a matter of fact I've got very good self-control,' said Gil, and Crispian heard the smile in his voice. 'I even managed to time rhythms to coincide with the vibration of the wheels—'

'For heaven's sake,' said Crispian, glancing down the corridor.

'—although it was touch and go when we hit that fast downhill stretch. It's considered the height of discourtesy to succumb to premature ejaculation with a total stranger, isn't it?' He sent Crispian his lazy smile and went unhurriedly back to their private carriage.

Crispian remained where he was. I can't take him on this journey after all, he thought. Not if he's going to behave like this all the time. *Join me,* he had said... *Join me...*And with the words, a shocking bolt of longing had seized Crispian—not romantically by the heart, but bawdily, between the legs.

Then he thought, no, it will be all right. Jamie's here. He'll keep Gil reined in. And Gil was making fun of me— he's always done that. Remembering this, he felt better, and was able to return to the private compartment and reach for the discarded *Times.* Jamie was in the other corner, apparently engrossed in a book, and Julius sat opposite, drowsy and unfocused from one of the bromides Gil's father had provided. Martlet had given Crispian several doses of the powders with a note as to how often they should be given. Julius seemed hardly aware of where he was; Crispian hoped he could keep him like that until they had got him onto the ship. If his father came out of the drugged stupor and realized what was happening, he might well resist.

Several times, as Crispian worked his way through *The Times,* he sensed Gil watching him. Once he could not resist glancing up. Gil did not speak, but there was amusement in his eyes, fixed on Crispian, and Crispian lowered his gaze at once.

As the train jolted its way across France to Marseilles, night began to fall. Crispian was deeply grateful for this, because it meant they would be able to board the ship in darkness.

CHAPTER TEN

Entries from an Undated Journal

W E BOARDED THE SHIP at Marseilles by darkness, and as we did so, I realized with panic and despair that my own darkness was starting to close around me.

I don't think anyone noticed—I had become very good at hiding it by that time. Perhaps they thought I was tired from the long journey and I mumbled something about feeling a bit travel-sick. Fortunately it was quite a small ship, probably with no more than thirty passengers in all, and I was able to get to my cabin with minimal fuss.

The crushing pain was already wrenching my mind, but when the pain stopped, the deformity was in place. That was when I felt lighter, stronger, filled up with power as if it had been poured into me from a jug. I could conquer the world, do anything I wanted. Stevenson's Mr Hyde, prowling the dim cobbled streets, had understood about that soaring exultancy, that deep strong wish to inflict violence, and I understood it too. During those darknesses, the longing to kill Crispian was almost over-whelming. But if I gave in to it, I knew I would not be sufficiently careful. I would not plan or bother to cover my tracks. I would simply slay him on the crest of that dark arrogance and glory in his death with no thought for the consequences. It could not be risked. Murdering Crispian could only be done when I was sane and in control.

So I spun the lie about feeling travel-sick and scuttled away to my cabin in the wake of a ship's officer. He moved quickly, presumably because he was afraid I might vomit on the clean floor. I kept a hand clapped over my mouth to foster this impression; you get used to practising these small deceptions; they're not praiseworthy, but they're necessary.

Once in the cabin I thanked whatever gods might be appropriate that we were not to share sleeping quarters. My quarters for the voyage consisted of a narrow room with a built-in bed and cupboard, a washstand and chair. It was airless and cramped already, and by the time we reached the Italian coast it would probably have turned into an oven, but I would have suffered a worse fate than baking below decks for the benison of that privacy. There was no lock on the door but the small chair could be wedged under the handle. I was shaking so badly by that time I could scarcely hold the chair, but eventually I got it in place, then threw myself on the bed and lay there, ready to do battle with the pain. It would pass in time; all I had to do was remain strong. Here it came—the crunching-bone agony, then the scalding feeling of power. There was a small oblong mirror fastened to the wall over the wash-stand, but I did not dare look into it.

The pain passed after two hours—a mercifully short time—and light began to trickle back into my mind. I splashed cold water onto my face from the ewer left on the marble washstand. There were towels and soap as well. I'll say many things against Crispian, but I have to admit he was never mean. The ship was small but the cabin was properly appointed and it looked as if passengers' comfort would be well catered for.

Restored and refreshed, I removed the chair from the door and went out. There had been mention of a passengers' lounge for meals, and the prospect of food and drink and the company of normal human beings was comforting.

1912

Crispian thought that considering the macabre nature of this journey, it was progressing reasonably well.

He hoped it would be uneventful, but they were only a few miles out into the Mediterranean when a storm blew up and most of the passengers were seasick. Crispian and Jamie managed to stagger up on deck, which was said to be the best place. Crispian did indeed feel better in the open, even with the rain lashing down, but Jamie hung over the side, retching and groaning, so Crispian left him to it, and made his way back downstairs to look in on his father.

Julius's cabin was hot and gloomy, and there was a slightly sour smell. There was a basin and ewer in the washstand cupboard, and Crispian guessed his father had been sick, like most of the passengers.

Julius was half-lying on the narrow bed, his shoulders hunched, his face to the wall, but he turned when Crispian came in.

'How are you feeling?' said Crispian.

Julius peered at him uncertainly. 'Crispian?'

His eyes were unfocused and his voice was blurred. He's not sure who I am, thought Crispian with a twist of apprehension, but, speaking in as normal a tone as possible, he said, 'I came to see if you were all right. Have you been seasick? Most people were.'

Julius frowned, then appeared to recollect his surroundings. 'Sick,' he said, as if trying out the word. 'Yes, I was sick.' He sat up a little straighter. 'Wretched storm,' he said. 'Still, you can't take to the sea without expecting a storm or two.'

This was so rational a remark, and Julius looked so much like his old self, Crispian relaxed.

'Ring for the steward if you need anything,' he said. 'I'll see you a little later on. We'll have supper here together if you feel up to eating.'

Julius nodded, then said abruptly, 'The Aegean Sea, that's where we're going, isn't it?'

'Yes.' Crispian had explained this on the train from Waterloo. He had brought an atlas and traced the journey out for his father.

'As long as it doesn't turn out to be the Styx,' said Julius, a glint in his eyes. Crispian's heart gave a thump of apprehension. 'Or even,' said Julius, regarding Crispian with his head on one side, 'the River of Jordan?' His eyes were no longer fogged, they were sharp and clear, and for a moment he was again the strong, powerful man of Crispian's childhood: the man who had headed Cadences Bank for so many years and wielded authority over so many people. 'Did you think I didn't know what was going on?' he said. 'Let's have honesty between us at least, Crispian.'

'We're being perfectly honest,' said Crispian. 'Jamie and I want to study foreign banking procedures. You've been working too hard and this is a recuperative trip for your health. Dr Martlet suggested it. I explained all that to you.'

'You always were a damn good liar,' said Julius, turning away.

Gil's cabin was on the same corridor, a little further along. Crispian hesitated, then knocked lightly on the door. His heart was beating a little too fast, which would be the result of that brief disconcerting interview with his father or even the seasickness earlier. He was just thinking Gil was not going to answer—or perhaps was asleep—when Gil called out to come in.

He was lying on his bunk, a book propped up, and he was wearing a silk dressing gown in dark red. His hair was disordered and the robe was slightly open at the chest. There was a faint scent of pine on the air, as if he might just have washed.

'I'm only looking in to see how you're feeling,' said Crispian.

'Never better,' said Gil, although he was pale and there was a faint beading of moisture on his brow. 'I've asked the steward to bring some chilled champagne, as a matter of fact. Finest thing in the world for seasickness, chilled champagne. It'll be here in a minute.' He considered Crispian. 'You could stay and drink it with me,' he said softly, and although he did not quite move over on the narrow bed as if to make room for Crispian, he somehow gave the impression of doing so.

'Champagne gives me indigestion,' said Crispian.

But as he went out he was aware of Gil smiling the narrow-eyed smile he remembered from the train.

❁ ❁ ❁

When they reached Nice, Gil proposed they dine at one of the restaurants on the famous Promenade des Anglais.

'At my father's expense, I suppose,' said Crispian caustically.

'Yes, of course. I certainly can't afford it, dear boy,' said Gil. 'But I do think we should sample some of the local delicacies while we're here.'

Crispian, who was writing a letter home, glanced up at him suspiciously. 'What had you in mind?'

'Bouillabaisse and salade niçoise,' said Gil, meeting Crispian's eyes guilelessly. 'Both famous dishes of this area.'

Jamie, however, requested to be omitted from the party. One had, of course, to eat, he said, but there were a number of famous works of art to be seen, and he would very much like to study them. 'I thought you two wouldn't be very interested in the museum,' he said, 'and I don't really want to explore the nightlife, so I thought I'd hire the services of one of the guides for the afternoon. The captain says they're always around the quayside, and providing one's careful they're generally trustworthy. There's an art gallery I want to see. I'll go out there with a guide on my own and have supper here with the captain and your father when I return.'

'In that case,' said Gil, 'Crispian and I will dine out. Give our regards to the paintings and the statues.'

Gil had been right about the bouillabaisse, which was delicious, and the Chablis they drank with it was excellent. Almost despite himself, Crispian found he was relaxing and enjoying Gil's flippant conversation.

'Here's to you, Crispian,' said Gil at one point, lifting his glass. His eyes were dark and glowing in the candlelit restaurant, and Crispian thought he was not completely sober. Then he thought he himself was not completely sober, either.

As if guessing his thoughts, Gil said, 'I'm fairly tipsy, dear boy. You'll have to take my arm to get me back to the ship.' He appeared to be perfectly serious, and when they left the restaurant and Crispian did take his arm, he was acutely aware of the muscles beneath the cloth of Gil's lightweight jacket.

They reached the ship around eleven and, as Crispian opened the door of his cabin, Gil leaned against the wall, watching him. It was infuriating to find this disturbing.

'Am I to be asked in for a nightcap?' said Gil. 'Because I've got a bottle of brandy in my cabin I could fetch.'

Crispian hesitated, intending to say he would have an early night, but heard himself say, 'Yes, we'll have a nightcap. Shall we call Jamie in as well?'

'Let's keep it just to the two of us.'

Gil poured the brandy and when he passed Crispian the glass his fingers brushed Crispian's hand, then lay against his palm for a moment. Crispian felt as if a thousand red-hot needles had slid under his skin. Oh God, he thought, I don't have these kinds of feelings for another man, I *don't*...He's teasing me, that's all.

He took the glass without speaking and went to sit on the narrow window seat beneath the porthole.

Gil's next words surprised him. He said, 'You're a good liar, Crispian.'

This was such a clear echo of what Crispian's father had said, that Crispian turned to stare at him. 'What do you mean?' he said at last.

'My father told me the reason for this trip was recuperative,' said Gil. 'He said Sir Julius had suffered some kind of "brain fever". That doesn't mean a thing. It could be a cover for anything from epilepsy to plain old-fashioned dementia.' He frowned, then in a more serious voice than Crispian had yet heard him use, said, 'But I've watched Julius since we left England and I don't much like what I've seen.' He regarded Crispian over the rim of his brandy glass. 'I've surprised you, haven't I?' he said. 'Did you forget I've studied medicine for four years?'

'I had forgotten for the moment,' said Crispian. 'But never mind. What is it you've seen?'

'For one thing, your father has episodes of gaze palsy—an inability of the eyes to move in the same direction at the same time. At times the upper eyelids are retracted—creating a fixed downward gaze as if he's constantly trying to examine his own lower lids. There's also photophobia—extreme sensitivity to light. He shies from almost all forms of light, doesn't he?'

'Yes.'

'There could be any number of reasons for those symptoms,' said Gil. 'I haven't the experience to know. It could simply be poor eyesight. He's perfectly rational for a large part of the time, but then a mental confusion seems to come down. Almost as if a curtain's lowered. Time seems to blur for him, as well—as if he loses whole segments of it.' He paused to sip his brandy. 'What's really wrong with him? And don't ask for my opinion, because I'm a disgraced, three-quarters trained medical student so I'm not venturing a diagnosis.'

Crispian paused, then in an expressionless voice said, 'He's in the final stages of syphilis.'

'Syphilis'. The word came out softly but it was almost as if something in the small, too-warm cabin recoiled.

'Dear God,' said Gil, staring at him. 'Syphilis. The roué's disease. I should have thought of it—I always heard he was a bit of a rip in his younger days, your father.'

'Apparently it can end in destroying the brain as much as the body—that's what's happening to him now,' said Crispian. 'Your father thinks he probably contracted it years ago and that it's been undiagnosed until now.'

'He's kept it hidden?'

'Yes. Your father also said it's a disease that can lie dormant for years, but that it nearly always comes back.'

'It does. I saw quite a number of cases when I was working on the wards at Guy's. We used to get a lot of sailors coming in for treatment so I learned quite a bit about it. And I remember a lecture—some German scientist came up with a drug a few years ago. If I hadn't drunk so much tonight I'd remember his name.' He frowned, clearly searching his memory. 'Ehrlich, that's it. Paul Ehrlich. He called his drug—I'll remember that in a minute, as well. Why does alcohol fog the brain? I know it was hailed as a miracle cure at the time—a "magic bullet", they called it. Salvarsan, that's the name. I don't think it's been very widely used. The mercury cure is still what most doctors try.' A glint of flippancy showed. 'A night with Venus and a lifetime with Mercury,' he said. 'That's the old saying. But even mercury's only a temporary cure.'

'Your father said the mercury cure wasn't worth trying,' said Crispian. 'He said the disease has progressed too far, and it's a painful cure anyway.'

'God, yes, it is. Even those hardened old sailors used to scream and beg the nurses to stop. But, Crispian, if my father said mercury wasn't worth trying, you can trust his judgement. He's a dry old stick, but he does know medicine.' He paused again. 'Not everyone dies from syphilis, but once it does get its claws in, it eats its way through flesh and nerve and brain tissue and...Julius is definitely in the final stage? The tertiary stage?'

'Yes.' Crispian remembered Gil's father using this term. 'He said it's progressed to neurosyphilis.'

'Dear God,' said Gil. 'Did he explain what that entailed?'

'It affects the brain,' said Crispian in an expressionless voice. 'There might be personality changes. But whatever happens, he'll end as a helpless maniac, probably more or less paralysed.'

'General paralysis of the insane,' said Gil, staring at him. 'Oh, Crispian, I'm so very sorry. The poor sod. Has he got chancres? The sores?'

'Some. He covers them up with scarves and gloves. His face was marked a while ago—blisters and sores—but they seem to have healed. For the moment, at any rate.'

'Does Jamie know the truth?' said Gil, suddenly.

'I used your father's term, "brain fever", to Jamie,' said Crispian. 'He doesn't know the truth, but he knows my father might be dangerous, that he has to be watched at all times. I had to tell him that much, because I needed an ally.'

'And as well as Jamie you got an ally you didn't bargain for with me,' said Gil. 'Well, even with an incomplete medical training I might be of some use.'

'I wonder if that's what your father had in mind,' said Crispian, and Gil grinned.

'More likely he wanted me out of England because of the hasty exit I had to make from Guy's.'

'Why did you have to make a hasty exit?'

'Do I have to say?'

'Perhaps better not,' said Crispian, a bit too quickly.

'How much does Julius himself know?'

'He hasn't been told he's got syphilis. But he's no fool.'

'Does he know he's dying?'

'I don't know.'

'And so,' said Gil thoughtfully, 'you've brought him all these thousands of miles to die. Is that in case it gets out that the head of Cadences Bank is gradually becoming helplessly insane?'

'Yes. If it becomes known, investors might take their money out. I don't suppose Cadences would actually crash, but it could be seriously harmed. That would mean people's lives would be affected—not just employees but people with small life savings.'

'Always that touch of *noblesse oblige*,' said Gil, lightly.

'Don't be so cynical.'

'But Cadences is strong enough to survive a few lost investors, surely? It's been going long enough.'

'It's not an easy time for any banking organization,' said Crispian.

'Ah. The Germans trying to corner everything they can,' said Gil. 'Aided by Austro-Hungary half the time.' He grinned. 'I've surprised you again, haven't I? You're thinking I'm not altogether the irresponsible shallow wastrel you thought me, and you're wondering if you should revise your opinion.' Before Crispian could think how to respond to this, he said, 'Is Julius likely to die while we're at sea?'

'Your father thought he probably only had a few weeks left. He said the deterioration had become rapid over the last six months. And I suppose once it reaches the brain—'

'So,' said Gil, his eyes bright and a faint flush across his cheekbones, 'for a few hours of pleasure with a handful of women, he's ended up with a filthy bone-nibbling, flesh-destroying disease that sends its victims scuttling into the shadows so no one will see its repulsive pawmarks. God, it's enough to make a man give up fucking for life. And don't make that prudish face, Crispian, because I know damn well there's nothing prudish about you.' In the glow from the cabin's lamp his eyes had a curious luminous quality like a cat's: Crispian could see the tiny golden flecks in the deeper brown. Neither of them spoke, then Gil put out a hand to Crispian.

Crispian's heart was beating like a steam-hammer, but after a moment, he moved away, ignoring the hand, not even looking at Gil. He managed to say, 'Gil, you do know I'm not—'

'Aren't you?' said Gil harshly. They looked at one another, then Gil said very quietly, 'Do you know, I believe I'm drunker than I thought. I'll go to my cabin and try to sleep it off.' He turned away and went quickly out.

Crispian listened to his footsteps dying away. His mind was in turmoil and he had to make a massive effort not to go after Gil. But somehow he forced away the desire to do so. This journey was for his father, who was going to die. It was for keeping Julius as safe and comfortable as they could manage, and it was also to protect Cadences and all its staff and investors. Nothing else should matter. Hell, thought Crispian, nothing else *does* matter.

But his emotions were still scalding through his entire body, and they were so strong they frightened him. I can't feel like this about another man, he thought, I simply can't. He forced his mind to recall girls he had known at Oxford—nice girls who were the sisters or cousins of friends and could be taken to lunch and with whom one might venture a daring kiss on the cheek. And there had been other girls who took it as a matter of course that things would go well beyond a chaste kiss or a respectful guiding arm. They worked in bars or clubs, those girls, and thought it ever so exciting to be smuggled into an undergraduate's room. They giggled a good deal, and although they did not precisely expect to be paid hard cash for the liberties they allowed, it was usually understood that some kind of generous gift would be forthcoming. Crispian had known several such girls and he had enjoyed his experiences with them very much. That was how it should be. It should not be this dangerous excitement, this pulsating desire because another man's hand had lain against your own for a few moments, or because glowing dark brown eyes, filled with secret promise, had stared into yours.

CHAPTER ELEVEN

London, 1912

SERENA THOUGHT IT WAS curious how one secret could bring about another. She and the Flaggs and Dr Martlet had kept the knowledge of Julius's insanity from the world for years—far longer than Crispian or anyone else had suspected. At first the attacks had been of quite short duration; Dr Martlet had talked about overwork and brain fever, and been reassuring. He had kept Julius docile with various draughts and potions at those times. Serena had agreed to it all, relieved to have the decisions made for her, but she had found it deeply distressing to see Julius, usually so vigorous and energetic, sitting meekly in a chair, staring vacantly at nothing.

The room at the top of the house had been Dr Martlet's suggestion; the spells of confusion were becoming more pronounced, he had said in the summer of 1910. It was possible they might spiral into violence. Serena had reluctantly agreed.

During the periods when Julius had to be locked inside the appalling room, Dr Martlet called at the house every day—sometimes twice a day. Mrs Flagg set meals on a tray, which Flagg carried upstairs. Serena knew quite well that without Dr Martlet and the Flaggs, Julius's condition would certainly have been known earlier. Crispian would have known, and Colm. The bank...She had never known a great deal about the running of Cadences—it had never been expected that she would—but it did not take much logic to see that investors in Cadences would be uneasy if they were aware its head had sometimes to be locked away for fear he injure himself. Even so, Julius had never displayed violence towards anyone until the night Crispian came home.

'I'm *that* sorry, madam,' Flagg said, challenged as to how Julius had got out of the room. 'Like I told Mr Crispian, the only thing I can think is that he finagled a key out of the workman when the lock was put in. He might do that, you know. He might have gone along to have a word with the man, friendly like, and the man, not knowing any different, would give him an extra key.'

'Yes, that's possible. It's not your fault, Flagg.'

After that attack, Serena stayed in bed for several days, pleading a bilious turn. In fact, she genuinely felt sick and on the third morning she had to rush to the water closet just off her bedroom, where she was violently ill. When the same thing happened the following morning and the one after that, a faint alarm stirred within her mind, but she managed to dismiss it and hid the bouts of sickness from Dora and Mrs Flagg.

But by then she was aware of another symptom—or, not a symptom exactly, more of an omission. She counted up the days, a small frown creasing her brow. One week after Julius's attack she should have felt the familiar ache in her womb; it should have been necessary to make use of the discreet padding arrangements kept in the bottom drawer of her dressing table. But she had not needed them and she still did not. Also, a swollen tenderness was starting to be apparent in her breasts, a feeling she remembered from the months before Crispian's birth.

It could not be that, it could *not*. She counted up the weeks again, this time using her diary to be sure, but the result was the same. Then she reminded herself she was forty-two and this was surely nothing more than the start of that last watershed of a female's life, the process that signalled the ending of child-bearing years. But the memory of Julius ramming into her body, brutally and convulsively that night, was still with her.

'I'm afraid there can be no doubt,' said Dr Martlet, four weeks later, having performed the hateful intrusive examination. 'You're going to have a child, Lady Cadence.' He sounded stern but he also sounded deeply sad, as if he thought he should have been able to prevent this.

'Are you quite sure about it?' asked Serena.

'I am. I'm sorry. I should have been firmer about Sir Julius, and I should have warned you...The male instincts are still strongly with him, it seems. I should have warned you he might want to—'

'You couldn't have known,' said Serena quickly, because it would be curdlingly embarrassing if he referred to the marriage act. Nor could she possibly let anyone know that Julius had forced her. Let Dr Martlet and anyone else believe this conception had happened during one of Julius's normal spells—one of the times when he was living in the house as usual, talking to people, behaving ordinarily.

Martlet did not press the point. He merely said, 'I shall take very good care of you.'

After Dora had shown him out, Serena sat by the window of her bedroom for a long time. Her mind was in turmoil. People said nowadays that the manner of a child's conception could not influence its character.

But what of a child fathered by a man at the height of insanity? A child conceived from out of that violent *darkness*.

Entries from an Undated Journal

There were no darknesses in Crispian's life. I always knew that. All that lay ahead of him were good and happy things. Inherited money and property, and let's not forget Cadences itself. I could see him very clearly indeed sitting in the bank's famous oak-panelled boardroom, presiding over directorial meetings, issuing orders, controlling the lives of so many people. And the thing that hurt most was that he would do it so well and all those people would like and trust him. They would like him right up until he died, and probably afterwards. Whereas it's unlikely anyone will mourn me, or even remember me after I'm dead.

It's a curious feeling to know so definitely when you're going to die. There are four and a half days left to me now. One hundred and eight hours. Or have I miscounted? Dear God, *have* I? No, I'm right. Why I should panic so massively at the thought I might have miscalculated a few hours, I can't think.

I believe if I could put an end to my life now and avoid what's ahead I'd do so, but it's impossible and, believe me, gentle reader, I've checked. I've bloody checked every fucking possibility and there's absolutely no way I can commit suicide...

Rereading that last sentence, it amuses me to juxtapose flowery Victorian or Austen-esque phrasing with stinging obscenity. In any case, they weren't so very prim, those Victorians, it was just that they had to appear to bow to the conventions of the day. I'll bet Charles Dickens sometimes had to restrain himself from adding a saucy paragraph or two when he chronicled the exploits of his street women and his gangs of ruffians. And let's not forget H. G. Wells and his numerous liaisons and free-thinking outlook, or Oscar Wilde...

I'm straying from the point. I'm trying to explain, to anyone who might read this, that there's nothing I can do to cheat the inevitable. But there's also the fact that I haven't entirely given up hope. I still have a tiny, absurd green shoot of belief that something will happen, that some long-odds, outside chance will rear up and come hurtling in like a *deus ex machina*. God in a machine, riding to my rescue? Some chance.

God was certainly nowhere to be seen during that sea voyage, and if anyone walked with me that day the ship docked at Messina, it was the Devil...

I sometimes think if any of the great actor-managers had witnessed my behaviour during that sea voyage, they would have whisked me off to their theatres there and then, and set me down on their lighted stages.

I was *good*. No, dammit, I wasn't just good, I was *inspired*. Believe me, David Garrick and Henry Irving had nothing on me, and as sure as God is my judge I fooled everyone. It's extraordinary how, once you adopt a role, it starts to become part of you. I think it's safe to say I almost became the person I was trying to portray. I wanted to become that person as well, I honestly did. I wanted to be normal. But every time I thought I might be within grasping distance the darkness would stir.

It was with me on the day the ship put into Messina and it was one of the times when I let it have its way—one of the times when it was too strong for me.

Messina is a very old city, but it suffered an earthquake a few years before our visit—1908, I think it had been—and a lot of it had been rebuilt. Even so, the traces of the ancient city were still visible. There were fragments of Greek and Byzantine influences, if anyone reading this likes that kind of historical detail. And, like most cities, you can walk along a modern street with smart new buildings, then turn a corner and find yourself in an ancient cobbled square, as if you've stepped back three or four centuries. I've done that many a time in London.

That day in Messina, there was one moment when I was in a broad street, with bustle and shops and people, and then the next moment I was in a dark narrow alleyway in the shadow of one of the ancient cathedrals. There was a service going on inside the cathedral. I could hear faint chanting voices and the sonorous notes of an organ. It sounded as if they were reciting the General Confession. It was in Latin, of course, and although I'm no scholar in the accepted sense, I remembered enough of my schooldays to translate most of it. *Mea culpa*, they were chanting. *Mea culpa, mea culpa, mea maxima culpa...*And even though the darkness had its teeth and claws into me, I stood there in that ancient corner of an old city, my mind splintering with pain, and found myself asking forgiveness for what I was going to do. It was very nearly medieval behaviour, like those sly, venal priests who traded in indulgences and sold pardons before the sin was committed. Like building up a credit balance with God. But I stood there and thought— God forgive me for what I can no longer help. Then I went, like that poor wretched creature Edward Hyde, deeper into Messina's Old Quarter to slake the hunger and reach the peace that always came afterwards.

I found what I wanted quite quickly. Any city has its women of the streets, and ports probably have more than most. The alley I entered was narrow and sunless, with tall deserted buildings on both sides, warehouses of some kind, their windows boarded up. Arched bridges spanned the street overhead and it was a slightly sinister place. But oh God, it was so very exciting to stand in a shadowy doorway, waiting. It was, in fact, an excitement that tipped over into actual sexual arousal. I write that without comment and once again the reader may judge me as he or she wishes. But I'll wager that a great many murderers—and murderers *manqué*—go to their macabre work in a semi-erectile state. The books don't describe that, of course.

As I waited, my heart thudding with anticipation, one or two people walked past, but I pressed back against the wall and none of them seemed aware of me.

There's a line from some Shakespearean play, I forget which one, but it goes, 'By the pricking of my thumbs, something wicked this way comes...' Those words resonated through my mind and, standing there, I understood what Shakespeare, wily old bard, had meant, because between one heartbeat and the next, I knew, absolutely and utterly, that my victim was approaching. That's something else the books about murderers don't relate. That in the last few moments, an instinct—almost primeval—tells you your prey is within your reach. *By the pricking of my thumbs, something tempting this way comes...*

Footsteps, quick and light, came towards me and I felt my fingers curl into predator's claws. This was it... In another few moments...I watched her walk along the street—there was a faint drift of cheap perfume, and anyone with half an eye could have seen she was a prostitute. She glanced over her shoulder as she went past the doorway where I stood—the quarry scenting the hunter, you see. That pleased me because her fear would lend an edge to what I was about to do.

I stepped out of the doorway before she could reach the far end of the alley, and caught her up. When I put my hand on her arm she turned sharply and fear showed in her eyes, so I smiled and held out a handful of cash. I have no idea how much money I was actually offering her, but the faint fear was instantly replaced by greed, so it was probably quite a lot.

Neither of us knew the other's language, and although I dare say I could have made myself slightly understood with a few Italian phrases, there was hardly any point, and the language of money is universal. She looked at the money, then she looked at me and nodded. She glanced up and down the street, which was deserted, then up at the buildings. Apparently satisfied, she pointed to the doorway where I had been standing.

If I had been in my normal frame of mind I would not have considered, for a moment, performing that act in such a public place. I'd like that understood. But as it was, I pulled her into the shadows and pushed up her skirt, unbuttoning my trousers with my free hand. Then I backed her against the wall and we strained and heaved and sweated together in that doorway. But since it's no part of this journal to record what it has pleased someone to call the slaking of fleshly lusts, I shall merely say the encounter was brief and achieved its culmination. Even with the lure of the money, she flinched several times, and once, just as I reached a climax, I slammed into her with such force she cried out in pain.

On a purely physical level I was satisfied. But on a wholly different level—on the dark plain where my other self walked—there was more I had to do to her. I *had* to. It was the only way to slake the insistent hunger and appease the agony in my head.

I did it there in the shadowy doorway, closing my hands round her neck—rather a coarse-skinned neck she had, I remember—and pressing hard into her windpipe. She choked and spluttered, flailing at me with her hands, trying to gouge my eyes, the vicious little slut. But I was too strong for her and within minutes spittle was running from her mouth and, as she jerked and fought, urine streamed down her legs and splashed over my shoes. That's from the spasms that strangulation causes and it's something that nearly always happens. In fact, I remember once in London—but I was much younger then and not so experienced.

It was only when her tongue started to protrude from her mouth and her eyes rolled up that the darkness began to loosen its grip. I let her fall to the ground, fastened my trousers, sufficiently calm by this time to feel annoyed at the mess over my shoes; they were handmade leather, bought in Jermyn Street. It was my own fault; I should have known better than to wear them.

I stepped back into the sunlight, and went briskly along the alley, back towards one of the cathedral squares. You'll note that I had no concern as to whether I might have left any damning evidence behind me—that's the weakness in my armour. Anything could have fallen from my pocket or my wallet that could have identified me when the girl's body was found. That's why I never made an attempt on Crispian during one of these darknesses.

Later

When I sat down to make this journal entry it was night-time. But now, as I set down my pen, I realize I have written all night, for I see that a thin dawn is breaking and it's the start of a new day. A new day. When I began writing a description of the Messina episode, I had a hundred and eight hours of life left to me. Now I have ninety-eight.

CHAPTER TWELVE

The Present

Everyone in Upper Bramley and the surrounding villages agreed it was a relief when Priors Bramley was finally pronounced safe and wholesome.

The news Ella had been dreading came on the final day of the decontamination operation. She had tried to pretend nothing would happen—that the body of the man would be too deeply buried, or the cleaning project would not go as far as Cadence Manor. But here it was, as clear as a curse, setting the little town buzzing like a hyperactive wasp. Human remains had been found, said people excitedly. Only a collection of bones, but unmistakable. No, it was not known precisely where the bones were— the police had not released much information yet. But the body was thought to have died around fifty years ago, so clearly someone must have been in Priors Bramley that last day—perhaps somehow trapped—and maybe overtaken by the tainting chemicals.

Even Upper Bramley's bored teenagers were sufficiently roused to take an interest, because this was the grossest thing you could imagine. A degree of rivalry sprang up among the fourteen- and fifteen-year-olds, as to who could tell the most ghoulish story about corpses with acid-corroded faces who wrapped bony fingers around people's throats and crushed them to their fleshless chests. The Red Lion, as usual alert to local mood and hearing this version, took spare-ribs off its menu and substituted vegetarian flan.

On the day the discovery was announced, Derek brought the details home, and told Ella about it over supper, which Amy had cooked and Ella suspected she would not be able to eat. But Derek, eating Amy's chilli con carne with what Ella felt to be insensitive enjoyment, reported that the entire council offices were agog over the news. The body was no more than a cluster of bones, of course, said Derek, but there were rumours about some of the bones being damaged.

'Does that mean it was a murder?' said Amy, wide-eyed.

'Not necessarily,' said Ella at once. 'He might have fallen downstairs or something.'

'"He"?'

'Or she. Figure of speech.'

'Actually, I believe it is a man's skeleton,' said Derek.

'Wouldn't it be cool if it turned out to be one of that old family who lived there?' said Amy. 'The Cadence lot. You always hated them, Gran. Maybe a black sheep turned up and one of the po-faced Cadences clonked him on the head. Or it was an illegitimate son who had to be silenced to protect the family's reputation. Or even—'

'The Cadences had long since gone by the 1950s,' said Ella repressively. 'It won't be that.'

'A man in my department said the police are going to do DNA and dental tests,' said Derek.

With Derek, there was nearly always a man in his department or in the Operatic Society or the Gardening Club, who knew more than anybody else.

Ella said, 'Probably it's just some old tramp who didn't know about the Geranos experiment.'

'And thought he'd found a good place to spend a few nights?' said Amy.

'Yes. They'll never be able to identify him, not after all this time.'

'This man at the office thinks they'll use carbon dating.'

'Carbon dating is a bit of a blunt instrument for anything after about 1950,' said Amy. 'Radiocarbon concentration was hiked up after then because of the thermonuclear bomb testing, specially in the northern hemisphere.'

'My word, imagine you knowing things like that,' said Derek admiringly. 'They're saying the bones were found in the old lodge house,' he added. 'A man in my office was talking to one of the CID chaps.'

Ella felt as if cold water had been flung straight in her face. She only just managed not to gasp. 'Did you say the lodge? The body was found in the lodge?'

'Yes. What's the matter?'

'Nothing. Just that I thought somebody said it was in the manor house.'

'No, definitely the lodge.'

The lodge, thought Ella. But we left the man's body inside the manor house. It was wedged in the chimney shaft—wedged in very tightly, as well. My mother saw it there, for goodness' sake. She told me so. It couldn't have moved, not unless...

She shut this thought off at once, but it was several moments before she could focus on what Amy and Derek were saying—something about dating bones by some scientific process Ella had never heard of. Amy appeared to know quite a lot about this.

Derek listened carefully, then said, 'Well, this man in my office says—'

Ella could not stand hearing what the boring man in Derek's stupid office had said. She said, very sharply, 'I should think a second-year student of archaeology would know more about dating human bones than a council accounts clerk.' Derek and Amy both stared at her for a moment but Ella was not going to back down. She said, 'You were sounding very teachy, Derek.'

'Was I? Sorry,' said Derek, mildly. He scraped diligently at his plate with his knife. Ella had tried to stop him doing that for years because cutlery against china made her teeth wince, but he still did it. 'Is there any more of this, Amy?' he said. 'It's very tasty. I didn't know you could cook.'

'I can do two dishes, chilli con carne and spaghetti bolognese,' said Amy, getting up to spoon out more chilli from the pot, which was keeping warm on the cooker. 'So make the most of it. But tonight I'll even do the washing-up.'

'Oh, your grandfather will help you with that,' said Ella.

'What's wrong with the dishwasher?' said Derek in a half-exasperated, half-humorous tone.

'I don't like putting the good china in it,' said Ella, annoyed he had not noticed she had set out her nicest dinner service in honour of Amy's cooking.

'Oh. Well, sorry, dear, no can do on the washing-up front. Rehearsal night and I promised to give Yum-Yum a lift.'

It was irritating of Derek to be rushing off to his silly rehearsals, although admittedly he was directing *The Mikado* as well as being in it. Ella was torn between relief that she had apparently hidden her anxiety from him so well and annoyance that he had not sensed something was wrong.

❀ ❀ ❀

Amy thought Gran had seemed a bit fed up this evening, which was why she had cooked her infamous chilli con carne. Gran did not seem to have much of a life, what with Gramps dashing off to rehearsals and talking about his office all the time, although she always said she was busy and Amy would be surprised at the hectic life she led. She had friends whom she met for lunch or coffee, said Gran, and then there was the reading group at the library and her gardening interests—she was on the committee of the Exotic Plants Society. And when the Operatic Society had a social evening she always helped with the refreshments.

'But tonight I believe I'll have a quiet evening, watching TV. I've got a bit of a headache anyway.'

'OK, I'll wash up, then go up to my room to do some work,' said Amy. 'I've got an essay I ought to finish for next term anyway. I keep putting it off.'

She went off to deal with the washing-up, leaving Gran to her headache. It was always very quiet in this house so Amy scooted up to her room to find some music to keep her company in the kitchen. She had managed to track down the music the tramp-man had talked about— *The Deserted Village*—and had booked it out to herself. It was classified in the library's reference section as an old vinyl recording, but at some stage somebody had dubbed it onto a CD—probably in case the original disc was broken. She had been interested in that stuff about the echoes between the music and the poem and Priors Bramley, and she wanted to hear the music.

She slotted the CD into the little player Gran kept in the kitchen, pleased to think that if she did happen to see the man again at least she could make an intelligent remark about it.

The music was extraordinary. It was not the kind of stuff Amy would normally listen to, but it painted vivid images in her mind. Whoever had originally recorded it—and it sounded as if it had been about a million years ago—seemed to have done so purely to preserve it; there was no actual singing, just a piano and, once or twice,

Amy thought, a violin and a flute and even some organ notes. She would have to get hold of the original vinyl disc if it was still in the library and see if there were any sleeve notes.

At first the music was a kind of merry hay-making, capering-peasants stuff. Probably the opera would have had gangs of village lads and lasses at this stage, with leather jerkins and dirndl skirts. There were tootling bird-chirruping sounds as well. But then it changed, subtly and gradually, and a threatening sound crept into the harmonies. Something's approaching, thought Amy, standing in the middle of the kitchen, the teatowel in her hands. Something menacing.

The menace came sweeping in—huge resonating chords like a thunderstorm or like the seven-league boots of a giant stomping over the rural idyll, sweeping cottages and barns aside in order to build his own mansion. Amy found it vaguely frightening. Then, little by little, it trickled away, and an eerie, achingly lonely theme took its place. This is the deserted village at last, thought Amy. This is the sad, lonely place that rotted away, like Priors Bramley's been rotting away behind barbed wire all these years. It's the decaying Cadence Manor where that man in the photograph lived. And it's the abandoned shops where nobody will ever sell bull's-eyes or interlock vests again. And the old church, quietly dying from dry rot and nobody caring...

She would love to play this on a really powerful player with good speakers so that it would belt out the sounds and you would get the full impact of the menace and the huge swathes of heartbreaking loneliness smacking you in the face. She was just thinking this when Gran opened the kitchen door.

Amy turned to say she had finished the washing-up. 'So I'll go upstairs and get to grips with my essay—' She stopped. Gran was grey-faced and pinched-looking. The hand holding the edge of the door was white across the knuckles as if she was gripping the wood too tightly.

Amy said, 'Gran, are you all right?' which was a rubbish thing to say because clearly Gran was not all right at all. Oh God, was she having a heart attack or a stroke or something? No, surely she was too young for that, and Dad always said she was disgustingly healthy, would go on forever, he always said proudly.

But right now Gran did not look as if she would go on forever. In fact she did not look as if she would go on for the next five minutes. Amy, trying not to panic, returned the deserted village to its remote desolation by switching the CD off, pulled a chair out from the breakfast bar, and took Gran's arm and guided her into it.

'What's wrong? Should I phone the doctor?' Who *was* Gran's doctor?

'Of course I don't need a doctor,' said Gran, but it came out a bit tremulously. 'I'm perfectly all right.'

'You didn't look it when you came in,' said Amy. 'For a minute you looked quite ill. Shall I get some brandy or make a cup of tea?' Tea, strong and well sugared, was good for pretty much anything.

'I will have a cup of tea,' said Gran, and Amy filled the kettle, thankful for something useful to do. 'I was just a bit surprised to hear that music,' said Gran as the kettle started to mutter its way to the boil. Her voice sounded a bit stronger although her eyes were still blurry. 'It came as a bit of a shock,' she said, looking at the CD player.

'It's just some music somebody in the library mentioned,' said Amy. 'It's called *The Deserted Village* so I was interested in hearing it because of Priors Bramley. It's based on an old poem. But it is a bit spooky, isn't it?' The kettle boiled and she poured water into the teapot. 'Have you heard it before?'

'Yes.'

'Really?' Amy looked round in surprise.

Gran said with an obvious effort, 'Somebody I knew used to play it—well, parts of it.'

This was instantly intriguing. Amy sat down in the other chair and pushed the cup of tea across. 'Who used to play it, Gran?'

'Oh, just a man I once knew.' The tea seemed to be reviving her. 'A long time ago, it was—before you were even thought of, Amy. Before your father was even thought of, as a matter of fact.'

'A boyfriend?' said Amy hopefully, but Gran gave the small laugh that Amy sometimes thought must have irritated the hell out of Gramps for the last forty years, and said, dear goodness, no, nothing like that.

'Just someone I knew. Rather an unpleasant man.' Amy thought she repressed a small shiver, but she only said, 'So hearing that music gave me a bit of a jolt.' She finished the tea and set the cup down. 'That was very nice,' she said. 'I feel much better. I'll just take one of my pills.'

Amy had no idea what Gran's pills were, but she said, 'Well, OK. But we could phone Gramps, you know. He'd come whizzing back from his rehearsal like a shot.'

'I don't want anyone whizzing back from anywhere.'

❊ ❊ ❊

After Amy had gone upstairs Ella sat for a long time, staring at nothing, the past tumbling through her mind.

The music was *his* music. Ella had recognized it at once, even though it was a very long time—over fifty years—since she had heard it. A deserted village, Amy had said, and the music based on some poem or other. Ella had never heard of the poem, but the music was unquestionably the music that had threaded itself through all the nightmares of her childhood, sometimes rich and sombre, as it had been inside St Anselm's that day, but at other times scratchy and cracked like an old gramophone.

Why had Amy made such a point of getting this particular piece of music and playing it tonight? It was hardly her usual choice. Was Amy taunting her? Surely not. Was someone taunting Ella through Amy? But who? Who else knew about the music?

Amy had said someone in the library had mentioned it. Had that been Clem? His parents had been a bit arty and highbrow—they had listened to the Home Service in the days when everyone Ella knew listened to the Light Programme. When Clem's mother was alive, she and Clem's father went to symphony concerts, taking Clem with them, which most of Upper Bramley regarded as very snobby.

A beat of apprehension began to pulsate inside Ella's head. Was Clem Poulter, stupid clucking old hen, playing some silly mind game? Perhaps even lending Amy the CD in the hope Ella would hear it? But how would Clem know what that particular piece of music meant to Ella? How would anyone know?

The CD was still in the machine, and, almost of its own volition, her hand reached out to the switch. There was a faint whirr of sound, then the notes floated out into the quiet kitchen. The homely scent of washing-up liquid and the faint spicy drift of Amy's chilli dissolved, and Ella was back in that long-ago summer afternoon, with the cuckoo calling in Mordwich Copse, and the scent of lilac and grass everywhere, and the squashy packet of sandwiches her mother had made in her bag. She was ten years old again, walking through a doomed village with her two friends, on her way to kill a man. She had waited nearly six months to kill him and the Geranos experiment had occurred to her as a possible way. She had not, at first, seen how it could be done, only that somewhere in the general disruption an opportunity might arise.

As the music moved to its conclusion the emotions that had driven her ten-year-old self rose fiercely to the surface again. She had felt no guilt that day and she felt none now, all these years later. What she did feel was anxiety verging on panic that after so many years his death might be traced back to her.

Because his death had not been the only murder that had happened inside Cadence Manor. The other one had happened on an autumn evening, that hour when the afternoon slides down into the evening. The sun had been setting over Mordwich Meadow and the scents had been the golden scents of bonfires and chrysanthemums. And on that autumn evening something had happened that no one had ever known about. Something Ella had never talked about, not even to her two best friends, Veronica and Clem.

CHAPTER THIRTEEN

Eᴌᴌᴀ USUALLY WALKED TO school and back home with Clem and Veronica and a few others. None of them lived far from the school, but one of the mothers generally went with them—they told each other you could not be too careful these days; you heard of such awful things happening to children. So they took it in turns to shepherd the children safely through the school gates, then went on for their shopping in Upper Bramley. 'And for coffee in Peg's Pantry,' said Ella's mother acidly. She was never part of the school-escorting or the shopping and coffee expeditions; she said she had better things to do with her time, and anyway she did not like coffee. Ella sometimes thought her mother would quite like to join in but had never been asked.

Usually the children reached home around half-past four, but on this particular autumn afternoon they were a bit later because they had to stay on to hear who was going to be in the end-of-term play. Ella stayed, too; originally she had thought she would like to be in the play, but when her name was not read out she changed her mind and saw it was a stupid, babyish play. Veronica was in it, of course; she was playing a princess, which Ella thought soppy. She would not have wanted to play a princess herself, and Veronica had only been picked because she smarmed up to the teachers.

A boy called Derek Haywood in Veronica's class was going to play the prince. He had only just moved to Upper Bramley so nobody knew him very well, but Veronica said his parents had been in an operatic society in the town where they had lived before, and Derek had been on stage twice already, singing in a children's choir. Clem said it was nothing to do with operatic societies or children's choirs; it was just that the teachers thought they should make a new pupil feel welcome. Clem himself had not been chosen to be in the play, even though he had sung 'Someday My Prince Will Come', and had got all the way through without forgetting the words. He told Ella he did not care and he was going to help write the programme instead. Ella could help if she liked, they could make it really good and have their names in it as the programme's authors. Ella did not particularly want to write a stupid programme but it would be better than not being part of the play at all, so she said yes. She thought Clem had not been picked because he did not look anything like a prince, whereas Derek Haywood was quite nice-looking.

It was an exciting afternoon. People who had been chosen were bursting with importance and telling their friends how good they would be. Then the mother whose turn it was to walk them home had to be told about it, and it all meant Ella was home a bit late.

Her mother was not exactly angry, but she was a bit annoyed. Where on earth had Ella been? When Ella explained about the play, she said, 'Oh, that. Are you going to be in it?'

'No.'

'Well, I don't suppose you mind. You wouldn't want to be bothered with a lot of play-acting anyway.'

'No,' said Ella again. 'But Clem and me—'

'Clem and I.'

'—we're going to write the programme. It'll be really good, Clem says.'

Her mother was not very interested in the play or the writing of the programme, Ella saw that. She was more bothered about Ella being late because she had to go out. The lady from the end cottage had been going to sit with Ella for the hour it would take, but because Ella was so late she could no longer do so.

'She says she has to be somewhere else,' said Ella's mother, 'so you'll have to come with me. Don't screw your face up like that, it's ugly and it's also very common.'

'Where are you going?'

'Priors Bramley.'

Ella stopped screwing up her face, not because it was ugly or common, but because the words 'Priors Bramley' brought back the remembered horror. She had not exactly forgotten about the man who had poured out the music in the church and sobbed so frighteningly, but after a while the memory had receded. There were all kinds of important things going on in her life—lessons and homework and the school play—and he had got pushed to the back of her mind. But as soon as her mother said this about going to Priors Bramley, it all came back.

'I can't come,' she said. 'I've got homework to do.'

'What homework?'

'Um, something for tomorrow's nature study.' She did not look at her mother when she said this, because Mum could always tell when she was lying.

'You don't have nature study until Friday,' said Mum.

'Well, no, but—but it's the serial on TV, *Children's Hour*. It's the last one tonight, so I don't want to miss it.'

She offered this last excuse hopefully, but her mother was not having it. Ella had not really thought she would. She said, 'I'm sorry, but I have an important errand and there's no one else who can come in to sit with you.'

'I don't need sitting with. I'll be all right on my own.'

'I'm not leaving you in the house on your own. Put on your coat, and you'd better fetch your gloves as well.'

'Where are we going in Priors Bramley?'

'To the manor.'

Ella turned round from rummaging in a drawer for her gloves. 'Actually to the house?' Nobody she knew had been inside Cadence Manor, so it would put her one up on the others, with their stupid play about princesses and silver curlews. It would even be worth missing the TV programme. Also, they could get to the manor across Mordwich Meadow, which meant they would not have to walk along the main street and past the church at all.

She asked how long the errand would take. Errands were things grown-ups did, and mostly you never found out what they were. 'I've got to run an errand,' they said, and that was all you were told.

'Not very long.' Mum's voice sounded a bit trembly. 'We'll be back for your television serial,' she said.

As they went along the little back lane towards the manor's side gate, Ella tried to think about the TV programme and not about whether the man from the church might be prowling around. On one side of Cadence Manor was what had once probably been a lawn. Veronica's family had a lawn in their garden where they sometimes put chairs and a table; Ella had had tea there several times. But this was a much bigger lawn, although the grass was so long it brushed the hem of her skirt and tickled her knees. They went towards the house, where a French window was partly open on one side.

And then, trickling into the glowing autumn evening, came sounds that sent fear scudding through Ella. Music. Music she recognized—music coming from what sounded like a record player like the one Clem's parents had. It was the music she had heard that day being played in St Anselm's church.

As they neared the house there was a movement beyond the French windows, and Ella's mother said, 'You stay here, Ella. You'll be all right. I have to just step inside the house for a moment to see someone, so you wait here like a good girl.'

Ella looked about her, trying to shut out the music. Cadence Manor was very old and there were a lot of trees everywhere. Under one oak, quite near the house, was a blur of blue, which might be gentians. You hardly ever found gentians, and it would be pretty good if she could pick some for nature study. She pointed to these.

'Could I get some of those gentians? Nobody'd mind, would they? It'd be extra good if I could take them to school for nature study.'

'I should think so,' said Mum, looking to where Ella was pointing. 'Only pick a few, though. And don't go anywhere else in the grounds.'

'I won't. I'll sit on that bit of crumbly wall when I've got them,' said Ella.

She watched her mother walk up to the house and go through the French window. As she did so, the music shut off with a scrape as if whoever was in there had lifted the needle off the record's surface and had not done so smoothly. The movement came again and this time an arm came up to the window, drawing thick curtains over it, almost all the way. As Ella watched, the movement was repeated at the two other windows. Whoever was in there had stopped the record and was shutting out the blazing sunset. Ella thought it was a bit peculiar. But the really peculiar thing was that no lights were switched on inside the room.

Ella went over to the blue fuzziness near the trees. They *were* gentians, and she picked several carefully. A couple of the roots came up with some of the flowers because of the dry ground; Ella thought she could put those in a plant pot and water them, so she wrapped her handkerchief around the roots to protect them, and then her scarf. There was what looked like deadly nightshade as well, growing a bit nearer to the house. Ella was not going to pick any of that; they had all been told it was just about the most dangerous plant there was. 'Belladonna', the nature study teacher had called it, warning them before a nature walk and showing a photograph. 'It means beautiful lady, but you have to remember that some beautiful ladies can be dangerous.' They had all laughed a bit embarrassedly, but they had promised to be careful.

Ella was not going to touch the belladonna growing in Cadence Manor's grounds, but she was curious to see the real thing. It would be pretty good if she could tell at school how she had found some. She had just reached the place where it was growing when a sound from inside the house made her turn her head. Had that been Mum's voice, calling out? Was Ella meant to go into the house? Perhaps she could go quietly up to the window and peep inside to see if Mum wanted her. If not, she could go back to the crumbly wall and Mum would not know she had looked in.

Still holding the gentians in the handkerchief and scarf she went forward, trying not to make any sound. The dry dead grass crunched under her feet but other than that everywhere was quiet, although once she thought something had moved within the old trees and she looked towards them, her heart racing. No, there was no one there, only the old trees with their trunks like gnarled faces. The curtains were still drawn but the French window was open, and Ella could see Mum. She was talking to someone. Ella could not see who it was, but it must be the person who had shut out the evening light.

She took a nervous step nearer and suddenly saw her mother was crying. This was dreadful. Mum never cried at home and she would never ever cry in somebody else's house. She was always talking about not making a scene in public. But Ella could see that her shoulders were shaking and she was wiping her eyes with her handkerchief. Whoever was in there had made her cry. This did not exactly stop Ella being so frightened, but it made her feel angry. She went nearer. Yes, Mum was crying quite hard. Ella took a deep breath and, pushing open the glass door, stepped through it.

The room beyond the French window was dim and musty-smelling, but there was a faint scent of something sweet overlaying the mustiness, as if whoever lived in this room had tried to smother it by pouring scent everywhere. It made Ella feel slightly sick.

Her mother turned and started to say, 'Ella, I told you to stay outside,' but Ella barely heard because her whole attention was on the other figure in the room. It was seated in an old-fashioned high-backed chair, this figure, but the chair was set against one window so it was difficult to make out the person's features. Ella squinted through the dimness, and saw some kind of high collar turned all the way up. Gloved hands, and dark clothes that fell in folds over the chair. And a blur where the face should be...Her heart started to thud and some of the anger trickled away, letting the fear back in. It was him. It must be. He was hiding from the light, exactly as he had done that day in the church. That was why the curtains were drawn and no lights switched on.

A harsh voice said very quietly, 'Get that bastard out of my house,' and Ella flinched, not so much at the word 'bastard'—although it was a very bad swear word indeed—but at the voice itself. It was a terrible voice, harsh and grating, as if the owner's throat was shredded into bloodied strips, or almost as if there was no throat there at all. She glanced nervously at her mother for guidance.

'You've had your last lot of money from this family,' said the faceless creature from its shadowy corner. 'And you've been well enough paid for your whoring. I bought that cottage for you. But there's no money left now, do you understand that?'

'You're a liar,' said Mum. 'You have money, all right. Plenty of it.'

'How dare you speak to me like that? Remember your place, Ford.'

Ford. That was how people used to speak to servants. As if they were scarcely even people, not even entitled to their own names. Some of the anger came back into Ella, and then the head turned towards her again.

'Does the child know who she is? Does she know what she is?'

'No,' said Ella's mother at once. 'She doesn't need to.'

'Get her out of my house,' said the voice. 'Or did you bring her here to gloat over me? Because if so—' The figure stood up, moving slowly, and came forward. For the first time Ella saw that the gloved hands held a walking stick.

'I'm not gloating,' said Ella's mother. 'I never have. I'm sorry for you. But it doesn't stop me hating you.'

'You can't hate me any more than I hate you,' said the figure. 'You ruined us all, you slut. And you—child—get out of my house!'

This last was aimed at Ella, and the stick was lifted, threateningly. Ella, frightened she was going to be attacked, flinched, stumbling backwards against the wall. In that moment her mother moved forward, screaming something. Ella couldn't make out all the words, but it was something about evil cruel monsters.

'Oh, you're showing your true colours now, Ford,' said the voice, and the stick was lifted again. Ella cried out a warning, but her mother had already dodged out of the way. Ella thought she would fall against the table, but somehow she regained her balance and lunged forward. Her fists were clenched and there was an expression on her face Ella had never seen before—a white twisted look of fury, like a snarling animal. It frightened Ella so much that she cowered back into a corner of the room, cramming her knuckles against her eyes so she could not see her mother's face, trying not to cry in case they heard her, but hearing herself sobbing anyway.

There was the sound of the stick clattering to the ground and of a piece of heavy furniture scraping across the dry floor and banging against something. A dreadful harsh cry came and then there was silence. Slowly and fearfully Ella took her hands away from her eyes. There was the room, shadowy and a bit dingy, with the furniture all the same—desk, cabinet, bookshelves, the gramophone on a small side table, its lid open. But the stick lay on the ground and the chair had skidded back against the fireplace wall. The dark figure was seated in it once again. But it's all wrong, thought Ella, trying to see clearly through her tears. People don't sit like that, with their head lolling to one side.

She looked across at her mother, who was standing at the centre of the room. Her fists were clenched, and her hair had come loose from the scarf; several strands hung over her face. Her face was shiny with sweat or tears, and although the snarling-animal expression was fading, it was still there.

But then her mother said, 'Ella?' almost as if she was not sure who Ella was.

'Yes. I'm here.' She whispered it in case the figure with its lolling head suddenly got out of the chair and came towards them. She did not dare take her eyes from it in case it moved.

'Are you all right?' said her mother.

'Yes.' Ella was not all right, but it was better to pretend.

'You'd better wait outside. I won't be a moment.'

'Is he all right?'

'He's—Yes,' said her mother. 'Oh, yes, quite all right. But wait outside.' It was the familiar, slightly sharp voice, and Ella went out and sat down on the step of the French window. She could hear her mother moving around inside the room. There was a bumpy movement that sounded like a piece of furniture being shunted across the floor, and then into the silence came the music once again.

Someone had started the gramophone record again. Had Mum done that? After a moment she came out, dusting her hands on the front of her skirt.

'Everything's quite all right,' she said. 'I'm sorry you saw that, Ella. But people sometimes say horrid things when they aren't well. It doesn't mean anything.'

'Should we get a doctor?'

'Oh, a doctor isn't necessary. I've even put the music back on. I expect you can hear it.'

'Yes.'

'But,' said Ella's mother, in a different voice, 'I think it would be better if no one knows we were here today. We don't need to tell anyone about it. Not even your best friends, do you understand that?'

'Yes.'

Ella thought she would not want to tell anyone about it anyway, and she specially would not want anyone to know how her mother had looked for those few minutes, all twisted and snarly. Still, she was glad they did not need to get a doctor, which would have meant going to a telephone box and perhaps being asked why they had been inside Cadence Manor. It sounded as if the man had just been knocked out. People did get knocked out, she had seen it on the television.

Neither of them spoke as they walked along the lane, but as they came to the stile on the edge of Mordwich Meadow, Ella's mother suddenly said, 'I believe I'll just sit down here for a moment, Ella. I'm not ill or anything, but my legs are a bit shaky.' She managed a half-smile. 'What they call reaction. It's quite nasty to be shouted at and threatened. So we'll sit here for a minute or two while I collect myself. I'll have a drop of my medicine, I think, then we'll go straight home.'

The medicine was kept in her handbag in a small bottle; she reached for it now and unscrewed the top. Ella waited until Mum had drunk two capsful.

'That's better,' she said, putting the bottle away. 'We'll go home in a minute.'

Ella wanted nothing more than to go home to ordinary things that would help her forget the way her mother had looked inside Cadence Manor, and that shadowy lolling figure sitting in the chair. There were lots of things to look forward to. The TV serial, and tomorrow she would be writing the programme for the school play, and on Friday was the nature study lesson, which she always enjoyed...

Nature study.

She said, 'I left all the gentians in that room. I dropped them on the floor.'

'For goodness' sake, that doesn't matter.'

'Yes, but I wrapped my hankie and scarf round them because of the roots. And it's my school scarf with my name on. You said no one must know we were here.'

They looked at each other and Ella saw for the first time that her mother was not just shaky because of being shouted at or because of drinking her medicine, she was frightened. This was the worst thing yet, because Mum was never frightened, not of anything in the world. But here she was, sitting on the stile, which normally she would never have done, her legs all floppy as if they had no bones in them, reaching for another dose of her medicine with hands that shook so badly she spilled some of it down her front. Her face was streaked with tears and she was frightened to death because Ella's scarf with her name was inside that room.

She mopped up the spilled medicine and tried to sit up straight, but she was still shaking, and when she spoke her voice was trembly. 'Oh God, Ella. Your scarf. Oh God, that's terrible.'

Ella could not see why it was so absolutely terrible as Mum seemed to think, but it seemed to matter to her very much, so she said, 'I'll go back in and get it.'

'No! You mustn't...' Mum tried to stand up and half fell against the stile. Her eyes had a foggy look as if she was not seeing properly.

'Yes, it's all right.' The thought of going back in the house filled Ella with horror, but she would rather do that than stay here with her mother being blurry and speaking as if she had a flannel in her mouth. 'What I'll do,' she said, pleased that her voice sounded quite brave, 'is I'll peep round the edge of the French windows and if he's there I won't go in. I'll come straight back and we'll go home before he can see us. But if he's not there I'll reach inside and pick up the scarf and my hankie—they were just inside the door. If the gramophone's still on no one will hear me anyway.'

'But—'

'It's all right, really it is. I'll run fast and I'll be back before you know I've gone.'

She did not say that by the time she got back her mother might have got over the blurriness. Before she could protest any more, Ella turned and ran as hard as she could back along the lane with the wall of the manor on her right, and then in at the side gate and across the tangly gardens.

She paused at the edge of the overgrown lawn to get her breath back. The curtains were still closed over the windows. Did that mean the man was still in there? She no longer felt so brave, but she remembered how upset Mum had been at the thought of the scarf being left in the house so she tiptoed up to the French window, trying to stay flat against the wall so as not to be seen. If the man was in there she would not go inside, and she and Mum would have to think what to do next. But if the room was empty Ella would dash inside, snatch up the scarf, and be outside again in a trice.

The music was still playing, but it seemed to be scraping over and over the same bit of tune. Had the needle got stuck? That had happened once on Clem's gramophone and it had sounded exactly like this. Surely if the man—or anyone else—had been in that room he would want to put the needle back in place? That must mean it was all right to go in. Moving very cautiously, Ella peered round the edge of the French windows, trying to see into the room. It was pretty dark but nothing seemed to be moving. And there were the flowers and her scarf, lying exactly where she had dropped them, just inside, quite close to the French windows.

She plucked up her courage and stepped over the threshold.

CHAPTER FOURTEEN

THE TOO-SWEET SCENT closed round her, but she tried to ignore it and went towards the scarf. In the corner of her eye she could see the chair where the man had been sitting, and she could see the stick on the ground nearby. Next to it was a soft dark cloth, lying in thick folds. Determinedly not looking at anything, Ella bent down to get her scarf, but doing so brought the bottom of the chair into her line of vision. It was then that she realized, with a jolt of new fear, that the man was still here. He was sitting in the chair, silent, not moving.

Ella's heart seemed to cartwheel up into her mouth, but she reached for the scarf because if she was very quick she could run outside before he could catch her.

Look at him before you run away, said a horrid voice in her mind. *Just one glance, then you'll see what he's really like...*
No! thought Ella. No, I mustn't do that.

But the whole world seemed to have slowed down and her legs were filled with lead like in a nightmare, and she could not move. The dreadful thing was that she really wanted to look at the man, to see him properly, instead of as the shadow he had been in the church.

Already it was easier to see through the dimness. She could make out a big marbly fireplace on the left of the chair, and rugs and tables. There was a door on the other side of the room, which was partly open, and Ella could see a big hall beyond it with pillars and a wide staircase. Should she run out that way? Would it be easier? No, she did not know who else might be in the house. She would go back over the lawn, the way she had come in. She would not look at the man, not even for a second, and in a minute her legs would start to move again. But again the evil little voice said, *Before you run away, look at him...You know you want to...*

Ella turned her head, and looked straight at the still silent figure. The music swelled maddeningly back and forth and a dreadful sick horror swept over her, because the figure in the chair was staring back at her; it had wide-open eyes that did not blink, and the mouth had fallen open. Hands in their dark gloves dangled down over the chair's sides.

Ella was absolutely frozen with terror and although she tried to look away she could not. The figure stared and stared at nothing, and Ella stared back. Her mind was whirling with fear and confusion, but she knew why the curtains had been shut and why the thick veil had covered the face earlier. It was a face you would want to cover all the time—a dreadful face, crusted with sores and scabs, the open mouth even showing scabs inside it.

But it was not the man from St Anselm's. The person in the chair—the person who had raised the stick and called her mother 'Ford' in that sneering way—was a woman, a very thin, very old lady, wearing an old-fashioned black frock that went down to her ankles and shawls of thick lace wound round her neck and over the top of her head.

Ella was very frightened indeed, but she managed to say, a bit croakily, 'I'm sorry to come in without asking, but I left my scarf behind.'

The woman was still not moving and this time, instead of forcing her unwilling legs to run from the room as fast as possible, Ella found she had taken a shaky step nearer to the woman.

'I need the scarf for school, you see.' Nothing. Perhaps

Mum had been wrong and a doctor was needed after all. Ella said, 'Um—are you all right?' She had no idea what to call the woman. At school they called the teachers 'miss', but it didn't seem quite right to call this woman 'miss'.

The woman still did not move. She did not even seem to hear or realize Ella was there. She must be unconscious, knocked out from when Ella's mother bounded forward to knock the stick away from her. Only—did your eyes stay open and staring if you were unconscious? And wouldn't Mum have fetched a doctor to her, no matter how much they should not have been here? Not if she knew the woman was dead, said Ella's mind. Dead people had their eyes open like this. Clem had seen his grandmother after she died, he had talked about it for days, saying how dead people stared at nothing for ever and you had to close their eyes.

Ella was not going to try closing this old woman's eyes, but she was becoming terribly afraid that the woman really was dead. Nobody who was living would sit like this, not speaking or moving, not trying to cover up that terrible face...

It was then that, with a teeth-wincing scrape, the music suddenly stopped.

Ella spun round. Standing just inside the room, the light behind him, was the figure of a man. All Ella could see was a dark outline, with a long coat, the collar turned up, but she saw that one hand was still resting on the gramophone on its small table. She could not see his face but she could see it was turned towards her and there was no mistaking him. This really was the man from St Anselm's. He was here in the room with her.

Ella gasped and it was as if the sound of her gasp released the frozen terror and she was finally able to move. She tumbled across the room and out into the clean sweet evening. As she ran across the lawn she risked a quick glance over her shoulder to see if he was coming after her. No, it was all right. She ran as fast as she could towards the side entrance, out through the little latched door, and along the lane to Mordwich stile, where her mother was waiting. She looked back twice more but the lane was deserted, and Ella reached the stile safely. There were pains in her chest from running so hard, but she did not care. She sank down on the grass, sobbing and shaking, but after a moment managed to gabble out to her mother that she had got the scarf and the hankie, and please could they go straight home.

Neither of them spoke on the way back to their cottage, but as they crossed Mordwich Meadow, Ella risked a glance at her mother. You killed that woman, she thought. I had my eyes shut when you did it because I was frightened so I didn't see you do it, but I heard it. I know what happened.

It was then that the really scary thought came into her mind.

The man had been in the house all the time. He would have heard the shouting between the old woman and Ella's mother. Had he been standing in that big cold-looking hall, watching? If so, he too would know what had happened.

❈ ❈ ❈

They had their cocoa and biscuits, and Mum began to look a bit better and to stop speaking slurrily.

They washed up the cups as they always did—Ella's mother said it was slovenly to leave dirty china in the sink overnight—and as they were putting them away, she said, 'Ella, when you went back for your scarf, what did you see in that room? I know it was dark in there, but did you see anything at all?'

Ella thought about saying she had not seen anything, but somehow the words came out before she knew it. 'I saw the old woman sitting in the chair,' she said.

'Ah. I thought you might.'

'I'm not absolutely sure, but I think she was dead.'

Her mother took so long to answer this that Ella began to think she was not going to say anything at all. But she sat down at the little scrubbed-top table, gesturing to Ella to sit down with her. 'Yes, she was dead,' she said. 'She was very old and very bitter and unhappy. She fell back and knocked her head on the mantelpiece. She was ill anyway—she had been for years and she might have died any day at all.' She reached out to take Ella's hand, which was not something she often did. 'I didn't kill her,' she said. 'Was that what you were thinking? It was an accident.'

Ella said she knew that, of course.

But I don't know it, she thought, not really. Because before I closed my eyes I saw your face, and I don't think I'll ever forget how you looked.

Mum was saying, 'But the worry now is that if anyone were to hear about what happened—that we were in the house with her when she died…People aren't always kind, Ella, and a lot of people in Upper Bramley—and all the villages—have been very unkind to me. One day, when you're older, you might understand. When I was young they used to call me cruel names.'

Barrack Room Brenda, thought Ella, still not speaking. I've heard that one at school more than once.

'What I'm trying to say is that if people heard, they'd believe the worst of me.'

'They'd think you killed that woman.'

'Yes. D'you know what happens to people who kill?'

'Um, well, prison, I s'pose.'

'Yes,' said Mum slowly. 'Yes, that's right. Prison. For a very long time. Years and years.'

'What would happen to me?'

Mum took even longer to answer this. Then she said, 'There's only you and me, you see. We haven't got any family you could live with. I'm afraid you'd be put in a children's home.'

'Like Bramley Gate?'

'Yes. Probably it would actually be Bramley Gate.'

'Oh,' said Ella blankly. She had seen the Bramley Gate children sometimes. When they went anywhere they walked in what was called a crocodile, led by a cross-looking woman who had a face like granite. They were silent and they all looked sad, and they wore horrid scratchy-looking grey uniforms, with their hair cut in ugly pudding-basin styles. Sometimes a group of them had to come to Ella's school for an exam and the boys mimicked them behind their backs. The girls said they looked like ragbags and told each other they would die if they had to go round looking like that. Remembering all this, Ella knew she would hate being in Bramley Gate more than anything in the world. She would hate Mum being in prison, as well, of course—she reminded herself how bad that would be—but she did not think she could bear living in Bramley Gate.

There was something else, as well. If Mum went to prison everyone would know. They would point to Ella and say, 'That's the daughter of that murderer. That's Brenda Ford's girl—Barrack Room Brenda, they used to call her.' And they would tell each other it would be better to steer clear of Ella Ford. 'Because you know what they say: like mother like daughter.'

And Ella would grow up with no life and no friends, permanently dressed like a ragbag, sneered at and made fun of...She dragged her attention back to what Mum was saying—something about being sure no one had seen them that evening.

'No one saw us go into Cadence Manor and no one saw us come out,' she was saying. 'So there's no reason why anyone will ever know the truth.'

'Oh, no,' said Ella obediently.

Lying in bed, later that night, she thought: but

someone does know. The man from the church knows. He was in the house all the time—he must have heard the shouting. What if he tells people he saw it all, that he saw Mum lunge forward, her fists raised? Would people believe that? Ella thought they would believe a grown-up—especially someone from Cadence Manor rather than a little girl from a cottage.

Was there a way she could make sure he never told anyone?

❀ ❀ ❀

It was about a week after that terrible evening that Ella's mother showed her a piece in the newspaper—the *Bramley Advertiser* it was called. It had local news in it, photographs of people getting married and stories about people in the villages, and lists of babies born or people who had died.

On one of the pages was a smudgy photograph of a lady with a severe expression and a long elaborate gown, standing outside a house that Ella recognized at once. It was Cadence Manor, only it was not Cadence Manor as it was now, but years and years ago when it had been tidy and nice, with lots of people living there. The newspaper said the lady in the photo was Lady Cadence—Serena Cadence—shown in her heyday and in the heyday of the Cadence family. Ella looked up the word 'heyday' in her school dictionary and it meant a time of great success or happiness.

The paper also said Serena Cadence had died at the family home, where she had lived a retired life for many years because of suffering from a long and debilitating illness. The long illness must be the marks on her face; Ella shuddered, remembering them. What kind of illness gave you marks like that? She looked up the word 'debilitating' as well. It meant something that made you very weak. But Lady Cadence had not been so weak she could not scream and threaten people with her walking stick.

The newspaper said there would be a private funeral service but also a public memorial service at St Michael's church, and told readers how Lady Cadence had been a lovely and gracious lady who had lived through stirring times and led a full and interesting life.

'Did she do that?' said Ella. 'Live through stirring times?'

'I suppose so,' said her mother, her eyes on the smudgy photograph. 'She lived through two world wars, although she did so in extreme comfort while the rest of us struggled and scraped to put food on the table.' Ella heard the vicious note in her mother's voice, and she was so worried that Mum's face would take on the snarly look again that she mumbled it was very interesting and thank you for showing her the article.

The article had not told the truth, though. Ella knew that, and she supposed her mother knew it as well. But the newspaper people would not be able to write that Serena Cadence had been a vicious old woman who called people bad names and frightened them half to death.

The really strange thing, though, was that the newspaper said Lady Cadence had died from her long and debilitating illness. It did not say she had died because someone had dealt her a vicious blow and she had smashed her head against a marble fireplace.

❀ ❀ ❀

Everyone at Ella's school had to go to the memorial service at St Michael's. The family deserved the community's respect, said the teachers. There had been a time—not so very long ago, either—when the Cadences had brought considerable work and prosperity to the area.

Only a few of the Cadence family were at the service. Clem's father said that was because the Cadences had almost all died out. Serena Cadence had not exactly been the last of her line, but there could not be many of them left. There were one or two distant cousins, he believed, but they were scattered around the world. Italy or Spain, so someone had told him.

Ella, seated near the back of the church, tried to get a good look at the members of the Cadence family, but it was impossible. They came in very quietly by the side door and sat at the front of the church, and all she could see was three or four dark-clad people. After the service the family went out through the same side door and were driven away in waiting cars. Ella wondered how she would feel if the man from St Anselm's was there, but he did not seem to be. She had not really thought he would be—he didn't seem like someone who'd be part of a crowd—and anyway he might not even be one of the family.

The school choir sang at the service and Derek Haywood had a small solo halfway through. Several of the congregation remarked on what a nice voice he had.

'I thought he screeched a bit on the high notes,' said Veronica afterwards, but she said it quietly because they had all been told to be solemn and quiet as a mark of respect to Lady Cadence.

'I thought he screeched a whole lot,' said Clem, who was still smarting at not being picked to play the prince, and not very inclined to admire anything Derek Haywood did. 'I should think Lady Cadence would come back from her grave to haunt him for screeching like that at her funeral.'

'People don't come back from the grave,' said Ella very sharply.

'How do you know? My father said she was an old witch. I'll bet she comes back to haunt Cadence Manor.'

The Present

Ella had not, of course, taken any notice of Clem's words, not then and not since. Lady Cadence had not haunted the manor, nor had she haunted Ella herself.

It was the music that had haunted her. She had never been able to forget how the needle had stuck on the record that day, and how the music had played the same section over and over.

The Deserted Village. She had not known then what it was called, of course. What she had known was that it must have been the man from the church who had taunted her on that last morning when she and Clem and Veronica had walked through Priors Bramley. He had known Ella was there and he had deliberately played that piece in St Anselm's for her to hear. *Remember this, little girl,* he had been saying. *Remember the last time you and I heard this music...? In Cadence Manor, when your mother committed murder...?*

Once or twice since that day Ella had wondered if she had been wrong, and if he had played it simply because he liked it. But she always pushed away this idea, because she did not want to ascribe to that sinister figure any of the softer qualities. When you have killed someone, you do not want to realize afterwards that they liked music.

What she had never been able to understand was how she could have heard the music on the day her mother went inside the poisoned village to find the lost wristwatch—the day the Geranos had burned her face. Because the man had been dead, he had been dead for a whole week. Ella had seen his body, broken and twisted at the bottom of the ruined chimney shaft, and her mother had seen it as well.

But on that afternoon someone had been playing his music in the deserted grounds of Cadence Manor.

CHAPTER FIFTEEN

The Present

GRAN HAD SEEMED PRETTY fed up since Amy played *The Deserted Village* CD last night, although Amy thought she was trying to hide it.

She wondered if she ought to ask Gramps if there was anything wrong. Dad would never forgive her if she did not keep him in the loop about Gran's health; he did not get emotional or embarrassing about her, but once or twice he said she had given him a really good, really secure childhood, which was something children did not seem to get so much these days.

Gramps was rehearsing tonight. He had gone out after supper, and Amy had been intending to go down to the Red Lion who were having a quiz night. One or two people from the library would be there, and Clem Poulter had suggested Amy join them. But Gran was looking white and pinched, and it seemed mean to leave her on her own, so Amy suggested she come along to the quiz too. It would mean Amy could not chat up any likely men, of course, though she was not sure she was yet back in a chatting-up frame of mind, even if there had been anyone around worth chatting up, which there was not.

But Gran said she would stay at home. She was not much of a one for quizzes. 'You go, though, dear. What time does it start?'

'Eight.'

'It's half-past seven already. You'd better go up to change.'

Amy was wearing her favourite scarlet cheesecloth shirt and jeans, and it had not occurred to her that she needed to change just for a couple of hours in a pub. But she brushed her hair and added a bit of lipgloss.

When she got to the Red Lion there were quite a lot of people there. Clem Poulter waved to Amy and beckoned her over to join his table. He made vague introductions to the people he was with, most of whose names Amy did not hear.

'I'm so glad to see you,' said Clem. 'I tried to get a couple of the local teachers to come along, but they couldn't or wouldn't. I tried to get Dr Malik as well, but a snowball in hell would have more chance. I don't think he's even heard of pub quizzes.'

'Who?'

'Didn't you say you spoke to him at that music lecture?' said Clem. 'He's staying here, so you'd have thought he could have been bothered to just walk downstairs and sit at a table, wouldn't you? He'd have been brilliant, and we'd like to win this quiz, wouldn't we, chaps?'

There was a rather half-hearted assent from the people round the table.

Amy said, 'Oh, him. I thought he was just somebody who wandered in out of the rain.'

'Eccentric academic,' said somebody on the other side of the table. 'He's some sort of expert on early church music or something.'

'You know my definition of an expert,' said Clem. 'Somebody who lives more than thirty miles away.'

'No, really, he's supposed to be very distinguished and knowledgeable.'

'What's he doing in Upper Bramley, then?' asked someone else, cynically.

'He's here to study St Anselm's musical history now that it's accessible again,' said Clem impatiently. 'I *told* you. Amy, what are you drinking? Oh, and we've ordered food for later.'

The quiz was fairly predictable, and Clem's table managed to scrape second place, although Amy never found out what the prizes were. She had gone up to the bar to ask where their food was, when she caught sight of Dr Malik coming out of the pub's tiny dining room. He was carrying a book and a sheaf of papers, and Amy had a sudden image of him eating his dinner with the book propped up against the salt cellar, oblivious to his surroundings. She watched him walk across to the stairs and wondered if she should try to catch his eye. She would like to tell him she had listened to the music they had discussed. Perhaps he would not want to know, though.

As if suddenly aware of being watched, he looked round. Amy smiled and Dr Malik hesitated as if unsure who she was. Then he seemed to remember, and smiled back. He appeared to consider what to do next, then instead of going upstairs, presumably to his room, he came across to the edge of the bar.

'Hello,' said Amy. 'We met at the lecture the other night.'

'I know. Second year, Durham University, yes?' His voice was as nice as she remembered.

'Yes. You told me about a piece of music based on a Goldsmith poem.'

'*The Deserted Village.* Yes, of course.'

'Well, I was interested because I've been helping with an exhibition of Old Bramley and I managed to find the recording in the library. It's a bit scratchy and bumpy, isn't it?'

'It's a very old recording,' he said, as if wanting to defend the music.

'It sounded it. I liked it,' said Amy, 'although it isn't the kind of thing I normally listen to.'

For some reason this made him smile, and his face stopped being serious and became much younger and slightly mischievous. 'I can believe that,' he said. 'But I'd be interested in your reactions—specially if you're delving into Priors Bramley's past.'

'I am, a bit.' Was he going to ask her to have a drink? If so Amy might as well take him up on it.

He said, 'I expect you're here with somebody, but if you've got ten minutes to talk about the village and the music...' He looked round the bar vaguely. 'We could go into the other room where it's quieter.'

It had not occurred to Amy that it was particularly noisy in the bar, but she said, 'I was with the pub quiz—I mean, I was with somebody's table.' This sounded so garbly she was annoyed with herself, and she said firmly, 'OK, thanks. I'll just tell them to hurry up with the food, then I'll be out.'

'I'll get you a drink. What do you have?' He said this a bit warily as if he thought she might ask for vodka laced with E.

'House red?' said Amy, and saw the flicker of relief.

His name was Jan Malik, and the book, which he propped on the edge of their table, was a hefty volume about early church music.

'Clem—that's Clem Poulter from the library, I think you met him—told me you were here because of St Anselm's,' said Amy, seeing the book.

'Yes, mostly. But I'm also interested in music and literature echoing its surroundings,' he said.

'Priors Bramley and *The Deserted Village*.'

'Yes. Not necessarily serious or obscure music, though. Modern stuff sometimes has a remarkable way of conveying a sense of place. Heavy metal often does it.'

Amy was so fascinated to hear someone who looked like a Pre-Raphaelite poet talk about heavy metal, she forgot to drink her wine. 'And St Anselm's is interesting on its own account anyway,' said Jan. 'It's an ancient church and it has quite an unusual history of music.'

'How old is ancient?'

'Well, there're a couple of mentions in one or two early monkish chronicles dating its origins to the early seventh century,' said Jan. 'And the church apparently had Ambrosian plainchant as part of the services until the late 1800s, which is why I'm curious about it. It's rare to find Ambrosian chant used so recently—it's virtually forgotten, except in Milan and parts of Lombardy. Occasionally I've taken postgraduate students to Italy to study it.'

Hell's boots, thought Amy, another university don. Only this one wouldn't quote Shelley, he would play music. She sent him a sideways glance and thought that despite his appearance, he would not be likely to lose his wallet when it came to paying for drinks or leave her to find her own way home in a taxi. Not that there were going to be any drinks bills or late-night taxis, of course. In any case he probably had a nice wife who taught Renaissance history or something, at an adjoining college.

Jan drank some of his wine, and said, 'Sorry, Amy, I'm getting carried away with my own subject. Tell me what you thought of *The Deserted Village.*'

'I liked it,' said Amy. 'I don't know any of the technical stuff, and I haven't read the poem it's based on, but it dredged up images really well. At the start I could see Priors Bramley, with people living ordinary lives, farms and shops and church, all like an Agatha Christie book, or *Cranford.* And then,' she said, warming to the theme, 'there's the bit where the music changes and starts to be quite menacing. I thought that'd be the feudal overlord stomping in, all droit de seigneur, grabbing village maidens and crunching up cottages. And the happy-milkmaid, kindly-shepherd rustic merriment dissolves, and in its place you get Edgar Allan Poe. Bats flitting through ruins and whatnot, and everything mouldering and decaying. The Fall of the House of Cadence.'

'Like Priors Bramley,' said Jan.

'Yes. My gran can just remember everyone being booted out of the cottages and shops, and Clem Poulter had a great-aunt who'd lived there all her life. I know there'd have been compensation and rehousing,' said Amy, 'but it's still anger-making, isn't it?'

'I'd like to talk to your grandmother to see what she remembers,' said Jan Malik. 'But it sounds as if it all mirrors Goldsmith's poem. That was written as a kind of a reaction to the Enclosure Act. In a lot of areas Enclosure forced a mass emigration of the poorer farming families into the cities. In the poem, only one person is left in the village of Auburn—an old widow, forced to gather watercress for food and brushwood to keep warm, but the one person left who knows its history and could pass on the tales.'

'That's seriously sad,' said Amy, after a moment. 'Good thing it's only fiction.'

'Is it, though?' said Jan softly. 'They found a body in Priors Bramley, didn't they?'

Amy stared at him, and for a moment something cold and unpleasant seemed to brush the back of her neck. 'But that was just someone who got stuck there—a tramp who passed out in a drunken stupor and wasn't noticed because nobody knew about him.'

'I wonder if that's all he was,' said Jan. 'What if he was "the sad historian of the pensive plain"?'

'Listen, if you're going to quote at me—because I suppose that was a quote—I'd better get another drink,' said Amy very firmly, because she was not sure she could cope with sad souls who scraped their sustenance from

watercress (watercress, for pity's sake!) or ancient histo-
rians dying in crumbling manor houses.

She got two more glasses of wine and carried them
back to the table. Jan lifted his with a half-salute that
might have been apology or merely thanks.

Amy said, 'I found photos of Priors Bramley before
they infected it with Geranos. There's a really good one of
St Anselm's and some of Cadence Manor.'

He appeared to accept the change of mood. 'Can I see
the photos sometime?'

'Yes, of course.'

'And,' he said, 'after that masterly precis you gave me
of the music and the village, I've got to ask what you're
reading at Durham.'

'Well, um, archaeology and anthropology.'

'Good subjects. Why are you so defensive about
them?'

'Was I? I suppose it's because when you say archaeology and anthropology, people mostly say, "But what
will you actually *do* with it?" Or they think you're going
to disinter Egyptian mummies and fall victim to a curse.'

'But there are masses of interesting possibilities,
surely? Even without field work and digs, there's museum
curatorships, research of all sorts, even TV—all those
Time Team-type programmes. They'd need advisers and
researchers on board for those. And the two subjects go
hand in hand, don't they? The history and the study of
buildings and the human race.'

'I love buildings,' said Amy, gratefully. 'Is St Anselm's
really seventh century?'

'Supposed to be. Built around 650, if you can believe
the chronicles.'

'Wow. The Romans had gone by then, hadn't they?'
said Amy, delving into her memory. 'They'd long since
conquered the blue and green misty island of all their
legends.' She glanced at him and saw a glint of amusement

in his eyes. 'Listen, it *is* poetic and it's far enough back to be really romantic.'

'I didn't say it wasn't romantic or poetic.'

'If you were lucky, there might be traces of the original structure of St Anselm's,' said Amy, thoughtfully. 'The timbers might be a bit crumbly, but the stonework ought to be still intact.'

Jan said, 'I'm going out to Priors Bramley tomorrow to take a look. To see if I can find any traces of…well, of anything that links St Anselm's to the Ambrosian tradition. Or that links Priors Bramley to Goldsmith's Auburn.' He paused, then said, 'Would you like to come with me?'

Amy stared at him. 'Is it safe to go in there now?' she said. 'Because if it is I'd absolutely love to. D'you mean it?'

'Yes. I've talked to the local council and they've disinfected everywhere until it squeaks, so anyone can go in. Oh, and in case you're wondering about me, I'm a relatively respectable senior member of Oriel College,' said Jan. 'And I don't normally issue invitations to people I meet in pubs. But you're studying archaeology and I'm chasing legends so it might be a useful exercise for both of us.'

'What about the body? The "sad historian" or whoever he was? Aren't the police still yomping around looking for clues?'

'They're still working there, but I've talked to them and explained I'm only here for a short while and I just want to look inside the church. They're fine with that. The body was in the old lodge house, anyway, which is quite a way from the church. They've got the whole of Cadence Manor and the grounds roped off so it's out of bounds to the public, but the rest of the village is open. I could pick you up somewhere, or meet you out there, if that's easier.'

Amy did not have a car and although she had open permission to use Gran's whenever she wanted, she didn't really want to do so for this. She thought Jan was probably giving her a tactful escape route, but she said, 'It'd be easier if you gave me a lift. I'm at the library until twelve tomorrow.'

'I'll pick you up there at twelve,' he said. 'Could I see the photos of the church at the same time? Thanks. And then you can prowl around the ancient stones of St Anselm's and tell me if they're Saxon. I dare say you can take photos or sketches as well, which will be useful for your thesis when you take your doctorate.'

'I wasn't going to take a doctorate—'

'Weren't you? Why not?'

Amy tried to think of an answer to this and could not. She tried not to think Gran would go up in smoke if she heard Amy was going out to Priors Bramley with a tramp she had picked up in a pub. Except that Jan was not a tramp, of course.

❈ ❈ ❈

Gran did go up in smoke. She had to be told about the Priors Bramley excursion because she expected Amy home for lunch each day after her library session. She was shocked to her toes to hear Amy was going off with a man she had met in the Red Lion.

'Who is he? What do you know about him? He sounds foreign. You can't be too careful these days, Amy. There was a girl in the paper only last week—'

'He's a quarter Polish. He's an Oxford don and he lectures at Oriel College. He's researching St Anselm's music for a paper,' said Amy, correctly guessing the mention of Oxford would go a long way to calming Gran's anxiety.

'Oh. Oh, well, perhaps...But what's he doing picking up a girl half his age?'

'I'm not half his age,' said Amy indignantly. 'He's only about, um, thirty-five.'

'Then he's quite possibly married,' said Gran, pouncing on this with triumph.

'It doesn't matter if he is,' said Amy. 'It's not a date, for pity's sake. We're only going out to Priors Bramley to look at the church.'

'Is it safe? Are they letting people in?'

'Jan says so.'

'I wouldn't have thought there'd be much to see. It'll probably be drenched in the disinfectant stuff they've been spraying everywhere.'

'Yes, but it'll be good field experience for me,' said Amy. 'I might even get an essay out of it for next term. I thought I'd ask Gramps if I could borrow his camera.'

'I don't suppose he'll mind. You'd better borrow my rubber boots, though. I wouldn't trust that stuff they've been using. And as well as that you'd better—Is that your grandfather coming in now? My goodness, Derek, you're late tonight.'

'Blame the Lord High Executioner,' said Gramps, dropping his jacket on a chair, and heading for the drinks cabinet. 'He can't, for the life of him, remember the words of "I've Got a Little List", at least not in the correct sequence. If we rehearsed it once we rehearsed it six times, Still, it's a whopping long song, and—Oh, are you going to bed, Ella? I'll just have a drink. And I might catch the end of *Newsnight*.'

It was a shame for Gramps, who always came in bright-eyed and happy from his rehearsals, to be greeted by Gran's indifference. He wanted to talk about his evening, telling little stories about people having tantrums, or the row between the stage manager and the prompter and who had said what to whom, but Gran hardly ever listened. She picked up a magazine, or went out to the kitchen to get tomorrow's meat out of the freezer or write a note for the milkman, and Gramps was left to watch *Newsnight* or read the evening paper.

Amy thought it was really sad when married people stopped being interested in each other's lives. Tonight Gran did not even give an excuse; she simply went up to bed, so, to balance things out, Amy asked about the rehearsal. Gramps brightened up at once—dear old Gramps; it did not take much to cheer him up—and switched off *Newsnight* to hunt out an old vinyl recording of the D'Oyly Carte company performing *The Mikado*, with somebody called Leicester Tunks singing the title role. Amy would find it very interesting, he said eagerly. He looked quite young and nice when he got enthusiastic like this, and Amy was pleased for him and managed not to giggle at Mr Tunks's name. She thought she might tell Gramps about *The Deserted Village* opera later. He would be interested in that.

They listened to the disc, and Gramps happily explained the plot of *The Mikado* to Amy, until Gran came down in a dressing gown to ask him to turn the music down because she had a headache and caterwauling opera singers did not help it.

❀ ❀ ❀

As Jan went up to his room at the Red Lion, he thought no matter how well you knew yourself, you still received a few surprises.

Amy Haywood had been a surprise. Jan had intended the investigation into St Anselm's and Priors Bramley to be a brief, more or less cursory inspection of the place, after which he would talk to the local choirmaster, if there was one, and maybe the local historian, if such a person existed and could be found. What he had not intended was that he should acquire an assistant in the shape of an enthusiastic archaeology student who had the most extraordinary looks he had ever encountered.

Amy would certainly not be everybody's idea of conventional good looks, but she was someone you would look at a second time and then a third. Jan had the thought that if you regarded the current stage of human race as being the edited article, Amy Haywood might be considered the director's cut. Or maybe the diamond hidden inside the rock, only visible to the really discerning eye. Hers was not a face men would be likely to sack cities for, or even want to take to bed—but it was a face men might want to take into their dreams.

Whatever she was, she was a one-off. *Sui generis*, thought Jan, smiling as he got into bed and turned out the light

CHAPTER SIXTEEN

JAN HALF EXPECTED, the next morning, to regret his uncharacteristically hasty invitation, but as he drove to the library he found he was looking forward to Amy Haywood's company.

He would not have been surprised to find she was not there, or that she had left some flimsy excuse, but she was waiting, wearing the jeans and scarlet shirt she had on last evening, with the jeans tucked into the tops of boots. She bounced out of the library and into the car, and although she was small and fine-boned she seemed to fill up the car with enthusiasm. She was not wearing anything as definite as sprayed-on perfume, but there was a faint, pleasing impression of clean hair and clean skin.

She had brought a large tote bag with notebooks and pens and a camera, which she said she was not sure how to work. 'Oh, and I've brought the St Anselm's photographs, as well. They're quite old—somebody's written "June 1930" on the back—so they're a bit faded, but the detail's quite good.' She burrowed in the tote bag.

'They're clearer than I expected,' said Jan, studying the photos.

'Yes, and d'you see there and there on the front? Those strips of vertical stone—pilasters—are very Saxon.

At least I think they are. I'll have to look it up to be sure. They might be fake, of course. Victorian pastrycook.'

Priors Bramley, when they got to it, was more desolate than Jan had expected. As they left the car on a grass verge and walked towards the cluster of buildings, he experienced a wave of loneliness and a feeling of isolation so strong that he felt as if Priors Bramley's past reached imploringly out to him. He did not believe in ghosts, but he did believe strong emotions could sometimes linger. God knew what agonies and fears had filled up this small pocket of land years ago. After all, this was a village whose residents had been forced to leave it before it was drenched in some lethal mix of poisons and then left to its own tainted remoteness.

A policeman on duty in the lane sketched a half-salute and seemed pleased at the small interruption to his day.

'We wanted to take a look at the church,' said Jan. 'I was told that would be all right.' He produced a small card, which he handed to the policeman, who glanced at it briefly, then stood up a bit straighter and said, 'Quite all right, sir.'

'Are the police still working at the manor?' asked Amy.

'Forensics are just finishing up. They've been searching the lodge, and the manor itself as well, of course.'

'I suppose they're trying to identify the body,' said Amy.

'Some hopes,' said the policeman. 'A tramp is most people's guess. Oh, you'll mind where you tread, won't you?' he added conscientiously. 'Everywhere's still sopping wet from the decontamination and it's a bit muddy and slippery in places. I'm supposed to warn everyone about that.'

'We'll be careful,' said Jan.

'What on earth does your card say?' demanded Amy as they walked away. 'Because it certainly impressed the policeman.'

'"Doctor of Ancient Music Studies and Medieval Church History",' said Jan and Amy suddenly felt inadequate. Clearly he would be regarding her as one of his students. When he got back to Oxford and the nice wife he undoubtedly had, he would say casually to her, 'I was latched onto by an eager young archaeology student while I was at Bramley. Durham, I think she's at. If she's ever in this area we'll ask her for a meal.'

And the nice wife would nod and think, aha, another breathless young thing who fell in love with you, and say yes of course they would invite the Durham undergraduate to the house.

At this point Amy reminded herself that she had eschewed men forever, and that from now on she was dedicating herself to her career and would most likely end up being a dessicated academic with no private life whatsoever and frumpy clothes.

At first it was not particularly disturbing to walk along the village street. The spraying was still drying out and there was a faint drip-drip of moisture from within some of the buildings. The ground was muddy, and despite the warm sunshine the air had a chill. Jan repressed a shiver.

Once Amy pointed to what looked like a faint glint of amber on the ground, like tiny specks of caramelized sugar. 'And there's a kind of sickly sulphurous taste in the air,' she said. 'Like bitterly cold metal, but with something very unwholesome just underneath.'

'The Poisoned Village,' said Jan, half to himself. Then, 'But it's more likely the chemicals from the decontamination that we can smell.'

'It's sad, though, whatever it is. It's only fifty years since this village was lived in and there were ordinary people who had lives and friendships. And now it's like a lost world.'

'That shouldn't worry you—you deal in lost worlds.'

'But this is a world people still remember,' she said. 'My grandparents remember it—and Clem Poulter. Even the shop signs are still in place. You can read some of the lettering. That bow-fronted one was a bakery. It's all spooky, isn't it?'

'Ghosts?' said Jan lightly.

'Well, not midnight groans and creaking coffins,' said Amy. 'And you needn't laugh, because there are ghosts here, only I think they're nice ordinary ghosts. All the people who used to shop, and scurry in and out of each other's houses, and gossip about what Mrs Whatnot at number thirteen was up to with the milkman yesterday. Don't look so quizzical, I do know it's centuries since people got up to things with the milkman.'

'And even longer than that since anyone cared,' said Jan, irresistibly drawn into the world Amy's word-pictures were painting, and preferring her cheerful homely ghosts to the lonely dispossessed shades he had sensed earlier.

'They'd buy all kinds of things we've never even heard of from these shops,' said Amy. 'There wouldn't be pizzas or sun-dried tomatoes or pasta, or vacuum packs of meat, would there?'

'Indeed not. This one was a butcher's shop, by the look of it,' said Jan. 'Scrag end of lamb, and brisket and brawn.'

'It's a lovely old place. I'll get a shot of it, shall I? What was brawn, for pity's sake? It sounds like a posh way of saying brown, or a make of hairdryer.'

'Pressed meat made from a pig's head.'

'I knew it would be something utterly disgusting,' said Amy gleefully.

'Remember that next time you eat sushi or fried squid.'

The tainted smell, once they were further along the street, was not so noticeable, but the occasional amber glint still shone here and there, and the brooding silence pressed down on them. Clumps of vegetation, flattened and pallid, still clung to walls like boneless fingers, scrabbling for life.

'Is the plantlife all dead?' said Amy, seeing this. 'I'm not very good on botany and stuff. Those trees look withered and there's hardly any grass anywhere. But what I know about plants could be written on a plate of brawn.'

'I don't think the trees are actually dead,' said Jan. 'But they look a bit sick.'

'I wonder if that's because of the stuff they've been spraying, or if the Geranos did something peculiar to the plantlife?'

'You're getting into John Wyndham's Triffid territory,' said Jan, smiling.

'I'll remind you of that when the plants start walking towards us.' Amy laughed.

The road was cracked and uneven, and in places had partially collapsed. Several times Jan reached automatically for Amy's hand, helping her across a particularly bad bit of ground, and every time he did so he was strongly conscious of the feel of her smooth young skin against his palm.

'It's all really eerie, isn't it?' said Amy. 'And you know the eeriest part of all?'

'The fact that there's hardly any colour anywhere,' said Jan. 'Everything's grey-green, except for those odd specks of amber.'

'*Yes.* Did the Geranos do that to the village? Leach all the colour away.'

'I should think it's more likely the decontamination. I'm not very knowledgeable, but I have a feeling they'd use bleach or chlorine. The church is just along here, on the left. We can't see it from here because the street curves round.'

'How do you know that?'

'I looked at an old Ordnance Survey map.' He glanced down at her and smiled. 'Basic research, Amy.'

As they went on, the colourlessness Amy found so eerie seemed even more noticeable. Here and there were occasional splashes of ordinary brightness—mostly from odds and ends of machinery or litter left by the recent workmen or the police investigation, once or twice from some rogue patch of plantlife—but in the main Priors Bramley was shrouded in misty grey-green shadows, and Amy's scarlet shirt was the only real note of colour.

'This looks like the curve in the road,' said Jan presently. 'We should see the church at any minute.'

'Clem said it had dry rot since anyone can remember,' said Amy. 'So it'll probably be almost completely crumbled away.'

But it was not.

Part of the lich-gate had gone, but the frame was still in place and also the small shallow seat. Beyond this was a Saxon cross, black and stark, and behind the church itself were the skeletons of several ancient trees, the massive trunks intact, but the branches withered in the way most of the trees seemed to be. These are cedars, thought Jan. Probably several hundred years old. They'd have had massive spreading branches shading the church, sheltering the graves and keeping everywhere cool and dim.

At his side, Amy said softly, 'It's still decaying, isn't it? Nowhere's actually dead, but it's all actively rotting. As if something diseased got into the marrow of the village— into the bricks and timbers and earth—all those years ago.'

But the ancient church of St Anselm, the church that for over a thousand years had clung to the ancient and rare tradition of Ambrosian plainchant, was still intact. Jan and Amy went warily up the path and peered through the low-arched doorway.

'We meant to go inside, right?' said Amy.

'Yes.'

As they went towards the doorway Jan realized his heart was beating fast, which annoyed him. It's a ruined old church, he thought, that's all. There won't be anything inside it. Anything of any value or interest will have rotted away or been looted and there'll be nothing to find. The music will long have gone.

But it had not.

❄ ❄ ❄

The instant Jan entered St Anselm's its atmosphere fell about him like a leaden cloak and he had the strong feeling that for all its centuries of worship, there had been deep unhappiness here. A darkness, he thought, that's what I'm sensing. A deep, lonely, despair.

The church was small, as he had expected, and very decayed. Parts of the roof had gone, but the thick stone walls were still standing and everywhere was cool and dim. The scents of damp and of dank plaster, and what Amy had called the tainted smell were very strong.

Rotting vegetation thrust up between the cracked stone floor, and some of the marble statues had fallen from their plinths and lay splintered in the aisle and apse. But the pews were still there, as if waiting for the worshippers who had once sat and kneeled in them, and the altar stood against tall windows, which were the traditional three-fold structure. Two of the windows were broken, and shards of glass clung to the framework, glistening like tiny icicles, but the central window was still in place.

Amy went forward to examine the altar, stepping warily through the debris, and Jan was walking towards a low archway to see what lay beyond it, when she called to him.

'Jan—look at this.'

'What have you found?'

'I don't know if it's of any interest, but come and see.' She was standing directly beneath the left altar window. Shards of glass lay everywhere, some of them quite large sections, still partly encased in thin lead strips. 'Look.' She pointed to a nearly oblong piece. The colours were faded almost to monochrome, but the picture was clear: a female figure in flowing draperies, seated at some kind of musical instrument.

'St Cecilia, almost certainly,' said Jan, studying it. 'Patron saint of music.'

'But look at the scroll thing over her head,' said Amy. 'It's musical notation, isn't it?'

'Yes, it is.' Jan went closer, heedless of the fact that the hem of his coat was trailing in the mud and dirt. 'Have you got a tissue or a handkerchief or something? Thanks.' He took the tissue and with infinite delicacy propped the piece of glass against the wall, then began to wipe the surface clean.

Amy offered him the rest of the tissue pack. 'Can you read the music?'

'Just about.' He peered closer. 'It's only very brief, and it could be anything, of course—'

'But it could be Ambrosian?' said Amy, hopefully.

He smiled at her. 'I'd have to compare it with known notation, but it might be from the Sanctus melodies.'

'That's good, is it?'

He smiled again, and went on studying the glass. 'The chants of the Mass are divided into the Ordinary—fixed points in the service, which don't change, and of which the Sanctus is a part—and the Proper where the texts change depending on the feast.' He delved in his pocket for a notebook, and began to copy the notes. 'It's a very simple, but very beautiful chant,' he said. 'And if I could match this with the Sanctus notation it could be definite proof of St Anselm's musical past. Can you get a couple of really clear shots of this?'

'I'll try.'

'Thanks.' Jan straightened up, pocketing the notebook. 'What a tragedy that this church was left to rot. The carvings are beautiful and the stained glass must have been exquisite.'

He returned to his exploration. Amy watched him for a moment, then concentrated on photographing the glass. She was pleased she had found it; Jan's eyes had glowed with fervour.

She finished photographing the glass, then took several of the altar.

'What you are doing?' said Jan, turning round as Amy clambered over the pews. 'Be careful—you could easily turn your ankle on those stones.'

'There's something shiny in that corner,' said Amy. 'Half under that window—there was a sort of glint when I took that last photo.'

'If it's the amber stuff again, don't touch it.'

'It's not the amber stuff.' She negotiated the pews with care. 'Good job I'm wearing rubber soles. Damn, I can't reach it. I probably shouldn't say damn in a church.'

'There's only the spooks to hear you.'

'I'll bet they've cursed a bit in their time. OK, I've got it.' She held up a small oblong plaque.

'What is it?'

'I don't know. It's filthy,' said Amy, screwing up her face in disgust. 'Wait a bit, I'll find another tissue. It's crusted with disgusting mould, but there was that sheen of something in the camera flash. I thought it might be brass or even silver.'

She bent over, cleaning the oblong industriously, then gave a soft hoot of satisfaction. 'Brilliant, it's inscribed. I thought it looked as if it was.'

'What does it say?'

'I think it's brass, like you see on church pews or pulpits. It says: "Donated by the Cadence family, 1920. 'I have learned to look on the still, sad music of humanity.'" Wow.' She scrambled back over the pews to show him. 'The Cadences are the family who used to live at the manor,' she said. 'They were some kind of merchant bankers, I think, or one of those ultra-posh private banks for the super-rich. I only know about them because of helping at the library,' she added, in case Jan thought she had any sympathies with plutocracy. She reached out to trace the engraved words with a fingertip. 'I suppose it could have come off one of the pews, but I wonder why 1920 was significant? To commemorate someone who died in the First World War?'

'They'd have named him in that case,' said Jan.

'True. D'you mind if I have a look to see if there're any more of these? If so, I might liberate one for the library's exhibition. I'll leave this one where it is, though.'

She went back to the altar. The Cadence family were all long since dead, including the man with dark hair and sexy eyes in the photo dated Christmas 1910. It would be interesting to know who he was, though. The line about 'the still, sad music of humanity' was disturbing. It suggested some kind of lesson learned or some deep tragedy. Amy would look it up at the library.

Jan's voice broke into this. 'Amy, it's half-past one. Are you hungry? How about I buy you lunch at the Red Lion as a thank you for helping me?'

'That's the kind of thanks I like,' said Amy. 'OK, we'll leave the spooks to themselves.'

CHAPTER SEVENTEEN

London, 1912

SERENA HAD RELIVED THE NIGHT when Julius attacked her over and over again. The dreadful thing was that it was not Julius's madness or his brutality she kept remembering: it was the way he had crouched sobbing in a corner of the room afterwards.

She sought for an emotion that would drive this memory out and that would also drive out the fear of the approaching birth, and after a while was aware of resentment—not towards Julius, but towards the child. She tried to quench this shameful emotion, but it stayed on her mind like a bruise. Julius might be dead by the time the child was born, but Serena knew that every time she looked at his son or daughter the painful memory of its father would taunt her. She did not think she could ever love this child. She did not think she could even like it.

Each morning she had violent spasms of sickness, so severe her insides felt as if they were being wrenched out. Her ankles and wrists swelled painfully and so grotesquely that in places her skin cracked and split. Serena hated this almost more than the sickness. She took to wearing loose teagowns with long, wide sleeves and trailing hems. The gowns were mostly sent from Bond

Street and Knightsbridge stores; Harrods and Debenham and Freebody were always so obliging. The dresses covered the swellings and sores quite well but, to make sure no one caught sight of them by accident, Serena told Dora and Hetty to keep all the curtains three-quarters closed. Yes, she said snappishly, she did mean all day long—she had a constant headache and the light hurt her eyes. She left her own rooms less and less. Dora and Hetty were young and spry, and quite able to scamper up and down the stairs with trays.

Guests to the house were discouraged, except for Dr Martlet, although when he suggested performing another of the embarrassing intimate examinations—'to make sure the child is in the proper position'—Serena discouraged him. She hated that kind of examination, with its fearsome instruments, but she was more afraid of what he would say if he saw the rash and the sores under her flowing gowns. So she said she was not feeling quite up to an examination today. They would consider it on his next visit.

Crispian had written to her twice, and Dr Martlet said he had had an untidy scribble from Gil. Julius had not written, but Serena had not expected that because Julius seldom wrote to anybody. Crispian's second letter was sent from Nice, although he said by the time it reached England they would probably be halfway round Italy. They were all very well and hoped to see a little of Nice while they were here. They had all suffered brief bouts of seasickness but Gil Martlet said cold champagne was helpful so they were taking a few bottles of Veuve Clicquot on board.

After reading this Serena told Mrs Flagg to serve a glass of chilled champagne at dinner each evening. It did not, in the event, help her own sickness a great deal, but she enjoyed drinking it so much she took to drinking a glass with her lunch as well. And since one glass made her feel better able to face what was ahead, she increased it to two glasses with lunch and three with dinner.

Dora and Hetty said having the curtains closed all day made the housework a fair trial. You could not see a hand in front of your face. Hetty had left a broom on the stairs the other day while answering the door to Dr Martlet, and Mr Flagg had missed seeing it and tumbled over it. His language had been shocking and Mrs Flagg had to rub his shoulder with arnica, which stank out the kitchen for an entire day.

Dora said it was becoming a nightmare to wait on the mistress, what with her trailing silks and chiffons. Dora was partial to a bit of silk, but not when the hems were dragged over the floor like a weeping willow, making a deal of washing and ironing because the mistress could not be doing with anything grubby.

'And silk scarves round her neck,' said Dora, over a midday dinner of Mrs Flagg's roast mutton.

'Ladies in the desert fold scarves over their faces,' said Hetty. 'I read about it in a novel. P'raps she's trying to start a new fashion.'

'Some hopes of that with madam never setting foot out of doors,' said Mrs Flagg, passing the potatoes to Flagg, because people had to eat, even if the mistress had taken to a diet of champagne, nasty windy French muck.

Dora, who liked to live in an atmosphere of friendliness, asked Mr Flagg to tell about the journey the master and Mr Crispian were on. Where would they be about now? Mr Flagg had a book of maps that showed where other countries were with little coloured pictures; Dora thought it was ever so interesting although you couldn't pronounce half the names.

'No, nor want to,' said Mrs Flagg, who could not be doing with Abroad ever since she and Flagg had taken a day trip to Ostend and she had been sick on the ferry crossing.

Flagg was pleased to be appealed to and he took out the atlas there and then, spreading it on the table so as to trace the route for the two girls.

'All those places,' said Dora, as she and Hetty pored over the map of Italy and the Adriatic Sea. 'Romantic, I call it.'

'I don't know about it being romantic, it'll be a long time before they get home,' said Mrs Flagg, setting down a rhubarb tart and reaching for the pudding dishes, while Flagg removed the atlas in case somebody spilled custard on it.

❀ ❀ ❀

Dr Martlet called most days, generally just after lunch, which Serena considered a very suitable time. He could be offered coffee, which Flagg generally brought upstairs, and then poured out. Today, however, it was Flagg's half-day and it was Hetty who carried in the tray and set it down. Serena did not trust Hetty to pour coffee, so she dismissed her and poured it out herself.

It was unfortunate that as she handed Dr Martlet the cup, the long sleeve of her gown fell back, showing her forearm. The rash was particularly bad that day, crusted and bleeding, and although Serena pulled the sleeve down at once Dr Martlet had seen it.

He stared at her arm and, in a voice of unmistakable horror, said, 'Lady Cadence, how long have you had those sores?'

'Not very long. A few weeks. My wrists and ankles tend to swell—I told you that.'

'Yes, but...May I look at your arm more closely?'

He did not touch her at all, but he looked carefully at the sores and asked if there were any others. 'On your body? Between your legs?'

'Oh, no,' said Serena quickly. 'This is only where the skin has cracked and become dry from the swelling. That's all it is,' she said, a bit desperately. 'I usually put hand lotion on, but I forgot it this morning.'

'Don't put lotion of any kind on,' he said. 'It won't help and it might make it worse.' He sat back, looking at her, and incredibly there were tears in his eyes. 'Oh, my dear Serena,' he said. 'I've prayed this wouldn't happen.'

He had always addressed her as Lady Cadence before, but now it was as if a mask, diligently kept in place all these years, had slipped. Serena was not offended because of his evident distress and concern. She said, 'But they're just patches of dry skin, aren't they?' Fool, she was saying to herself. You know what it is; you knew almost from the first appearance of the marks.

Dr Martlet sat very still for a moment, then he said, 'I'm afraid it's something far more serious than that.'

Serena heard herself say, 'I've got the same disease as Julius, haven't I?'

She willed him to say of course she had not; that it was just dry skin, or some condition resulting from the pregnancy. She was even hearing the comforting words in her mind.

Gillespie Martlet said, 'Yes, I'm afraid you have.'

Serena sat very still for several minutes. Then she said, 'Once, you told me that the disease my husband has can eventually affect the brain. Will that happen to me?'

'In your husband's case,' he said, 'the disease went untreated for far too long. He hid it from us all. For years, perhaps. In your case, though, we know about it early enough to try a number of treatments.'

'How effective are the treatments, though?'

'Some can be very good,' he said, but Serena heard the note of evasion.

She said, 'But if they aren't effective—it could encroach on my brain?'

'Yes,' he said. 'Yes, it could.'

1912

Before they left England, Dr Martlet had told Crispian the
syphilis was encroaching on Julius Cadence's brain. 'I've
been measuring the progress of it as far as one can measure
such a thing,' he said, 'and it seems to me that there's been
quite a rapid deterioration in the last three months. It's by no
means a constant process, though, so it might slow down.'

'But not reverse?'

'I'm afraid not,' said Martlet. 'Crispian, you need to know
that now it's reached this stage—now the disease has a firmer
hold of him—there will probably be episodes of violence
and also extreme personality changes. Those episodes will
become more pronounced and more frequent. And—I'm sorry,
Crispian—but in the end you may find that not only does he
not know you, you won't know him. He'll turn into a stranger.'

But as the ship left Italy and began the long haul
around the coast of Greece, Julius seemed almost normal.
They docked briefly at Patras, where Jamie went ashore to
explore the ancient cathedrals and pursue the tradition of
Byzantine music in the city. Crispian went with him, interested to see something of the place, leaving Julius with the
ship's doctor, who did not want to come, on the grounds
that once you had seen one port you had seen most of
them. He would spend his afternoon quietly on the ship,
Dr Brank said, although he would be very grateful if
one of them could bring back a bottle of the local wine.
Perhaps a couple of bottles, in fact, or maybe best make it
the round half-dozen while they were about it. He was by
way of making a collection of wines of the world.

'It'd be ungenerous to refuse that request,' said Gil,
and accompanied Crispian and Jamie for the first half-
hour of the exploration, then proceeded to vanish.

By half-past four, Jamie and Crispian, meeting by
arrangement in one of Patras' squares, began to worry that
something had happened to him. They set off to scour the

city, finally running him to earth in a dim subterranean room where he was involved in a card game with six sinister-looking men of uncertain nationality and dubious probity.

Told they might miss the ship's departure, he said, 'Balls, dear boy. The ship would never sail without its wealthiest passengers.'

Pressed for an account of his activities, he said he had gone into the wine shop in quest of the doctor's wine, had there been recognized as English, considered as a result to be lavishly rich and forcibly enlisted in the game that was in progress below the shop. Crispian and Jamie knew how it was with card games, he said; once you started playing, time ceased to exist.

'But it's been nearly five hours,' said Crispian, furious.

'That proves my point.'

He was unrepentant and amiable, and on the way back to the ship counted his winnings with satisfaction. After this, he listened with apparent interest to Jamie's description of how he had managed to find a conservatoire devoted exclusively to Byzantine music and had been able to hear a little of one of the classes.

Crispian, who for the last couple of weeks had been deciding that Gil was not nearly as wild as gossip painted him, realized angrily he had been wrong. Gil was every bit as wild, and he was untrustworthy and reckless as well. Those strange and disturbing moments of closeness—intimacy, if you wanted to call it that—that had passed between them could be ascribed to nothing more than Gil's mischievous streak. Crispian would put them very firmly from his mind and he would certainly not allow them to happen again.

❈ ❈ ❈

They were several days out into the Aegean Sea when the last shreds of sanity fell away from Julius Cadence.

He and Crispian had been having breakfast together; Julius had been calm and lucid for several days and that morning had started to talk to Crispian about Cadences. Crispian, drinking his coffee, even wondered if it was possible the doctors might have been wrong about his father's condition. He appeared pleased to be with Crispian, and he was wearing one of the linen jackets purchased for the trip with a silk scarf. His hair was brushed neatly and there was a faint scent of the expensive soap he always liked to use.

'When I think what's ahead, Crispian,' he said, drinking his coffee, 'I'm worried for the bank. There're storm clouds gathering in Europe—you know that, of course?'

'Yes, certainly.'

'If there's war it'll affect the financial institutions. War always does.'

'Will there be a war, d'you think?' Please let this conversation go on, thought Crispian. Please let him stay like this—lucid and intelligent.

Julius said, 'Yes, I think there's going to be a war. And, other considerations apart, Cadences may have to ride out what's called hyperinflation after it—that's something that frequently follows wars. Your grandfather saw it happen after Crimea and the Transvaal, and to a lesser extent I saw it happen after the Second Boer War. Prices increase so rapidly that currency loses its value, you see. Coinage becomes debased. Cadences has never yet suffered an actual bank run, but if this war that's brewing ravages its way across Europe, as the politicians say, then it might do so in the aftermath.' He frowned, then said, 'Not all wars are fought on battlefields.'

Crispian thought: this is the man whose brain, according to old Martlet, is being slowly eroded by disease. How sad it is that my father should talk so lucidly and with such concern about a run on Cadences, when I have brought him out of England to avoid that very possibility.

Suddenly Julius said, 'I do know what's ahead, Crispian.'

'You mean if there's a war?'

'I don't mean the war. I mean me. I'm ill, aren't I? No pretence, now.' For a moment the familiar imperious impatience showed.

Crispian said carefully, 'You were working too hard. That's why we've come on this sea trip. Dr Martlet thought it would do you good.'

'Ah. Ah, yes, sea trip. But you can't always trust the sea.' He looked uneasily about the small dining room, and an expression came into his eyes Crispian had never seen before. He felt a lurch of apprehension.

'I don't like travelling,' said Julius suddenly, and hunched over, wrapping his arms around his body as if hugging a pain. 'I don't feel safe.'

Crispian searched for something soothing and ordinary to say, but before he could speak Julius straightened up. The sunlight fell more strongly across his face and with a deep stirring horror, Crispian understood properly what Martlet had meant about his father turning into a stranger. I don't know you, he thought. Someone else is waking behind your eyes.

Julius stood up, pushing the chair away, and the silk scarf round his neck fell slightly open. For the first time Crispian saw the lesions in full, livid on the skin of his father's throat. Like open sores, he thought, and although he tried not to flinch, his father saw the revulsion.

But he said, 'So now you've seen what I am. Dear God, if you knew how I scheme and struggle to stop everyone from knowing and seeing—'

'It doesn't matter—' began Crispian, reaching out a hand, but Julius was already pushing his chair back. 'I can't bear you to see it,' he said, and with a gesture that was infinitely pitiable, he scrabbled at the scarf to cover his throat again. 'I can't bear anyone to see it. I know what it is, even though that old fool Martlet tried to pretend. But you see, Crispian, it might be better not to give it a name.' The sly darting look showed again. 'Once you give something a name,' said Julius, 'it makes it real. Did you know that? The priests will tell you that to exorcize a demon you first have to name it...But I've never named my demon, Crispian, I've never dared...'

He tailed off and Crispian, moving slowly, got up and began to edge his way to the door, intending to call Gil or Jamie, or the ship's doctor. He had reached the door when the sly look vanished and wild glaring madness took its place. Julius was making flailing, uncoordinated gestures with his arms as if fighting off an invisible assailant. The cups and plates were swept to the floor, most of them smashing, and Julius sank into a tight huddle in the corner, wrapping his arms about him, his head hunched over. In a sobbing whisper, as if talking to himself, he said, 'I never name it, that demon...I won't call it by its name, no matter what it does to me, because if I do it will destroy me completely...'

Pity closed round Crispian's throat, but he managed to get into the corridor and to shout for Dr Brank, who came almost at once, Gil at his heels.

They took in the situation at a glance, and Gil went straight to the corner where Julius crouched, and took his arm. 'Let's get you back to your cabin, sir,' he said, and through the dizzy horror Crispian was aware of thinking it was a pity Gil seemed to have abandoned his medical training because there was a gentle kindness in his voice he had never heard before.

But when the three of them tried to move Julius he fought them savagely, emitting cries that were half sobs, half roars of rage. After a few moments, the doctor said,

'Can you two hold him while I get something from my surgery?'

'Yes, but what—'

'Only one thing to do in this situation,' he said tersely, and without waiting for them to answer, sped from the dining room.

Crispian assumed he would bring a bromide, but when he returned he was carrying an oddly shaped jacket made of canvas. Crispian did not immediately understand, and it was Gil who said, 'Oh Jesus, you're going to put him in a straitjacket!'

'I'm afraid it's the only course of action,' said Dr Brank grimly. 'And you'll have to help me.'

In his corner, Julius gave a cry of rage, and tried to twist out of Gil's hands.

'He knows what it is,' said the doctor. 'Sir Julius, I think you've had this on before, haven't you? But it'll only be for a short time—just until you're calmer.'

Julius was gripping the doctor's hands, and Crispian saw the man wince. Julius said, 'Don't name it, will you? Don't say aloud what I am.'

The doctor was busy with the straps, and it was Gil who said, 'We won't name it, sir. There's no need to do so anyway.' He looked at the doctor. 'For pity's sake, can't you give him a shot of something? Laudanum, if you haven't anything else.'

'The condition prohibits laudanum,' said the doctor in a low voice. 'Now then, Sir Julius...'

The terrible garment was fashioned a little like a narrow jacket, but the sleeves were almost twice as long as normal sleeves. Crispian held his father while the doctor and Gil managed to pull the jacket over Julius Cadence's head and force his arms into the sleeves. He fought them for all he was worth, lashing out, and once his fingernails raked a scratch down Gil's cheek. Gil swore, but held on, and between them they wound the lengthy sleeves round his body, and then—to Crispian, worst of all—looped a thick crotch strap under his legs and secured it at the back.

'We'll have to carry him,' said Dr Brank. 'You take his legs, Martlet. Cadence and I will carry his shoulders.'

'His cabin?' said Crispian.

'No, bring him to my surgery. I can keep a better watch on him there.'

Julius was still fighting when they finally laid him on the narrow bunk in the doctor's rather sparse surgery.

'He'll wear himself out quite soon,' said the doctor. 'Then we can take the straitjacket off. You two go and have something to eat. I'll stay with him.'

'That's rubbish about laudanum,' said Gil to Crispian as they went out. 'I've seen it used on syphilis patients at Guy's perfectly effectively and safely. Anyway, if it'll calm that poor wretch down, I'll pour vinegar down him. I tell you what, dear boy, the minute that drunken old sawbones comes out, I'm back in there with the laudanum.'

'How will you get the laudanum?' said Crispian suspiciously. He would not be surprised if Gil said he intended to steal it from the dispensary.

'Private supply,' said Gil. 'And don't put on your prudish look, Crispian. I suffer from insomnia at times. Laudanum allows me to sleep and get some rest.'

Entries from an Undated Journal

There was precious little rest for anyone on that ship as it began to crawl its way along the Turkish coast.

I had looked forward to that part of the expedition— I thought it would be interesting and rewarding to see a little of those exotic lands. The sultans and caliphs and viziers. The covered squares and onion domes, wreathed in their ancient legends. And the people of the old stories—Tamerlaine and Suleiman the Magnificent. There's magic in the very words, isn't there? You, who read this, must agree with me, even though you know, by now, that I'm a self-confessed murderer. But murderers can have souls and appreciate the finer things of life. We aren't all Jack the Ripper characters, walking around with dripping knives in case a likely victim presents him or herself. I always thought him rather an exhibitionist, that man, whoever he was, although the popular press must take some of the (dis)credit, because they seized on the whole thing with the glee of ghouls and sensationalized the killings. 'Subtle' is not a word one could ever apply to those newspapers, not then and not now. Still, one can't really blame them, because scandal was ever popular, and the ordinary people have always loved a juicy murder. Charles Dickens knew that when he gave his Fat Boy that marvellous line: 'I wants to make your flesh creep.'

But as for that part of the voyage that took us to the Turkish coast—I must confess I felt somewhat cheated that I couldn't enjoy it as I had hoped. Actually, my memories of those weeks are somewhat blurred. I do know the darkness descended on me quite heavily around then, but I also know I was very cunning and I firmly believe I fooled them all. I've said earlier in these pages that I was a consummate actor, but when I look back on those days—on the stifling nights in that stuffy cramped cabin—on the hot smell of tar from the decks and the oakum in the huge coils of rope—I do believe I gave a remarkable performance.

Later

After I finished the above entry, I made a search of this place where I'm spending my last days. Quite why I did that, I can't explain, because I surely know every last inch. The search didn't take very long, of course, but the curious thing is that I found something, and as God—or the Devil—is my witness, I don't believe it was there earlier.

There's a cupboard opening out of this room. A cupboard so almost-seamless and so flush with the wall I never suspected it was there. But an hour ago I laid the flat of my hands on every inch of the walls and moved slowly around them. And halfway along the long wall near my bed I felt a difference in the surface. Seams, joins, lines making up a definite shape. The shape of a door? No, too small. Even so, I explored along the seams until I realized it was a large, deep cupboard.

Believe me, I have examined this room so minutely I wouldn't have thought so much as a cobweb could have escaped my attention. But this cupboard had escaped it.

It's roughly four feet high and perhaps two feet wide. Inside it goes back for about two feet, and then there's just a blank wall. There's nothing stored inside it, which is slightly surprising. So what is it? And what's on the other side of that wall at the back? I sat for a long time trying to work this out.

The thought of escaping is so tremblingly fragile an idea I dare not let it take shape in my mind—I certainly dare not commit it to these pages. Not yet...But, oh God, oh God, let there be a way out of here.

There are three and a half days left to me—eighty-four hours—and I've decided to fill them by dividing the rest of my story into segments and allotting one or two segments to each day. It's unbearable to contemplate the prospect of reaching the end of my story with hours—perhaps as much as a day—of life left, and nothing with which to fill the time.

CHAPTER EIGHTEEN

Turkish Coast, 1912

THE DAYS ON BOARD ship were filled with a variety of things, but for Crispian the worry about their situation overrode everything else.

Jamie, who took a gloomy view of most things, had already said they were in dangerous waters.

'And I don't just mean the Aegean Sea,' he said. 'I mean this threat of war.'

'But the Balkan League's supposed to have settled all the turmoil,' said Crispian, knowing it had done no such thing.

'I know, but it's a very fragile alliance between those countries,' said Jamie. 'And any or all of them might decide to wage outright war on the Turks. On the Ottoman Empire. If that happens—if the Ottoman Empire mobilizes its armies—we'll be trapped out here.'

'It should be all right,' said Crispian. 'They're turning the ship round today to go back to Athens. The captain thinks it's too risky to go any further.'

The conversation took place in the ship's small bar, with Gil lounging in the padded seat under the porthole, drinking what Crispian thought was ouzo.

Crispian had been reading the English papers picked up in Rhodes. The papers were a week old, but he was working his way through them because they made him feel in touch with home. He finished *The Times'* potted version of the history of the Ottoman Empire, which the paper's editor apparently thought its readers would find edifying, and threw the paper down.

'Personally,' said Gil, 'I find the Turkish Empire rather fascinating, never mind *The Times'* correspondent casting thinly veiled aspersions at its decadence. I'm all for a bit of decadence. Sultans and harems and concubines. And you have to admit the silk garments they wear are sumptuous. Very dramatic.'

'It'll be dramatic if war does break out between the Balkan States and the Turks,' said Crispian. 'Because the Greeks will seize all the islands in the Aegean and they'll control shipping and we won't get out.'

'But who said life was ever meant to be safe?' enquired Gil, carelessly. 'I feel definitely drawn to the Turkish culture.'

'What about the religion?' said Crispian, half-amused, half-exasperated.

'I'm a pagan at heart, dear boy, or hadn't you realized?' said Gil, reaching for the ouzo bottle again.

'Their music is rather beautiful,' said Jamie, picking up *The Times* and rifling the pages. 'Byzantine plainchant and the liturgical rites of the Eastern Orthodox Church. If we do risk putting into any of the Turkish ports, I'd rather like to delve a bit into that.'

'You'd take that risk, then?'

'I'm not a risk-taker,' said Jamie, with his rare, sweet smile. 'You know that. I'd like to hear some of the music at its source, though.'

Crispian was about to reply when running footsteps came along the deck outside, and Brank, the ship's doctor, fell gasping into the bar.

'Dear me,' said Gil, 'you're in more than a usual hurry to get a drink tonight, and in fact—' He broke off, seeing Brank's face. 'What's wrong?' he said, and even through his concern for what the doctor might be about to say, Crispian heard how Gil's voice suddenly sharpened and saw how he sat up straighter.

'Mr Cadence—it's Sir Julius,' said Brank.

'Ill?' It was Gil who rapped out the question.

'Oh God,' said the doctor, and his hands were trembling. 'Oh dear God.'

Again it was Gil who moved fastest, going swiftly along the decks to Julius Cadence's cabin, the other two at his heels. They reached the cabin, and Gil went in. Crispian paused in the doorway, horrified, Jamie behind him. He heard Jamie's gasp of distress, but he had no room in his mind for anything other than his father.

His father. It took several moments for Crispian to be sure that it actually was Julius Cadence in the room. It was as if a wholly different person crouched in the corner, arms wrapped round its body, head turning from side to side, and a dreadful blank unseeing look in the eyes. Crispian, his mind spinning, thought, This is the worst yet. He doesn't know any of us—dear God, I don't think he can even see any of us.

He became aware of the doctor babbling at his side, tripping over his words in his anxiety to explain what had happened.

'... and I left him on his own for most of the day, I admit I did that, Mr Cadence, Mr Martlet,' Brank was saying. 'But he was so tranquil after breakfast, a little sleepy, perhaps, but nothing out of the—'

'Had you given him bromide this morning?' said Gil, who had kneeled at Julius's side. Crispian saw his father give a start of surprise as Gil grasped his hand.

'Bromide? Yes, it seems to soothe him, make him comfortable. You suggested it yourself,' said Brank to Gil. 'You remember how you said a mixture every morning...' He turned his head as Julius said something in a whisper.

'What's he saying?' said Jamie, still in the door of the cabin.

'That it's dark.' Gil was staring at Julius very intently.

'Dark,' said Julius again, and this time the word came out louder. 'It's everywhere now. All round me. I knew it was creeping after me—I've known it for a long time. But now it's everywhere. Soon I shan't be able to breathe for it.'

Gil was still holding Julius's hand between his own. 'You're all right, sir,' he said. 'Quite safe. We're here. Tell me what you're feeling? Are you in any pain?'

'I always feared the darkness,' said Julius as if Gil had not spoken, and began to rock to and fro like a child in pain. Crispian had the impression that his father was not talking to any one of them. 'It's followed me for so long. Like a thick black shadow. Like a monstrous bruise hiding in corners, waiting to pounce.'

Crispian went to kneel on his other side. He said, 'Father—it's me. Crispian.'

Gil said, very softly, 'I don't think he can see you. Can't you tell that?' He leaned closer to Julius again, moving a hand back and forth in front of his eyes. 'You see?' he said. 'No response at all.'

'Father—'

'Uncle Julius—'

Crispian and Jamie spoke together, then stopped. Gil said, very gently, 'There's no point in talking to him, either.'

'Why?'

'I don't know exactly what's happened,' said Gil, 'but it's my guess that the disease has finally touched a vital spot in his brain—perhaps given him a seizure.' He sat back on his heels, and incredibly Crispian saw the glint of tears in his eyes. 'The poor sod,' he said softly. 'Whatever happened, it's rendered him blind and deaf.'

❀ ❀ ❀

Eventually they managed to reach Julius by means of tracing letters on the palm of his hand to form words that made up simple sentences.

It was Gil who suggested this. 'I should have thought of it for myself,' said Crispian, half angrily.

'No you shouldn't,' said Gil. 'I'm the one with medical training.' He glanced angrily at Brank. 'I saw it done once at Guy's. It was a different disease, but the patient became blind and deaf in much the same way. But I think it works only if there's some spark of understanding left, and if Sir Julius has had a stroke...Still, we can try.'

Slowly and with infinite patience, Gil traced a series of words on the palm of Julius Cadence's hand. Short, simple words, reassurance, questions. *Friends here...Any pain? Can help...*

It seemed to Crispian that it was hours before his father showed any understanding of what Gil was doing, but then gradually, as if the darkness he had described was dissolving, he turned his head in Gil's direction. When Gil again traced out the word 'pain', then sketched a question mark, he nodded.

'Head hurts,' he said.

Crispian, watching closely, thought Gil spelled out, *Can help.*

'I'll fetch something for the pain,' said Brank, clearly relieved to have an excuse to leave the cabin.

Gil relaxed. 'I think there might be a faint glimmer of sight remaining,' he said to Crispian and Jamie, who were both watching. 'But it's impossible to know for sure unless we test him with strong light straight onto his face.

And at the moment he's so confused and frightened, that would be inhuman. Crispian, I'm so sorry.' He put out a hand to Crispian, and Crispian, scarcely realizing what he was doing, took it.

'Could it improve?' he said.

'I don't know.' Gil released his hand quite naturally and gently and, as the doctor came back, said, 'What's the qualified opinion, Brank? Will this improve?'

'Honestly, I've no idea. I've never encountered this before.'

'You're a ship's doctor,' said Gil, with an edge to his voice. 'Swashbuckling across the seven seas with lust-filled sailors. I'd have expected you to come across syphilis quite often.'

'Yes, I have, but I've never seen it in this advanced stage,' said Brank. He was looking at Julius. 'If we had more medical equipment on board to perform tests we might find out a bit more. As things are, there's not much we can do.'

'What's that you've brought him?'

'A double dose of the bromide with an opiate in it.'

After a few unsuccessful attempts, Crispian managed to close his father's fingers round the glass and guide it to his mouth. He was relieved that his father seemed to understand he was meant to drink.

'What do we do?' said Crispian, as they went out of the cabin, leaving Julius lying on the narrow bunk sliding into a drugged sleep.

'First, we head for the whisky,' said Gil, leading the way back to the passengers' lounge and reaching for the bottle and three glasses. 'I don't know about you two, I intend to get drunk.' He poured the whisky and sat down. 'Actually, I think all we can do is not look too far ahead.'

'You think he might come out of this?'

'It's not out of the question. But someone will have to be with him almost constantly. Throughout the day, at any rate.'

'We can arrange that,' said Crispian.

'We'll work out a rota,' said Jamie. 'What about the nights?'

'If he has a good measure of bromide around ten o'clock each evening he should sleep the sleep of the innocent for hours,' said Gil. 'If that drunken old fool Brank won't administer it, I'll break into his surgery and mix it myself.'

'I'll help you, if you have to do that,' said Jamie, and Crispian shot him a grateful look.

'At least that would mean we could all have an ordinary night's sleep,' said Gil. 'But I think one of us had better move into the cabin next door, so there's always someone at hand.'

'I'll do that,' said Crispian at once. 'I'll get my things moved at once. It will only be for the next two weeks, anyway, then we'll be at Athens. There'll be a good hospital there and a British Embassy.'

For the next two nights the arrangement worked well. Crispian was intensely grateful to Jamie and Gil, who shared in the often pitiful, but frequently tedious, task of looking after Julius during the day. His mental state immediately following the seizure had been fairly good—he seemed to understand what Gil called the skin-writing, and answered questions put that way quite sensibly. But after two days he seemed to become suddenly more helpless and dependent; it was necessary to wash and dress him, feed him, and, at suitable intervals, take him to the small water closet, which was shared by them all. There were long periods when he simply lay on his bunk, staring up at nothing, and it was impossible to know what he was thinking.

'Or even,' said Gil, 'if he's thinking at all.' He looked at Crispian. 'He's withdrawing into some dark world of his own,' he said. 'I don't think we can bring him back now, Crispian. I think this is the start of the end.'

It was Jamie who cut up small squares of different fabrics and put them in Julius's hands so he could feel the different textures.

'It was just an idea I had for him,' he said to Crispian, a note of apology in his eyes. 'Have you noticed that since the seizure he seems to like the feel of the silk scarf he always wears to cover the...that he always likes to wear? So I thought since the sense of touch is probably the only sense still remaining to him...'

'I hadn't noticed,' said Crispian. 'And I should have done. Thank you, Jamie.'

Jamie's brown eyes were sympathetic. 'Crispian, we'll cope. Until we reach Athens, we'll cope somehow.'

'I must have been mad to bring him out here in the first place,' said Crispian, with an impatient gesture. 'But I honestly thought it was the right thing to do. I thought we needed to be safe from prying eyes, inquisitive newspapermen who'd want to tell the world that the head of Cadences Bank was—' He shook his head angrily. 'But I didn't expect this development.'

'None of us did,' said Jamie. 'And of course it was the right thing to do. We all agreed on it. Old Martlet agreed—your mother agreed. And you couldn't risk Cadences. If the newspapers had once found out...I understand why you did it and if your father was his normal self, he'd understand it, as well.'

Crispian began to believe they would reach Athens without further incident and hand his father over to the care of doctors. But several nights after Jamie's idea about the pieces of cloth, Crispian woke with a start and knew at once that someone was in the cabin with him. He half sat up, not unduly alarmed, assuming it was one of the crew or Dr Brank to say there was a problem with his father. But wouldn't they have knocked or called out? The cabin was practically pitch-dark because the faint glimmer of moonlight on the sea stopped Crispian from sleeping, so he always drew the cover across the porthole. As his eyes adjusted to the darkness he saw a figure standing motionless and silent by the door, the head turned towards the bed.

Crispian's first thought was of Gil and the night when Gil had opened champagne and suggested Crispian stay in his cabin to drink it with him. He heard again his own stammered excuse about perhaps doing so another night, and he saw Gil's slant-eyed smile.

Was this to be that night? Was Gil in here with him, and if so, how did Crispian feel about it? But he knew, almost at once, it was not Gil; he had no sense of Gil's presence—none of the instinctive recognition that takes place on some indefinable level of perception within the human mind. It was then he saw a faint glimmer of colour from the intruder's neck as if the sheen of some fabric was showing up in the dark cabin, and recognized it at once.

It was the scarlet and blue silk of his father's scarf—the scarf he always wore to cover the sores on his neck and chest. The scarf that, even in his present, increasingly confused state, he groped for, winding it determinedly round his neck as if it were a charm that would hold the dark disease at bay.

Crispian got cautiously out of bed, moving slowly because Gil and Dr Brank had both thought Julius could sense people's movements and he did not want to alarm him. Somehow Julius must have found his way out of his cabin and felt his way the few steps along to Crispian's. Sleepwalking, perhaps? The result of too many of Gil's bromide mixes? Or something simpler—trying to feel his way to the lavatory without calling for help?

Reaching for his dressing gown, Crispian glanced at the faint rim of light round the porthole, but decided not to waste time fumbling with the awkward catch. He would simply take Julius's hand and trace out the 'C' he used to identify himself and which Julius had come to understand. Then he would lead him out to the passageway and back to bed.

He slid his feet into the slippers by his bed and stood up. Almost at once the figure seemed to stiffen.

He *has* sensed that I've moved, thought Crispian. We were right about that.

But as he went forward, the figure seemed to stiffen again. As if it were watching him. As if it had sight.

Sight.

Crispian froze, the sudden fear that this might not be Julius after all engulfing him. Very softly, he said, 'Gil?' praying Gil's light mocking voice would answer. But it would not, of course, Crispian already knew that. 'Jamie?' he said. 'Jamie, is that you? Is something wrong?'

Nothing. But the resonance of his voice seemed to thrum like a shivering cobweb on the air or as a plucked violin string thrums long after the sound has died away. Crispian knew the dark figure was aware he had spoken. But he was remembering his father's frightening strength the morning they put the straitjacket on him, and fear prickled the back of his neck. He moved towards the door, hoping he could reach it and get to the passageway outside to call for help. But as he did so, the figure moved, darting across the room. One arm was hooked tightly round Crispian's neck, half-choking him, and the other came round his body, pinioning his arms. Crispian fought to get free, but Julius's arms were like iron staves and he could scarcely move. His lungs struggled for air and his senses swum, but he managed to kick out with a backwards jab and felt his foot encounter flesh and bone. But Julius hung on, and a hot, mad excitement seemed to emanate from him.

He's enjoying it, thought Crispian in horror. He's enjoying the power over me.

A red mist danced crazily before his eyes. The arm around his body suddenly moved upwards and his attacker's two hands closed around his neck. Crispian clawed at them, but they were like steel traps and he could not prise them free. There was an agonizing pressure on his windpipe and blinding, hurting lights cartwheeled across his vision. He half fell but his assailant's body kept him standing upright.

The red mist whirled and Crispian had the feeling of being sucked down a black tunnel. With his last shreds of strength he threw out an arm, hoping to reach something—anything—he could use as a weapon. His hand caught the oil lamp on the little ledge; he felt its cold brass outline, then he heard it crash to the floor, knocking books and shaving things with it.

At once the pressure on his windpipe lessened, and this time Crispian managed to wrench himself free. He fell back, gasping and coughing, his throat and lungs on fire, unable to stand, but air rushing blessedly back into his body. For several moments all he could hear and feel was the drumming of his own blood in his ears, but then it cleared a little and he became aware of a clumsy fumbling movement by the door, then of the faint light from the passageway trickling in. He's trying to get out, thought Crispian, and on the crest of this thought managed to half sit up and turn his head. The figure was framed briefly in the doorway, the glint of the silk scarf glancingly visible, then the figure seemed to shake its head like an animal coming up out of water and went blundering down the corridor.

Crispian stood up, but his legs felt as if the bones had been pulled out and he was still gasping for air. He fell forward, half on the bed, half on the floor, but this time he managed to reach the overturned oil lamp, and to bang it hard against the floor. In a cracked, still-coughing voice, he shouted for help.

Gil was the first to arrive, with one of the crew hard on his heels. Dr Brank, blinking, appeared next, and then Jamie, whose cabin was at the far end.

'Julius,' said Crispian, still in the cracked, gasping voice. 'Tried to attack me...Don't know where he went.'

'We'll find him,' said Gil in the same moment as Jamie said, 'Are you hurt?'

'Please find him,' said Crispian. Then to Jamie, 'No, I'm not hurt at all.'

❀ ❀ ❀

They found Julius in his cabin.

'He's asleep,' said Gil. He bent down to roll back an eyelid. 'And his pupils are contracted.'

'Not so much as I'd expect, though,' said Brank, leaning over to make his own examination. He frowned, then gestured to them to come out of the cabin.

'I don't think he's very heavily drugged at all,' he said. 'I think it's possible he could have woken and found his way to your cabin, Mr Cadence.'

'Would he have known what he was doing, though? Where he was going,' said Jamie.

'He might,' said Brank. 'In fact, I think Sir Julius may be retaining a lot more understanding and sense than we realized.'

'Balls.'

'What?' Brank, who had been reaching in a pocket for his flask, looked at Gil and blinked.

'I said balls,' said Gil. 'He's retained no more sense than you do when you're drunk, and probably a sight less.'

'Dammit, Martlet, I should think I know more about a patient's condition than a pipsqueak medical student.'

'You'd think so, wouldn't you?' said Gil, unperturbed. 'But when they did let me loose on patients at Guy's at least I didn't attend them in a drink-sodden state.'

'Now, see here—'

'Stop it, both of you,' said Crispian impatiently. His voice was still hoarse but he was able to speak sharply. 'Brank, are you suggesting my father still has understanding?'

'He might have.'

'But we gave him the bromide at ten o'clock,' said Gil. 'If you hadn't been sozzled last night you'd remember I told you about it. Plain tried-and-tested bromide each night to help him sleep. But,' he said thoughtfully, 'I'll admit he may have developed a tolerance to it.'

'Rot. He's fooling the lot of us. I think he tipped the opiate away without you knowing. That's not the appearance of a man who's in a drugged sleep,' said Brank, jerking an angry thumb at the cabin door. 'I think he's trying to fool you.'

'Why?' demanded Crispian.

'Because,' said Brank, meeting Crispian's eyes squarely, 'he wants you out of the way.'

'What on earth for?' said Jamie.

'How should I know? Some unfathomable reason of his own.'

'But that would be the behaviour of a madman—' Crispian stopped.

'I said I thought he had retained some sense,' said Brank tersely. 'I didn't say he had necessarily retained any sanity. I'm sorry to say it, but I think he's in the grip of madness and he's got all the cunning of the genuinely insane.'

Gil said furiously, 'He's in the tertiary stages of syphilis, the poor wretch, and his brain is disintegrating. He had no idea what he was doing tonight. He groped his way out of his cabin for some muddled reason and, when he encountered someone, he panicked and tried to defend himself.' He paused, thrusting his fingers angrily through his hair. 'Haven't you the imagination to understand how it must have been for him? He can't see, he can't hear, and all he knew was that something reared up out of that silent *smothering* darkness he's suffering. Of course he lashed out. But then, when Crispian somehow fought him off, he managed to get out and found his own cabin again.'

'Fortuitous if he's really blind,' said Brank, drily.

'Jesus Christ, man, it's only next door! But I'll allow he might have a thread or two of vision left.'

'None of this is helping,' said Crispian. 'I'll see the captain in the morning and ask what we'd better do. It's less than two weeks before we reach Athens, and if my father really has sunk into a mad confusion he'll need watching every minute.'

'Yes, he will,' said Dr Brank. 'And I'd like to say here and now that I refuse to take any further responsibility for him. If there's a conventional medical emergency I shall, of course, treat him. But I have no experience or training whatsoever in the treatment of the insane.'

'Surely simple common sense and kindness—' began Jamie.

'It's not enough,' said Brank. 'To my mind Sir Julius is mad in an entirely different way from what any of you believes. I think he's deeply dangerous and I think he should be restrained. But it's no longer my concern.' He pushed past the younger men, opened the door, and returned to his own quarters.

Entries from an Undated Journal

I've said several times in these pages that I was never mad and, truly, I never was. The thing I called the darkness brought its own strange distortions, but it was never madness in the accepted sense.

But when I look back now, I think I may have been a little mad on the night I crept into Crispian's cabin and tried to strangle him. That was the first time I wondered if the darkness might have overtaken me without my being aware of it.

That worried me quite a lot.

CHAPTER NINETEEN

'I'M SORRY,' SAID THE CAPTAIN next morning, facing Crispian, 'but I'm not prepared to make the journey back to Athens with a madman aboard. It's too far. Anything could happen.'

'You accept Brank's diagnosis then?'

'I have to. He's the ship's doctor, the official medical authority, and I have to take his judgement.' He frowned. 'That being so, we'll have to put into port as soon as possible and you'll have to disembark. Alexandroupolis is the nearest.'

'I've never heard of it,' said Crispian.

'No, you probably wouldn't. It's a small port, close to the Greek/Turkish border, but just inside Greek territory. It's mostly used for cargo ships, and it's quite difficult to navigate. But I've done it in the past and I should be able to get permission.'

'But that part of the world is a seething hotbed of unrest,' said Crispian, horrified. 'You can't just throw us off the ship out here. The Balkan League is collapsing—all the newspapers agree on that. There's even a suggestion that it's mobilizing its armies.'

'There's also a strong suggestion that the Ottoman Empire is doing the same,' said the captain. 'I'm aware of all that. But guidelines to masters of ships in this situation are clear. Sir Julius has already had to be restrained in a straitjacket, and last night he apparently tried to strangle you. He could start on the crew next. You'll have to leave the ship at Alexandroupolis.'

'But we'll guard him,' said Crispian, a bit desperately. 'There are three of us—we can manage it between us until we reach Athens. And if the ship's carpenter fits a bolt on his cabin door—'

'Mr Cadence, sailors are a deeply suspicious breed. They won't like this business of madness—well, they don't like it now. They know something of what's been happening. The second officer has reported some of them are already gathering in angry huddles and talking furtively. I can't let that go on.'

Crispian stared at him and thought: I'm on the high seas, in waters that might explode into a messy, complicated war any day. It's not Britain's war—not yet—but that won't count. On top of that, I'm trying to restrain a man who's tried to kill me, and now I'm being told there could be a mutiny brewing.

'Alexandroupolis should be safe enough territory,' said the captain. 'I remember there's a railway actually on the quayside, so if the hospital in the town isn't able to help, you can take Sir Julius to wherever they suggest by train.'

He's washing his hands of us, thought Crispian.

The enormity of what might be ahead was almost overwhelming, but after a moment he said, 'Yes, I see. How long will it take to get to this Alexandroupolis place?'

'Two days, on my reckoning. Less, if I can manage.' In a kinder voice than he had yet used, the captain said, 'There's a small English community there. You should be safe enough.'

'You don't give me any choice,' said Crispian coldly.

'Believe me, Mr Cadence, I wish there was another choice. Can the three of you restrain Sir Julius for the next two days? Brank tells me he's still very strong, despite the illness. If he were to break out and wander about the ship in his present state—'

'We can manage while we're on the ship fairly well,' said Crispian. 'It will be once we're ashore in Alexandroupolis that the nightmare will start.'

Entries from an Undated Journal

People talk about things being a nightmare or having lived through a nightmare, but most of them have no idea what it's like actually to live through one. I had talked like that myself, more than once. But it wasn't until we went ashore at Alexandroupolis and travelled on to the little township of Edirne that I came to understand the real meaning of living a nightmare.

Crispian made all the decisions and dealt with all the arrangements. Of course he did. I don't know the details of everything, but I do know he handed out money with that arrogant carelessness I found so repugnant. He always thought problems could be solved by money. It annoys me to say this, but most of them can, of course. Give someone sufficient money and he or she will do whatever you want. It was the *way* Crispian did it that I hated. As if he was a better, less coarse person than anyone else. Almost as if the money had somehow purified him, washed away any scummy imperfections, while the rest of us had to wallow around in the grit and grime of ordinary humanity.

I remember very clearly that it was mid-September when we finally stepped ashore at Alexandroupolis. I also remember standing there for a moment and absorbing the scents of that hot quay—the unmistakable sea tang, but also the scents of that particular country. Each country has its own scent, of course. I do know it's mainly to do with the climate and the food that's eaten and grown, but I like to think there's something else as well: that the essence and the history of a country permeates its air.

But standing there that day, with the hot eastern sun on my skin, I experienced a longing for England that was so sharp and strong it was nearly painful. You may think this impossible and even mad—mad! there's a word!—but I ached for the feel of thin silken rain against my face and the crunch of dead leaves under my feet.

The hospital at Alexandroupolis, when finally we reached it, was less than useless—hopelessly inefficient and old-fashioned—and the doctors and nurses found it difficult to hide their hostility. No one actually said so, and the language barrier was a difficult one, but there was the definite impression that they regarded us as lordly English travellers who expected everyone to bow and scrape and tug mythical forelocks. (Crispian again, you see?) Still, somewhere in that suspicious old building must have been someone with a speck or two of humanity—or perhaps it was just that someone could speak a word of two of English and understood what we wanted. Because eventually we found ourselves with the address of some kind of semi-military, partly British hospital in a place called Edirne, and we got out to a railway station where Crispian did his I-am-rich performance again, and we obtained a railcar to ourselves.

But on that occasion Crispian was probably cheated. The railcar was small and hot; it smelled of urine and sweat, and of years of dirt. There were seats of a kind—slatted wooden benches, which were appallingly uncomfortable. It was a very long time before the train finally started on its journey, but when it did it was truly dreadful. It shook and jolted so violently that it was a minor miracle the carriages stayed linked. By the time we got to Edirne all of us had been travel sick. Can you imagine being sick—I mean actually vomiting—in a closed carriage with no washing facilities of any kind? And certainly no privacy. Looking back, I have no idea how long that journey lasted, but it felt like hours. All I remember now is the wet sour smell of the vomit on the floor—of trying not to stand in it—and of my own heaving stomach and the skewering pain in my head over one eye.

But at last we crossed the border into Turkish territory.

None of us knew that the worst part of the nightmare was still to come.

Edirne, 1912

Crispian had found himself frequently dreaming of England on their travels, but never more so than during the squalid rail journey to Edirne. As the train rattled its way through the strange countryside he looked at the others, one by one. They had all been sick during the journey and they all looked ill. Gil was white-faced and uncharacteristically silent; Jamie was exhausted and withdrawn, and Julius was restless and clearly distressed, despite the triple dose of bromide Gil had given him before they set off.

But the journey had to be made; the Alexandroupolis hospital had said Edirne had a military infirmary—only very small but certainly it could provide the care that the poor English milord needed. And Crispian thought a military base, no matter how small, might afford some protection if the seething cauldron they were stepping into finally erupted into war.

Edirne, when they reached it, weary and grubby, was better than he had dared hope.

'It's a bit of a hybrid place,' Jamie said, as the train seemed to near the end of its run. 'I read something about it on the ship. It's been a centre of learning in its time. The Ottomans got their hands on it about five hundred years ago, and they've populated it with quite a lot of immigrants: Hungarians and also a thriving Jewish community. There's even a rabbinical seminary.'

'We can spend our evenings there when we want to relax, and get drunk with the rabbis,' observed Gil, drily.

The hospital turned out to be in a kind of enclosure, part of an ancient Ottoman fort.

'We're all walking on hot bricks, of course,' said Raif, the young doctor who had greeted them, who had examined Julius, and whose English was better than Crispian had dared hope. 'And we think we might be in for some dangerous times. But you're welcome to stay, and if you have to be in this country at the moment, this fort is probably about the safest place. It's withstood many a battle over the centuries. There are several of your countrymen—also women—here. There'll probably be room for the three of you in the same wing.'

'You can look after my father?'

'We can probably make him comfortable and see he doesn't harm anyone or himself,' said Raif. 'I don't think you can hope for more than that.'

'I don't.'

'Don't be too downcast. There have been some surprising remissions, even at this stage. He might astonish you yet.'

'Is the war situation as grave as the newspapers say?'

'Far worse,' said Raif.

❀ ❀ ❀

All thoughts any of them had of returning to England were swept overwhelmingly away when all the endeavours of countries like France and Austro-Hungary failed to dissuade the Balkan League from finally taking arms against the Ottoman Empire. Both the League and the Turks mobilized their armies. Early in October Montenegro declared war, and shortly afterwards, the other states in the League followed suit.

At a time when the English countryside would be golden and amber, and scented with apples, Greek naval and army detachments seized almost all the islands of the eastern and north Aegean Sea, effectively controlling all exits.

Crispian knew that whether his father died or whether he lived on in this dreadful blind mindless state, they were all trapped in the ancient Turkish fort until the war was over.

Entries from an Undated Journal

Earlier today I reread some of the notes I made during those appalling weeks, and I was shocked to see how bad my writing was. I was never a particularly good penman at the best of times. The content is all good, of course, but the execution isn't always immaculate.

But some of the pages from those weeks are very nearly indecipherable. I can also see there were several places where I had to break off abruptly because someone was coming. Some pages are quite badly creased as well, because I would thrust the journal into one of its hiding places. I always kept it well concealed, of course—I didn't trust anyone on that ship or, later, inside the Edirne fort— but concealment became increasingly difficult and I had to change the hiding place more than once.

They never found the journal though, not then and not since, and that affords me such satisfaction, even now, even in this place, with three days left to me.

Three days.

Today I explored that cupboard again, with the tantalizing blank wall at the back—the wall that should lead somewhere but that, even by my most careful reck- onings, can't lead anywhere. But although I tapped and even hammered at it, and although I explored its surface minutely, I could find no way of breaking through to the other side.

Will three days be long enough to finish my story?

Or will that nibbling darkness overtake my mind before the three days are up?

❧ ❧ ❧

A long time after that journey to Edirne, I came across the poems of Thomas Hardy. A remarkable writer, Hardy. He understood about the darkness, all right. One poem called 'The Interloper' has an epigraph—a kind of subtitle—which struck such a chord in my mind I think it's gone on resonating ever since.

'And I saw the figure and visage of Madness seeking for a home.'

The figure and visage of Madness. Think about that, my unknown reader. Imagine seeing the figure and the face of Madness starting to take shape. The darkness of the spirit becoming flesh. I've seen it all right, which is why I can write about it. The real horror is that the figure doesn't materialize all at once, in one huge smack-in-the-face vision so that you fall down in a fit there and then and lose all comprehension of the world. It's nothing so merciful. It steals up on you, so that at first you think your eyes are playing tricks. Then you think it's just a shadow you're seeing. You spend weeks, months, trying to convince yourself you're perfectly sane. But finally you come to understand that a slow inexorable madness is creeping over you, nibbling away at your brain as it comes...

I mustn't get sidetracked, though. Nor must I allow myself to get too far ahead with this account. I must space it out, so that the days are filled. Because the clock is ticking relentlessly, and in three days—seventy-two hours—I shall hear death approaching.

Death. My death can no more be avoided than the stars can be halted in their courses.

CHAPTER TWENTY

The Present

CLEM POULTER'S LITTLE dinner parties could no more be avoided than the sun could be prevented from rising each morning. Even if you were not on the guest list, it was impossible not to hear about them. Meeting Veronica in the supermarket, Ella was not best pleased to learn from her that Clem was in the planning stage of one of his evenings.

'It's next Friday,' said Veronica, who this morning was wearing what Ella considered an impossibly inappropriate outfit, consisting of leather trousers, a woollen jacket and a quantity of gold jewellery. The fact that the gold was almost certainly genuine did not make it any better. In fact, Ella thought it rather vulgar of Veronica to be flaunting nine carat in the middle of Sainsbury's halfway through the morning.

Everyone knew, without the parade of gold necklaces and nappa leather, what a very good thing Veronica had made out of having two husbands. The first had been discarded via the divorce courts and the ceding of a five-bedroomed house into Veronica's name, and the second had died from a perforated stomach ulcer, leaving behind what Derek referred to as 'an entire battalion of insurance policies'. At the time he had said he could very easily visualize Veronica checking the insurance policies with one hand and stirring arsenic into the coffee with the other. Ella had thought this remark in very poor taste, but the Operatic Society had been rehearsing *Cosi Fan Tutte* at the time, in which there was apparently a lot of arsenic-quaffing, so the remark could be partially forgiven.

Veronica cornered Ella to say Clem had phoned her last evening to invite her to the dinner party. Oh, Ella had not been invited? Well, doubtless Clem would get round to it. He had meant to have it a couple of weeks ago but he had had that shocking cold, so he had postponed. The invitation was seven thirty for eight, and Veronica had decided to wear a trouser outfit because Clem said there were to be games afterwards. She had a brand-new one—silk, with satin lapels on the jacket—and when she tried it on in the shop the assistants had all said how youthful and sexy and elegant she looked.

'If there're games, at least he won't be forcing his dreadful music on the guests,' said Ella, because once Veronica got onto the subject of being youthful and sexy and elegant they would be here all morning.

'No, but I wouldn't put it past him to stage a session of Murder or Sardines,' said Veronica, and went off to the wine section.

Ella watched her for a moment, seeing how the vain creature teetered along the aisles in her absurd high heels and paused to ostentatiously examine the labels on wine bottles. She would be hoping people were looking at her and speculating on who would be drinking the wine with her. As if, thought Ella crossly, anybody gives a damn. Ella certainly did not give a damn who drank special-offer Pinot Noir in Veronica's over-furnished house, nor did she give a damn about Clem's stupid dinner party with its even more stupid games, whatever they might be. She and Derek would probably not be able to go anyway; as well as *The Mikado,* Derek was very busy with some sort of audit at the council offices. Amy said he was looking quite haggard, poor old Gramps, but to Amy's generation anyone over forty looked haggard.

If anyone was entitled to look haggard at the moment, it was Ella herself, what with all the worry about whether Clem and Veronica would keep their nerve if questioned about the body found at the lodge. She was not sleeping very well, and in the ragged sleep she did get she saw the dreadful face peering over the ruined tumble of bricks in Cadence Manor. Sometimes she saw Serena Cadence with her staring dead eyes and ravaged face, and sometimes Serena's face turned into that of Ella's own mother, with the scars livid and ugly on her skin.

She had no idea if the police had identified the man's body yet, or if they had found her watch with the damning initials, ELF, and the date of her birthday. Initials and date together would show she had been inside Cadence Manor during the two days between her birthday and the closing of the village. It was what Derek would call 'a very small window of time'.

Ella was annoyed with Derek. She thought she might reasonably have expected him to notice she was preoccupied, but he had not, though she did not want him asking awkward questions. Amy had noticed. That very morning she had asked if Gran was all right, because she was looking a bit moth-eaten. Ella took this to mean slightly unwell in Amy's vocabulary, and said she was perfectly all right—well, maybe a bit tired, what with one thing and another.

'What things?'

'All sorts of things. You don't realize what a lot I have to do,' Ella said. 'There's the running of this house—all the shopping and washing and ironing.'

Amy said, 'But you've got a washing machine. And a dishwasher. And there's someone in Lower Bramley who does an ironing service. She's put a little poster up in the library. She'll collect and deliver, and it's not very expensive.'

'It's not just that,' said Ella quickly. 'There are all my various activities. I lead a very busy life, you know. A very fulfilled life,' she added hastily, in case this sounded grumblesome.

'Oh, I see,' said Amy, in the blank voice of someone who did not see at all.

Walking round the supermarket, trying to keep a distance from Veronica, Ella remembered Amy's words and suddenly wondered if other people were thinking she seemed moth-eaten. She could not risk anyone wondering if she had a secret worry. People were so gossipy, and she was quite a well-known figure in the district, what with helping Derek's operatic people on their social nights, what with the Gardening Club and the library group, and helping in the Oxfam shop for an hour on Friday mornings.

At this point she caught sight of herself in a mirror display. She did look a bit drawn, although supermarket lights were invariably unfriendly. Still, it would not hurt to book a hair appointment when she got home. Quite apart from looking moth-eaten, standards had to be maintained and Ella liked to look smart. And even without silly dinner parties with childish games (to which she would not go, even if Clem asked her), in her busy and fulfilled life there was generally something to look forward to.

❀ ❀ ❀

Clem Poulter was pleased to have one of his little dinner parties to look forward to. Everything had been so dreary of late, what with his cold and the horrible chemical mist hanging over Priors Bramley, and the unpleasant discovery of the body. He was a bit worried about that, but only a very little bit. What had happened all those years ago had been the purest accident. They certainly had not deliberately pushed the man into the ruined chimney shaft. Clem had wanted to go down there in case there was something they could do for him, but the church clock had already been striking twelve and they had known the plane with its sinister cargo would be approaching.

A bit of frivolity would go down very nicely at the moment. Some of the things he wrote in his Jottings were often quite frivolous, even a bit quirky; the trouble was that people did not always understand that kind of quirkiness, which was why Clem got stupid rejections for his articles, with magazine editors and feature writers politely saying they did not think his work was quite what they wanted at the moment.

He always blew a mental raspberry at the people who sent him these letters, and planned that one day he would assemble his Jottings into a book and everyone would marvel at his powers of observation and acuity of character-drawing. This last phrase pleased him so much he hunted out his spiral notebook to write it down before he forgot it. His father had been a great one for writing your thoughts down; diaries and journals were the very cloth of history, he used to say.

Clem thought that one day his own diaries and essays might receive the acclaim they deserved. They would give future generations an insight into the last half of the twentieth century and the first part of the twenty-first, and researchers would say things like, 'We'd better consult Poulter on that point.' Academics would argue the merits of the Poulter Journals against other learned sources.

But in the meantime, and since the library was not very busy this morning, Clem spent a happy half-hour drafting out the menu for his party. There would be eight people—ten if he included Ella and Derek, which he supposed he would do in the end; it was not worth Ella's ice-queen sulking if he left them out. In any case, he wanted Amy to come, partly because he enjoyed her company, but also because he suspected Amy might be a good lure for Dr Malik. To have Dr Malik as a guest would be a real coup.

Ten people meant extending both leaves of his table and he would have to borrow two chairs from Mrs Williams next door. But ten was a satisfying number and Clem enjoyed cooking. He was just frowning over the advisability of a seafood starter—you could depend on it that someone would claim a shellfish allergy—when Amy scooted across to his partitioned cubbyhole to say there were two policemen asking to see him.

This was faintly alarming, but when Amy brought them in Clem waved them to chairs and asked how he could help.

'I dare say it's this wretched business of the—um— body you've found, is it?' Which was a ridiculous thing to say, because what else would it be?

But they took it at face value, and said it was indeed, sir, and very puzzling.

'And there's now an added complication,' said the older of the two men.

They had told Clem their names and ranks when they came in, but he had been in too much of a fluster to take it in properly, other than to register which was the inspector and which the detective sergeant.

'Complication?'

'There's a second set of remains been found,' said the inspector.

'What kind of—You mean another body?' said Clem.

'I do. This time inside the manor itself.'

'And,' said the sergeant, 'it looks as if it's from the same era as the first one. Fifty years old, is our guess.'

Clem felt as if he had been punched in the face. He stared at the two men, then realized his mouth was gaping open as if he was the village idiot, and said, with an effort, 'You mean there've been two bodies lying there in Priors Bramley all these years? *Two?*'

'Two,' affirmed the sergeant, pulling out a notebook.

'And that being so, Mr Poulter, we'd like to find out a bit more about the history of Priors Bramley,' said the inspector.

'History? I'm sorry, I don't quite see—'

'I should have said Cadence Manor's history,' said the inspector. 'The family who lived there and so on. Local people who might have been involved with them—helping out on a domestic level at the house, maybe. A bit feudal, I know, but it's how life was in village communities, even as late as the 1940s and 1950s. Between ourselves, Mr Poulter, we're having trouble enough identifying one body, never mind two. We've scoured the missing persons lists, but they haven't yielded anything helpful so far. And so, you being the local librarian, we thought you might put us onto some archive stuff.'

'We'll be looking at the old newspapers as well, of course,' put in the sergeant.

'You'll find a lot of those here,' said Clem at once. 'It's always been my pride to keep a copy of every issue of the *Bramley Advertiser*. I like to think of myself as keeper of the area's history, you know.'

'Do you indeed, sir? Very admirable. And I hear you're mounting an exhibition of Old Bramley, so very likely you'll have unearthed a lot of quite useful stuff already.'

'Well, yes, I have,' admitted Clem. 'At least, Amy— that's Amy Haywood, who's helping out—has done.' He peered over the partition to see where Amy was and waved to her to come over.

Amy, listening to the inspector's explanation, was horrified to hear another body had turned up. 'It's surreal, isn't it? Like a whodunnit where the author chucks a new corpse in every twenty pages in case the reader's getting bored,' she said. 'I don't mean that to be disrespectful, but the bodies are from pretty far back, aren't they?'

'About fifty years ago, we think, miss. We're waiting for forensics before we can be sure, though.'

'Well, I've got a ton of boxes that I'm sorting through,' said Amy. 'But there's a million more in the basement.'

'We'll take a bit of a look at what's in the basement, if that's all right, sir.'

'Inspector, you can have the run of the entire library, as far as I'm concerned,' said Clem. 'If you want to go down there now you can have the keys.'

'You keep the cellars locked, do you, sir?'

'Yes, on account of security and fire hazard,' said Clem, who had been on a Health and Safety course. 'You never know who might sneak down there during the day when you aren't looking. There are peculiar people around, Inspector, even in Bramley.'

'Especially in Bramley, if two murders were committed fifty years ago and nobody knew about them,' said Amy, as Clem rummaged in his cabinet for the cellar keys.

'We don't know that it was murder,' said the inspector. 'There could be an innocent explanation.' He took the keys and nodded his thanks to Clem. 'The cellar door's in the hallway, isn't it? I thought I saw it. There's no need to come down with us, Mr Poulter. We'll find our own way. No need to put you to trouble.'

'It's no trouble,' said Clem earnestly.

Amy said, 'Clem, I think the inspector's trying to say tactfully that they'd prefer to do their own delving.'

'Quite right, miss,' said the inspector. 'Although if it does turn out to be murder, Mr Poulter's not likely to be the killer, not with both bodies having died over fifty years ago.'

Clem managed a nervous laugh and said, well goodness, he was hardly likely to have been murdering people when he was only nine.

'You'd be surprised at the things some children get up to, though,' said the inspector. 'None of us will ever forget the Jamie Bulger case. And there have been other cases of child murderers.'

Child murderers. But what they had done that day had not been murder. There was nothing to worry about. Clem watched the two men descend to the cellars, then returned to his cubbyhole and retrieved his plans for Friday evening. He would not dwell on all this police stuff. Instead he would concentrate on his menu and on the games his guests might play.

✿ ✿ ✿

Veronica generally found games at dinner parties boring.

She did not, however, find games in the bedroom the least bit boring, particularly with the new and exciting man with whom she had so unexpectedly and so thrillingly become entangled. It was a relationship that had considerable promise, so Veronica was going to acquiesce to any requests he might make. Well, within reason.

When, over the Pinot Noir, he broached the possibility of a little role-playing, she said at once she had an open mind.

'I don't think anything is wrong between two people who...' She paused. Better not use the word 'love', not yet, at any rate. 'Between two people who understand one another.'

He nodded, and looked pleased.

'I wouldn't do anything actually pervy, though,' said Veronica, who thought it as well to make this clear at the outset, even though it was not possible to think of him wanting to do anything in the least pervy.

But he said at once, 'No, of course not. I was thinking of something like slave girl and master?' It was said with a diffidence that Veronica found endearing, but the diffidence was somewhat counteracted by the admiring glance he sent over her figure. 'I think,' he said, 'you could carry a slave-girl costume off very well. Lots of silk veils and gold bangles.'

'And not much else?' said Veronica, with a giggle.

'Of course not. I'd very much like to see you in silk veils, Veronica.'

'I'll go up and get changed,' said Veronica, delighted.

'Shall I see you in the bedroom in fifteen minutes?'

'Make it ten.' There was no point in being coy, not after their other evening together, and he would like her to be enthusiastic; men always did.

He smiled. 'And when I come upstairs, you'll be Berenice?'

Last time, he had told her that the name Veronica was a corruption of Berenice. 'I'd like to call you Berenice sometimes,' he said. 'It could be our private name.'

Veronica thought this was really brilliant, because once you got into private names it meant you were well on the way to a real commitment.

So when he suggested the slave-girl thing, she instantly said she would *love* to be Berenice tonight.

It was strange how the name made her feel entirely different. Berenice was quite a wicked wanton lady; Veronica had a feeling Berenice might be capable of all kinds of excesses.

In the bedroom she undressed quickly and foraged in the dressing table for suitable slave-girl accessories. There were two or three silk scarves—good ones, bought in Italy—which she draped around her body. And she had some chunky gold bracelets which she put on, fastening one round her ankle. What else could she do to heighten the image? How about that gold luminous eye shadow bought years ago for a ladies' night at her second husband's masonic lodge. At the time her husband had thought it a touch vulgar, the miserable old killjoy, so Veronica, in those days wanting to be a good wife, had not worn it. But it was still in the cupboard, and she smoothed it on her eyelids. It smelled a bit musty but it looked wonderfully exotic.

'Berenice?'

He was coming up the stairs now, and hearing him whisper the name made the fantasy spring into life. He had an extraordinary way of saying 'Berenice', almost purring it. Veronica, languorously arranged on the bed, waited for him to come in and tell the slave girl what she must do. Here he was now, smiling with pleasure at the costume she had fashioned, nodding with approval at the soft light from the bedside lamp she had switched on.

'Berenice,' he said softly, and stood in the doorway for a moment, savouring what he was seeing. Then he moved to the bed.

❊ ❊ ❊

It was extraordinary the heights to which his imagination took them. Veronica remembered how, on their first evening together, he had almost seemed to become a different person. It was happening again tonight, and it was exciting and just a tiny bit frightening.

The veils worked tremendously well, although it was annoying to find her eyes beginning to sting from the eye shadow. She tried, a bit furtively, to see her reflection in the mirror over his shoulder in case her eyes were red. She would throw the shadow out and buy some new stuff in case they played this game again.

They might play other games as well. Perhaps she could be a saucy French parlourmaid to his squire of the manor. There was a black miniskirt in the wardrobe from years ago; she could fluff it out with lots of frilly petticoats.

Black stockings and her highest, spikiest heels, of course. She smiled, thinking how sexy she would look and how he would not be able to resist her.

'Something's amusing you?' he said, turning his head on the pillow.

'I'm planning another fantasy for you,' said Veronica, wriggling with delighted anticipation at the prospect.

'What is it?'

'It's a surprise. I'm still working out the details of my costume,' she said, wondering if she could fashion a cap from a couple of lace doilies, and trying to remember if Sainsbury's sold feather dusters.

CHAPTER TWENTY-ONE

Eʟʟᴀ ᴡᴀs ᴠᴇʀʏ ᴄᴏᴏʟ with Clem when he phoned her the following day to invite her to his party. Just a small gathering of friends, he said, so of course Ella and Derek must come.

'I don't know if we can manage it,' said Ella, who was not going to enthuse over a last-minute invitation. 'We both have a lot on at the moment, and with Amy staying—'

'I've invited Amy,' said Clem. 'And she thought you'd be free. And I've got a really scrummy meal worked out—a delicious recipe from a Brittany fishing village.'

'Derek can't eat shellfish,' said Ella at once. 'Shellfish upset his stomach. Don't you remember the time you served clam chowder—'

'There won't be shellfish,' said Clem, who did not want to hear again the grisly details of Derek's rebellious intestines after the clam chowder episode. 'Do come, Ella. It will do you good.'

'I'll see,' said Ella, irritated that Clem thought she needed something to do her good. 'I'll phone later to let you know,' she said, preparing to put the phone down.

'Well, make it this evening at home,' said Clem. 'I'll be in all night. My rehearsal for Friday's meal, you know. I always like to do a dummy run with a new recipe, in case—'

'Yes, you always tell us that,' said Ella, who had sat through many a meal at Clem's house, glassy-eyed at the saga of how he had adjusted the juniper berries after his dummy run or how he discovered there was no lemongrass in his spice cupboard.

'And I'll be busy here at the library all day,' went on Clem. 'I want to tidy up the cellars after the police visit. I expect Amy told you all about that.'

Ella discovered that rather than putting down the phone, she was gripping it so tightly it dug into her hand. She managed to say, 'Amy didn't mention anything about the police. D'you mean they came to the library? What did they want?'

'My dear, didn't you know?' said Clem. 'They've found another body.'

Ella felt as if something had dealt her a hard blow across the eyes. She said, 'Another body? You mean a second one?'

'You wouldn't have thought it, would you?' said Clem. 'But apparently there is another one and they've just found it. I got a real shock when they told me. They said it was inside Cadence Manor itself, so it must be the man we saw that morning. You know, Ella, when they found the one at the lodge, I assumed it was a tramp—a coincidence—because our man couldn't possibly have crawled down there—'

'Let's not talk about it on the phone,' said Ella, quickly. People insisted phone systems were computerized and automated these days, but there were always reports about them being tapped. It was mostly royalty and football stars, but it went to show you could not be too careful. 'Why did the police come to you?' she said.

'To look in the library's archives.'

'I didn't know you had any archives.'

'Of course we've got archives, we're a library, for goodness' sake.'

'Why were the police interested in the archives?' demanded Ella.

'In case it helped them identify the bodies,' said Clem with exaggerated patience. 'I don't think it did, but they went through some old newspapers. I suppose they were looking for reports of anyone vanishing around the time Priors Bramley was closed.'

'Newspapers?'

'We've got quite a lot of the back issues of the *Bramley Advertiser,* although most of them were transferred to microfiche when that Middle Counties group took them over.'

Ella's mind was working furiously. She was not overly worried at the police enquiries, because surely they would be part of normal routine. Even if the body was identified—either body—it would not matter. But a tiny nagging doubt made her say, 'Clem, are you sure they didn't find anything? I mean anything that might lead back to us—to what happened?'

'Such as your watch?' said Clem. 'No, I don't think they found anything. But, I've been thinking, Ella, perhaps we should tell them what happened that day.'

Ella sat very still. Then she said, as lightly as she could, 'Oh, I don't think that's necessary. And after so long it might look a bit peculiar.'

'I don't see why. Specially since there's another body now.'

'The one in the lodge has nothing to do with us,' said Ella quickly.

'I know, but if we gave a description—of our man, the one in Cadence Manor, I mean—that might help them identify him at least.'

'Don't be stupid,' said Ella sharply. 'None of us can remember what that man looked like—'

'Can't you?' said Clem very quietly. 'I can. In any case, it's all in my diaries.'

This time Ella felt as if her chest had been punched. 'What do you mean?'

'My Jottings, you know.' He gave one of his silly giggles and Ella hated him. 'So I can look it all up. In fact I could even let the police see the entry. I know it'll be a bit simplistic—I was barely nine—but it'll be reasonably accurate.' He paused and, when Ella did not reply, said quite seriously, 'Ella, I think we must bite the bullet on this. We didn't do anything really wrong that day. That man threatened us and we were frightened and defended ourselves. His death was a tragic accident.'

'I suppose you're right,' said Ella slowly.

'I am right. It's no good being intense and neurotic about it all these years later.'

'I'm not. But, Clem, don't do anything about talking to the police until we've discussed it again,' said Ella. 'And I'll let you know about Friday's fish supper,' she added, thus relegating pretentious Breton seafood recipes to their proper place.

She replaced the phone firmly, but she could not get up because her legs had turned to cotton threads and she felt sick and dizzy.

Clem's diaries. He had frequently said they would one day be part of Bramley's history, but Ella had never taken them seriously. She did not think anyone had. Derek once said Clem fancied himself as a modern-day Samuel Pepys, which was a waste of time and energy, to Derek's way of thinking, and Clem Poulter would have done better to occupy his time with something more useful. Who would ever want to read the ramblings of a local librarian? demanded Derek, laughing.

Remembering that, Ella thought: the police would want to read them, that's who. Not all of them, but certainly anything around the time Priors Bramley was sealed off.

It was starting to seem as if the diaries might have to be destroyed. Burned or buried or shredded. But where were they? Did Clem sit at a desk or a table and write them into a book? Surely most people used computers for writing almost everything nowadays? Derek had bought Ella a laptop last year; it was very smart and sleek, and it was nice to be able to refer casually to it, to mention having emailed Andrew designing his bridges in Africa, or talk about having ordered something on-line. She wrote the occasional letter on it, as well, although other than that she did not use it very much.

But Clem might use a computer regularly. There had been no such things when they were children, but he might have put those early, childhood diaries onto a computer recently. Ella knew that could be done; Derek often talked about scanning documents onto hard disk. Would Clem have done that?

She forced herself to take deep, calming breaths, and presently she saw exactly what she must do.

❉ ❉ ❉

She was surprised to discover there was a deep, secret satisfaction in behaving absolutely normally that evening, so that neither Derek nor Amy suspected anything.

Ella cooked and served supper as usual. As they ate, Derek was banging on about something to do with the office. She hardly listened, but a word or two got through and it sounded as if the audit had uncovered something suspicious.

'Clear case of fraud, from what I hear,' said Derek, shovelling forkfuls of food into his mouth. 'That'll mean the sack and probably prosecution. And all for a paltry couple of thousand, apparently. Shocking, isn't it? Now if I was of a criminal turn of mind and planning to defraud the local authority—'

'Amy, are you going out tonight?' said Ella, because once Derek got onto the subject of how thoroughly he would defraud the local authority if he had a criminal mind, he would go on for hours.

'I thought I might wander down to the Red Lion,' said Amy, leaning over her plate so that her hair tumbled forward over her face. 'Why?'

'I like to know what's happening, that's all.'

'Meeting your academic again, are you?' said Derek.

'He might be there,' mumbled Amy.

'Well, don't come home on your own very late,' said Derek. 'No, I know it isn't very far to walk, but you can't be too careful. A man at the office was telling me—'

'Amy will phone one of us if she wants picking up,' said Ella, who was still managing to appear ordinary, but could no more cope with Derek's man at the office tonight than she could cope with his silly tales about how he could defraud the local authority to the tune of half a million, if he put his mind to it.

'I'm rehearsing tonight, don't forget,' said Derek. 'Technical run-through for lighting cues. You won't believe this, but last week the stage manager—'

'If you've finished eating, I'll clear away and Amy can fetch the pudding,' said Ella, getting up.

'Well, I wouldn't mind another helping of stew before I have any pudding,' said Derek, and Ella winced because it was not stew they were eating; it was an Elizabeth David chicken casserole with corn-fed farm chicken and fresh basil and tarragon.

❀ ❀ ❀

Clem had stayed at the library a little later than usual this evening so he could see what the CID men had been up to yesterday in the cellars.

The library closed at five, and by half-past the two girls who manned the loan desk had gone. Clem often walked round the silent rooms on his own before locking up. He liked feeling that this was his domain and the books in their serried ranks were his possessions. Sometimes he spoke to the books in his mind, exchanging a genteel word with Miss Austen, perhaps apologizing to her if she had been put on a shelf cheek by jowl with some raunchy slash-and-gore book or bodice-ripper; sketching a military-style, heel-clicking salute in the direction of war books, or humming a snatch of a Northumberland folk song as he went past the shawls-and-clogs section. It was behaviour that Clem thought of as whimsical, although he suspected most people would have said it was Mr Poulter being slightly dotty.

Tonight, however, he went straight down to the cellars, switching on the lights and descending the stone steps with care. He did not much like cellars, which were usually cold and damp, but he did like the feeling that cellars had a life of their own. They housed secrets and memories, and romantically minded people said if you stood very still and concentrated very hard you could sometimes actually smell the stored-away memories and tragedies and comedies, and the lost loves and forgotten hopes. Clem tried to do this now in case he could write a little article about it, but his recent cold had affected his sense of smell, and all he got was mildew and the disinfectant the cleaners had sloshed around on their last spring-cleaning session. It was a sad day when history and cobwebby romance were smothered by Jeyes fluid and Dettol.

The newspaper archives were on the far shelf in thick leather binders, one for each year, neatly labelled and stacked in date order, all the way back to 1908, when the paper had started. It did not look as if the police had disturbed them. But if newspaper accounts alone were what they wanted, they could use the newspaper office's microfiche.

The boxes were all labelled as well, mostly with the year their contents related to, or with a general heading, such as 'School Registers' or 'Town Hall Re-modelling' or the recent twinning of Upper Bramley with some unpronounceable Polish town. It was a bit of a miscellany, and it looked as if the police had searched some of these boxes, although they had been quite tidy about it. The only box they had left out of place was the one labelled 'Cadence Manor'. A note was taped to it saying, 'Contents checked by DS Barlow, nothing taken away,' and the date was scribbled at the bottom.

Clem thought it would not hurt just to peep inside the box. It was so packed with photographs and newspaper cuttings the cardboard was starting to split, which was a pretty good excuse to check it. He lifted out a bundle of photographs, wondering if he would suddenly come across the face of the man they had sent to his death that day. It was fifty years ago but Clem thought he would recognize him. There had been an odd, deformed look to his features.

But the photographs here were mostly stilted family groups, and the only person he vaguely recognized was old Lady Cadence, Serena, who had died when Clem was a child. He studied the photos of her: she had been quite nice-looking, although a bit severe. He remembered going to her memorial service at St Michael's.

There were a few letters tucked into large manila envelopes alongside the photos. Clem opened these because you never knew what might be grist to the writer's mill. There was a batch of general reports about Cadence Manor from someone who had lived there and seemed to think it necessary to make some kind of regular accounting. Across the corner of one of these was an impatient scrawl that read, 'Do wish C would stop this irritating habit of thinking he must account to me for every last farthing!'

It was interesting to speculate who 'C' could have been, but it was not what Clem was looking for. He opened a few more envelopes, most of which contained household accounts, and finally, finding nothing pertinent, switched off the light and went back upstairs. He might go through the Cadence Manor material properly sometime, but not now because tonight was earmarked for his recipe rehearsal. People thought he fussed and finnicked about his menus, but Clem did not mind that because the proof of the pudding would be in the eating, or, in this case, not so much the pudding as the Breton fish dish, which was a kind of bouillabaisse. Clem was going to serve it on the gold-edged plates that had belonged to his great-grandmother, and accompany it with what the recipe book called 'a medley of spring vegetables'. He'd provide crusty bread to mop up the sauce, as the French did.

He called in at the supermarket, filling his wire basket with the ingredients he needed, exchanging a few words with the check-out girls. They were always interested in his little evenings.

'My word, Mr Poulter,' they said tonight, 'that's an unusual lot of things you've got. One of your dinner parties, is it?'

Clem, pleased to think they had noticed, told them all about the new recipe he was trying. It made for a pleasant little exchange and the supermarket was not very busy at this hour, although two shoppers in the queue behind him tapped the counter and said very loudly that some people wanted to get home, *if* he didn't mind.

In the end, he did not reach his house until almost seven o'clock. He distributed his shopping in the fridge and larder, and made a cup of tea, which he drank while listening to the evening news on the kitchen radio. After this he assembled his ingredients for his fish dish, using scaled-down portions. It would take an hour to simmer, then he would eat it himself, making notes about seasoning and thickness of the sauce. It would make his meal very late and he was already quite hungry, but it could not be helped.

He bustled happily round the kitchen, chopping parsley and tarragon, pleased he had remembered the bay leaves. You could hardly ever buy fresh bay leaves but there was a house on the way back from the library that had a very lush garden; the owners were, in fact, cronies of Ella's, all of them belonging to one of those arcane gardening societies. In their garden was a bay tree, which very obligingly grew at the edge, near the footpath. More than once, on his way home, Clem had discreetly reached over the hedge to pluck two or three of the leaves from the flourishing bay tree. He always made sure no one was watching, of course; it would never do for anyone to see nice Mr Poulter from the library pilfering something, even if it was only a couple of bay leaves.

❧ ❧ ❧

Amy left to go to the Red Lion shortly after seven, calling cheerfully that she would phone if there was a problem about getting home, and no she would not walk along the streets by herself late at night, Jan would probably drive her home anyway, and would Gran for goodness' sake, please stop *fussing*.

Derek left soon afterwards, phoning somebody he referred to as Pish-Tush to say he would pick him up as arranged. He told Ella he would not be very late getting home, and went off singing about being a wand'ring minstrel he, a thing of shreds and patches. Ella would be glad when this stupid *Mikado* was over and done with.

She gave them both a quarter of an hour, then put on her coat and went out.

CHAPTER TWENTY-TWO

CLEM STIRRED EVERYTHING into his dish, squeezed in a few more drops of lemon juice, tasted it, and nodded approvingly. The dish could now safely be left to simmer for forty-five minutes. It tasted very good and the lemon juice would give it that extra zing.

It was nearly eight o'clock by this time and he was ravenous, but he was not going to spoil his first taste of the fish by scoffing bread and cheese. He would wash up the utensils he had used, which would pass some of the waiting time.

He remembered Amy had returned that unusual recording that morning, and that he had then booked it out to himself, thinking he might play it as background to his little party. *The Deserted Village*, it was called, and Amy had said it was really creepy the way it made you think about Priors Bramley and see it as it must have been all those years ago. Dr Malik had put her on to it, she said.

It would look well if Clem could talk about the music at the party. Jan Malik had not, at first, seemed inclined to accept the invitation; he had started to frame a sentence about being busy, but Clem very artfully mentioned that Amy would be there. Malik had paused, then said, 'I suppose it wouldn't hurt to allow myself a night off,' and Clem had thought, aha! Remembering this, he fetched his current journal from his bedroom and, seated at the kitchen table, made a neat little entry. 'Dear Diary, yesterday noticed definite *frisson* between our visiting Oxford don and a certain young lady who helps out in the library...May well try to promote good relations and more *closeness* between them—if only to annoy E.H.'

He added a couple of brief paragraphs describing how he had gone down to the library's cellars and found the old photographs and papers. You had to get all these things down before you forgot them.

It was by now a quarter past eight and Clem was so hungry he was starting to feel slightly sick. He would have a glass of wine and listen to the CD. He put it on the stereo, propping open the sitting-room door so he could hear it while he got on with his cooking. He was enjoying the opening sequences—all rustic gambolling and May Day frolics but with the hint of something nasty lurking in the wings—when the doorbell rang. This was unexpected and vaguely annoying, but when Clem tiptoed into the hall to peer through the side window it was even more unexpected and annoying to see Ella outside. He hesitated, wondering if he could keep quiet until she went away, then realized she would have seen the light on and might even have heard his music. He would have to ask her in. But first he darted back to the kitchen and closed the journal, pushing it behind the plate rack, then scurried back to open the door.

It was probably a bit mischievous to take her into the kitchen, but Clem wanted to keep an eye on his casserole. Most people liked kitchens—they said it was friendly to sit at somebody's kitchen table or perch on a breakfast bar and talk while cooking was going on—but Ella always let it be known she thought it very common to sit in a kitchen. But since she had called on Clem out of the blue, tonight she would have to put up with it.

Clem indicated the cooker with its bubbling dish. 'My recipe rehearsal.'

'I'm not interrupting, am I?' She looked towards the sitting room where the CD was still playing and the composer had just started to infuse his Merrie England imagery with subtle menace. Clem switched the stereo off, and came back to explain that the fish was not quite ready but he would be eating it for his evening meal in about half an hour. In the meantime, would Ella like a drink? A glass of wine? He had opened a bottle for himself and one glass would not hurt if she was driving. Or she could have sherry, if she preferred, said Clem. He believed he had some Harveys Bristol Cream somewhere.

Ella had driven here, but did not think one small drink would matter. 'I'd like sherry, if it's no trouble.'

'None in the world,' said Clem, trying to quell the thought that, given two options, Ella would always choose the slightly more troublesome one. But he went into the dining room to find the bottle and hunted out a couple of glasses from the chiffonier. Serve Ella Haywood sherry in cheap glasses and you got the entire saga of how she had bought a complete set of Waterford Crystal for her and Derek's wedding anniversary.

'I hope you're coming on Friday evening,' he said, returning to the kitchen.

'Yes,' said Ella. 'We find we can both make it.'

'Good. And my recipe is working out a treat. I dare say you can smell it, well, you can't avoid it, can you? That's the trouble with fish.' He poured sherry for himself as well. On an empty stomach and mixed with the glass of wine he'd had earlier it made him feel vaguely light-headed.

'Actually,' said Ella, 'I came round to see if you were serious about telling the police what happened that day in Priors Bramley.'

'Yes, I was. I honestly think,' said Clem, 'that we've got to do it.' He felt very noble saying this and also it would make a good entry in his journal. 'Today I made a decision to perform an honourable and selfless act,' he would write.

'Yes,' said Ella slowly. 'Yes, I do see that it had better be done.'

'We wouldn't go in unprepared. We'd work out what to say beforehand; stress that we were very young and frightened that morning—that the man threatened us.'

'He did threaten us, didn't he?'

'God, yes.' Clem shuddered and swigged down more of the sherry.

'I suppose,' said Ella, 'it ought to be all three of us telling the story.'

'You mean Veronica, too?' Clem had not thought about this. 'Would she agree?'

'I think I could talk her into it,' said Ella. 'You'd better leave her to me, though. I've got to phone her this evening, as a matter of fact, so I'll ask.'

Clem was very happy to leave Veronica to Ella on this occasion. Veronica, once she got going on the phone, was apt to talk for anything up to an hour, and although Clem enjoyed a gossipy conversation as much as anyone, tonight he wanted to concentrate on his menu.

After Ella had gone, he returned to stirring his fish. He added salt, spooned out a bay leaf that had floated to the surface, and thought how unlike Ella it was to turn up unannounced. It was even more unlike her to change her mind. People were odd; you thought you knew them and then they did something that surprised you.

He had expected a real tussle over telling the police what had happened, but Ella had capitulated without any fuss. Or had she? The more Clem thought about it, the more he remembered all the times he had discovered that Ella had her own agenda, even over the smallest things. He would not put it past her to have some plan to turn this situation to her own advantage, although he could not think how. Still, he was not going to be fooled by Ella

Haywood's little plottings, not he! He smiled to himself. Over the years Ella often thought she had fooled him, but she never had.

❀ ❀ ❀

Ella had often fooled Clem Poulter over the years, and she knew she had done so tonight. She smiled to herself as she drove home.

She had gone to his house prepared to give him a second chance, but as soon as she went into his kitchen, she had known that the time for second chances was past. He was playing that music, the music Ella had heard so many years ago in the over-scented room of Cadence Manor with Serena Cadence, dead-eyed and terrible, seated bolt upright in her chair. And he was doing so deliberately and maliciously. When Ella rang the doorbell she had seen him peep through the hall window, then dart back into the house before letting her in. He had seen who was on his doorstep and seized the chance to administer one of his vindictive little jabs, switching on the stereo so the music would greet her when she walked in. In some way he knew what the music meant to her. Ella could not think how, but clearly she had been right to suspect him of giving Amy the CD. It was sad because it meant the plan Ella had worked out—the plan she had hoped would not be needed—was now imperative.

It was a quarter to nine when she reached her own house. As she got out of the car she waved a friendly greeting to some neighbours across the street, out walking their dog. If asked, they would be able to confirm the time she had arrived home.

She went into the house, satisfied that the plan was already under way. She dialled Veronica's number. It was slightly irritating of Veronica to take so long about answering, and even more irritating that the silly creature was breathless and giggly when she did answer.

'I spent the evening with my new friend,' she began coyly. 'And he's only just left, actually, so when the phone rang I was—'

'I won't keep you a minute,' said Ella, quickly. 'But I've just got back from Clem's house, and he's in one of his flaps about the pudding for Friday evening.'

'Pudding?' Veronica sounded bewildered. Ella supposed if she had been cavorting around the bedroom with her current man it would be difficult for her to switch her mind onto puddings.

She said, 'Clem wanted my advice about what to serve. We've been looking through his cookbooks, but we haven't found anything. Then I remembered that lovely meringue dish you did once and I told Clem I'd get the recipe from you. He thought it would be just the thing.'

'Meringue,' said Veronica blankly. Then, 'Oh, *meringue*. Yes, he can have the recipe with pleasure. Will tomorrow do? I can drop it into the library. Because at the moment the bedroom's like a battlefield and—'

'Tomorrow will be plenty of time,' said Ella. 'I've got to go out to his house first thing because I promised to lend him my crystal dessert set—the one—'

'—that Derek bought when you were in Portugal,' said Veronica. 'I know. Can you call for the recipe on your way to his house?'

This was exactly what Ella wanted. She said, 'Is nine o'clock too early?' and braced herself for another of Veronica's suggestive remarks, but Veronica said, in a perfectly ordinary voice, that nine o'clock would be quite all right.

Ella replaced the phone and sat very still, reviewing all the details of the plan. It had been right not to hide the fact that she had called at Clem's house tonight. She might easily have been seen by one of his neighbours—she had been seen by a couple of her own. And Clem might even have made a phone call to someone—anyone—after Ella left, although that was not very likely. He was a bit of a Scrooge at times, old Clem; he made as many phone calls as he could from the library rather than his own phone.

And there were the sherry glasses. Clem might not have washed them up; he might just have put them in the sink for later. Ella's fingerprints would certainly be on them, along with DNA from her lipstick. But she thought her story about a recipe was completely credible and she would have Veronica's backup over that.

The only person who could contradict the story was Clem himself, of course. But by about half-past nine tonight Clem would not be able to contradict any story at all.

❁ ❁ ❁

It was nine o'clock when Clem finally ladled out the fish in its rich sauce. It looked very good indeed, the consistency just right, the smell appetizing. Another of his triumphs. He sighed happily, fished out the other two bay leaves, dropped them into the bin, then buttered a wedge of crusty bread. He set the plate on the kitchen table; he would eat here, and this time he would listen properly to *The Deserted Village*.

The first mouthful of the fish was excellent, creamy and sharp, and the cadences of the music rose and fell as he ate. It was evocative music. The village and *its* people were pretty much doomed, that was the burden of the song. As he listened, he could almost imagine himself back on that long-ago morning when they had walked through the deserted village street, hearing the church clock chime, listening for the plane bringing the Geranos. It was odd how it had become known that Geranos was harmful; Clem had never actually heard of anyone being damaged by it. Still, governments and councils had been cagey in those days, and they had been able to be cagey. Not like now, when so much information had to be available to everybody.

He forked up a second mouthful of the fish. On further tasting it was actually a bit salty. Or was it? Clem's recent head cold had blunted his sense of smell and also his sense of taste. He frowned, trying to decide. It *was* salty. In fact it tasted almost bitter. Had he put in too much seasoning after all? Clem got up to pour a glass of the chilled wine from the fridge and sipped it, hoping to sharpen his palate. No, it made no difference. He would be very annoyed if, after all his care, his beautiful dish had not worked and something else had to be quickly fudged up for Friday. He carried on eating, trying to think what he could cook in its place. He could not serve this to his guests, that was for sure. The bitterness was becoming more strongly pronounced, in fact it was almost acrid. His whole mouth was starting to feel hot and his throat was prickling.

He got up to get a glass of water and the entire room tilted and spun all around him. Clem gasped, and clung to the edge of the sink. Something was wrong with the food—something was very wrong indeed. Sickness welled up and he retched violently, leaning over the sink, spluttering and shuddering helplessly. Dreadful. He managed to run the tap to wash the disgusting mess away and felt slightly better. A bad bit of fish, most likely. In that case, it was just as well he had been sick and got rid of it. In a minute he would tip the whole panful of food down the outside drain and flush it away with disinfectant and bleach. He would most likely throw the casserole dish away as well. He never wanted to eat fish again in his life.

He tottered back to the kitchen table but a dreadful cramplike pain twisted his stomach before he got there.

He doubled over, sweat pouring from him, and as he did so he felt the inside of his throat tightening and swelling. Dear God, this was more than a bit of food poisoning— he was really ill. He would have to get to the phone to summon help—a doctor—ambulance...

He was sick again, shamefully and messily, the wetness spattering all over the floor. Clem shuddered, but the pain tore through his guts again and he was beyond caring about the mess. If he could just get to the phone—

But he could no longer stand up and the phone on its cradle by the hall door seemed a thousand miles away. He felt dreadfully dizzy, but he managed to crawl a couple of feet towards the phone. Almost there, almost...

The pain slammed into him again and he curled over it, clutching his stomach and moaning. His throat and mouth seemed to fill up with thick suffocating flannel and he clawed at the air, gasping. The kitchen shivered and blurred, and there was a dull roaring in his ears. As he fell to the floor, the music wound its way to its eerie conclusion and faded into silence. But Clem could no longer hear it.

❉ ❉ ❉

Ella was friendly and ordinary when Derek came home, with Amy shortly after him. She listened to all they had to say and, when asked about her own evening, said she had gone round to Clem Poulter's house. He had wanted her help with a recipe, would you credit it? All that boasting he did about planning his menus and here he was, two days before a dinner party, rushing round like a demented hen to find a pudding.

'Make him one of your apple pies, why don't you?' said Derek, who had switched on the television news and was only half listening to what Ella was saying. Ella did not bother to say apple pie was hardly the kind of thing Clem would want to serve. She did not, of course, say that there would not be any party anyway. She merely said she had promised to collect a recipe from Veronica and take it round in the morning.

'I'll do that if you like,' said Amy, who was curled up on the hearthrug, drinking a mug of the tea Ella had made for them all. 'Then I can take it into the library when I go in after lunch and save you the bother, Gran.'

Ella had a sensation like skidding uncontrollably over a patch of ice in a car. They said there was always one small item you overlooked. Was this it? Then she heard her voice saying, 'I think he wants the recipe first thing, Amy. He's going to collect the ingredients on his way in to the library. And I said I'd lend him my crystal dessert set as well, so I'll need to pack that up and drive round with it.'

'Oh, OK.'

The moment passed and Ella felt safe again. Derek had started his usual running commentary about the news: the state of the country and what the government ought to be doing, and he and Amy entered into a lively argument about some policy the Home Secretary had just announced.

Ella relaxed, but she was shaken. It just went to show you could not plan for absolutely everything. To reassure herself, she went back over what she had done that day. It had been so easy to pluck several leaves from her own garden that afternoon—not bay, which gave such a good flavour to cooking and which Clem swore by, but leaves from another bush entirely…

When they bought this house Ella had been very taken with the fact that it had a conservatory. Very nice, she had said. They would spruce it up and make it into an orangery with rare Mediterranean plants. Derek had said however much sprucing up you did and whatever names you gave them, conservatories were apt to become dusty and filled with dead flies, never mind being drearily unused during winter. But Ella had had it freshly painted and added ruched blinds and cane furniture ordered by catalogue from Heal's. She tried her hand at growing a few of the rarer, more tropical plants in there, and one of her real successes was an oleander bush. Several members of the Exotic Plants Society had admired the oleander very much; one of the ladies actually had the very same variety of oleander in her garden, she said—Petite Red, a dwarf variety. It was nowhere near as luxuriant as Ella's, however, although having this greenhouse—beg pardon, orangery— probably made it easier. Hers had to be taken into the house in a big pot during the winter, which was a bit of a nuisance, particularly when you had to be so careful with oleanders. They were regarded as one of the most poisonous plants in the world. Ella did know that, did she?

Ella had not known it, but she was not going to admit it to the Exotic Plants crowd.

Earlier, casting around for a means to deal with Clem, her eye had fallen on the bright splash of colour in the orangery. Oleander, one of the most poisonous plants in the world...A tiny pulse of excitement began to beat. In a cluttered kitchen, with a complicated recipe to follow, the oleander leaves might just about pass for bay. As Ella considered this, another fragment of memory swam into her mind, something the Exotic Plants woman had also said about her garden.

'We inherited a lovely bay tree from the previous owners of our house,' she had said, 'but I do wish it wasn't so near the road. D'you know, people actually reach over the hedge to steal the leaves? Can you believe that? In fact, the other week you wouldn't believe who I saw taking some—No, I mustn't say.'

She broke off hopefully, and at least half the assembled company urged her please to say, just in confidence, just among friends.

'Mr Poulter from the library,' said the woman. 'He looked round to make sure no one was watching, then he leaned over the hedge and broke off a handful of bay leaves.'

Remembering that conversation, Ella thought it just went to show that you never knew what seemingly innocent part of your own life might one day come in useful.

Even so, before putting her plan into action she made very sure of the facts, looking up oleander in Derek's *Encyclopaedia Britannica*.

Its full name was *Nerium oleander*. It was a Moroccan and Mediterranean plant, described as an evergreen shrub in the dogbane family, *Apocynaceae*. Ella already knew this because she had looked it up in preparation for the Exotic Plants afternoon. What she had not known was the strength of what the encyclopaedia called its toxicity. There was a list of the substances oleander plants contained. Ella did not recognize any of them and she could certainly not have pronounced them, but the burden of the song was that if you ate enough you would almost certainly die, and very quickly too. Ella read it all carefully, paying particular attention to the quantities believed to be fatal. As well as the leaves, the bark, it seemed, contained a substance called rosagenin, which was apparently known for its strychnine-like effects.

Before going to Clem's house, she went into the orangery and, wearing her kitchen gloves, plucked a number of the leaves. Then, with extreme care, she scraped off some of the bark, and sealed everything in a small freezer bag, which she tucked in her handbag. It should be easy enough to stir the contents into Clem's casserole. He had made enough fuss about telling everyone how he was cooking it this evening, and Ella thought she would be able to make some excuse to go into the kitchen or to find a reason to get him out of the room.

In the end, it was easy. He offered her a glass of sherry and went bumbling out of the kitchen to find the bottle and the glasses. While he was gone Ella tipped all the leaves into the casserole, along with the bark scrapings taken from the stems. There was even time to stir it all round before Clem came back with the sherry.

❀ ❀ ❀

Lying in bed that night, Ella found it difficult to sleep. She was not specially troubled by what she had done because Clem, stupid poultering old hen, had signed his own death warrant.

What was bothering her was the unpleasant task that now lay ahead, because she would have to drive out to his house, conspicuously bearing Veronica's recipe and the dessert dishes, and discover his body. And then find those stupid diaries and get rid of them before anyone saw them.

Would it actually be a body she found, though? Supposing he had recovered? Supposing he had managed to summon a doctor or an ambulance?

She finally managed to get to sleep, but her dreams were troubled and the eerie music of *The Deserted Village* ran in and out of her consciousness like quicksilver.

CHAPTER TWENTY-THREE

NEXT MORNING, DEREK left for the office at half-past eight, as usual. In his own words, he liked to be at his desk on the tick of nine. You had to set an example in these things.

Amy was in the bathroom when Derek left, washing her hair. To Ella's mind Amy washed her hair far too often. Her mother, said Ella, would have considered Amy was washing all the nature out of it.

Amy said, 'Yes, but this morning my hair smells a bit of the Red Lion's seafood platter,' and Ella found she had to grip the banister because her heart had done its breathless little skip. It was going to be a nuisance if this business with Clem resulted in her heart performing gymnastics every time anyone mentioned eating fish.

She left Amy to her shampooing, saying she would nip round to Veronica's house for the promised recipe, then go on to Clem's.

'It sounded good, that pudding of Veronica's,' said Amy, coming downstairs with her hair wrapped in a towel. 'Have I got to dress up for this bash at Clem's?'

'No, but I hope you won't turn up in jeans,' said Ella, wrapping up the dishes she was supposed to be lending Clem. It was a nuisance to have to do this, but it was important to act innocently.

Veronica had the meringue recipe ready. She was a bit puffy-eyed this morning, but she invited Ella in, saying there was surely time for a cup of coffee.

'Actually, there isn't,' said Ella. 'Can we make it another day? I promised to get this stuff round to Clem before he leaves for the library.'

Driving away, the recipe in her bag, Ella was increasingly nervous about what was ahead, but it had to be faced. She parked outside Clem's house, and saw with mingled relief and apprehension that the curtains were all closed exactly as they had been last night, and that a pint of milk stood on the front doorstep.

Again, it was important to behave naturally, so Ella rang the doorbell and then, when there was no response, plied the knocker. She stepped back, looked up at the curtained windows, then consulted her watch, frowning slightly. Anyone watching would think she was calling on Clem by arrangement and was annoyed to find him either not at home or still in bed.

Ella tried the doorbell again, then walked around the side of the house, trying to quell the nervous clenching of her stomach muscles. This was going to be the tricky bit, the *unpleasant* bit. She pushed open the wrought-iron gate, which Clem's fancy had led him to paint a virulent pink. Here was the back of the house, with its little terrace and the pink chairs that matched the gate. There was the big patio window that opened off the dining room. Ella looked through the window, shading her eyes against the sky's reflection in the glass.

Nothing seemed to be out of place in the dining room. That left the kitchen window to be looked through, and the kitchen, it had to be said, was the likeliest place for Clem to be. Ella stepped back and looked up at the bedroom windows, and again she looked at her watch in case anyone was in sight. Then, taking a deep breath, she stepped up to the small kitchen window with its looped

and swagged blind and the row of African violets in pots
on the sill.

For a moment she thought there was nothing to
see, and the possibility that Clem had got himself to
bed last night and died or was lying helplessly ill in his
bedroom rose up. He might not even have eaten the food
at all, although Ella did not think that was very likely. She
leaned closer to the window, trying to see the entire room.
Oh God, he was there all right. He was lying on the
floor by the kitchen table, and there were all kinds of
mess round him: crockery that had crashed to the floor,
the results of sickness...Ella found herself gripping the
window ledge. Stupid, she said. You know what you've got
to do. Everything's worked out.

She went quickly to the patio window and, taking
off one of her shoes, smashed it as hard as she could
against the glass, as close to the latch as possible. The
tough double-glazed glass splintered, and several splinters showered out and stuck in the leather driving gloves
Ella had been careful to wear. She brushed them off and
dealt a second blow, then a third. At the third blow, a
large section of the glass fell inwards, smashing onto the
floor, and she was able to knock out several more and step
through.

She walked warily across the dining room and
opened the door into the kitchen. The first thing to strike
her was the stench. Dreadful. She snatched a tissue from
her pocket and clapped it over her mouth, and, trying to
remain calm, leaned over to feel for a pulse in Clem's wrist.
There was a bad moment when she thought something
fluttered under his skin, then she realized it was her own
pulse, skittering like a trapped bird. He was lying half on
his front, hunched over. Should she move him to check for
a heartbeat? But his skin was cold and flaccid, and when
Ella lifted his wrist there was a board-like stiffness to his
arm. Rigor mortis? She was annoyed to realize she had

not thought of that, and it was not the kind of thing one knew about instinctively. But she had the impression that it generally set in six or eight hours after death. She had left Clem shortly after half-past eight. If he had eaten the poisoned food soon after she left, he had presumably died around nine or a bit after. That seemed to fit.

Ella straightened up, and looked round the kitchen. In a minute she would phone for an ambulance but first she must find the diaries, Clem's stupid self-indulgent journals with God knew what damning content. She was still not entirely sure if they existed, but she went systematically through the house, opening cupboards and wardrobes, peering under the beds. She was starting to panic. Supposing after all he had put them on a computer? But when she went into the little boxroom, there they were, potential dynamite, neatly stacked inside a small cupboard. Ella's first reaction was relief and then shock that there were so many. Had he written one a year, for pity's sake?

No, there looked to be about twenty or twenty-five of them—one book would cover roughly two years.

They were not diaries in the strict sense, but leatherbound notebooks. Ella took several out at random and sat on the edge of a chair, looking at them. Morning sunshine streamed into the bedroom and dust motes danced in the light. There were faint sounds from the street—the slam of a car door, somebody calling out a greeting, the bark of a dog in a neighbouring garden.

Ella only half heard these noises, because her whole attention was on the notebooks. 'My Jottings' Clem had called them. Sometimes, if he had had a drink, he would call them 'chronicles'. Whatever they were called, Ella supposed you might, if you were of a romantic disposition, consider that fragments of the past were captured inside these books, although having murdered the author twelve hours earlier, romantic was the last thing she was feeling.

She opened the topmost book and saw at once that Clem had not made an entry every day; he had simply written accounts of events that seemed to him interesting, a couple of pages here, an odd sentence there, all with a date heading at the top. Sometimes he had not written anything for several weeks. Ella turned the pages, realizing that even though she would be able to find Clem's original account of the man's death at Cadence Manor, removing that one book would not be enough, because it looked as if Clem had sprinkled references to it through the whole of his journals.

Even on his fiftieth birthday he had harked back to it. 'A landmark birthday this one,' he had written.

A time for retrospection, for taking stock. Writing this, I look back over the things I've done and wonder if decisions were made rightly and if actions taken were correct. That last day when we were all in Priors Bramley, for instance… Could we have acted differently when that man chased us…? And how much were we to blame for his death? That's an uncomfortable thought, but it's one that sticks in my mind. The past is always distorted when one views it from the present—and memory spins its own illusions— but as I grow older I find myself wondering if we fought that man too hard—if one of us gave him one push too many…

One of us gave him one push too many…

I've even wondered at times if his purpose was not as sinister as we believed. What if he was simply some poor soul whose wits were not entirely sound—some remnant of the Cadence family, even—trying to be clumsily friendly, maybe trying to tell us to get out before the Geranos bomb was dropped?

Ella closed the book with a snap. Clem's notes were absolute rubbish; that man had been evil and malevolent, and even though Clem could not have known that, Ella had certainly known it. She had no qualms at all about having killed him.

She had no qualms about having killed Clem, either, particularly now she had read this. And she was deeply relieved she had found these notebooks because if Clem had been able to hand them to the police, the truth of that day would certainly have come out. There would have been probings into the past—into Ella's childhood. The never-forgotten image of Serena Cadence, dead and terrible in the dim over-sweet room, rose up. It should have faded with the years, that ghost, but it never had.

All these notebooks would have to be destroyed. Ella had been prepared for this and had brought two folded-up plastic carriers in her handbag. The diaries would make a fairly bulky package, but anyone seeing the bags would assume, if they thought about it at all, that it was shopping.

The first diary had been written shortly before Clem's ninth birthday, and had ended when he was eleven. Ella thought Clem had probably got bored with it at times, only returning to it when something of real interest had happened. There was an account of the school play—that had been the year that Veronica played the princess and Ella got to know Derek. She frowned, closed the book, and began to put the whole lot into the carrier, checking the dates as she did so to make sure they were complete.

But they were not. The diaries ended with an entry dated last year and the book was written to the last page. So unless Clem had suddenly stopped writing, which seemed unlikely, there must be another one somewhere. He would surely have described recent events: the opening up of the village and the finding of the bodies. Ella frowned and rechecked, but there was definitely not a current one. The possibility that it might be in his desk at the library or that he had, after all, begun using a computer occurred to her. She would search again, but first, she moved a pile of magazines onto the empty shelf of the cupboard so it would not look as if anything had been removed.

She checked the bedrooms again, even looking under Clem's pillow this time, but found nothing. By now she should be phoning the paramedics. If anyone had seen her break in they might later remember there had been quite a long delay before the ambulance arrived. She scoured the dining room and then the sitting room, again opening cupboards and cabinets. Nothing. Finally, she stood in the hall, unwilling to re-enter the kitchen. Don't be squeamish, said her mind sharply. You know you've got to go in. Do it. Don't think about what's lying there on the floor. Don't even look at it.

Pressing the tissue to her mouth again, she opened the door and went in. Terror engulfed her at once. He had moved—Clem had moved. Oh God, thought Ella, staring at the twisted figure, oh God, he's still alive and he knows I'm here and he's trying to crawl towards me for help. And then she saw that of course he had not moved. It was just that the clouds had cleared and a spear of sunlight had fallen across the kitchen, giving an eerie semblance of movement to the prone figure.

She opened cupboards and drawers. Nothing. She dare not waste any more time; she would have to make that phone call to the ambulance. And then she saw it— the missing journal, thrust behind a plate rack, clearly done hastily because several corners of the pages were slightly creased. Ella seized it thankfully, and glanced inside. Yes, it was the current one. The final entry read, 'Dear Diary, yesterday noticed definite *frisson* between our visiting Oxford don and a certain young lady who helps out in the library...May well try to promote good relations and more *closeness* between them—if only to annoy E.H.'

Fury rose up in Ella. You thought someone was your friend—you trusted him—and all the time he had been sniggering and plotting behind your back. She thrust the journal into the bag with the others, then headed for the phone in the hall.

'Emergency, which service, please?'

Ella had thought this out, just as she had thought out the other parts of her plan. No longer troubling to quench panic, she asked for an ambulance. 'Quickly.'

When the ambulance service, calm and efficient, came on, she said in a breathless voice, 'I'm at a friend's house. Mr Clement Poulter. I've had to break in. He was lying on the floor and I thought—oh God, I thought he had just fainted, but now I think he might be dead—anyway, deeply unconscious. So please can you come...'

'That's all right, madam,' said the voice. 'Can you give me the address?' A pause while a note was made. 'We'll be with you in about eight minutes. Can I just get your name and address in the meantime? And can you give me any more details about Mr Poulter's condition?'

Ella knew they generally kept you talking while the paramedics were on their way. It was something to do with maintaining calm or making sure you were not a hoaxer. Or, if you were the sufferer, making sure you stayed conscious, of course. Whatever it was, it meant she could sit down on the little hall chair, and establish some of the details of her plan.

'I'd arranged to call,' she said. 'Some dishes I was lending Clem—Mr Poulter. Only he didn't answer the door and the milk was still on the step and the curtains drawn...So I went round the back and I saw him through the kitchen window, lying on the floor.'

'You did the right thing phoning at once,' said the voice, and Ella thought, oh, if only you knew!

She said, 'I just thought he'd fallen over—broken an ankle or something. I smashed the window to get to him.'

'Very resourceful.' The voice was warm and approving.

Ella remembered that these calls were usually automatically recorded.

She gave a half-sob and said, 'But I saw almost at once that he was—um, well, if he isn't dead he's deeply—*deeply*—unconscious. I said that, didn't I? And he's been dreadfully sick and—and so on.'

'Our people are used to all that kind of thing,' said the voice.

'You're very kind,' said Ella, meaning it. 'And, oh, wait, I can hear the ambulance now. Do I ring off?'

'Just let them in and then come back to me when they're in the house.'

As Ella unlocked the front door, admitting a burly gentleman and a youngish woman, she thought that you heard all kinds of horror stories about the NHS and the emergency services, but they certainly seemed to be corning up to scratch for Clem. Fortunately, however, it would be much too late for them to save his life.

❀ ❀ ❀

Amy was horrified when Gran returned home white-faced and tearful, with a dreadful story of how she had found Clem Poulter dead on the floor of his own kitchen. Amy was not entirely unfamiliar with people zonking out on the floor and paramedics having to be called, but in her world the cause was usually drink or drugs. It was impossible to associate Clem Poulter with either of these things, however.

'You broke into his house?' she said, rushing to make Gran a cup of tea. 'You actually smashed a window and climbed in? Gran, you're amazing.'

'I did it without thinking,' Gran said. 'Oh, that's a nice cup of tea, Amy. I think I'll take a couple of paracetamol as well.' She drank the tea gratefully. 'I could see him quite clearly through the patio windows,' she said. 'He was lying on the floor in a dreadful huddle. I suppose I could have phoned the police right away—in fact that's probably what I should have done—but all I could think of was getting to him at once.'

'I think it was brilliant of you,' said Amy warmly.

'Well, I've known him so long, oh dear, since we were children. I'll have to phone Veronica, and somebody will have to let the people at the library know...I think I'll just give your grandfather a ring first. He'll know what's best.'

'I could tell them at the library,' said Amy. 'The girls there would know who to contact.'

'No, I'd better do it,' said Gran. 'It's my responsibility, Amy. He was one of my oldest friends. He'd want me to do everything I could for him.'

❀ ❀ ❀

Everyone in Bramley was deeply saddened at the death of nice Mr Poulter from the library. Shocking, they said. Some kind of food poisoning, seemingly. It just went to show you could not be too careful with shellfish. The Red Lion removed its seafood platter from the bar menu at once, and chalked spaghetti bolognaise on the board instead, which, as the harassed manager said, could surely offend no one—well, apart from people who knew how it should be spelled, so would somebody please find a dictionary and rewrite it *correctly*.

But when the results of the autopsy were made known, it appeared that nice Mr Poulter had not died from food poisoning at all, but from a different kind of poisoning altogether. The leaves of *Nerium oleander*, the Mediterranean plant from the dogbane family, *Apocynaceae*. The inquest followed three days later, at which it was concluded that Mr Poulter, eagerly trying out a new recipe for a dinner party, had mistaken the very harmful toxic oleander leaves for the entirely harmless and flavoursome bay leaves.

Ella, wearing a grey outfit (black, she felt, would have been overdoing it), gave subdued evidence of having called at Clem Poulter's house early in the evening to discuss recipes, and of arranging to return early the following morning with a recipe and some dessert dishes. Mr Poulter had been cooking the meal then, she said, and had told her he would be eating some for his supper that night. She had not particularly looked at the dish, but she had thought it smelled very tasty and she had...she paused to stifle a sob...she had thought how much they would enjoy eating it at the little party. She would like to add her appreciation of the paramedics who had come out very promptly and been very kind.

'Thank you very much,' said the coroner approvingly.

A member of the local Exotic Plants Society testified to having seen Mr Poulter plucking bay leaves from the tree in her garden on several occasions. Pressed for more detail, she said, with reluctance, that it was without her permission, although she would certainly have given it if asked, and she had never bothered to confront him with it. A few bay leaves were neither here nor there. Well, yes, she said, with even more reluctance, she did have an oleander bush growing near the bay.

'Could Mr Poulter have mistaken one for the other?' asked the coroner.

'Not if he was paying attention,' said the Exotic Plants woman. 'There's a definite difference.'

'But if he wasn't paying attention? If, for instance, he was taking the leaves furtively, trying not to be seen. Looking up and down the road.'

'I suppose it's possible.'

The coroner supposed so, as well. He drew a little thumbnail sketch for the Court of Clem Poulter standing outside the Exotic Plants house, sliding one hand over the hedge to what he thought was the bay tree, his eyes on the road in case anyone came along, not paying sufficient attention to the leaves he was actually taking. He then directed the jury to bring in a verdict of Death by Misadventure, and himself added a rider to the effect that it was very dangerous to steal plants and experiment with them for cooking purposes. The body, he said, could now be released for interment.

Ella had gone to sit in the town hall's little public gallery by that time—Veronica had saved her a seat. It was annoying to see that Veronica had had no qualms about wearing black, in fact add a lace veil and she would look like a Victorian widow, apart from the skirt, which was unsuitably short, and the heels, which were impractically high. Amy, surprisingly, had turned up in a black pinstripe trouser suit with a cream silk shirt. Ella had not even known Amy had brought such a garment with her, but she noticed how well the outfit suited her, even with her slightly outlandish looks, which were, of course, down to Amy's mother, the girl Andrew had married entirely against Ella's advice, and whom Ella had never much liked, although Derek always said she was lovely.

After the inquest Veronica wanted to go on to lunch. 'Amy too, of course,' she said. 'We'll have a bar meal at the Red Lion and a couple of drinks in Clem's memory, dear old Clem.'

Ella thought she had better agree. You never knew who might be watching and taking mental note. She noticed Dr Malik on the edge of the crowd; for a moment it seemed as if Amy was waiting for him to approach her but he merely gave her a half-smile, nodded a brief, polite acknowledgement to Veronica and to Ella herself, and walked away.

'I didn't know you knew Jan,' said Amy to Veronica.

'We're the merest acquaintances,' said Veronica.

Ella was glad she had agreed to Veronica's suggestion about lunch, because when they got to the Red Lion
several others seemed to have had the same idea and the
bar was full. Ella was greeted on all sides, with everyone
wanting to commiserate and ask how on earth she must
have felt, actually finding Clem's body, poor old Clem,
silly old bugger, wouldn't you know he'd end up doing
something like this? And how about a drink to speed him
on his way?

Accepting the drinks, Ella felt herself surrounded by
friends. It's all right, she thought. No one suspects. I've
buried the journals in the garden, right under the spot
where Derek always has a bonfire for garden rubbish.
She had done it the previous morning when Derek was
at the office and Amy at the library, digging quite deeply,
then shovelling earth over the notebooks. They would be
mouldering away already, and later in the week she could
prune the hedges and tell Derek they needed to have a
bonfire at the weekend to burn the cuttings. It was not
exactly the time to prune but that could not be helped.
And even if anyone had seen her actually burying the
incriminating diaries, they would have assumed she was
simply tidying up that patch of garden.

I've got away with it, thought Ella. I'm free.

CHAPTER TWENTY-FOUR

London, 1912

SERENA WAS STARTING to feel as if she would never be free again. She was certainly beginning to think she would never feel well again.

When Dr Martlet next called, she was fretful, complaining about the sores on her face and neck.

'It's very distressing. Surely there's something you can do? I've always looked after my complexion so carefully. As a girl they used to say my complexion was as good as Lillie Langtry's.'

'I remember how you looked as a girl,' he said softly.

'The porcelain look, it was called, and very fashionable. Not that one particularly wanted to be compared to the Langtry hussy, but still...' Serena frowned. 'Surely there's something you can do? It's only in the very early stages, isn't it? I know you couldn't help Julius, but he'd had it for years, only no one knew.'

'Lady Cadence—'

'I distinctly recall you saying if you had known, you could have helped him.'

'Helped, but not cured,' said Dr Martlet. 'There's no cure for syphilis.'

'Then am I to end like my husband?' She was aware that fear was making her voice hard and ugly.

'I shall do everything I can for you.'

'That,' said Serena, fighting back mounting dread, 'does not answer my question.'

'The disease waxes and wanes,' said Dr Martlet after a moment. 'You know that—I explained it. That's how Sir Julius was able to keep it from everyone. It can be quiescent for months, even years. I'm hopeful that will be the case for you.'

'So am I,' said Serena coldly.

'When it's at its height there are some remedies that can be tried,' he said, speaking rather reluctantly. 'And we can and will do so after the birth.'

The birth...The dark memory rushed back at Serena yet again. Julius's face, twisted into the mask of a frightening stranger, forcing into her...Then sobbing like a bewildered child ashamed of itself.

'I should prefer to try the remedies now,' she said in the same cool voice.

'It wouldn't be advisable to try any of the treatments at the moment,' said Martlet. 'And the sores will disappear after a time.'

'Only to return.'

'Not necessarily. The difficulty is that almost all of the remedies we could try might harm the child.'

Harm the child. The memory clawed at Serena again and this time a dreadful idea etched itself onto her mind like poison.

She said sharply, 'Dr Martlet, if you will not do what I'm asking, our association must end and I must find a physician prepared to help me.'

Martlet flinched as if he had been dealt a blow. With the air of a man yielding to intolerable pressure, he said, 'Very well.'

'You'll arrange treatment?'

'Yes. But there are only two possibilities. One is a fairly new drug they say is producing some good results with early syphilis. It's been developed by a German scientist: Dr Ehrlich. But it contains arsenic, which is poisonous in the wrong quantities.'

'When I was a girl people occasionally used weak solutions of arsenic to whiten their hands,' said Serena. 'So I have no especial fear of it. But I don't think my husband would want me to take a German drug. He doesn't trust the Kaiser, you know.' Despite the extraordinary and macabre circumstances, there were still rules in marriage, and one of them was obedience to a husband's wishes.

'I'm not altogether sure I trust the Kaiser either,' Martlet was saying. 'To my mind this obsession he has with the idea of German Imperialism clouds his judgement. All those speeches about what he calls a place in the sun for Germany. Still, that doesn't mean we should doubt Dr Ehrlich's work.'

'Oh, no,' said Serena politely. 'But I still don't care for the sound of it. Is there nothing else?'

'Well,' said Dr Martlet, with even more reluctance, 'there is something called the mercury cure.'

'Mercury doesn't sound particularly unpleasant. Isn't it sometimes called quicksilver?'

'Yes. I've never actually administered it—I've never even seen it administered—but I will be straight and tell you it's not pleasant. I think it's possible to give it by injection, but as far as I know most physicians make use of an infusion box. The box is about so big.' He described with his hands a squat structure, roughly oblong in shape, to Serena's eye like an oversized chair. 'The patient is enclosed inside it for a number of hours and a mercury solution is heated underneath. The mercury turns to vapour so that the fumes are absorbed into the skin and lungs. It's a little like the principle of inhaling friar's balsam from a boiling kettle for a bad chest.'

'I understand.' Serena did not think this sounded so terrible.

'Lady Cadence, this is a painful and exhausting treatment,' said Martlet very earnestly. 'And I really am concerned about the risk to the child.'

Risk to the child. There it was again, the trickle of acid into her mind, a little stronger this time, a little more insistent. Serena stared at Dr Martlet and thought: but what you don't know, you stupid man, is that I don't care about the child. And if this treatment dislodges it before it can even draw breath—

She snapped off this thought before it could develop, but the child had stirred uneasily and a dull pain rippled through Serena's stomach. She ignored it and said, 'Please tell me about this mercury treatment. Could it be administered here?'

'I should think so,' said Martlet. 'It would be a bit of an upheaval, but the equipment could be brought by carriage or carter. I'd have to call in a colleague to supervise everything—probably someone from Guy's. How would you feel about that?'

A strange doctor who would need her to undress, and who would see the ravages of the disease...Who might make one of those painful intrusive examinations to determine the unborn child's condition...I can't bear it, thought Serena.

But a moment later, in the remote voice she used for giving orders to Mrs Flagg or Hetty and Dora, she said, 'I should have no objection. I understand the risks. Please arrange this mercury treatment for me as soon as you can.'

'Lady Cadence,' he said, 'are you sure?'

'Perfectly sure,' said Serena and again felt the child move restlessly.

❀ ❀ ❀

The equipment for the treatment was conveyed to the house a week later.

Gillespie Martlet's colleague from Guy's Hospital was a portly gentleman who brought with him the aroma of cigars and claret. With him came his assistant, a youngish man, who carried the contraption up the stairs with Dr Martlet's help. Dr Martlet suggested Flagg should be called, but Serena could not bear any of the servants to be part of this or to realize what was happening, and she had given them all the afternoon off. Dora had told her Mr Flagg had bought tickets for an afternoon performance at one of the music halls. Serena had said, 'I hope you have an enjoyable afternoon,' and had called Flagg to her room to give him a small sum of money. 'Perhaps you could have afternoon tea somewhere after the music hall,' she had said, and Flagg had said that was very kind, milady, and they might go along to Lyons Corner House at Marble Arch, which Mrs Flagg always thought very genteel and where the cakes were particularly good.

Dora and Hetty had cleared out a small room on the second floor the previous day. It had been a nursery-maid's room when Crispian was small and Jamie used to stay with them, but it had been unused for years.

'The doctors have said a separate room must be set aside for the actual birth,' said Serena to Dora. 'I know it's a good four months away, but since Dr Martlet is bringing a medical gentleman to the house, the room had better be ready for him to see.' This explanation had seemed to satisfy Dora, and the walls were washed down and the floor thoroughly swept. Flagg, puffing like a grampus, carried in a bedstead, which Hetty made up with clean sheets. There was a marble washstand in the corner with clean towels and soap, and before the servants went off to their music hall Hetty brought a can of hot water, wrapped in flannel to keep it warm.

Serena had been aware of the child stirring all through the morning, almost as if it knew something distressing was ahead, and when the wooden contraption for the treatment was carried in, something at the pit of her stomach clenched in painful spasm. She gasped and bit her lip, but the pain passed and no one seemed to notice. The portly doctor, who was introduced as Mr Josiah Jex, listened to her heart with a stethoscope and looked into her eyes and ears.

'No dizzy spells, Lady Cadence? No palpitations or swoons? Good. Now then, I believe Martlet is a little concerned about giving this treatment to a lady in your condition, but you seem fairly robust to me. Your pulse rate is a little fast, but I dare say you're apprehensive about what's ahead. Very understandable. I'll make sure the little one is just as healthy before we go any further, though.' He placed the stethoscope on her stomach to listen to the baby's heartbeat, then nodded and straightened up.

'Is it all right?' said Serena, trying to read his expression.

'Oh, yes,' he said, reassuringly. 'A perfectly good regular heartbeat. I think we can proceed. You understand what we're going to do, I think? Martlet explained it all?'

'Yes.'

The wooden box had been set in the centre of the room. Serena hated it at once. It was about the height of her shoulders, roughly square in shape, with a hole at the top where the head of the patient would protrude. At the front was what looked like a hinged flap, with a catch to hold it in place. The whole structure was mounted on small legs so that it stood about eight inches off the floor, and underneath it, on some kind of metal sheet, was a grid like a flattened brazier, with small pieces of charcoal laid out on it.

'I'll ask you to undress down to your underthings,' said Josiah Jex. 'First we shall paint a mercury solution directly onto the worst affected parts. Rather cold initially, I'm afraid, but I'll be as gentle as I can.'

The mercury felt cool and not unpleasant against her skin, but when he asked her to lie back on the bed and spread her legs apart, Serena said, 'Must I?'

'We do need to treat all the areas,' said Jex, glancing at the assistant. 'We'll be very quick and very gentle, I promise.'

'We're very used to treating people,' added the young assistant. 'Ladies and gentlemen both.'

They spoke kindly, but Serena thought that of all the humiliations and discomforts she had had to endure, this was the worst yet. To lie on a narrow bed, wearing nothing but a chemise and drawers, while two men moved their hands intimately between her thighs and saw the ravages the disease had inflicted on her skin, was deeply embarrassing and shameful. They both wore thin cotton gloves, but Serena could still feel their hands through the fabric. Josiah Jex's hands were warm and fleshy, the assistant's thin and probing. Several times she flinched as they applied the mercury with a small soft brush, but she managed not to resist or cry out. She was thankful that Dr Martlet had waited outside for this part of the treatment; these two men were strangers and she was unlikely to see them again, which made it seem impersonal. But when finally she was allowed to sit up, her whole body felt as if it had been punched.

'We'll leave the room for you to undress completely,' said Jex. 'Take everything off, please, and then get inside and close the door like this.' He demonstrated the hinged door at the front, which opened into two parts, the top flap folding down when the subject was seated inside. 'We'll give you fifteen minutes then we'll come back.'

Serena was grateful for this small privacy. She took off the chemise and silk drawers, opened the hinged flap of the wooden structure and forced herself to squeeze inside. It smelled worse than anything she had ever encountered, but she sat on the wooden bench as instructed. There was hardly any space and it was necessary to keep her feet tightly together and to cross her arms over her body. But it was not as uncomfortable as she had feared and the wooden seat had some kind of covering that softened it a little. By now she was strongly conscious of the child's distress, and of the pain spiking through her lower stomach. But I'm ignoring you, Serena said to it.

The two doctors returned, inspected the box and the grid on which it stood, and at a nod from Jex, the young assistant kneeled down to set light to the charcoals.

'This is like a fumigation process, if you're familiar with that,' said Jex. 'There's mercury in a small tank at the bottom of the box—you'll be resting your feet on it. We've lit the charcoal directly underneath and as the heat rises the mercury will vaporize—turn to smoke. The fumes will soak into you and you'll breathe them in as well. That seems to be burning quite well now,' he said to the assistant.

'How long must I be in here?' asked Serena.

'Three or four hours, I'm afraid. You won't be able to open the door because you won't be able to reach out to the catch, but we'll stay in earshot, of course.'

'You won't remain in the room with me?'

'I'm afraid we can't. If we inhaled all the mercury vapour we administer...' He made a gesture implying it would be harmful. 'And we'll have to keep this door closed to prevent it seeping out to the rest of the house. But don't worry. We'll look in at intervals to make sure you're all right.'

'And to see that the mercury's staying at the right level of heat,' said the assistant. 'But there's no danger of fire, Lady Cadence. Sometimes we need to add a little more charcoal or mercury halfway through.'

'We'll hear you if you call out,' said Jex. 'Stay as calm as you can. It'll soon be over and you'll quickly recover.' He nodded to her and the two men went out, closing the door.

The room was very quiet, apart from the occasional sizzling from the charcoal, and several times Serena thought the mercury in the tank spat as it bubbled from the heat. The only other sound in the room was the ticking of the clock, which Jex had moved to the windowledge where Serena could see it.

At first she thought nothing much was going to happen, and that all the talk about pain and exhaustion was purely for the doctors to surround themselves and their remedy with a degree of mystery. The small container of mercury under her feet was certainly warming up, but it was not burningly hot or even particularly uncomfortable. Her skin was starting to tingle where the mercury had been painted on earlier, but that was all. It's bearable, thought Serena. I'll get through it. But will the child get through it?

The clock's hands pointed to two o'clock. Normally she would have just finished her lunch and be drinking a cup of Mrs Flagg's excellent coffee. She would like some coffee now; Dr Martlet had told her to have only the very lightest of breakfasts and no lunch. She had done as he said, but she was used to a substantial lunch and she felt slightly light-headed.

It was half-past two. The inside of the box was beginning to feel uncomfortably warm and Serena began to fear it would overheat and she would burn. They had said they would come back at intervals, but how long would those intervals be? And if she shouted, would they really hear? The house was large and the doors were heavy and close-fitting. She moved restlessly, trying to get more comfortable, but the box was too small to permit much movement. She managed to get her arms into a slightly different position, and as she did so the mercury fumes finally started to rise. There was a smell like hot tin in her nostrils and a stinging sensation when she breathed in. Serena felt even more light-headed and had the impression of a thin mist forming in front of her eyes. She had no idea if there was actual mist from the hot mercury or if it was just the result of its fumes on an empty stomach clouding her vision. Her skin was starting to feel as if it was being scraped with a knife, but it was still all bearable.

Mr Jex looked round the door just then, asking, was she all right—was she in much pain?

'Only a little,' said Serena, relieved to hear her voice came out fairly normally.

'Sure?'

'Yes. It's unpleasant but not unduly so. I can bear it.'

'Good,' he said, and went out, closing the door.

But if Serena was bearing it, the child was not. It was churning inside her—the word 'threshing' occurred to her—its movements sending ripples of pain across her stomach and spiking down between her legs. She moved again, but the pain was building up into a vicious wave, and she cried out and instinctively tried to hunch over but could not because of the cramped space. This was part of the cost she must pay for curing the repulsive disease Julius had given her. But what about the child? Was the child going to be part of the cost she would pay? Serena, sobbing and moaning, was beyond caring. The mist was partly obscuring her vision again and the stench of hot metal was making her feel sick.

The pain receded and she gasped with relief, sweat running down her face, but now the mercury vapour was soaking into her skin, down and down, as if it was scouring her body, trying to find the core of the disease. Serena moaned, and tried to withstand it, but it reached deeper and deeper, until she had the impression that her very bones were bubbling and seething.

The child was like a hard, heavy lump at the pit of her stomach. It's dying, she thought. It's dying or it's already dead. She had no idea if it was her own pain or something in the mercury vapour that was causing the child's distress, and she no longer cared. Because you'll never love it, said her mind. Remember? You'll never love it and you'll never even like it. It was perfectly true. She could scarcely even think of the child as human any more. It was as if the thing in her womb was nothing more than a black twisted lump of disease. She shuddered and pushed this nightmarish image away, and she thought she lost consciousness for a time because when the mist cleared slightly the clock was showing a quarter-past three.

The clock's hands had reached quarter to four when a warm viscous fluid began to seep between her legs, and agony tore mercilessly through her lower body. Tears ran down her face, this time not from the burning pain of the mercury on her skin and within her bones, but because of the little lost life that was leaching away. 'Forgive me,' she whispered to it. 'I know you're dying, and I'm so sorry...'

Sweat streamed down her face and ran stingingly into her eyes. She gasped and clenched her fists. She would not call for help, she would not...But there was a dreadful pressure between her legs now. The child was thrusting its blind, fumbling way out of her. Serena tried to lean back, tried to widen her legs to ease the brutal pushing, but the box was too narrow and she could not. Blood trickled down her legs and she sobbed with the agony and, finally, with the loss.

"I don't want you,' she said to the child. 'I never did. But I'm so sorry you've got to die before you're born. I'm so dreadfully sorry...'

The clock had reached half-past four when she began to scream.

Gillespie Martlet and Josiah Jex agreed later that it had been a narrow thing with Lady Cadence. A very unpleasant business indeed, although, as Mr Jex said, she had been most straitly warned of the risk she ran.

'Certainly she was warned,' said Dr Martlet, who was rather white around the lips and had discarded his starched high-necked collar halfway through their endeavours to revive their patient and stop the bleeding. Dear God, he had forgotten how much blood a damaged, aborted foetus could bring with it! That was what came of practising medicine from the dignified confines of a Wimpole Street consulting room, of course; you no longer dealt with the voidances and the exudations of the human body. Gillespie Martlet, who for the last two decades had been more accustomed to advising delicate ladies to take care of their fragile constitutions, and to exchanging bluff but deferential pleasantries with corpulent gentlemen about their fondness for rich food, had found the last two hours an appalling experience.

Lady Cadence—Serena, whom he had loved from afar in a perfectly respectful and entirely chaste fashion for more than fifteen years—had screamed like a trapped hare, and when they dragged open the mercury box's door, she had been seated in a pool of blood and amniotic fluid, writhing and struggling. And the child, the poor half-formed, half-crushed foetus, half in and half out of her body...

Between them, Dr Martlet and Jex had carried her to the narrow bed in the corner of the room, sending the young assistant for hot water and cloths. He had taken so long that Jex had almost gone huffing down the stairs himself, but he had finally returned with a canister of water and towels, gasping his apologies, but explaining that there appeared to be no servants anywhere in the house.

'No, of course there aren't,' said Martlet, remembering. 'She sent them out for a half-day's holiday. She didn't want any of them knowing what was being done to her this afternoon.'

Jex, his hands busy about his patient, grunted that in his experience servants generally knew more about their masters and mistresses than anyone else, and added it was a pity there was not a sensible woman in the house to help them. But they would manage, he said, eyeing the prone figure on the bed.

They did manage, but it was, as they later admitted to one another, a very close-run thing indeed. It took their combined knowledge and Jex's skill to remove the foetus without damaging Serena Cadence's uterus. As the forceps, hastily snatched out of Jex's bag, closed around it and he prepared to withdraw it, there was a nightmare moment when it seemed to squirm and resist.

'Oh God,' said Martlet again, recoiling, one hand over his mouth. 'Jex, it can't possibly be alive...'

'Five months, didn't you say?'

'Yes, but—'

'I've known them survive at five months,' said Jex grimly. 'But this little one hasn't, and from the look of it, that's God's mercy.'

They piled pillows under Serena's feet to stem the bleeding, but even so, the sheets and the mattress were soaked, and the stench of stale blood quickly filled up the small room. Martlet, feeling slightly sick, reflected that this was something else you lost touch with from a smart consulting room.

Much later, the servants returned, and the sensible maid, Dora, left to sit with her mistress, the three gentlemen sat in the downstairs drawing room.

'And,' said Dr Martlet, 'I think Lady Cadence—and Sir Julius—would permit us a little of their brandy.' He poured the brandy, his hands still shaking.

'A very good brandy,' observed Josiah Jex, swilling it round in its balloon glass to release the ethers. Without looking up, he said, 'She understood what happened, didn't she?'

'That the child was lost? Yes, of course.'

Jex paused, then said, 'Have you told her she was pregnant with twins and she only aborted one of them?'

'Not yet,' said Dr Martlet. 'But undoubtedly it will be a great comfort to her.'

CHAPTER TWENTY-FIVE

London, 1912

T RUST MADAM TO CHOOSE the most troublesome way of travelling,' said Flagg crossly, dragging two large wicker hampers from the big larder into the kitchen. 'No consideration for other folks, as per usual. And why are we jaunting off to the wilds of nowhere all of a sudden? That's what I'd like to know.'

Hetty, who had been directed to help him, said most likely madam wanted to shut herself away at Cadence Manor until after the birth.

'More like she's shutting herself away because she contracted you-know-what from the master, the old rogue,' said Flagg, straightening up from the hampers, one hand to the small of his back.

'Flagg, I'll thank you not to refer to such matters while I'm cooking madam's lunch.'

'I speak as I find,' said Flagg. 'We all know what ailed Sir Julius, and why Mr Crispian and Mr Jamie took him off to foreign parts before he could go completely mad and ruin the bank altogether.'

'I don't know about ruining the bank, I call it tragic what happened to him,' said Mrs Flagg, stirring the caper sauce, which was to go with the halibut.

'Tragic my foot. He sowed the wind and now he's reaping the whirlwind,' said Flagg, who had been making an inventory of the wine cellar and was always inclined to quote the Old Testament when he had taken a nip of Sir Julius's port.

'Well,' said Mrs Flagg, who could not be doing with Flagg when he became biblical, 'I don't care for Cadence Manor, and I don't mind who hears me say so. It's the back of beyond, that place; no shops to hand and never a soul to exchange a bit of gossip with. I'd much rather madam stayed in London, with Dr Martlet scampering round every five minutes to make sure she hasn't suffered a finger ache. Dora, if you've nothing else to do at the moment, you and Hetty had better see there's plenty of greaseproof paper for packing the provisions. I'm taking as much as we can manage, for if Mr Colm's kept the larders at the manor properly provisioned it'll be the first time ever.'

❀ ❀ ❀

Serena had not realized she wanted to leave London until she had actually said the words aloud to Dr Martlet. But as soon as they were out, she thought, yes, of *course* that's the answer. Away from London, away from the annoying noises and people plying the door knocker, and Flagg and Hetty having to turn them away because she did not want to see anyone, not like this. And perhaps at Cadence she could find a way to think of this child, this lone little survivor of twins, as an ordinary baby.

Dr Martlet had at first been doubtful about her leaving London, but finally he agreed. 'Perhaps after all it would be best. It will be quieter and I can make sure you're looked after by a doctor in Bramley. If you've completely made up your mind?'

'I have. My husband's cousin, Colm Cadence, lives in one wing of the place. He looks after it for us.'

'Yes, Gil's mentioned him.'

'He's painfully shy, poor Colm. Very scholarly. He lives for his work and I wouldn't want to disturb that, but I suppose some arrangement can be reached. Cadence has more than one wing.' It pleased her to say this, to visualize the manor house behind its high walls. One of Julius's ancestors had built it and the Italian influence was evident, even though it was slightly battered nowadays— in fact very nearly shabby.

Dr Martlet was of the opinion that her health was sufficient to withstand the journey, which Serena would make by car, since she could not face a train journey, even with a private railcar. 'The child's heartbeat is steady and good,' he said, having listened to it during one of the rare examinations Serena permitted.

'Mr Jex said that about the heartbeat a few hours before the other child was lost,' said Serena, rather acidly.

'Yes, but...' Martlet straightened up, folding the stethoscope into his bag. 'Lady Cadence, the heartbeat Mr Jex would have heard was that of the twin who was still alive. This one you're still carrying. We can be reasonably sure that there was only the one heartbeat for him to hear that day. The other twin—the lost one—was already dead.'

Already dead, thought Serena, her mind going back to that day. That lurch of panic and distress I felt when they brought in the mercury apparatus. It happened then, of course. That's when it died. Of fear? Could unborn babies feel fear?

'And,' Dr Martlet was saying, 'we hadn't realized you were carrying twins, mostly because—'

He broke off, and Serena said coolly, 'Because I wasn't permitting the examinations you wanted to make? Yes, I understand that.' She would not apologize, but at least this would make acknowledgement of the facts.

'As for the other—ah—problem, the mercury treatment seems to have alleviated a great many of the symptoms,' said Dr Martlet. 'Better than I dared hope, in fact, particularly since it was not as long a session as Mr Jex wanted. But perhaps after the birth we can try again.'

Try again. A second spell of being enclosed in the bad-smelling wooden contraption, the hot stench of tin in her nostrils, the feeling that her entire skin was being scraped raw, the sensation that her bones were blistering. Never, thought Serena. Even if this disgusting disease tears me into tatters, all hell's furies won't force me to endure that a second time. In a vague voice she said they would have to see.

'Have you been able to write to Sir Julius or Crispian to tell them what's happened?' asked Martlet.

'If you're referring to the loss of the child, I haven't told them anything at all,' said Serena. 'None of them knows about the pregnancy.' The thought that Julius might never know, hovered unspoken. Serena said firmly, 'And in the light of what has just happened I'm inclined to be cautious about telling them even now.'

'Ah. Yes. Perhaps you're right.'

'But I've written to let them know I'll be at Cadence Manor for the next few months. I've sent the letter to the shipping office at Athens. The ship was due to call there in a few weeks' time, did you know that? They're going a little way along the western coast of Greece, Crispian says.' The places Crispian wrote about had an exotic ring; Serena would not have cared to travel so far herself, but she looked forward to Crispian's letters. He wrote vividly and well.

'As long as they don't get too close to the Turkish coastline,' said Dr Martlet, frowning slightly. 'That area's been in a state of turmoil for years. The Ottoman Empire has had sovereignty over the Balkan Peninsula for centuries and now the Christian countries are trying to oust them, that's what it really boils down to.'

'Crispian asked the man from Thomas Cook if the area was safe before they left,' said Serena, who had not really followed the complicated squabbles of the people in these outlandish places. 'He told Crispian the trouble—the fighting—had died down.' She had not been especially concerned, because Thomas Cook could presumably be trusted to know what was happening in most parts of the world.

She added comfortably, 'And I dare say Crispian and your son—Jamie, too—are more than a match for any foreign quarrels. And Thomas Cook were quite definite that the—what is it called?—the guerrilla warfare had died down.'

'Yes, the Balkan League was hailed as the solution to all the problems,' nodded Dr Martlet. 'It's a complex business, though, and I wouldn't trust the present peace, not if a dozen Leagues had been formed. The Turkish people are quite warlike, although they have an interesting culture, I've always thought.'

'I suppose so,' said Serena vaguely. 'Anyway, Crispian said as long as they didn't actually go ashore in Turkey they would be perfectly safe.'

Edirne, October 1912

Crispian knew they were very far from safe in Edirne. Even so, he thought they were as comfortable as they could be, given the circumstances. Their rooms in the fort were a bit sparse and facilities were basic but adequate.

'I think we're lucky to have somewhere to sleep at all,' Jamie said. 'I'd been imagining bedding down in a ditch.'

'As far as I'm concerned,' Gil said later to Crispian, 'I'm perfectly happy with any bed, providing I have a glass of wine, a loaf of bread, and thou beside me in the wilderness.'

'I think there's a book in the original poem's list,' said Crispian, who had taken a minute to recognize the quotation.

'Oh, bugger the book, as long as I've got the bread and wine. And,' said Gil with a sideways look, 'I'd quite like thou beside me, as well.'

'I wish you'd stop this,' said Crispian angrily.

'Stop what?'

'Making these—these stupid mischievous flirting remarks.'

'What makes you think it's only mischievous flirting?' said Gil very quietly, and walked away before Crispian could think how to respond.

Despite the war being waged beyond the city, none of them had any real sense of danger. Various reports of battles fought and won or lost filtered through, but the thick walls of the old fort and the presence of soldiers created a sense of security.

'It's false security, though,' said Jamie. 'At any minute we could be faced with hordes of marauding Balkan armies.'

'But the war's nothing to do with us,' said Crispian. 'It's Serbia, Greece, Montenegro and Bulgaria who're fighting against the Ottoman Empire.'

'Try telling that to the Balkan armies when they erupt into this courtyard,' said Gil. 'And before you start any of that damn-it-chaps-we're-British stuff, let's remember we're actually inside the ancient Ottoman capital. Personally, I think we've been lucky to escape unscathed this long.'

But the sprinkling of English civilians in the fort—most of them doctors or journalists, or simply other stranded travellers—did not agree with Gil's views. They told one another it would soon be over. Mark their words, they said firmly, the troubles would die out, normal life would be restored, and one would be allowed to get on a ship and go home. They talked wistfully of England, and wrote letters intended for their families, which they optimistically took to the shipping office. Gil said the letters would not even get as far as the Aegean Sea, never mind across Europe and into England.

'The Greek navy's had control of every island in the Aegean for nearly a month. It won't let so much as a postage stamp out.'

For nearly three weeks what Jamie called 'the false security' continued. They explored the town in their various ways, often not seeing one another until they met for dinner. After dinner, along with some of the other English civilians, they gathered in the largest of the courtyards to drink the thick sweet coffee that was brewed, and eat the tiny honey-and-nut pastries served with it. The fierce glow of the dying sun sent banners of crimson across the skies and bathed the ancient stones with rose and gold. Jamie found this deeply moving, and talked about Kubla Khan's ancient sacred Alph or the fire-streaked skies of Aegia, and likened himself and the others to the pilgrims who had set foot on the golden road to Samarkand. Told by Gil that Samarkand was at least a thousand miles further east, he said he was talking metaphorically, if not even metaphysically, and Gil had no romance in his soul.

Gil fell into the way of lending a hand in the hospital block, which was bracing itself for an influx of wounded men. On several occasions he was found to be absent from his bedroom all night; challenged by Crispian, Gil demanded to know where did Crispian think he had been.

'Helping in the infirmary, I suppose.'

'You have such a beautiful innocent nature,' said Gil. 'Don't you know that nurses work in infirmaries, and nurses are frequently attractive and very affectionate.'

'You're spending some of the nights with a nurse?'

'Several of the nurses. I've never practised exclusivity.'

'Gil, there's a war raging within a few miles of us!'

'All the more reason for a little light entertainment,' said Gil.

Jamie had spent more time in the town than the other two; he got to know some of the Jewish community, and talked with the scholars, printers and musicians.

'He'll end in converting to Judaism, if you're not careful,' said Gil.

'I think he's just interested in their culture and knowledge,' said Crispian. 'He's very like his father, my uncle Colm. You never met Colm, did you?'

'I did, actually. Those Christmas house parties at Cadence Manor. I was asked to a couple, if you remember. Colm generally shut himself away from the frivolities, but I met him.'

'I'd forgotten that,' said Crispian. 'Colm's spiritual home is probably an Oxford college or a library somewhere, and Jamie's the same. He shouldn't really be working at Cadences at all.'

'At the moment I'd give a good deal to be cleaning the lavatories at Cadences,' said Gil. 'Anywhere but here.'

Once or twice they accompanied Jamie to performances by one of the choral societies within Edirne. Seeing Jamie rapt and silent in the cascades of the unfamiliar music, Crispian thought: I shouldn't have let him come on this mad voyage in the first place. And then, as the music poured out, he gave himself up to it, finding it moving and beautiful. Like balm anointing the soul, he thought. Like a silencing hand laid over a discordance. The images of home came strongly and painfully to him: London with its clatter and bustle and impatience; the oak-panelled rooms of Cadences Bank, with their air of quiet activity; Priors Bramley and the old manor house; the scents of the Oxfordshire meadows; the village street, with the smell of freshly baked bread; the serene old church behind the lich-gate, with dappled sunlight lying across the grass...

He spent a large part of each day with his father, but he was not sure if his father knew who he was—or even if he knew Crispian was there. One of the attendants found an old Bath chair and wheeled Julius outside to enjoy the sunshine, even taking him into Edirne's centre. Crispian was grateful for this, and several times wheeled the Bath chair himself, sitting in one of the ancient squares with the mosques and the glimpses of onion domes, trying to describe the surroundings to his father using the skin-writing. Sometimes he thought there was a flicker of understanding, and once or twice he thought he saw a glint of sly malevolence in the sightless eyes.

'I don't think there's any sight left to him,' said Raif, with whom they had become friendly by this time. 'I think the disease is too deep into his brain now.'

'But you can't be sure there's no sight?'

'Not completely, no.'

For most of the time Julius lay on his narrow bed in a side room of the infirmary, staring blindly up at the ceiling. But as the weeks went by he became prone to fierce rages, rearing up from the bed and blundering round the little room, clutching wildly at whatever came within reach and hurling it from him. Sometimes the rages lasted for several hours, after which he would subside in a corner of the room, crouching in a huddle, covering his face with his hands, and sobbing.

The second time this happened Raif came in search of Crispian.

'I regret,' he said, 'that you won't like the methods we've used to restrain him. But last time we were afraid he would injure himself and we wouldn't be able to get near enough to treat him. Certainly we couldn't get near him to administer any kind of sedative. The strength of a person in the grip of genuine mania—' He broke off and shrugged. 'You will have experienced that for yourselves already, I suppose. The strength of the insane can be as much as the strength of three men put together.'

Crispian said, 'What, exactly, have you done?'

'You had better see. He's not in his usual room, because...well, you will see. Perhaps you would prefer one of your companions to come with you?'

Crispian was deeply grateful for Gil's presence that evening, but, as they went along the narrow corridors and down a flight of shallow stone steps, he was aware of a churning apprehension and he was very conscious that they were inside a place whose history stretched back into the days when caliphs and sultans had thought nothing of inflicting what was called exquisite torture on anyone transgressing their laws.

The passages were lit by flaring torches thrust into wall sconces. Edirne had some electricity but it was erratic and this was one of the times it had failed. Dark shadows danced grotesquely across the walls as they went deeper.

As the doctor opened a door halfway along a stone corridor, Edirne's dark past seemed to surge forward and to Crispian's first horrified sight it was as if Julius had fallen into the hands of those long-ago avengers. He was seated on the floor; there were blankets and cushions for him, but thick iron gyves with chains attached had been clamped round his wrists and ankles and the ends of the chains were driven into the wall behind him.

'He's chained up,' said Crispian, turning to Raif. 'Did you have to do that to him?'

But even as he said the words, Julius made a snarling bestial sound, and lunged forward as if aware of their presence, as if he intended to attack whoever was there. The chains tautened at once, scraping across the floor with a sound that made Crispian flinch.

'It's not often we're forced to make use of the fort's ancient equipment,' said Raif defensively, 'but we could see no other way. Truly, we shall release him as soon as this seizure passes. We'll have to keep him more heavily sedated from then on.'

'He's right,' said Gil quietly. 'There was nothing else they could have done. Crispian, come away. He'll come out of this—he'll become docile again.'

'But we can't leave him down here in the dark...'

'It's dark for him anyway,' said Gil. 'It's forever dark, as far as he's concerned,' and this time there was such infinite pity in his voice that Crispian looked at him in surprise.

'Mr Martlet is right,' said Raif. 'The mania will work itself out, and Sir Julius will be submissive again.'

Submissive. That dreadful, almost childlike, obedience. Crispian said, 'Can I stay with him until he comes out of it?'

The doctor hesitated, and it was Gil who said, 'Better not. It won't make any difference to him.'

'Again, Mr Martlet is right,' said Raif.

'All right. Will you tell me when he's taken back to his own room?'

'Of course.'

They went out and, without speaking, walked back along the dim passageways. But when the doctor left them to go to the main infirmary, Gil reached for Crispian's hand, and for the first time Crispian did not push him away.

He said, 'Are you spending tonight with one of your nurse friends?'

'Not necessarily.' Gil paused and turned to look at Crispian. They were much of a height; in the flickering light, tiny red pinpoints of light seemed to dance in Gil's eyes.

Like the eyes of a devil, thought Crispian. Or is he?

After a moment, he said, 'I'd better find Jamie and tell him what's happened.'

Gil made a gesture with his free hand as if to say, it's up to you, but he released Crispian's hand and went to his own room without speaking.

CHAPTER TWENTY-SIX

Edirne, October 1912

THE FALSE SECURITY SOON ended. At the beginning of October martial law was proclaimed in Edirne, and Mehmet Siikrii Pasha, who was to command the military operations from Edirne, arrived at the fort. With him came soldiers and a hybrid crowd of people fleeing to the relative safety of the city. Crispian, with Gil and Jamie, went out to help with the influx of exhausted people whose villages had been ransacked and burned by the invading Bulgarians. Crispian found it heart-rending to see how they clung to the few belongings they had managed to save, and even more heartrending that none of them complained. They hoped to return to their homes soon, they said. Migration was a legacy of the Prophet.

'It's a legacy I wouldn't want,' said Gil, when Crispian reported this. 'And I've just heard that they're going to impose a curfew on the city. It'll come into force two hours after sunset each day.'

'They're saying the Pasha is trying to arrange for women and foreign visitors to leave,' said Jamie. 'In case we find ourselves in a siege situation.'

They looked at each other.

'Could we possibly leave with them?' said Gil at last.

'We'd have to do it soon, while trains are still running,' said Jamie. 'If we leave it much longer we'll really be trapped. Some of the soldiers are already saying they're expecting orders to requisition wagons and carts. But where would we go?'

'I don't know. Presumably deeper into the Turkish countryside until we got to a British Embassy. And what about Sir Julius?' said Gil. 'He couldn't make that kind of journey, or any kind of journey. Personally, I think we're as well here as anywhere.'

Crispian said, 'You two could leave. I'd have to stay here with my father.'

'If you stay, I'm staying,' said Gil at once. 'Jamie?'

'I certainly wouldn't leave either of you here.'

'There you are then,' said Gil to Crispian. 'All for one and one for all. And as Jamie says, where would we go? We're a hundred miles from the coast, and even if we got there, we'd never get a ship, not now.'

At night, as they sat in the courtyard, they could hear gunshot. It sounded frighteningly near, but Gil thought that was just an illusion of the heat and stillness of the night. Several days later, wounded Turkish soldiers began to arrive, brought on carts and wagons, some of them already dying. Gil worked with the doctors, and Crispian and Jamie tried to help where possible, acutely aware of their ignorance, but at least able to act as messengers. Crispian organized a small team who knew the town and could fetch supplies. 'While supplies still last,' said one of the doctors, rather grimly.

It was around then that some of the soldiers began to use what Raif told Crispian and Gil was sulphur mustard.

'Don't let it get near you,' he said. 'Don't even breathe the air. We don't know very much about it yet, and we aren't sure which side is using it. What we do know is that it causes the most horrific burns.'

'What can we do for them?' asked Gil.

'Not very much. The poor wretches don't even know they've been burned until hours later, by which time it's often too late to do much to help them. We can't bandage the burns—we can't even touch them. Soldiers are a stoic race,' said Raif. 'But the men suffering from these burns cry out in agony for hours on end.'

'But they recover eventually?' said Crispian, listening with horror.

Raif shrugged. 'It depends on the degree of the burn and the length of time they're exposed to the stuff. It can lead to death, usually because the lungs become damaged. Also it can destroy the sight. There's also a belief that even if they recover, they're vulnerable to growths later in life.'

'Cancer?'

'Yes. It's appalling stuff,' said Raif, sounding angry. 'Vicious and often fatal.'

The escalation of the war was a massive blow, but there were two more to come.

The first of these fell in early November when the Bulgarians, determined to take the stubborn town of Edirne, cut off the town's water supply.

'But there's a river and there are wells,' said the doctors firmly. 'We'll use those.'

The second blow was very different, and Crispian thought none of them could have foreseen it.

A Bulgarian plane had just flown over Edirne, showering leaflets, which Raif translated. It read, 'We have surrounded Edirne with a thousand guns. Come and surrender.'

'Will Edirne surrender?' asked Crispian.

'Not without a strong fight.' Raif frowned, then in a voice Crispian had not heard him use before, said, 'Mr

Cadence, there is a different matter I have to raise with you.'

'Yes?' Crispian waited, expecting to hear something about his father.

'It's about your cousin. Mr James Cadence.'

'What about him?' said Crispian, slightly startled.

'These last weeks he has often gone out by himself. Do you know where?'

'In a general way. He's got to know several people in the Jewish Quarter. He's interested in their way of life, particularly their music. Why?'

'An hour ago I was asked to talk to you. This is very difficult, but it seems it's not only the Jewish people of Edirne your cousin formed friendships with. If the information is right, he's made some very unwise acquaintances.'

'What on earth do you mean?'

'In any country, any city, in a time of war, there's a very particular kind of occupation,' said Raif, 'undertaken by people who appear to be ordinary civilians. They would say, those people, that they contribute as much to a war as men fighting on a battlefield. They...' He paused, apparently searching for the right words. 'They give information about the people among whom they live. They give it to the enemies of those people. You understand what I'm trying to say?'

'No, I don't,' said Crispian. 'Clearly you're talking about spies, but I don't see what that's got to do with Jamie.'

'Mr Cadence, your cousin was this morning caught passing information about the military activities inside this fort to a known agent of the Bulgarian armies.'

Crispian felt as if an invisible hand had flung icy water into his face. He said, 'That's impossible. There must be some dreadful misunderstanding. You must have the wrong information—or someone's playing a cruel trick.'

'The Pasha's men who brought in the intelligence do not think there is a trick. They are sure the charge against Mr James Cadence is based on sound fact. They will try to find out more, but you must understand there are larger issues for them to deal with. One Englishman...' Raif made a gesture, indicating that Jamie's transgression, if transgression there had been, was not very high in the pecking order. 'I will ask them to talk to you,' he said.

'I think you'd better, and as soon as possible.'

'I'm very sorry indeed about this,' said Raif, 'and I hope it will be found a mistake. All of us here like you. We have come to respect and trust you.'

'Jamie wouldn't act as a spy,' said Crispian. 'It's a ludicrous idea. He's a gentle person. Someone must have misunderstood something he said or did. The language difficulties could have caused a genuine error. Or perhaps someone even wanted some kind of revenge on him—or on me or my father.'

'That is certainly possible. Rich Englishmen are often targets for the unscrupulous.'

'Where is Jamie now?'

'This is where we have a problem,' said Raif slowly. 'We've been told that a small group of people on the outskirts of Edirne have him.'

'You mean they're keeping him prisoner? But that's not permitted.'

Raif spread his hands. 'In wartime rules can change. And we know of these people. They work in secrecy but the Pasha's men know they exist.'

'Who are they? How many are there?'

'In the main they are Turks. There could be fifty or so of them, perhaps more. Some are guerrilla fighters but all are fiercely loyal to their country and their race. But they are all what I think you would call extremists.'

Extremists. Fierce men—probably also some women—who changed the rules of war. And Jamie, quiet unassuming Jamie, whom Crispian had regarded as a brother, was in their hands.

'Can we get to him? Get him back here?'

'I don't know.'

'God, man, we must! The British Embassy—' Crispian stopped, remembering how very isolated they were, how virtually impossible it would be to even get a message to an embassy. 'Do they intend to keep him prisoner until the war is resolved?' he said. 'Until Edirne is no longer under siege?'

'Mr Cadence, it is not just a matter of imprisonment for your cousin. The people who are holding him follow the old ways of the Turks. And there is a very particular punishment they reserve for spies.'

❀ ❀ ❀

A very particular punishment.

The doctor's words went through and through Crispian's brain as he and Gil made their way to the small square on the edge of the city. Neither of them was sure of their own safety, but two of the Pasha's soldiers had been rather grudgingly allotted to escort them, which Crispian thought was probably as safe as they could get.

'Which is to say not very safe at all,' said Gil.

They had managed to persuade Raif to accompany them, to act as interpreter. At first he had refused. 'There is too much here I must do,' he had said. 'So many injured people who need me.'

'We need you,' said Crispian. 'We need you to interpret for us. Please. If it's a question of money—'

'It is not a question of money,' said Raif coldly. 'It is a question of who has more need of me and at the moment that is the injured soldiers. Also, I do not care to be seen assisting a spy against my people.'

'My cousin isn't a spy,' began Crispian hotly, but Gil broke in, laying a hand on Crispian's arm.

'We'll do it by ourselves,' he said. 'We're outcasts here, that's very clear. Somehow we'll manage, though.' He turned away, but before he got to the door, Raif said, 'Wait. That was discourteous of me. I will come with you and I will translate what's said by the captors. But my name must not be used. These people who hold your cousin must not know who I am.'

'That's a reasonable enough condition,' said Gil.

'And if, after an hour's time, you have no success I shall return here, even if I do so on my own.'

'That's also reasonable,' said Crispian.

As they got ready for the journey, Gil said quietly, 'I thought that would get him.'

'What?'

'Our indifference. The implication that we could do it without him.'

'Thank you,' said Crispian gratefully.

'Save your thanks until we know whether we can get Jamie out of this. I should think we can trust Raif, can't we? To translate everything honestly?'

'Yes, I think so.'

'And Jamie?' said Gil. 'I suppose there couldn't be any truth in the charge of spying? Not even the smallest speck?'

'Not even the smallest speck,' said Crispian angrily. 'It's absurd. Are you ready? We'd better set off.'

But before they could do so, Raif came to them.

'Is something wrong?' said Crispian, seeing the expression on the doctor's face.

'Later you might think of it as something that is right. I'm sorry, Mr Cadence, but the night staff have just told me that during the night Sir Julius sank into a deep coma. So far it hasn't been possible to revive him. They have tried and I have just been with him and I have tried as well.'

'Oh God,' said Crispian, and for a moment he had to turn away from both the doctor and Gil, because the emotions struggling inside him were almost too much to bear. He put out a hand to the wall, because he was not sure if his legs would support him. Anger and sorrow and bitterness coursed helplessly through him, but after a moment he was able to straighten up and turn back to the others.

'Is he dying?'

'I think so.' Before Crispian could ask the question, Raif said, 'I think he has a few hours of life left. Not longer than that.'

'Oh God,' said Crispian again, and looked at Gil. 'What do I do?'

'If you stay here I'll try to get Jamie freed—' said Gil, but Raif interrupted him.

'You must both go,' he said. 'These people will take more notice of family. Sir Julius can't be helped, not by any of us. He's already far beyond us. Also, I don't think we will be away very long. Your discussion with the people who are holding him won't be a lengthy matter.'

Gil said, 'They'll either agree to release him right away or they'll refuse?'

'Yes. And if they refuse, you won't be able to change their minds. I think we will be back here in two hours— three at the most.' In a friendlier voice than he had used since breaking the news about Jamie, he said, 'Sir Julius is not likely to die until late tonight at the soonest. You will be in good time to be with him at the end.'

It did not take very long to reach the place where Jamie was being held. The Pasha's men clearly knew the way, and Crispian's party were taken to one of the old parts of the city.

Sarah Rayne 305

'D'you sense we're going nearer to the fighting?' murmured Gil to Crispian.

'Yes, but I think it's probably because we're going to the outskirts of the city.'

Buildings huddled together and there were dark, sinister-looking alleyways with archways overhead. Neither Crispian nor Gil had been to this part of Edirne before, and Crispian noticed that the Byzantine influence was stronger than elsewhere. Despite the fighting and the threat of food shortages, the narrow shops still had displays of beautiful, jewel-coloured silks and exotic pottery, and stalls and booths were selling food.

'Probably not for much longer, though,' remarked Gil.

Between the buildings they glimpsed the onion domes and minarets of the mosques and prayer halls, and all round them was the strange, unfathomable language. On the air came the distinctive thin wailing that Crispian recognized as either people being called to prayer or people already engaged in prayer. The scents of cooking and exotic spices and oils lay heavily on the air and people looked at them curiously as they went past doorways and shops.

And somewhere in this bewildering maze of alleys and buildings, Jamie was being held by people who believed he had given information to Edirne's enemies. People who, according to Raif, followed the old ways of the Turks and had a very particular punishment for spies. But what?

As they were led through the streets Crispian tried to imagine what Jamie must be feeling but he was unable to do so.

Jamie Cadence's Journal, Edirne, 1912

When I think of how I worked out the details finally to destroy Crispian in Edirne, and how I failed, I'm consumed with such fury it almost overwhelms me.

It's quite difficult to set out a proper account, and earlier, I was aware of nervousness because this is the morning I've allotted to describing what happened in Edirne. The day I'll have to relive the nightmare in these pages. So here it is. The truth.

CHAPTER TWENTY-SEVEN

Jamie Cadence's Journal

I STARTED TO EXPLORE Edirne soon after our arrival—when I had got over being sick from that vile railway journey, that is, and after we had settled into our quarters in the fort. I'll admit Crispian did well in arranging that.

It took a great deal of courage to go outside the fort on my own. I don't think many people would venture into a maze of narrow streets in a strange land, knowing nothing of the language, and with the country on the brink of war with half a dozen of its neighbours. But I did. Neither Crispian nor Gil thought it very unusual: they both considered me something of a loner.

As I walked through the streets, I drew myself little maps so as not to get lost, and quite soon I sought out the Jewish community, using their music as the basis for approaching them. No, that's not an accurate statement. I didn't 'use' the music; I was genuinely interested. They have a wonderful legacy of music in that city. A choral society of Maftirim was founded there in the seventh century and a great many gifted cantors have come from the area.

Jewish people have endured much abuse and ill treatment over the centuries, but I've always liked them.

They're courteous and warm and interesting. And among that particular Jewish community were a number of very scholarly men—elders—who could understand and speak English. That was what I wanted. I was accepted by them quite early on—the eccentric Englishman from the famous banking house, caught in the country through the fortunes of war.

From there it was easy to identify others who were not so scholarly or courteous. Extremists, they were called, those fiery-eyed, dark-visaged men and youths, and the few women who were with them. I never sorted out their nationalities, but I think they were mostly Turks and a few Greeks. They were all working in their own ways to defeat the Bulgarians and the Montenegrins, and all the other people who wanted to take over Edirne and everything that had once been part of the ancient Ottoman Empire.

The remarkable thing is that they trusted me. They were pleased—perhaps also flattered—that this Englishman who had so much money (ha!) sought them out and wanted to understand about their war and their plans. Ah, the English understood about empires and the losing of them, they said. I spent long afternoons with them, seated in their small, hot houses. Usually one of the English-speaking Jews would be there, but not always, and one or two of the younger men had a phrase or two of English. I was able to listen with apparent absorption to everything. Even with the language barrier, it was plain that these were people who would fight with every means at their disposal, and who would ignore the ordinary rules of warfare. Do ordinary rules operate in warfare, though? I wouldn't know. I've never fought a war, except my own private wars with the darknesses, which I usually lost anyway.

Sometimes I went to their houses at night as well, avoiding the evening meal in the fortress with Crispian and Gil and the others, pleading a headache from the heat of the day. It was easy to say I was retiring to my room and then to slip out of the fort—I knew all the ways in and out by that time—and skulk through the dark streets. On several of those nights my own darkness walked with me. Once, it was so strong I believed I saw its shadow, loping alongside me on the ancient stones. Henry Jekyll seizing the hapless Hyde's mind yet again, twisting and deforming and dredging up the shameful bloodlust, or Thomas Hardy's figure and visage of Madness seeking a home.

I killed again that night. I don't suppose anyone who's read this far will be surprised. It wasn't a particularly imaginative killing. I simply stood in the shadows of a tall building, waiting for a likely victim, and in the end a young boy came along. I usually prefer a woman when I'm killing but there was little chance of a lone female in that part of the world. The boy put up quite a fight, but I overcame him, of course. What did Raif and that drunken sot on the ship, Dr Brank, say? That genuinely mad people have the strength of three men? They were talking about Julius but they might as well have been talking about me. I certainly had the strength of three men, that night. And, as in Messina, the fight and the eventual killing were deeply arousing. I pondered that afterwards, because although killing a woman always brought me to helpless arousal, I hadn't expected it to be the same with a man. But since I'm shortly to die (sixty hours left now), I may as well admit I was aroused by the boy's struggles.

It was as I returned to the fort, the hunger slaked, the darkness dissolving, I suddenly saw the perfect way to get rid of Crispian. Tonight, if I had left something of Crispian's on the boy's body, he could have been traced and charged with the murder. It wouldn't have mattered if anyone had seen me either, because Crispian and I are superficially alike. And it would have been easy to have stolen something from his room—a cufflink, perhaps.

He was always vain as a cat about the way he looked and dressed. Even in the fortress with the Bulgarian armies bombing the town and people starting to worry about food supplies, he donned a dinner jacket each night, with studs in the cuffs. People make jokes about the British dressing for dinner in the jungle to preserve standards, but it's exactly what Crispian did in Edirne. Gil Martlet did too, but that was because he wanted to go to bed with Crispian. Each to his own brand of gratification. As for Crispian's feelings about Gil, I never had a clue, because he gave nothing away. Personally, I always thought him a cold fish when it came to emotions.

The idea of committing a crime in Crispian's name—of arranging for him to be charged with some serious transgression—took firm root in my mind. So, when I got to know the Jewish musicians and the Turkish extremists, I didn't tell them my real name. I said I was Crispian Cadence. And from there, I took pains to let it be known that I and my companions desperately wanted to get out of Edirne, that we would do practically anything to return to England. We would pay handsomely, I said hopefully. When that brought no response, I amended it to say we would do anything at all that would lead to our freedom. Living in the fort, alongside the soldiers and the Pasha's aides, was very tedious; there was no privacy to speak of. Everyone knew everyone else's business.

At first I thought there were no Bulgarian spies inside Edirne or, if there were, they had not been told what I said or were not prepared to take any risks with an unknown Englishman. There was also the chance that the real meaning of what I had said had been lost in translation.

But shortly after the Bulgar armies surrounded Edirne, one of the extremists I had met approached me with a proposition. He was quite a young man, formerly a student, I believe, although I have no idea what his nationality was. Speaking in fragmented English he managed to explain he had friends outside Edirne who would pay very well indeed for information about the workings of the fortress and the movements of the Pasha's men. It might not be payment in actual money, I was to understand, but in the creating of a safe passage out of the town and onto a cargo ship for myself and the other Englishmen. That was what I wanted, yes?

'Yes,' I said very emphatically.

For the next ten days, working with infinite care and patience, I began to feed this man details of life inside the fort. The times of guard duty on the main entrance, the hours when there were only a couple of men guarding and when the guard changed over. He said something about those being vulnerable times. Later I managed to get into the Pasha's room when no one was around, and stole a file of letters, which I passed on. I have no idea what the letters said—they might simply have been lists of provisions or dull records—but the very fact that I was prepared to court such danger added to my credibility as a spy.

Still pretending to be Crispian, I then deliberately became careless. I handed over papers in public places, I behaved with furtive nervousness, and I let damning remarks drop among my Jewish acquaintances, then looked guiltily around as if to see who had heard or understood. After a time I got quite annoyed that no one did anything, because there I was, spying away for all I was worth, passing on information about the workings of the fortress, and nobody did a damn thing to stop me.

What I wasn't prepared for—what I don't think anyone could have been prepared for—was that my plan would go so disastrously wrong; that I would be the one caught and charged as a spy. I had assumed that at some stage Crispian would be hauled off to face some kind of inquiry. Instead, they pounced on me while I was in the town, and they seemed to have been watching for me

without my realizing it. Also—this was a bitter blow—
they addressed me by my real name. When and how they
discovered I wasn't Crispian I have no idea, and it no
longer seems to matter.

There were four of them and there was no possibility
of resisting them. Even if I could have got away, where
would I have gone? A bewildered, slightly angry air of
innocence was clearly my best attitude, except that I didn't
even get chance for that. They half dragged me to a dim
cellar with the smell of stale sweat emanating from the
walls. Then they locked the door and went away.

I tried the door at once, of course, rattling it and
shouting furiously to be let out, but the room was too far
below the ground for anyone to hear me, and the door
was massively thick oak, with a lock that resisted all my
attempts to smash it.

I sat down in a corner of the room and wondered
what they would do to me.

Edirne, 1912

The Pasha's guards took Crispian, Gil and the reluctant
Raif to a tall old building, marching them through a
low archway into a large square, enclosed on all sides by
rearing stone walls. At one end were a group of about a
dozen men, all seated at a long table. There was an air of
hasty tribunal about the situation.

'Dear God,' said Gil softly, 'it's like a court.'

'What does he say?' said Crispian, as a youngish man,
clearly the leader, stood up and began to address incom-
prehensible words directly to them.

'That they have no quarrel with us, but that the one
who is of your family has sinned against the ancient law
of treachery and betrayal.' Raif sent a glance of apology to
Crispian. 'I know it sounds biblical, but I told you these
people keep to the old ways.' He listened for a moment,

then said, 'We're being told that if we try to interfere we will be asked to leave. They're being quite polite about it.'

'Oh, good,' said Gil sarcastically.

'Are they going to try Jamie?'

'I think so. They will regard it as a solemn ceremony.'

'But is this kind of proceeding permitted?' demanded Crispian. 'I mean—is it lawful? Can't we call in some kind of authority?'

'Mr Cadence, we're not in England where you can call for policemen or lawyers. Edirne is being besieged by half a dozen countries, all of them our enemies who want to destroy it. These people believe your cousin sold secrets to those enemies. I doubt you would find a single person in this city who would lift a finger to help him.'

'But he's innocent,' said Crispian, helplessly.

'Is he? Can you be sure of that?' Raif turned away and Crispian looked at Gil, who shrugged as if to say, Don't look at me, I don't know if he's innocent or not.

The men at the table had been murmuring to one another, but quite suddenly they sat up straighter and turned their heads to a door in a corner of the square. It was flung open and Jamie was brought out. Crispian had been having wild ideas of somehow rushing the men around the table and snatching Jamie away, but he saw at once it would be impossible. Jamie was heavily guarded, and his ankles and wrists were manacled.

'He's very frightened,' he said softly to Gil.

'So would I be in his shoes. He's managing not to show it, though. They'll respect that.'

But in the rapid interchange of words that followed, it did not seem to Crispian as if Jamie was being accorded much respect at all. Raif translated as much as possible, but at times the dialogue was so fast it was difficult for him to keep up.

'Also,' he said, 'the leader speaks with a strong...' He paused, clearly searching for the word.

'Accent? Patois?'

'Yes. I cannot follow it all.'

But what they could all follow was that the men around the table were now nodding solemnly and raising their right hands. The leader made a show of counting the hands, then walked to the centre of the square, standing directly in front of Jamie. One of the older men joined him.

'He is to act as interpreter for your cousin,' said Raif. 'See, they are beckoning us to go a little nearer so we can hear what's being said. But I'm very much afraid they've agreed he's guilty and they're going to pass sentence.'

A silence fell on the square. Then came the words, then the voice of the translator.

'James Cadence, we find you guilty of spying. Of selling or giving away information about our country in a time of war—information that could lead to its enemies possessing the country. Therefore you will suffer the punishment our fathers meted out to those found guilty of betraying our country and our people to enemies.' A pause. 'The ancient rule sets down that whichever part of the body committed the sin shall be cut out.' Then, as cold horror washed over Crispian, the man said, 'Since you are guilty of speaking secrets that would aid our enemies, tonight at sunset your tongue will be cut from your mouth so you can never speak again.'

CHAPTER TWENTY-EIGHT

The Present

JAN MALIK HAD BEEN glad to keep out of all the gossip and speculation surrounding the death of Clem Poulter.

He was not asked to give evidence at the inquest, and he had only been questioned by the police in the most cursory way. This was fair enough; he had met Poulter on only a couple of occasions. But for the sake of politeness and Amy Haywood he went to the hearing, sitting quietly at the back of the little public gallery. Amy was with her grandmother, who gave evidence of having found the body and was clearly distressed by the whole thing. Jan, who had half-wondered whether to ask Amy to have lunch with him afterwards, saw it would not be appropriate.

Amy smiled at him in a subdued, half-guilty way, as if she thought a smile might be out of place on such a sombre occasion. She had abandoned the jeans and cheesecloth, and was wearing a black pinstripe trouser suit and cream silk shirt, which made her look unexpectedly responsible. Her hair was brushed into a shining waterfall and clipped back. But there was still the impression that she had not been cut from quite the same cloth as the majority of her species. Jan studied her covertly, supposing she was linked up to some grubby young man in Durham, who made selfish and careless love to her half the night and did not appreciate her.

Immediately after the inquest, back at the Red Lion he scribbled a brief note to her, explaining he would be travelling around over the next few days in search of more traces of Ambrosian plainchant in the area. He would be back at the end of the week, he said, and maybe they could meet up for a drink if she was still in Upper Bramley. He wrote four drafts of this without hitting the right note of casual friendliness, and was about to embark on a fifth when he realized he was taking a great deal of trouble over a casual acquaintance. After this he folded the current version in an envelope, found her grandmother's address in the phone book and posted the note before he could change his mind.

Amy thus satisfactorily dealt with, he set off to scour the surrounding villages. He took the sketch he had made of the glass shard found at St Anselm's, along with the scrap of music notation. The photographs Amy had taken were in the same envelope. Amy. There he was, back again with his feline *sui generis* girl.

The first three villages he explored yielded no clues, but on his third day he found a church about twelve miles east of Upper Bramley, dedicated to St Luke the Hospitaller. Prowling absorbedly through mildewed parish records provided by a helpful churchwarden, Jan found something that delighted him.

It was a brief account of how, at Christmas 1920, St Luke's Choir (mixed) had travelled by charabanc to join the choir (male) of St Michael's, Upper Bramley, at the dedication of a newly installed organ at St Anselm's in Priors Bramley. This appeared to have been quite an event, and the diligent chronicler—Jan thought it might be the choirmaster—recorded that the choirs had joined together for two hymns, *Nunc, Sancte, nobis Spiritus* and

Rerum, Deus tenax vigor, which Mr Cadence had particularly requested be sung.

Jan, who had been bent over the small table in the vestry, sat back, smiling. There were only four hymns universally attributed to St Ambrose, and these were two of them. Good for you, St Luke's, he thought, making notes of dates and names for further investigation, because he had not expected to find such clear evidence of the plainchant being used into the twentieth century. It was a strong tradition of the Roman Catholic Church, and the churches in this area were almost entirely Anglican. Even if the notation on the St Anselm's stained glass was the Sanctus, it would most likely be a left-over fragment from the Popish days before Henry VIII swept Catholicism out of his realm.

The first hymn, the *Nunc, Sancte, nobis Spiritus,* appeared to have taken an extra verse unto itself for the occasion: a stanza from Wordsworth's famous poem 'Tintern Abbey', which Mr Cadence had also asked be included. The diligent chronicler, clearly wishing to record all the details, had written the extra verse out in full:

> I have learned
> To look on nature, not as in the hour
> Of thoughtless youth; but hearing oftentimes
> The still, sad music of humanity,
> Not harsh nor grating, though of ample power
> To chasten and subdue.

The still, sad music of humanity. It was the strange troubling line on the plaque in St Anselm's and, viewed logically, it was not a particularly unusual or remarkable find. Some long-ago member of the Cadence family had wanted to include a few lines from a favourite poem at a special church service. Where's the big deal? Jan's students might have said.

But Jan was suddenly curious about this unknown Cadence gentleman. Nineteen twenty. For a moment, his hands still resting lightly on the faded pages, the scents of old timbers all round him, he felt the past brush against his mind. Nineteen twenty, with half the world still recovering from the Great War.

Who were you? he thought, staring back at the faded, slightly foxed pages. And why did that piece of Wordsworth mean so much to you that you not only had it set to music that had virtually vanished, but you also caused a line from it to be engraved into the fabric of the church?

❋ ❋ ❋

Jan's curiosity about this enigmatic Cadence man took strong hold of him over the next couple of days. He reached Upper Bramley and the Red Lion too late that night to do anything about it, but early next morning he headed for the local newspaper offices. If the donation and dedication of St Anselm's organ had been an event worthy of those records, surely it had been worthy of an article in the *Bramley Advertiser*.

It was not really part of his research; it was merely an interesting byway that might sprinkle in a few extra details about the area's tradition of plainchant, and it would not add anything. But it was all bound up with the deserted village—the desolate poisoned Priors Bramley—and Jan wanted to know more.

The *Advertiser*'s staff were helpful. The paper had been in existence in 1920, they said, in fact it had started in 1908. Oh yes, all issues had been preserved on microfiche—that had been done ten or fifteen years ago when the title was bought by a big newspaper group. If Dr Malik wanted the actual newspapers, they were stored at the local library. Mr Poulter—oh dear, poor Mr Poulter—had been meticulous about record-keeping.

'I really only need to look at a few copies,' said Jan. 'I'll try the library first.' He told himself this was because it would be quicker, not because Amy might still be working there.

She was not—she'd left to concentrate on her holiday essays—but one of the girls on the desk thought it would be fine for Dr Malik to have access to the newspaper archives.

'We're taking day-to-day decisions as we think best until Mr Poulter is replaced.'

'I was so sorry about his death,' said Jan conventionally.

'So were we. He'd been here all his working life—well, you could say the library and Upper Bramley actually *were* his life, I suppose. Sad in a way, isn't it? Still, all the old papers are in the cellars. The police were there a week or so back—looking for clues about those bodies. I don't think they found anything useful, though.'

'Do they know who the bodies are yet?'

'If they have, nobody's been told. They didn't take any of our records away and they didn't say the public couldn't have access.'

As Jan surveyed the archived copies of the *Bramley Advertiser* in the dingy cellars, the unshaded electric light casting a hard radiance, the feeling of the past reaching out swept over him again. This is how history preserves itself, he thought as he began to turn the brittle pages. Not because anyone folds it in camphor or lavender, or scatters magic charms in and out of the creases, but because so much of it gets written down. Originally it was recorded in home-made ink on curling brown parchment, then in newsprint. Nowadays it's hard disks and memory sticks and video tapes. As he scanned the headlines and the articles about local events, he thought this was the real heart of history. This parish-pump news, this miscellany of trivia. This England...

The *Bramley Advertiser* had originally been a fort-nightly publication and had not achieved the dizzying heights of being produced once a week until 1922. Jan started his search at the beginning of 1920. The dedication of the new organ would have been a significant event in the villages. Surely the paper would have reported it?

But it had not. He went through the entire batch of papers from the start of 1918 to the end of 1922 but found nothing. This was vaguely irritating, but he was sufficiently used to dead ends in research not to be too daunted. It was possible his eye had missed a small para-graph. But even if he had, it did not matter.

But the image of that shadowy man who had clearly cared deeply about music and had found some reso-nance in Wordsworth's words had lodged in his mind. He wanted to know more. It would have to be the digital age after all.

The microfiche at the *Bramley Advertiser* was available, and Jan was shown to a small room with a table, chair, and desktop viewer. It took him some time to fathom the database system, but eventually he mastered it, and typed in 'Cadence', and also 'Cadence Manor' as search requests.

This elicited quite a number of references to the Cadence family in general, and Jan read them diligently. In the main they were reports of how Sir Julius Cadence or his wife had opened some local event, or smudgy photographs of parties at the manor house. But there was nothing linking them to St Anselm's, and mentions of the family itself trickled to almost nothing by 1930. Perhaps the upcoming generation had simply married and gone away, or perhaps the men of the family had died in the Great War. There must be a war memorial, and he should see if any Cadences were listed on it.

He was just thinking he would have to admit to a dead end as far as the *Bramley Advertiser* was concerned when his eye was caught by a much later article that the search request had turned up. It was headlined 'Distressing Incident at Cadence Manor', and the date was the late 1940s. It could not have anything to do with what he was looking for, but none the less he called it up on the viewer's screen.

It was not a very long article. Jan skimmed it, at first with only slight interest, then with growing attention.

DISTRESSING INCIDENT AT CADENCE MANOR

Police today issued a statement that a violent assault had been made on a local girl in the grounds of Cadence Manor—the ancestral home of the once-famous banking family.

The assault on young Brenda Ford (19) has shocked the community, and Miss Ford, interviewed briefly at her home, could only tell our reporter that she had been on her way to her home, having spent an evening with two friends in Priors Bramley village. She was taking the well-known local short cut around the manor towards Mordwich Meadow, intending to cross Crinoline Bridge, when the man attacked her. Miss Ford, who suffered some bruises and a sprained wrist, managed to beat him off and to run away.

Since recent reports that German spies could still be hiding out in rural backwaters, there has been some concern that Miss Ford's attacker may have been just such a person. However, police have said this is very unlikely and have advised the public not to panic.

The article was interesting for its insight into the mood of English village life in the years after the Second World War, with people still suspicious of strangers, and any incidents of this kind instantly put down to Germans unable to make their way back to their own country. Probably if it had not been for that, the incident would not have been reported.

But the real interest was in the attached photograph. It was clearly an existing snapshot that the paper had made use of, and it showed Brenda Ford in a garden. She was smiling rather warily, as if she did not much like having her photo taken but as if she was prepared to indulge whoever was wielding the camera.

Allowing for the difference in ages and hairstyles, it might have been a photo of someone Jan had just recently met. Amy's grandmother. Ella Haywood.

❊ ❊ ❊

'It wasn't part of my research,' said Jan, seated opposite Amy in a corner of the Red Lion. 'But I thought you might be interested in it.'

'So that's my great-grandmother,' said Amy, propping up the printout Jan had made from the microfiche, and studying it with interest. 'I never knew her—I think she died ages before I was born. She's very like Gran, isn't she?'

'Yes.'

'Poor old great-grandmamma Brenda, being attacked and thinking it was a German spy,' said Amy, still looking at the printed photo. 'Could I borrow this to show Gran? I'm sure she'd be interested. I don't think she's got any photographs of her mother. Actually, I don't think she's got any of her father, either. If she has, I've never seen them. I could let you have it back.'

Jan started to say he did not particularly want the printout back, then realized her returning it would set up a further meeting and said, 'All right.'

'And now tell me how you got on grubbing around the churches for music and musical legends,' said Amy.

'I think I found the source of that engraving at St Anselm's,' Jan told her. 'At least, I found a reference to it.' He told her about the report he had found at St Luke's, describing how the choirs had joined forces, and how some unknown Cadence man had apparently requested the Wordsworth stanza be set to music and added on.

'That's brilliant,' said Amy, her eyes glowing. 'I'd love to know who he was, wouldn't you? I know the Cadences aren't the last of the Romanovs or anything, but they're starting to sound really romantic and mysterious. Imagine it: they were once a famous banking house, only they went bust, and when you think about that crumbling old manor inside the poisoned village...'

'You shouldn't be studying archaeology, you should be writing Gothic fiction,' said Jan, smiling. 'When did the Cadences go bust?'

'I don't know. They were going strong in the early 1900s, I think, because there's a lot of references to them in the library archive stuff.'

'And in 1920 one of them donated an organ to St Anselm. Don't laugh at me, one of us was going to make that pun sooner or later.'

'Well, anyhow, they're not around, now,' said Amy, still grinning. 'Maybe the Wall Street Crash got them. When was that?'

'In 1928 or 1929, I think.'

'D'you know what I'm thinking about that plaque?'

'That it probably came off the organ itself?'

'Exactly. And I think,' said Amy, 'that I might go back to St Anselm's to see if there's anything else among the rubble. If the police have stopped searching Cadence Manor I might see if I can get into the grounds as well.'

'Why the manor particularly?'

'I'd like to find out a bit more about the Cadences. And houses say a lot about their era and the people who lived in them. Even ordinary houses like we live in.'

Jan said, 'Benjamin Britten wrote an opera based on Henry James's story *Owen Wingrave*. The theme running through it is "Listen to the house".'

'I love that,' said Amy, at once. 'What does the house say?'

'The central character comes from a family of soldiers, but at heart he's a pacifist, and he struggles with that while the voice of the house tells him he should fight in the Great War like his ancestors would have done.'

Amy said, 'Even ordinary houses have a voice about people who've lived in them.'

'They do, don't they? I've got a tiny house on the edge of Oxford, which is supposed to have been a farm labourer's cottage when it was built,' said Jan. 'I keep meaning to track down its origins.'

'You should,' said Amy, enthusiastically, trying not to take too much notice of the fact that he had said 'I' and not 'we'. 'Start with land searches and work back.'

'You do dash from one thing to the next, don't you? Like quicksilver.'

'Well—'

'Don't worry about it. Quicksilver is very attractive.'

'Really?' said Amy.

Jan had been about to reach for the Red Lion's bar food menu but he looked across the table at her. As their eyes met, he said, very softly, 'Oh yes, really.' Then, before she could think how to respond, he said, 'It's half-past twelve. Shall we have some lunch while we're here?'

CHAPTER TWENTY-NINE

AMY WAS PLEASED to have the small piece of family history from the *Bramley Advertiser* to show Gran. She had been a bit glum since Clem Poulter's death, poor old Gran; several times Amy had caught her staring blankly into space, and even Gramps said, 'My word, old girl, you're looking a bit pasty-faced these days.' Amy thought for a moment that Gran would throw something at him, which might have been disastrous since she was chopping parsley at the time. But if Amy had been married to a man who called her 'old girl' and said she was 'pasty-faced', she would have tipped the entire saucepan of parsley sauce over him and added the gammon steaks as well.

Gran merely said, 'Oh, I'm just a bit tired. And I was very upset at Clem's death,' and Gramps looked contrite and said at once that of course she was upset, he had been forgetting about poor old Clem. How about Ella coming along to the rehearsal that evening, just to cheer her up?

'No thank you,' said Gran, a bit too quickly. Then, seeing his expression, said, 'But it was a very kind suggestion, Derek.'

Gramps went off to his rehearsal, singing about the flowers that bloomed in the spring, but doing so in a muted voice out of respect to Clem Poulter. He would not be very late back, he said.

Gran glanced at Amy and said, 'Your grandfather and I have been married for forty years, and it's difficult to be enthusiastic about light opera for forty years. He's an enthusiast, though.'

Amy, who had already forgiven Gramps for the 'old girl' comment, thought this was actually one of the endearing things about him; he loved his rehearsals and the performances with almost a childlike delight. She hoped if she was ever married to someone for forty years she would still be able to share his enthusiasms, whatever they were. Even if they were grubbing around churches for fragments of obscure music and arcane legends...

By way of taking Gran's mind off Clem Poulter's death, Amy fetched the printed article about Brenda Ford—it was difficult to think of the eager smiling girl in the photo as anybody's great-grandmother. She wore her hair in a roily bob and looked as if she might start singing a Vera Lynn song any minute.

'She wasn't hurt in the attack,' explained Amy, passing it over. 'But I was really interested to see her. I don't think you've ever shown me any photos of her.'

'I don't believe there are any,' said Gran. 'Things get lost when you move house, of course.'

She read the article and looked at the photograph for a long time, and the spooky thing to Amy was that Gran seemed to turn whiter and whiter as she did so. Oh God, was she going to have another of those peculiar turns?

'Attacked,' said Gran at last, and Amy heard how she was trying to sound normal. 'Attacked in the grounds of Cadence Manor. How shocking. It doesn't sound like a serious attack, though, does it?'

'I bet it was only the German spy scare that got it into the paper at all,' said Amy.

Gran appeared to make a huge effort. She handed the printout back to Amy as if she wanted to put it away from her as quickly as possible. 'I don't know much about my mother's life,' she said. 'She died when I was still in my teens. But I do know people weren't always very kind to her. They made up cruel stories.'

'What kind of stories?'

'Oh, the kind of stories people did make up in those days if a woman lived on her own.'

It sounded to Amy as if Great-grandmamma Brenda might have been a bit of a goer, which was rather intriguing. If that was so, it was small wonder Gran never mentioned her. She was quite old-fashioned when it came to morals.

❀ ❀ ❀

After Amy had gone up to her room Ella sat by the fire, thinking.

Life could be extremely unkind. Just when you thought you had got rid of all the dangers that might disrupt your neat and orderly life—when you had gone so far as to feed poisonous leaves to one of your oldest friends and bury fifty years' worth of his diaries in your garden—something came bouncing out of nowhere and smacked you in the face. It was deeply unfair. It was even more unfair that a fragment of her mother's life should make its appearance on the scene, like a gibbering and accusatory ghost.

But there was no cause for panic, because there was nothing in that article that might cause people to see a link between Ella's mother and the Cadences. Even though people had whispered about Brenda Ford being a bit of a slut, they had not actually known much about her. So logically it could not matter that Dr Malik had found that old newspaper article. Or could it? Clearly Amy had been interested, and if she or Malik started delving a bit deeper…

Ella's heart bumped into its erratic rhythm at the thought of what those delvings might uncover. Three murders. The recent one of Clem Poulter, and the two in the past. Bizarrely, it was the two in the past that caused her heart to skitter like a scrabbling rodent: the death of the man the day Priors Bramley was poisoned and the death of Serena Cadence in her dim, over-scented room inside the manor.

❃ ❃ ❃

By the time Ella was fourteen her mother was a complete recluse.

She said repeatedly that the scars from the Geranos had ruined her life. She had become an object of pity, she said, and there was no point in life any longer.

'I'm marked forever because I caused Serena Cadence's death,' she said. 'I'm marked almost exactly as she was. There's a terrible justice in that, Ella.'

Ella thought something might be done about the scars. There were all kinds of plastic surgery procedures nowadays, she said. Why couldn't they make an appointment with their GP to ask about it?

Her mother refused point-blank. In any case, the law would eventually catch up with her, she said, no matter what the doctors did to her. One day people would find out she had killed Serena Cadence and then they would shut her away forever.

'...Even though she was a mean-spirited, cold-soulled bitch who deserved to die. And they say there's always something a murderer misses. Remember that, Ella, in the future, when you think you're safe. Things happen— even after years and years. Somebody says something or remembers something, and people put two and two together. Remember that.'

Ella tried to say that what had happened had been an accident. Mum had not meant to smash that frowsty old woman's head against the marble chimney breast. She herself had not meant to push the man into the derelict chimney shaft.

'Didn't I?' said her mother, and quite suddenly and terrifyingly there was a sly glint in her eyes. 'And didn't you? How do either of us know what the other did or meant?'

'I do know,' said Ella, trying not to feel frightened, trying to beat down the memories. 'And even if it did all come out—it won't, but say it did—we'd just tell the truth. People would believe us.'

'No, they wouldn't. I'm the local bad girl. They'd like to have something against me.' This was said with a kind of gloomy relish. 'They'd like to see me in prison.'

'I wouldn't be put in prison, would I?'

'No, but you'd be put in one of those young offenders' hostels. It'd be years and years before they let you out.'

After a while Ella stopped trying to reason with her. She went off to school each morning, thankful to be out of the dingy little house and out of range of her mother's angry despair and defeat, and thankful, as well, to be away from the constant reminders. I'm a murderer, you're a murderer...sometimes her mother's words beat such a fierce tattoo inside her brain, Ella thought it might explode.

And then, shortly before her sixteenth birthday, her mother suddenly changed tack. She sat down at the little kitchen table, straightened her shoulders almost in the way she used to, and said, 'I'm going to confess.'

'Confess?' Ella had been making toast for breakfast before setting off for school, and she did not immediately understand. Confession conjured up vague images of two girls at school who were Catholics and had to confess sins every week. 'Confess what?'

'I'm going to confess that I murdered Serena Cadence.'

It could not be allowed. Ella was conscious of a tumble of confusing emotions that morning, but out of the jumble, one definite feeling came uppermost. Her mother absolutely could not be allowed to confess. It probably would not be taken very seriously—it was a long time ago, and Brenda Ford had since been damaged physically and mentally by the Geranos—but it might be looked into to some extent. And once that happened, once the police started delving into the past, they might discover there had not been one murder, but two.

That morning Ella instinctively made a start to shut her mother up. She crushed up three of the tranquillizers prescribed by the GP and stirred them into the cup of tea her mother always drank at breakfast. This could not be regarded as a long-term solution, but it could be used to send her mother into a drowsy stupor for hours at a time. It would do until Ella could either talk her mother out of her mad idea, or...

Or what?

Or until she could find a way to keep her mother quiet forever.

❀ ❀ ❀

When she was seventeen Ella opted to stay at school for an extra year to take what the school called 'business studies'. It was a year-long course, consisting of shorthand and typing and a smattering of bookkeeping. The school was pleased it could offer this to girls who did not want to try for university places. One or two boys took the course as well, generally because knowing shorthand was useful for the police force or journalism, but in the main, it was aimed at girls. The teachers, while conscientiously proclaiming themselves in sympathy with the vibrant sixties and equality for women, said it remained the best thing for girls. The idea was for them to work as shorthand typists or secretaries for a few years until they settled down with some nice man. Ella's mother, told about the plan, said dispiritedly it was no doubt a good idea since Ella would have to make her way in the world.

Ella found the course quite hard, particularly the book-keeping classes, but she persevered. Clem was going to try for a university place so he had gone up into the sixth form to take A levels. He would get a Bachelor of Arts degree and he might become a writer or a journalist, he thought.

Veronica left school altogether and got a job behind the make-up counter at the local pharmacist. She said it was to mark time because eventually she wanted to work in fashion or the beauty industry. She quite fancied fashion journalism, actually. Ella did not think selling cheap make-up was likely to get Veronica onto the staff of *Vogue* or into a Mary Quant boutique, but she did not say this in case it sounded bitchy. Several people commented that Veronica seemed to have a lot of boyfriends and hoped she was not heading for an unfortunate experience. Still, working in a chemist's ought to be useful on that score.

Ella thought she might sort of have a boyfriend herself by this time, because shortly after her eighteenth birthday Derek Haywood, from the fifth form, started to take her to the pictures once a week. This was quite gratifying because his parents lived in a big detached house, and Derek was going to study for some accountancy exam or other, which sounded important. Accountants were professional people who wore smart suits and had their own offices. Veronica thought Ella was mad to go out with somebody who was almost two years younger, but she entered into the spirit of things and brought make-up samples from the cosmetic counter for Ella to try. She said Ella should wear mascara because her eyelashes were a bit pale. Men liked the sooty-eyed look, even if it was only

Derek Haywood from the fifth form, said Veronica. But Ella thought the mascara made her look like a panda and Derek now seemed to think it a settled thing that they went to the cinema every Saturday anyway, so sooty eyes would not make much difference.

At intervals her mother remembered that she was going to confess to killing Lady Cadence, but each time this happened Ella doped her tea with tranquillizers. The GP never questioned the constant repeat prescriptions. When Ella visited him to discuss it, he said it was all very sad, and he was not surprised poor Mrs Ford suffered from depression so severely. Ella should try to get her to go out. He could refer her for psychiatric help, if Ella wanted, but there was likely to be a long waiting list.

'Oh, I don't think she needs that,' said Ella, terrified. 'But the tranquillizers do help quite a lot. I'm very careful that she doesn't get dependent on them.'

The doctor said that was important, wrote the prescription, and was relieved that there was a caring intelligent daughter to cope with poor Mrs Ford, whose condition did not really fall into any NHS pigeonhole.

The business studies course was nearing its end when Ella went home one afternoon and found her mother huddled on the settee, her face twisted with pain, moaning.

'What's wrong?' said Ella, hanging up her coat on the back of the door. It would be annoying if her mother decided to be ill tonight because it was Derek's last day at school before he started in the local council offices with his accountancy career. They were going to have a small celebration.

'Pain—stomach,' said Ella's mother. 'Dreadful. Can you call a doctor?'

Ella sat down and studied her mother thoughtfully. She looked quite ill—she was flushed and her eyes were bloodshot. A bowl stood on the floor near her. 'I was sick earlier,' said Brenda, seeing Ella look towards this. 'I thought I might be sick again and not get to the sink this time.' A fresh spasm of pain twisted her again and she hunched over, gasping.

'I think it's appendicitis,' she said, when the spasm eased a bit. 'The pain's in the right place for it.'

Appendicitis. That was something that was easily dealt with, providing it was caught in time, Ella knew that. But what if it were not caught in time? A sudden image of what it might be like if Mum were not here glinted tantalizingly. No more living on a knife-edge, worrying if her mother would start talking again about confessing to murder. No more lying to the GP to get extra tranquillizers, and surreptitiously stirring them into cups of tea. She would be safe for ever—safe in this little house, because she was eighteen, about to finish her business course and get a job.

She said, 'How long have you been like this?' These days Mum was always still in bed when Ella went to school, so she seldom saw her until the evening.

'Felt a bit seedy yesterday. Didn't want to worry you, though. Then last night the pain started...It's been getting stronger since breakfast. I'm fairly sure—' She broke off to deal with another wave of pain. 'I'm fairly sure it is appendicitis,' she said after a few moments. 'So you need to get a doctor—ambulance.'

'Yes, of course.' The cottage did not have a phone. Brenda had often said they should have one, but Ella had always discouraged it because she was frightened that while she was at school her mother might suddenly ring the police and tell them about Lady Cadence's death. She said, 'I'll go down to the callbox and phone the surgery.'

'Quicker to ask next door,' said Mum. 'Now they're on the phone they won't mind.'

'They're away,' said Ella at once. 'Don't you remember? But it won't take me long to go down to the callbox. D'you want anything while I'm gone?'

'No—'

'You'd better have a hot-water bottle,' said Ella. 'And aspirin.'

The kettle took a long time to boil on the old-fashioned stove. Ella watched it and thought if this house really did belong to her, she would try to make a smart shining kitchen with a modern cooker. She took her time about filling the bottle, then dissolved two aspirin in water. After that she fetched a blanket from the airing cupboard. Mum seemed feverish, she said, and you had to keep warm when you were feverish. By this time it was after six, which meant the surgery would be closed.

'I'll go down to the phone box now,' said Ella.

Phone boxes were notoriously unreliable. Even in a law-abiding place like Upper Bramley they were occasionally vandalized, and even if they were not, they were often out of order. People said it was a sad joke how you could never find a phone box that was working.

The phone box on the corner looked all right, but the receiver cord was very frayed. Ella had brought change with her and she dialled Derek to explain she might not be able to meet him because her mother was poorly. No, it was nothing very serious, she thought, but she was going to ask the doctor to come out, just to be sure.

'Can I help at all?' said Derek, clearly a bit nervous at being confronted with illness, but obviously aware that it was polite to ask.

'Oh, no, I can manage,' said Ella. 'It's nice of you to offer, though.'

'Will you still be able to come to the pictures on Saturday? It's *West Side Story*.'

'Yes, I should think so,' said Ella. She rang off, considered the frayed cord, then tugged on it as hard as she could. It frayed a bit more, then came partly away from the receiver. At first look it did not seem too bad, but when she lifted the receiver there was no dial tone. Good. Very good indeed.

It was easy to tell her mother she had made the call—the line had been very crackly, she said, but she thought she had got through and left a message for a doctor to call. Oh yes, she had stressed the urgency. Well no, she had not actually mentioned the possibility of appendicitis because they were not sure about that. It might turn out to be just a tummy bug. In the meantime, she would refill the hot-water bottle, and perhaps Mum could try some warm milk with a dash of brandy?

It was eleven o'clock before Ella finally agreed to try phoning again. The message mustn't have got through, she said. Yes, she would go out to phone again, of course she would.

This time, she walked all the way to the High Street to the phone box near the post office. It took fifteen minutes. She dialled the number of their doctor's surgery, and there was a series of click and buzzes, which Ella supposed was the call being transferred to whoever was on night duty. When a man's voice answered, she said she was a bit worried about her mother who was being sick and having a bit of stomach pain. Yes, she looked as if her temperature might be higher than normal. She did not have a ther-mometer, but her mother was certainly flushed and her skin felt hot.

'Probably no more than a bug,' said the voice at the other end. 'How much of an emergency is it, do you think?'

'She didn't want me to call you,' said Ella. 'But I said better to be on the safe side.'

'Give her a good dose of soda bicarbonate or AlkaSeltzer. Something of that kind,' said the voice. 'And plenty of fluids. I'll put her on the rounds for tomorrow morning. But you'd better ring back if it gets worse during the night.'

'Thank you very much.'

It did get worse. Shortly after 1 a.m. Ella's mother became delirious. She began to talk about the past, the words pouring out, as if a dam had given way. Ella sat in the little bedroom, helplessly listening, wanting to shout at her mother to stop, because she did not want to hear any of this, she did not want to know about it.

But towards three the torrent of words slowed to a meaningless mumble, and Ella breathed a sigh of relief. She fetched a bowl of tepid water to sponge her mother's face and neck. The Geranos scars stood out like angry raised lumps, but there were mottled patches between them and Brenda seemed to be having difficulty in breathing. Ella nearly gave in and ran out of the house to hammer on the neighbour's door, to ask them to call 999 for an ambulance. They were not away, of course, that had just been a delaying tactic. But she did not. She sat it out.

By the time the doctor arrived it was mid-morning and Brenda Ford was deeply unconscious. An ambulance was summoned. Ella, crying real tears by this time, went in the ambulance, carrying a small bag with overnight things.

The bag was brought home unopened. Brenda Ford died that night from sepsis brought on, the doctors believed, by a ruptured appendix. There was a post mortem and an inquest, and everyone was very kind. Veronica's parents asked Ella to stay with them, and Derek Haywood's parents asked her to their house for meals or to spend a Sunday.

It was very tragic to lose a mother at such an early age. Everyone said so. What nobody said, because nobody knew, was that it was actually very liberating for Ella. She no longer had to worry about anyone knowing her mother was a murderess. Going through her mother's papers after the funeral, she consigned everything to the fire. There must be no clues anywhere.

She was over eighteen and legally allowed to inherit the little house outright. Armed with a certificate for 120 w.p.m. shorthand and 60 w.p.m. typing, she got a job in the typing pool at the local education offices. She did not have much money but she had enough. There was a tiny insurance policy on her mother's life, which helped, and she was able to whitewash all the walls in the house. Derek's mother gave her some spare bales of curtain fabric.

Eventually Ella and Derek married. Ella sold the cottage and his parents gave them £2,000 as a wedding present towards a better house. Ella kept it spick and span, and everyone said she was a wonderful wife and Derek was very lucky. Life became placid and safe. It stayed that way for a great many years.

Until now. Until Jan Malik found an old newspaper article—an article Ella had not even known existed—and Amy, with the careless impetuosity of youth, started asking questions. It was becoming plain that Amy would have to be watched very carefully.

CHAPTER THIRTY

T HREE MURDERS, THOUGHT Ella. The man from St Anselm's, Serena Cadence, and Clem Poulter. I committed two of them. My mother committed the third.

For the hundredth time she went over everything she had done, but she could not see that there was anything to trip her up. Clem's death had been firmly put down as 'Accidental' and the file had been closed. Ella did not think the coroner's verdict was likely to be re-examined. As for the two bodies, the police were said to be going on with their enquiries, but most people seemed to think the case would soon be closed. A man at Derek's office said 'Death of two unknown men' would be the eventual verdict. Derek relayed this information to Ella and Amy.

'It looks as if the excitement's all over,' he said. 'I don't think they've identified either of the bodies. Probably they were just a couple of tramps who were hiding out in the ruins.'

'It'll go down as a Bramley mystery,' said Amy. 'People will come on murder weekends and anoraks will try to solve it for years ahead. In about a hundred years' time there'll be television programmes, re-examining the evidence and invoking technology we've never heard of, and pronouncing who the bodies were.'

'What an imagination you have,' said Derek admiringly. 'Ella, where does she get her ideas?'

'I don't know.'

'Are you both going to Poulter's funeral? I can get an hour or two clear to come with you. I think I should. I've known him since we were all at school. I'd like to pay my respects to the poor chap.'

'Of course I'm going,' said Ella. 'Amy's coming as well.'

The funeral, which was held at the local crematorium, was a gloomy affair. Veronica said it was difficult to know how to behave, because it was so ghoulish, so utterly outside one's experience. She could not stop thinking of Clem, happily stirring his fish casserole all by himself that night, planning how he would set the table for the guests who would never come.

When the coffin slid back behind the curtains and the organist struck up the final hymn, Veronica dissolved into a very showy spate of crying, which Ella thought displayed a shocking lack of self-control. Veronica always had to draw attention to herself, though. Several of the men went over to comfort her; Ella was glad Derek was not one of them.

After the service finished some people hung about hopefully, because generally at a funeral somebody would make an informal announcement about all mourners being welcome back at the house or the Red Lion to drink old so-and-so's health. But for Clem, who had no family, nobody seemed to have taken on this responsibility. Ella was annoyed with herself for not having thought of it; she could have put on a very nice little buffet lunch—Amy could have helped—and Derek could have taken an extra hour from the office to hand round glasses of wine.

As it was, Derek, who had come in his own car, went back to his office to deal with some cock-up somebody had apparently made over the planning budget, and Amy thought she had better devote what was left of the afternoon to working on one of her holiday projects. Veronica was standing in the car park, explaining to anyone who would listen that she had not driven here because she had known she would be far too upset to drive back afterwards, and ostentatiously looking up the number of the local taxi firm on her mobile phone. Ella felt bound to offer her a lift. They dropped Amy off, then went on to Veronica's house.

'Have you got time for a cup of tea or even something stronger?' said Veronica. 'We should at least raise a glass to Clem, shouldn't we?'

In Veronica's too-warm sitting room, drinking tea, Ella felt better. Life was gradually but surely sinking back into normality. Clem was out of the way with an unthreatening verdict of Accidental Death pronounced on him, and it sounded as if the police investigations into the bodies at Priors Bramley were petering out.

Veronica had finished her tea and was drinking vodka and tonic, which Ella thought a bit louche at three o'clock in the afternoon. She suddenly set down her glass and said, 'Ella, there's something rather strange about Clem's death.'

A prickle of alarm scudded across Ella's skin. 'What?'

'And the more I think about it, the stranger it seems.'

Every nerve-ending in Ella's body jangled like alarm bells, but she said, 'What kind of strange?'

Veronica appeared to take a moment to organize her thoughts, then said, 'It's Clem's diaries. They've vanished.'

The alarm bells screeched through Ella's entire body, momentarily blotting out every other sensation. Then, making a massive effort, she said with a little laugh, 'Oh, Clem's famous diaries. But they were only ever part of Clem's fantasies about becoming a writer.' Careful, she thought. Don't be too sneery. You've just been to the man's funeral: you ought to be awash with sentiment. So she added, 'Dear old Clem and his journals and jottings. But we all knew they didn't actually exist.'

'But they did,' said Veronica.

'Are you sure?' said Ella. 'How do you know?'

'Because he showed them to me one night. It was only two or three weeks ago, actually. I was quite flattered. He was usually as secretive as MI5 about anything he wrote.'

'Why did he show the diaries to you?'

'We were at his house—he was thinking of having his kitchen refitted and I was advising him on colours. Some people say I have quite a good eye for colour, you know. Oh dear, poor Clem, now he'll never have his grand new kitchen. Anyway, we had a drink or two,' said Veronica. 'Well, we had more than one or two. He got a bit maudlin and talked about how he'd been an observer of life since he was a child. He'd always lived life from the sidelines, he said. But he didn't mind, not really. He saw himself as a—what was that man's name who wrote those famous diaries hundreds of years ago?'

'Samuel Pepys?'

'That's the one. He took me up to his spare bedroom. Honestly, Ella, I've been in a few bedrooms in my time, but that's one I never expected to go into, not that it counted, because Clem was hardly—'

'You saw the diaries?' said Ella. 'You actually saw them?'

'Yes. Leather-bound notebooks, all stacked in date order. They certainly weren't fantasies, I promise you. He said they were his life's work and he talked about how he would live on through them when he was dead.'

'Did you read any of them?' demanded Ella, then realized her voice had been much too sharp.

But Veronica did not seem to notice anything wrong. She said, 'No, I didn't, but I'd have liked to, because I'll bet there was some juicy stuff in them. You remember what a shocking old busybody his father was. Always listening to people's conversations and sneaking peeks at letters if he came to the house. I remember once, my parents invited him and Clem for Christmas, and my mother said afterwards she was sure he had gone into the bedroom when he went up to the loo and looked through my father's bank statements. I bet he told Clem all kinds of things, and I bet Clem wrote them all down.'

'Such as?'

'Well, *I* don't know. Local scandals, I expect, and don't say there haven't been any, because there are scandals everywhere. Things about us, I dare say. Certainly things about me.' She gave the stupid coy giggle that always rasped on Ella. 'And there'd be things about our parents, I imagine, and your mother. In fact, very likely quite a lot of things about your mother. She was supposed to have been a bit of a girl, wasn't she?'

'No, she wasn't,' said Ella at once. 'People were unkind about her, that was all. Just because she lived on her own and my father died when I was a baby and nobody in Upper Bramley ever knew him—'

'Oh, Ella, even if you were illegitimate what does it matter?' said Veronica, sounding slightly exasperated. 'There's no shame in it these days. Good Lord, the word's almost vanished from the dictionary.'

'I was not illegitimate,' said Ella angrily. 'And anyway, how do you know Clem's diaries weren't found?'

'Because I'm the executor of his will,' said Veronica. 'Didn't you know that?'

Ella stared at her. 'I didn't, as a matter of fact,' she said. 'So?'

'So I went into the house with the solicitor straight after the inquest. The house will have to be sold, of course, and most of the money goes to various charities—education of illiterate adults and that kind of thing, mostly. But they're going to see if they can trace any relatives first. I think there's a distant cousin in Australia. The solicitor's an executor as well and he'll do most of the work, I expect, but I'm supposed to know what's going on and agree to things.'

Ella wanted to scream at the stupid woman to stop talking about trivialities, but she said, quite calmly, 'And what about the diaries?'

'They weren't in the house. I looked absolutely everywhere and they'd gone.'

'Why were you so keen to find them?' said Ella.

'Well, partly because I thought they might make spicy reading—I told you that already. But also I thought the local history society or something might have been interested in them. So I wanted to make sure the coroner's people hadn't thrown them away by mistake. Clem would have hated it if his precious diaries had been consigned to some municipal rubbish tip, you know that.'

'Yes,' said Ella. Would the silly prattling bitch never come to the point?

'I asked the solicitor about them and he checked with the coroner's office. They'd been through the house before the inquest—not a police-type examination, but they had to make sure there was nothing suspicious, nothing that might make it necessary to actually set up a police investigation.'

'Yes?'

'At first they thought I meant just a day-to-day diary,' said Veronica. 'Addresses, dentist's appointments and stuff like that. The coroner's man had found one of those by the phone. But I said no, there were at least twenty leather-bound books, and I told him where they'd been. But he said there definitely hadn't been anything like that, he'd have remembered, and he certainly wouldn't have let them be destroyed. They're not allowed to destroy anything without the executors' permission in that situation.'

'It is a bit odd,' said Ella, after a moment. 'Probably there's a perfectly ordinary explanation, though.'

'I think it's more than odd,' said Veronica. She was watching Ella. 'I think it's extraordinary and quite thought-provoking that those diaries seem to have vanished. Specially since you were the one who found Clem's body that morning. That's the really thought-provoking thing.'

❀ ❀ ❀

As Ella drove away from the over-heated, fussily furnished house, her mind was in turmoil. She was not overly worried that a solicitor and a coroner's official apparently knew about the diaries; what worried her was Veronica's sly hints that it might have been Ella herself who had taken them. Did Veronica think Ella was worried that Clem might have recorded what had happened in Priors Bramley all those years ago? If so, it was odd she had not said so. But she could not suspect Ella of anything worse than taking the diaries. She could not possibly suspect her of killing Clem. What motive would there be?

Still, it might be as well to find out exactly what was in Veronica's mind, although it was to be hoped Ella would not have to deal with Veronica in the same way she had dealt with Clem.

❀ ❀ ❀

It had been a bit naughty to tease prim, correct Ella, Veronica acknowledged that. She did not really think Ella had pinched Clem's diaries and destroyed them— there was no particular reason for her to do such a thing, although it was still peculiar that the diaries had vanished.

Veronica had only been having a bit of mischievous fun, although on reflection perhaps she ought not to have mentioned Barrack Room Brenda. That might have been going a bit far and Ella had looked quite upset when she left. Veronica would phone tomorrow and apologize. She would say she had been a bit squiffy on account of drinking in the middle of the afternoon, and that Clem's funeral had upset her. It would not actually be a lie, and Ella would understand and forgive her.

Meantime, there was an early evening guest to prepare for. Veronica, washing up the teacups and the vodka glass, felt a little thrill of excitement. He would be here around six—cocktail hour, if they wanted to be posh, although it sounded as if posh was the last thing they would be.

They were going to have one of their games; he had suggested it when he phoned yesterday. What he thought was that he would pretend to be an unsuspecting caller at her house—there for some innocent ordinary purpose— and she would be the sex-mad housewife luring him in to have her evil way with him.

'D'you mean like here to read the gas meter?' suggested Veronica, who was quite getting into the spirit of these games and had read a couple of fairly raunchy books to get a few ideas on her own account. 'Or mend the washing machine? Or sell insurance?'

'Whatever you like, Berenice,' he said, letting his voice sink into a lower key over the name.

Shivers ran all over Veronica's body. Really, this was the most extraordinary, unexpected thing that had ever happened in her life.

She had dashed out early that morning to buy a low-cut scarlet top, and after Ella had gone, she put it on. She had a black skirt which was a bit tight nowadays, but which exactly fitted the role he wanted her to play. Industrial strength make-up, and a slash of really vivid lipstick. Dangly earrings and some clunky necklaces, and she was ready. She positioned herself at the window to watch for his arrival.

Here he came now, walking up to the front door. Veronica, watching fondly, thought you could almost say the sun came out and cast a rosy glow on the whole street, just because he was here.

The game went brilliantly well. Veronica adopted a breathy, slightly accented voice, and they made love up against the washing machine, and then again on the sofa.

As he got washed and dressed afterwards, he said it had been marvellous, and she had been wonderful, really tarty and exciting. She played the slut to absolute perfection, he said. Veronica thought this was a remark a lot of people would have considered insulting. Coming from him, it was nothing of the kind, of course. It was said from inside their private world, the vivid exciting make-believe world *he* could create. It was a world where different rules and standards applied.

CHAPTER THIRTY-ONE

Edirne, 1912

'THE RULES ARE DIFFERENT here,' said Gil as he and Crispian stood in a corner of the courtyard, horrified at the sentence just pronounced on Jamie. 'There's a war raging and we're in the East, and this is the old Eastern way of tailoring the punishment to the crime. In some areas if you're caught stealing they cut off your hand. But for them to do this…this mutilation to Jamie without a proper trial, without letting him even try to defend himself…'

'Raif, what do we do?' said Crispian in a low voice, his eyes on the men around the table, who were now in earnest conclave.

'There's nothing any of us can do,' said Raif, but he looked shaken. 'Even if we could call out the entire military personnel from the fortress, by the time they got here it would be too late.'

'They said sunset. That's more than an hour away. Surely there's time to get help? Can't we at least try?'

Raif frowned, then said, 'Yes, all right. You two had better stay here, though. I'll go faster on my own and I might be able to get in to see one of the Pasha's aides. But don't hope for too much. Also,' he said, 'while I'm there I can collect some medical supplies to bring back.'

'Raif, if we don't free him—if they carry out this sentence—will they drug him first?'

'I don't know. They probably would do if the crime was anything other than spying. Or perhaps if he wasn't a foreigner. I'm sorry,' said Raif, 'but being English won't have helped him.'

Gil, seeing Crispian's expression, said, 'You can't blame them. Imagine how we'd feel if England was about to be invaded and someone from Turkey or Greece sold military secrets to the enemy. You wouldn't fall over yourself to rescue him and nor would I.' He looked at Raif. 'Do the best you can,' he said.

Jamie had been taken back into the stone-faced building. Crispian had tried to gesture to him, implying they would rescue him somehow, but he had no idea if Jamie understood or had even known they were there. After the door banged shut, he went to speak to the interpreter, hoping he and Gil would be allowed in to see Jamie.

But the interpreter was implacable. 'No,' he said. 'No visitors to the prisoner allowed. We do not know you; we have no cause to trust you.'

They returned to the courtyard and sat in one corner, watching everything that happened.

'I still don't believe Jamie's guilty,' said Crispian. 'But if he is, what was his motive?'

'Money, I suppose. Isn't it at the root of everything?'

'But he doesn't need money.'

'Don't be naïve, Crispian. Everyone needs money.'

'But he had only to ask me—I'd have given him anything he needed.'

'Perhaps that's why he wouldn't ask,' said Gil. 'But if he did do it, it was more likely to be to find a way to get back to England.' He shrugged. 'Perhaps there was some offer of forged papers or something of that kind. I'm only guessing, though.'

Gradually the shadows lengthened and the first glow of the setting sun began to colour the ancient stones. The Englishmen were hot and exhausted, thirsty and hungry, but they did not dare leave the courtyard.

The sun was setting in a blaze of crimson and amber when Crispian suddenly said, 'Something's starting to happen,' and pointed to where several of the men who had formed part of the makeshift jury were lighting small bronze lamps set high on the stone walls. The flames leaped up in the hot dry air, tinting the night sky, and the scent of rancid oil drifted across the courtyard. Four men carried out a rectangle of wood, about ten feet long and half as wide. Chains were driven into each corner.

'Manacles,' said Gil softly. 'They're going to chain him down.'

Crispian glanced towards the courtyard entrance. 'Raif's not coming back, is he?'

'It doesn't look like it. We're on our own, Crispian.'

'I'm glad you're here,' said Crispian, suddenly.

'Believe me, I'd rather be a thousand miles away.'

The men tilted the wooden rectangle and, as they did so, a single plangent note from somewhere inside one of the buildings rang out. Crispian's skin crawled with fear and repulsion.

'Jesus Christ, that's the grisliest thing I've ever heard,' said Gil.

'What is it?'

'It sounds like the Last Trump. In fact—' He turned sharply as there was a flurry of movement from beyond the main entrance. Raif, accompanied by a young man, came in, half-running.

'He hasn't done it,' said Crispian, sick with disappointment. 'No soldiers, nothing.'

Raif ran across to where they were sitting. 'I couldn't get anyone to help,' he said. 'I'm sorry. It's not that no one cares, but a spy in wartime...' He gestured, indicating the indifference of the Pasha's men.

'Yes, I see,' said Crispian. 'He's going to have to endure it, isn't he?'

'Yes.'

'Will it kill him?'

'I don't know. It's not a...an injury I've ever encountered. There'll be considerable blood loss, and the shock to his entire system will be immense. There're quite a lot of nerve fibres in the tongue, and also muscle.'

'It'll be very painful,' said Crispian, conscious of the lameness of this remark.

'Yes. But I've brought what I could to help him afterwards.' He indicated the small bag he had with him, then said, 'Mr Cadence, I had a moment to look at your father. He still lives, but the coma is deepening.'

Crispian tried to focus his mind on his father, lying in his dark silent world, but his whole awareness was for Jamie. They were bringing him out at last, and a drumbeat had started up from somewhere—a dreadful hollow rhythmic tapping that made the hairs lift on the back of Crispian's neck. He thought he had never heard anything filled with such menace. The torchflames burned up, throwing huge elongated shadows across the courtyard, so that for a moment it seemed full of monstrous prowling creatures.

Jamie was not manacled this time and he was struggling fiercely, but Crispian could see the men were holding him tightly. The drumbeat increased and a thrumming tension built up in the square. Crispian was aware of sweat prickling his scalp and sliding down between his shoulder blades.

The guards snaked the chains round Jamie's wrists and ankles, pinning him to the wooden board. Then they fastened an iron brace round the upper part of his head, like a travesty of a coronet, then a second, smaller one, round his neck. The ends were driven into the board, holding his head absolutely immobile. The neck circle seemed almost to be choking him and Crispian found himself swallowing convulsively.

One of the men moved to stand behind the board, reaching around it and thrusting his fingers knuckle-deep into Jamie's mouth, dragging it wide open. Jamie jerked and let out a cry of mingled surprise and pain, and a trickle of blood ran from the corner of his mouth. The other man stood in front of him, and Crispian saw for the first time that he was holding a jagged-edged clamp with serrated edges.

'They could have spared him the sight of that,' murmured Gil. 'My God, I'd like to tear their own tongues from their mouths.'

They were inserting a wedge into Jamie's mouth, forcing it impossibly wide. His eyes were straining from his head and sweat was running down his face, gluing his hair to his forehead. Even in the crimson light his skin had taken on a grey pallor.

The single trumpet note rang out again and, as if a signal had been given, the man with the clamp stepped forward and thrust it down into Jamie's mouth. Crispian could no longer see what they were doing because they were bending low over their prisoner, but he could see Jamie struggling against the manacles and he could hear him choking and gagging and trying to cry out for help. He flung himself against the restraints, but they held firm.

And then there was a cold snapping sound and Jamie screamed with dreadful high-pitched screams. Like an animal, thought Crispian with sick horror.

'They've done it,' said Gil softly. 'Oh God, they've really done it.'

The men stepped back but Crispian could not see them properly because his eyes were streaming with helpless tears and sweat was pouring down his face, half-blinding him. When his vision cleared he saw that Raif and Gil had both crossed the square and were kneeling at Jamie's side. The chains that had held him in place seemed to have been removed, but he was slumped against the wooden board. Crispian was not sure if he was conscious. The lower part of Jamie's face was covered with blood, but it was possible to see that his mouth was bruised and dreadfully swollen, distorting his face.

Crispian was horrified to feel his mind swing between pity and shameful repulsion, because in those moments he had the eerie feeling that it was no longer Jamie who lay there, no longer the cousin he had known since they were both small, but someone quite different. He shook his head to dislodge this feeling but an image stayed with him: an image of Jamie shying away from the world and living the rest of his life in some dark, dreadful half-existence.

❀ ❀ ❀

After Raif and Gil had applied the remedies Raif had brought, the Pasha's men found a cart, onto which they lifted the barely conscious Jamie.

Crispian had expected resistance to this, but Jamie's captors simply turned their backs and they were left to wheel the cart away.

'They have inflicted the punishment,' said Raif, as Crispian glanced back at the little knots of watchers. 'They have no further interest in him, and they will return to fighting the war now.'

When they reached the fortress infirmary, Jamie was taken to a narrow room near the main ward.

'There's not a great deal we can do except try to ease the pain,' said Raif.

Crispian, staring down at his cousin, forcing himself not to flinch from the swollen distorted face, said, 'I should go to see my father, shouldn't I?'

'Yes.' Raif glanced at Crispian. 'Sir Julius may rouse a little near the end. Don't let that upset you. And on some level he might understand you're there. If so, that would be a great comfort to him.'

Entering his father's room was, Crispian thought, like going from one nightmare into another. Both Jamie's room and this one were dimly lit, but where Jamie had been moaning with the same dreadful formless sounds he had made in the square, Julius lay still and silent. A nurse was with him. She smiled at Crispian and indicated to him to sit near the bed, then went out. A low lamp was burning in the corner, shutting Crispian and his father into a dark intimacy in which he could hear his father's light, regular breathing. After a moment he took Julius's hand. It lay cool and unresisting against his palm.

The night dragged on. Several times a nurse looked in, and Gil and Raif both came in as well. Occasionally soft footsteps went past the door and Crispian's mind strayed from his father to Jamie, lying at the far end of the corridor. Jamie, mutilated and damaged forever, because the Turkish extremists believed he had spied on them and sold information to the Bulgarian army waiting outside the city. Do I believe he did that? thought Crispian, and still did not know.

Shortly after 2 a.m. he became aware of a change in his father's breathing. It was slowing, becoming laboured. Did that mean he was dying? Crispian went to the door and managed to signal to a nurse, who appeared to understand what he was trying to tell her because several minutes later a doctor Crispian half recognized came into the room. He examined Julius briefly, then shook his head and patted Crispian's shoulder comfortingly.

Crispian took this to mean his father was sinking into death and the doctor was sorry but there was nothing that could be done.

'I hope you'll just slide out of life gently,' he said very softly, taking Julius's hand again after the doctor had gone out. 'I don't know if you're even aware I'm here and you probably can't hear me. But if you do know and if you can hear, I want to tell you I'll miss you because I love you and I always did.' A memory of his father's robust character made him add, wryly, 'Even when you were at your most difficult and cantankerous.'

Incredibly there was a flicker of movement in the withdrawn features on the pillow. Crispian's heart jumped, and he glanced towards the door, wondering if he should summon the doctor again. He felt an unmistakable pressure from his father's hand and Julius's head turned slightly on the pillow, as if searching for something—for the light?

Very softly, in a whisper so fragile it sounded as if it could dissolve into nothing at any minute, Julius said, 'Crispian?'

Sight and hearing had failed Julius before they had come to Edirne, but Crispian said, 'I'm here,' and pressed his father's hand firmly.

'Good son, Crispian,' said Julius faintly. 'So proud.' He turned his head again, as if trying to see. 'Always so proud of both my sons,' he said.

Both my sons? Crispian stared at his father, not understanding.

The fragile whispering came again. 'Don't think Colm ever knew,' Julius said. 'Hope not. Fay wouldn't have told him—she promised she never would.'

Fay. The lady of the faded photograph on the desk at Cadence Manor. The lady who had been Jamie's mother and whose name had always seemed to Crispian to belong to a rose romance. Horrified comprehension was unfolding. The long-ago, long-dead Fay—the woman Crispian's own mother had thought frivolous and unsuitable—had been his father's mistress, that was what his father was meaning. It was the only thing he could mean. And he had said 'both my sons'. Did he mean Jamie had been his own son and that Jamie was Crispian's brother? Crispian's mind was reeling.

'Tragic the way Fay died, though—never forgotten it,' whispered the frail voice. And then a dry gasping came from Julius's lips, and his head fell to one side.

Jamie Cadence's Journal

When my memories of those weeks inside the fort at Edirne come back to me, they do so in crimson and black images, streaked with clawing agony and filled with the deepest, bitterest anger and despair any man ever knew.

At first I thought I was going to die. For a long while I wanted to die. I believe I tried to do so. I remember that Raif and the nurses tried to feed me cold liquids. I have no idea if they were a form of anaesthesia or simply for sustenance, but whatever they were I turned my head away from them.

'It will heal,' Raif said to me. 'Jamie, the wounds will heal—they're healing already. Your face is dreadfully bruised and swollen still, but that will get better in time. As for the other aspect—well, the human race is remarkably adaptable. Remember you can still see and hear, both huge blessings. Speech can be made in other ways. You'll find a way to talk to your friends, your family.'

Family.

Julius died shortly after my punishment by the extremists. Crispian came to tell me. He hated coming to visit me, I saw that at once. He found me repulsive. I knew if I looked in a mirror I would find myself repulsive, as well. But they kept mirrors away from me and I was glad of it. I was afraid I might recognize the reflection that looked at me from a mirror. I had the deep conviction that what had been done to me would have brought that other deformity to the surface—that the darkness would be stamped on my face forever and the world would finally see it.

Crispian said they had buried his father in the courtyard and after he went I lay thinking about Julius, wondering what his will would contain. Would he have left everything to Crispian, perhaps with some kind of trust fund for Crispian's mother? Or would he have left something to me—the son he had never acknowledged—the son born of a long-ago affair that my mother tried to surround with moonlight and roses and a noble forswearing of true love?

Which is utter and complete rot, of course. By the time I was seventeen and had sorted the pieces of the past into their right order, I guessed the truth about my mother and Julius Cadence. A case of simple lust, probably in more or less equal measures on both sides. I may as well be honest and say she was a bit of a slut, my mamma, although to look at her photographs you'd never know it because she looks like the Lily Maid of Astolat or an unawakened Victorian heroine. As an aside, I always suspected that in his early teens Crispian had a romantic admiration for her. Several times I caught him gazing at the photograph, looking moonstruck. He was inclined to be a touch mawkish when it came to the emotions; I often wondered how Gil Martlet dealt with that. Assuming he did deal with it, of course, for I never knew the truth about those two.

One truth I do know is that Julius and Fay gave their affair a spurious air of morality by wrapping it up in protestations of love and devotion and implausible rubbish about being soul mates. Julius's thoughts were more likely on the lines of: let me have a few nights in your bed, my dear, and we'll preserve the decencies by telling each other we're wildly in love. Fay probably thought, I'm married to somebody who's the next best thing to impotent, I'm going mad with frustration, and you'll do as well as anyone.

They wouldn't have used those exact phrases, but I'm fairly sure that was the burden of the song. Over the years I've tried to see my mother in a favourable light, but when I remember what she did to me, it's impossible.

CHAPTER THIRTY-TWO

Jamie Cadence's Journal

IF I WERE FANCIFUL I might say I've felt my mother's presence near to me while I've been writing this journal. I've even thought she might have guided me to make that search earlier when I found the cupboard with its apparently flimsy back section. She would certainly have told me to see if I could use it to get out. She believed in sweeping aside obstacles if they were barring the way to something you wanted. She said as much to me on the day she died.

'Never let anything get in the way of a thing you want, Jamie.' That's what she said that day, her voice blurry with pain. 'Never let *anything* get in the way...'

I was seven years old and it was the end of a long hot summer. I had been at Cadence Manor with Crispian since our school holidays started; I always spent almost the entire summer there—everyone thought it so kind of Sir Julius and Lady Cadence to include me in Crispian's life, to ensure we were at the same school and that I was so often at Cadence Manor. I was a poor motherless child, they all said, and shook their heads over the tragic death of Fay Cadence when I was little more than a toddler.

I thought I was a poor motherless child, as well. It's what I was told by everyone, including the man I thought was my father, Colm Cadence. If I could get a sneer into the writing of that name I would, because I despised him for years. He was a man who never swept aside an obstacle, a man who, instead of making a living for himself and his wife, was content to live on his cousin's charity. He was weak, impractical and gutless. When I was younger I used to wonder how someone like my mother ever married such a milksop. When I was older I realized it was the Cadence money she was after. It was a pity she hardly got any of it. It was more of a pity that I got even less.

Colm lived at the manor, in one wing that he had made his own, and received an income in return for work so light it was virtually non-existent. He was said to look after the place and act as his cousin Julius's agent, but it was simply another example of the Cadence arrogance, of Julius playing lord of the manor. Colm never had any pride, though. People said he had buried himself in the country, among his books and manuscripts, and told one another that he had never got over the death of his beautiful young wife.

It was part of family folklore how the beautiful Fay had died young, how she was forever enshrined in the heart of Colm and everyone who knew her. Even at the age of seven I knew I had to speak of Mamma with reverence and respect, and I knew I had to look at her photograph regularly so I would never forget what she looked like.

That summer was one of those long hot drowsy ones that seem to go on forever, but I think there were only a few days left before Crispian and I would return to school. I remember I was running across the lawn to meet him— we were going down to the lake—when Flagg, who had been butler to Crispian's family since before he was born, came out of the house and called to me. My father was asking for me, he said. Would I please come up to the house at once? This was annoying, but perhaps it would not take long. I went obediently; I was always an obedient child.

After the glare of the afternoon sunshine, Cadence Manor was dim and cool, and my father—that's to say the man I thought of as my father—was waiting for me. He said, 'Jamie, there's someone you must see. Come through into my rooms.'

We crossed to the door leading to the small wing where he spent most of the time, and this was interesting because, as a rule, neither Crispian nor I was allowed in there.

'Your father has his work and his studies,' everyone said. 'It's important for him to be left in complete peace and quiet.'

So this would be something to tell Crispian afterwards. We often made up stories about what was in these rooms. I was better at that than he was. It usually started with a princess being held captive by a wicked enchanter and the two of us having to hack our way through thick undergrowth to rescue her. Or it was a hideout for bandits or jewel thieves and we helped the police catch them. Or it was a lost prince who had been usurped by a greedy uncle or cousin, and whose throne and kingdom had to be restored.

But at first sight the rooms were not much different from the rest of the house. They looked a bit like the ones in the wing where we normally lived, only the other way round. I had recently read *Through the Looking-Glass*, and I felt a bit like Alice tumbling through the glass that day. As we went up the stairs and along the top corridor there was a dreamlike quality to everything. Everywhere was very quiet and slightly dusty and cobwebby as if no one ever came in here to clean it. There was not much furniture, but what was there wasn't glossily polished like the furniture in the rest of the house. I remember thinking that if my Aunt Serena could see this she would be icily angry because she was very particular about everywhere being clean and polished. My father was holding my hand quite tightly, which was unusual, and he was not speaking.

And then we went into a big room at the back of the house, and I stopped thinking about Alice and the looking-glass and about this being a prison for an enchanted princess.

The curtains were drawn, but pinpoints of light showed through the thick fabric in places. Dust motes danced in and out of the dimness and there was a sickly, too-sweet smell. Pushed against the far wall was a bed with thick hangings of the old-fashioned kind, partly drawn. I hesitated in the doorway and looked at my father for guidance because I had no idea what was expected of me.

'She's over there in the bed,' he said. 'She wants to speak to you. But you'll have to be very brave, Jamie.'

I was perfectly ready to be brave, especially if this turned out to be an adventure I could boast about later to Crispian. So I went over to the bed, not feeling especially nervous, more curious.

The hangings were open a very little on the side that did not face the window, and as I approached I became aware of a figure lying in the bed. A very thin figure, it was, with a cloud of hair spilling over the pillows, but with a thick veil over its face. That was when I started to feel frightened.

A hand came out to me as I stood by the bed—a thin hand that ought to have been slender and smooth but that was mottled and scarred. I had the wild idea that something had partly eaten the hand, which was surely absurd.

'Take her hand,' said my father's voice just behind me. 'She won't hurt you; she can't hurt anyone. She's very ill—dying—and she wants to see you and say goodbye.'

'Who—'

'Oh, Jamie,' said a voice from the depths of the bed. 'Jamie, don't you know who I am. I'm your mother.'

The dim room, the dust motes, the thick drapes and the too-sweet scent whirled madly around me. My mother had died a long time ago—so long I could not remember her. Did this mean that what people in church said about dying was wrong? That all those stories about people falling asleep and going to live with Jesus and being happy, were not true? That instead of that, they lived on in dark dusty bedrooms, their bodies crumbling away like this thin hand seemed to have crumbled away?

I tried to back away from the half-hidden thing in the bed, but my father was there to stop me. 'Say goodbye, Jamie,' he said, and kneeled down beside me. 'Take her hand and tell her you love her and you'll always remember her.'

'No,' I said, terrified, and trying to pull free. 'I won't.'

'Oh, Jamie...' It was a breath of sound from within the bed and, terribly and fearsomely, the figure half raised itself, stretching out its hand. 'I only want to say goodbye—I only want to see you, just this last time...So handsome, so bright and clever...Julius must be so proud of you.'

Julius. The name skittered across my mind, and I thought—insofar as I thought at all—that she meant Colm, but was confused.

She leaned nearer and the cloud of hair swung slightly to one side. The veil—a thick black veil—slipped to one side. I was dimly aware of my father lunging forward, fumbling to push it back into place, but it was too late. I had seen the face the thick cloth had been hiding. I screamed and ran blindly from the room.

❋ ❋ ❋

He found me some time later, huddled in a corner of my own room, not crying, but hunched on the window seat, knees drawn up to my chest, arms hugging them; staring out of the window at the orderly grounds and lawns, and the faint glint of the lake through the trees.

'I'm sorry I lied to you,' he said hesitantly. He was never good at speaking to me—he was never good at speaking to anyone.

Because I had been brought up to be polite, I said, 'I don't understand.'

'Jamie,' he said, sitting awkwardly on the end of the window seat, 'your mother didn't die when you were small. She's lived at Cadence Manor for a number of years.'

'Why did you tell me she was dead?'

'Because she had a—an illness that she and I both knew was killing her,' he said. 'A dreadful illness that—It disfigured her. Do you know what that word means?'

'No.'

'It scars the skin and spoils it,' he said, and even through my anger and distress I heard his sadness. 'Little by little it destroys flesh and skin and sometimes even the brain...' He broke off, and I saw him dash one hand across his eyes. 'She couldn't bear people seeing,' he said. 'She was so very beautiful, you see. So we arranged for her to live here without anyone knowing. I would look after her. We didn't think it would be for very long, you see. Just a few months, perhaps a year. But it's been four years.'

'But now she really is dying?'

'Yes.'

'I don't want to see her again,' I said. 'Could you tell her, please. Say I'm sorry.'

'Yes.'

'Unless she's dead already? Is she?'

He turned to look at me and there was an expression in his eyes that, just for a moment, made me feel cold and uncomfortable. 'No,' he said. 'She's not dead yet. But I think she will be by this time tomorrow.'

'Yes, I see. Thank you for telling me.' I got off the window seat. 'I'll go and find Crispian now, if you don't mind, sir,' I said. 'We were going down to the lake.'

❀ ❀ ❀

It was nice by the lake that day. Sunlight glinted on the water and we skimmed stones across the surface, competing to see who could skim the furthest. Crispian had no idea what had just happened; I don't think he ever found out.

We made plans for fishing in the lake and thought we might even be allowed to swim in it, although Crispian said it might be too muddy and choked up with weeds. And all the time I was seeing that terrible face and the reaching hand with the scars and sores.

I think she did die that night, my mother, because I awoke in the middle of the night and heard hurrying footsteps and the murmur of voices. But in the morning everything was exactly as it always was, and I never knew when they took her body away or where they buried her. I never knew, either, if the other people in the house—Julius and my Aunt Serena and Flagg and his wife—knew she was there, but I suppose they must have done. I can't see how Colm could have coped otherwise.

It wasn't until I was thirteen that I realized my mother had not been confused over the names that day at all. She had said Julius must be proud of me, and she really had meant Julius, not Colm.

It was Christmas Eve when I found out the truth. There was a houseful of guests at Cadence Manor. Julius liked giving big house parties and he was a jovial and generous host; in fairness I have to say that about him. One of the men made a vaguely bawdy remark, which Crispian and I were not meant to overhear, about it being a wise man who knew his own offspring.

'And I dare say Julius, old rascal, has one or two colts not in the stud book,' he said, and somebody else responded with a remark about not housing them in your own stable. There was some half-embarrassed, half-sniggering laughter.

Something clicked inside my head, and the next morning I asked Julius about it. 'Sir, I've been putting a few facts together,' I said politely. 'And I'd very much like it if you could reassure me about something.'

'Yes?'

'I've got it into my head that Colm Cadence might not be my father.'

There was a very long pause. Then he said, 'I can't reassure you, Jamie. He isn't your father.'

'Yes, I see. I thought he wasn't. You're my father, aren't you, sir?'

He took a bit longer to answer this time. Then he said, 'Yes, I am.'

It was the truth, pure and simple, although as Oscar Wilde (I think it was Wilde anyway) said in one of his plays, the truth is rarely pure, and never simple.

'How did you know?' he said.

'Oh,' I said, deliberately vaguely, 'just one or two things I heard.'

'I see. Well, I hoped you'd never suspect, Jamie, and I certainly hoped you'd never ask me that question. But I promised your mother if you ever did, then I would answer you truthfully.'

And *that* was when he handed me all that rubbish about them having been so intensely in love they hadn't been able to help themselves, and how Colm had been impotent. He didn't put it quite like that about Colm— he might even have thought that at thirteen I wouldn't understand. I understood perfectly well, of course. No one who went to a boys' boarding school and shared a dormitory with ten others was ignorant of the basic facts of life by the age of thirteen, and in a good many cases a lot younger than thirteen. So I was quite clear as to what he meant.

But I sat politely in his study for the next half-hour and listened to him telling me how lovely and sinless and warm my mother had been, and how painful it had been to end the romance, and I thought: you bloody lusting old hypocrite.

But there was one other question I had to ask, and I have to be honest and record that this, really, was the main thing I wanted to know.

'Sir, since I'm your son as much as Crispian, does that mean I'll one day own Cadences with him?'

'Oh, no,' he said at once. Instant reaction, immediate rebuttal. I think I hated him more at that moment than at any other.

'Oh, no, Jamie,' he said again. 'I'm sorry, but that isn't how things work. Crispian's my legitimate son. My heir. I'll make sure you're looked after, of course, but you won't inherit Cadences.'

'I see,' I said. 'Thank you anyway, sir.'

So there it was. I was Julius's son as much as Crispian but I wasn't going to get what Crispian would get. The banking house, Cadence Manor, the money and the power.

Unless, of course, Crispian were to die. That was the thought that came, unbidden, into my mind and, once there, it stuck. I thought, if Crispian were no longer here, I'd have everything. There'd be no one else to inherit it. I'd be the obvious heir and no one would raise an eyebrow.

The lake at Cadence Manor has long since dried out, but in those days it was quite deep. We had already made plans for fishing and swimming at Easter, and I was careful to make regular mention of them—of how I was going to ask for fishing rods for my birthday next February so we could try them out. And, of course, whatever I had, Crispian had as well.

It was easy to push him into the lake. I did it clumsily and inefficiently, and all that happened was that he was drenched. He got out almost at once, of course, and I pretended I had slipped on a patch of mud and knocked into him. I cried so they would think I was ashamed and remorseful at what had happened.

I wasn't ashamed or remorseful at all. I was furious because Crispian hadn't drowned. It was my first attempt to murder him. But as you know by now, my unknown reader, it wasn't my last.

❀ ❀ ❀

These were the memories that coursed through my mind in the infirmary inside Edirne. The clearest was how the veil had slipped from my mother's face that day, and how I had run sobbing from the room. It never faded, that memory.

But it wasn't until I saw the same marks on Julius's face that I realized my mother must have died from syphilis. It was a scaldingly bad thought, but it explained why she had been hidden away all those years. Not just vanity, although I dare say that came into it, but shame. The shame of having contracted a sexual disease, although whether she got it from Julius or he got it from her, I have no idea.

And here's the real agony: it's a disease that can be inherited. Not always and not necessarily severely. But if the mother has syphilis during pregnancy there's a strong danger of the child displaying some symptoms. And when both parents have it...

It doesn't always mark the face, syphilis. Sometimes it marks the mind. Like a smeary pawprint of black disease stamped into the brain. Distorting it and dredging up darknesses.

Darknesses. You can see, can't you, why I hated my mother and my real father so much?

❀ ❀ ❀

It was later that night when the Pasha called everyone inside the fortress together and told them that the siege of Edirne was likely to continue for some time yet. I wasn't among the people. Even if I had been pronounced fit to leave my room I would have stayed away because I didn't want to face anyone. But Crispian and Gil were there, and Raif had interpreted the gist of the speech for them. Boiled down to the bones, it meant that Edirne remained an island of resistance, and was still being attacked by the Bulgarians, who were determined to possess the ancient Ottoman capital.

Supplies were dwindling, but the Pasha had pledged that in the event of a siege, the fortress would not surrender for a period of fifty days. God knows why fifty, as opposed to any other number, but that's what he said.

'So,' said Crispian, 'we're stuck here for a good while yet.'

I shrugged. It made no odds to me whether I was stuck inside a Turkish fortress or in a British castle.

'The Pasha has promised the sick people will be given the best of what there is,' Crispian said. 'We'll make sure you're all right, Jamie.'

I nodded.

'But,' said Gil, who was lounging on the end of the bed, 'I think there's going to be a good deal of hardship ahead. The supplies of food are already running low. It's being said that provisions will have to be rationed. If it goes on for long we could be facing what's virtually a famine. I'm afraid,' he said, 'that we have a very difficult and painful time ahead.'

CHAPTER THIRTY-THREE

Cadence Manor, Early 1913

SERENA CADENCE KNEW she had a difficult and painful time ahead.

The actual birth of the child—the twin that had survived the brutality of the mercury treatment—did not especially worry her, even though she knew it would be painful and exhausting. It was what lay beyond the birth that was so frightening.

Dr Martlet had tried to reassure her. He had said after the birth they might try the mercury procedure again or consider the new German drug. Salvarsan, it was called; he had been able to read some of the reports on it. The outlook was really very promising, he said.

Serena listened politely but she knew he was lying. The outlook was not promising at all. She *knew* what this disease did. She had seen it ravage Julius's body and then shred his mind, and the images were sickening ones. But what was far worse was the macabre memory of Fay Cadence.

There had only been one occasion when Serena had seen what lay beneath Fay's shawls and veils, but even that brief glimpse had sickened her. A nightmare figure, she had thought. The skin had been ravaged and corroded;

the lips and eyes distorted by the scars and sores. Was that what lay ahead for Serena herself?

Dr Martlet said very firmly that it was not. It might take a very long time for the disease to develop; it might be quiescent for years. In fact, it might remain quiescent and never trouble her in the future. The changes that her pregnancy was currently creating had brought it to the surface, that was all. After the birth, it would recede. But Serena saw the look in his eyes when he said this and she knew that what had happened to Fay—and later, Julius—would eventually happen to her. It was not an absolute certainty, but it very nearly was. And it was a bitter and cruel irony that Serena, of all people, should become afflicted with a tart's disease, with a sickness that infected libertines and whores.

Fay had been a whore. No matter how Colm tried to pretend otherwise and Julius tried to make excuses, Fay had been a cheap little tart. Even so, they had all done their best for her, including Dr Martlet, although the treatments he had tried had proved useless. At last, Julius and Colm had come up with the idea that Fay should live permanently at Cadence Manor. The west wing was a separate suite of rooms, said Julius; poor Fay could be entirely private. And Dr Martlet, so absolutely trustworthy, would go down regularly and give her what help he could.

It had been the only possible solution. The fact that one of the family had contracted such a shameful illness could not be made known. Serena thought they had all been clear about that. Fay had sobbed with despair, but in the end had agreed to the plan. Her life was over in any case, she said, and all she could do was die quietly and unobtrusively somewhere. Cadence Manor would do as well as anywhere else for that. Serena had been unable to decide if Fay was being courageous in the face of death or simply hysterical and attention-seeking. The vain little creature was so self-centred it was perfectly likely she did not believe she would die.

Whatever her real emotions, Fay had gone docilely enough to Priors Bramley. It would not be for long, Dr Martlet said privately to Colm and Julius. A few months, perhaps. A year at the very most. Colm had gone with her, of course, and Serena had detailed one of the older maids from the London house to live at the manor with them. She was a rather dour woman, a Miss Crossley, not very popular with the other servants, unlikely to gossip in the village or form foolish friendships with local people. When Fay died, Crossley could either be retired on a small pension or she could remain at the manor if she wanted, as a caretaking housekeeper.

The family continued to use Cadence Manor for the summer and for the big Christmas house parties Julius liked to give and Serena always tried to avoid. She had thought Fay's presence would provide an excuse, but Julius said the west wing was remote and contained, so Fay could safely be left to her seclusion. Life must go on as normal and the rest of the manor was big enough to house their guests. As for Jamie, he need never know the real facts, said Julius. Looking back, Serena was glad they had kept the truth from Jamie. He had been only a toddler then, and for him to see the nightmare thing his mother had become was unthinkable.

The only unsatisfactory thing in the plan was Fay herself, who must needs confound Dr Martlet's prediction and linger for four long years. When she eventually died, a trustworthy and incurious undertaker from London came down the next day and arranged a discreet funeral at a church some ten or twelve miles away. St Luke the Hospitaller, it was called, and there was a brief private burial. Julius attended, but Serena was in London. She did not travel down for the funeral because it was important not to attract too much local attention. Also, it was a hot August that year, and the journey would have been exhausting.

And then, more than a decade later, Fay's ghost returned. A diseased ghost. Because it turned out that the light-minded slut had slept with Julius. She had actually allowed Serena's husband into her bed, and the seeds of her filthy, unpredictable illness had been passed to Julius. And, years later, Julius had given it to Serena so that Serena herself was now under sentence of death, living in seclusion at Cadence Manor, exactly as Fay had done.

She wandered through the rooms, finding grisly traces of Fay everywhere. At the back of a housemaid's cupboard was a stack of mirrors, five or six of them, hidden away so Fay could not accidentally catch a glimpse of her reflection. In the bedroom that had been hers, shawls and veils were folded in a drawer. Lavender bags had been tucked into the folds, but when Serena opened the drawer the indefinable scent of disease and death drifted out.

That's what's ahead of me, she thought. They'll have to hide the mirrors and keep the curtains closed. Eventually I'll give orders that the gas jets burn at the lowest possible glimmer even on the darkest of evenings.

A few years ago Julius had wanted to install electricity in the manor, but it had turned out to be too expensive for the old fabric and, remembering this, Serena was grateful. She was not grateful for very much else, though.

The west wing where Fay had lived for those four years had long since been rearranged and cleaned out, and nowadays Colm lived there, pottering contentedly among his books. If his dead wife's shade walked those rooms, he did not seem to notice. He and Serena shared lunch or dinner a few times after her arrival, but she had never found Colm easy to talk to and he seemed to have grown nervous and almost hermit-like with the years. He was still looked after by the dour Miss Crossley, who had nursed Fay all those years ago; Dora said there had been a few battles in the kitchen between Mrs Flagg and Old Crosspatch.

'Her name is Miss Crossley,' said Serena.

Dora said that was as maybe, milady, but to everyone downstairs she was Crosspatch, and was there anything else needed tonight, milady, on account of it being her night off. She and Hetty were going along to the Red Lion.

'No, nothing else,' said Serena, and Dora went off, very pert, for her evening. Serena heard them giggling as they went under her window and hoped they were not heading for trouble. Dora had always been a good, well-behaved girl, but Hetty was apt to be flighty, there was no denying it.

After the first few weeks, Serena and Colm, by tacit agreement, kept to their own parts of the manor; Colm with his books and his memories and ghosts in the west wing, Serena in the east wing. Really, it was better that way; conversation at meals could be so tiring and Serena had noticed Colm looking at the wine and brandy decanters, which Flagg now placed at her hand without being asked. It was nothing whatsoever to do with Colm if she took a glass or two of good wine with her lunch and dinner, or if she enjoyed a little brandy after her food. Brandy was good for the digestion, everyone knew that.

Sometimes she thought the disease was not progressing at all; sometimes she even thought it was retreating. But then a morning would come when the unforgiving sunlight poured into the rooms and she was forced to hunt out the shawls and veils to wear, or to lie in sick despair on her bed, her skin on fire, her bones in grinding agony.

And every day the child Julius had forced on her, that black knot of disease inside her body, grew a little bigger and a little stronger. I hate you, said Serena to the child. Why couldn't you have died that day with your twin? Why can't you die now, before you're born? The words whispered inside her head like a secret echo. Die before you're born...*Die before you're born*...

378 WHAT LIES BENEATH

At some point, the whisper changed to, *I'll make sure you die before you're born...*

❧ ❧ ❧

The scullery at Cadence Manor was, as Mrs Flagg often said, a gloomy old place.

'Dismal from floor to ceiling, and always has been, and how I'm to make a meal fit to send to table on this rusting old stove is a mystery.'

They were just sitting down to their midday dinner— a good leg of roast pork it was, and for once the Crossley woman had unbent sufficiently to help out. Flagg was serving himself apple sauce, when there was a cry from the main hall, following by a bumping tumble.

'Sounds like the mistress,' said Flagg. 'Taken a fall, that's my bet. We'd best see what's happened.'

What had happened was that Lady Cadence, poor soul, stumbling around in the dim, curtained hall, had tripped at the head of the stairs and gone headlong down to the half-landing. The sound even brought Mr Colm from his part of the house, spectacles pushed up onto his forehead, his hair rumpled round his head like an astonished baby.

Lady Cadence was lying a bit twisted, saying weakly she did not know how it had happened; she had been coming down to the dining room, and she must have stumbled over that bit of rug at the top of the stairs.

Miss Crossley was dispatched to send a message to the local doctor to come up to the manor at once, while Hetty and Dora carried the poor mistress to her bed, with Flagg and Mr Colm in anxious attendance.

Later in the servants' room they all agreed it was fortunate that all madam had suffered was a sprained ankle. With the child due to be born so soon it was a miracle she had not done some irreparable damage to it.

Miss Crossley told Hetty to make sure no dangerous bits of rug were left lying around for folk to trip over, and when Hetty declared hotly that she had not left no rug nowhere, Miss Crossley warned Mrs Flagg the lower servants were becoming impudent.

❈ ❈ ❈

The news that Sir Julius had died in a heathen country nobody had heard of reached Cadence Hall shortly after Christmas. Lady Cadence had a letter telling the news, and asked Flagg to let the servants know.

There had been some sort of funeral service. For once Mrs Flagg and Miss Crossley were united in hoping it had been a proper Christian burial because you never knew what might go on in those outlandish places. Mr Crispian's letter had asked if a memorial service could be arranged at St Anselm's, so Flagg was sent down to the village to ask the vicar please to come up to the manor to discuss this.

The service took place in early January and they all attended it except Miss Crossley, who had to stay behind with Lady Cadence. Madam would have liked to go, said the Crosspatch, but of course the icy weather made it inadvisable in her condition. Dr Martlet, who had travelled down from London, said there was no question of her attending, even though St Anselm's was only a five-minute drive into the village. Lady Cadence must stay in the house on her bed, he said firmly.

She stayed there until the birth of the child a few weeks later. It was a boy, and everyone was very thankful that he seemed sound and whole. A child torn from its twin in the womb, and whose mother had tumbled down the stairs only a few weeks earlier, might have been damaged in some unthinkable way.

❊ ❊ ❊

Serena named the child Saul, for no other reason than that she thought the name unusual and pleasant, and he was christened at St Anselm's on an early spring day with crocuses starring the fields.

Recovering slowly from the birth, Serena had the feeling that Saul hated her. He cried when she went near him, and struggled if she tried to feed him. Dora, who had brothers and sisters, took over his care, along with a village girl engaged by Miss Crossley. Serena was aware of guilty relief that she need have very little to do with him. Sometimes she thought Saul, even at this age, had a deep sense of loss that he could not understand—a loss for the small barely formed little thing that had not survived. When he cried it seemed to her there was an uncontrolled and frustrated fury in the sounds.

But Dr Martlet told her Saul was healthy and sound. There were no signs of him having inherited the disease both his parents had suffered from, he said firmly.

Serena believed him until one bright May afternoon when sunlight streamed into the nursery and she saw, for the first time, the faint tracery of scars around Saul's mouth.

Jamie Cadence's Journal

There's no point pretending I behaved well during those weeks in Edirne when the food supplies were so low. Everyone around me thought I was wonderful, but actually I was behaving appallingly. I was selfish and self-centred, and I used my mutilation shamelessly to make sure I got the best of the food there was—and there wasn't much of it for anyone. The Pasha's men stood guard over the stores, and people subsisted on handfuls of rice and bowls of some liquid concoction I believe contained boiled-up vegetables—mostly onions, from the smell of it.

But I was an invalid, a victim of misguided hatred, and everyone was sorry for me. I was given the best of everything.

The days blurred into one another. My mouth was healing; sometimes I still spat blood but that lessened as the weeks went by. The pain was much easier as well, although I didn't let them know that. I gave a performance of a man nightly suffering the torments of the damned.

But there's one day I'll always remember and that was the day I demanded a mirror. They made excuses at first, pretending there were no mirrors to be found, saying they had forgotten and would bring one later. But in the end they gave in.

I have a half-memory of someone—I think it was Gil—surreptitiously turning down the oil lamp. He might as well not have bothered, because let's not pretend about this: I was deformed. There's no other word for it. There were—and are—appalling scars round my mouth and although most of the torn flesh had healed, even then, it had done so lumpishly, twisting my mouth into something dreadfully close to a snarl. For several appalling moments, in the erratic light of the oil lamp, it was as if something from one of the ancient grisly fables of the world's dark ages stared out at me from the glass—or a mistake, occasionally made by nature, such as can sometimes be seen shambling pitiably through freak sideshows...

'It's not so bad,' said Crispian, watching me, and I looked at him and felt the familiar surge of hatred towards him. Because it was bad, it was very bad indeed. 'You'll grow accustomed,' he said. 'And there'll be small tricks— little illusions you can use. A scarf, a deep-brimmed hat.'

'Even easier, grow a beard,' said Gil.

❀ ❀ ❀

The beard turned out to be not possible—the flesh around my mouth had been so badly damaged the hair didn't grow. I didn't come to terms with how I looked then, and I never have. Perhaps I haven't tried hard enough to accept the results of what was done to me.

I see I haven't mentioned the darkness for the last few pages of this journal. It didn't trouble me in the weeks following the punishment, but it was still there. I knew when I had completely healed it would flex its claws and rip into my mind. And on the day I saw my altered reflection for the first time, it seemed to me that I had somehow been turned inside out: that the inner darkness I had struggled against had been scraped away from inside my skin and smeared over my face for the world to see.

Crispian found a child's slate and chalk, so I could write down anything I wanted to say. Never anything about being mistaken for a spy—I never referred to that. It would have been too easy to spin an elaborate tale and make some vital, damning mistake along the way. So I never once referred to it. No explanations or apologies.

It was soon apparent that no one believed the spy accusation. Or did Raif? Yes, I think he was suspicious. But Crispian and Gil and the other English people in that beleaguered city certainly thought I had been pursuing one of my quests for knowledge—music or some obscure area of Eastern art—and that I had given the wrong impression, to the wrong people. A tragedy, they all said. Absurd to imagine someone so quiet, so scholarly—never a trouble to anyone—could be involved in spying. Appalling that an innocent man had endured such extreme brutality. They said it several times to one another, and also to Crispian, and then they felt they had assuaged their own consciences and went off to deal with getting through a siege in the depths of winter.

I should point out to anyone who hasn't journeyed to the Turkish-Greek borders that winter there is not a pleasant experience. Winter in England can be rather cosy—roaring fires and mulled wine, spiders' webs frozen into exquisite lace patterns on frosty mornings, and hollied Christmases with laden dinner tables. That's if you have money, of course. If you're poor, you shiver in doorways and beg in the streets, and hate the pampered rich with their fur-lined gloves and warm houses.

There was nothing cosy about that winter in Edirne, with the war raging and food supplies dwindling by the hour. Inside the fort huge fires were built in the old stone hearths and even in the inner courtyard, but they didn't do much to combat the unforgiving iron coldness. Christmas was celebrated in a rather bleak fashion among the European community. I didn't go to the festivities; I wrote on the slate that I was in too much pain that day. Crispian and Gil went and said later it had been a brave attempt at merry-making but not very successful. A few people had tried to sing carols but nobody had joined in with any real enthusiasm. There had been tiny measures of a fiery drink that Crispian said tasted of aniseed and would probably make him sick, but that Gil said was ouzo, and perfectly palatable. As to what the food had been, they had no idea.

I wrote, 'Meat?'

'Well, there was definitely some sort of meat,' said Gil. 'But whether it was horse or donkey, or whether they'd caught a Bulgar and boiled him, I wouldn't know.'

'Whatever it was you had two helpings,' said Crispian.

'And I was glad to get it,' said Gil. 'By the end of the Twelve Days we might be eating rat. Raif says some of the soldiers are setting up a shooting alley outside the cellars. Don't shudder, Crispian. Rat is probably regarded as a great delicacy in some parts of the world. Jamie probably knows which ones,' said Gil, glancing at me.

I shook my head.

'Well, whatever it is, we might have to eat the rats before they eat us,' said Gil. 'Because I don't think the food's going to last out much longer.'

'The Pasha will surrender soon,' said Crispian confidently. 'He'll have to.' He was as arrogant as ever. I suppose he couldn't imagine he would be expected to endure this siege for long.

'Lay you five pounds the old boy doesn't surrender until the fifty days are up,' said Gil. 'Those were his orders and he'll follow them to the letter.'

'Done,' said Crispian promptly.

I nearly took Gil's bet, but later I was glad I hadn't because Gil was right. The Pasha followed orders almost to the hour, and did not surrender the fortress and Edirne until the end of March. But it was a grim three months. By the end of January people were gaunt and hollow-eyed, and—let's not be squeamish—rather smelly. What water there was—mostly taken from wells—had to be preserved for drinking. Sanitation was primitive in the extreme, which was unfortunate in light of the onion broth that still appeared at almost every meal. It can have very dramatic effects on the human gut, onion broth. The entire fort— probably the entire town—stank to high heaven by the time February was under way.

Living inside a fortress that's being besieged is an extraordinary experience. I've tried to think of a parallel, but I don't think there is one. Not even prison compares to it. The sense of isolation is absolute. There are no newspapers or letters, no communication with the outside world at all. The only thing that came to us from beyond the city's confines was the sound of the guns and cannons constantly bombarding the city. People died and were wounded; families were torn apart, there was wailing of grief and anger on all sides, and dozens of small fires broke out from the shelling, and caused minor damage.

By the end of February Gil and the soldiers really were shooting the rats, because people were ready to eat anything. I don't know if I actually ate any rat, but I wouldn't be surprised. There comes a point when you're so agonizingly hungry—when your stomach is twisted by cramps all the time—that you don't question what's on the plate; you just wolf it down.

Gil said messages were smuggled in and out by the Pasha and his aides, but they were almost entirely in code so it was no good trying to intercept any of them. When Crispian asked how he knew this, Gil said, oh, he occasionally met up with some of the soldiers in one of the bars that somehow remained open.

'And the rumours get wilder all the time,' he said.

'D'you know what I find so terrible,' said Crispian, having taken a moment to digest the fact that Gil met up with soldiers in bars. 'It's the way this has become almost commonplace. We're hardly hearing the incessant bombardment from the guns and we're becoming impervious to the deaths—the fires, the destruction and suffering...If you look out of a window on almost any night, you see little groups of people carrying dead bodies. You don't know if they've been killed by shells or if they're dead from starvation, but either way they're just tumbled into graves.'

'We'll all end up being tumbled into graves if those go on much longer,' said Gil. 'Because if a burst of cannon-fire doesn't get us, we'll die from starvation.'

'But we're no longer shocked by any of it,' said Crispian. 'Even those appalling burns from that stuff that's being used—'

'Sulphur mustard,' said Gil.

'They scream with the pain, those poor wretches who've suffered burns,' said Crispian, half to himself. 'I can hear them sometimes from my window.'

I did not tell the others, but I heard the screams, as well. Sometimes, in the depths of those nights, unable to sleep, hearing the agonized sobbing from the other rooms, I used to imagine the sounds were coming from my own soul.

'But we're accepting it all,' said Crispian, with angry despair. 'That's what sickens me. We're seeing it as normal—we're hardly even upset by it any more.'

I wrote, 'Speak for yourself,' on the slate, and Crispian sent me one of his intense looks that usually heralded the start of some deep and searching discussion. Gil just winked at me and went off somewhere.

It pains me to record this, but during those weeks I don't think I ever heard Gil complain and I don't think I ever saw him give way to anger or fear. Somehow he maintained that air of flippancy all the way through. I suspect it was a mask, and I suppose he was trying to appear in a favourable light to Crispian. I don't know if it did him any good with Crispian, who, as far as I could make out, remained in chaste celibacy in his own bedroom every night. Gil could have been in half a dozen bedrooms every night, for all I knew, and probably was. Even war and famine don't prevent people from fornicating. I shouldn't think anything ever prevented Gil.

But one day it would all end—I clung to that thought. And then we would be back in England, and England meant Cadences—the bank, the old manor, the money...everything I wanted and had been cheated of having. Everything Crispian was preventing me from having.

'Crispian's my legitimate son,' Julius had said to me all those years ago. 'My heir. I'll make sure you're looked after, of course, but you won't inherit Cadences.'

*You won't inherit Cadences...*The words still reverberated in my mind even after so long. To Julius's ghost, I said, Oh won't I, though?

It was almost the end of May before we were finally able to leave Edirne. And although it's probably unusual to record gratitude to a man you intend to kill, in the name of justice I have to admit that when we finally got back to England, Crispian did everything he could to help me.

❄ ❄ ❄

Crispian had always known that when they finally got back to England he would do everything he could to help Jamie.

In the infirmary within the fortress, Raif had told Crispian that Jamie's wounds would eventually heal. Then he said, 'But I'm afraid his face—his mouth—will always be...' He paused, obviously searching for the word.

'Scarred?' said Crispian.

'Misshapen?' said Gil. 'Deformed?'

'Deformed,' said Raif. 'That will always be there. I am sorry, but there is nothing I can do about that.' He paused again, then said, 'Has he ever offered any explanation as to why they believed him a spy?'

'No,' said Crispian quickly. 'And I haven't asked him. I don't think I'll ever be able to.' He looked at Raif and said, 'You don't believe he was innocent, do you?'

'Mr Cadence, I have no opinion. I heal bodies. Souls and minds I leave to others.'

Souls and minds. Many times during those weeks, Crispian felt as if the images of famine and suffering and loss were etching themselves on his mind as if corrosive poison was dripping onto it.

'When you reach England, what will he do, your cousin?' asked Raif.

'There's a place in the country where he could live,' said Crispian.

'Your family's house?'

'Yes.' An image of Cadence Manor, remote and quiet, flickered on Crispian's mind. He said, 'I think it's what he'll want. I'll find some kind of work for him, though. He'll need to be occupied.'

'While you go off to fight the war that is coming?'

'No,' said Crispian. 'No, I shan't fight in it.'

'No? I thought the British were great ones when it came to fighting wars.'

'We are. But after what I've seen here I'm too sickened by violence. I won't fight in this war.'

'You surprise me,' said Raif.

'I surprise myself.'

CHAPTER THIRTY-FOUR

Jamie Cadence's Journal

CRISPIAN DID NOT OFTEN surprise me, but he surprised me over his decision not to fight in the war against Germany.

We learned about the declaration of hostilities with Germany at Cadence Manor. I remember we were all in the big drawing room and the early August sunshine was streaming through the French windows. Crispian and Gil—Gil was often at the manor in those days—were arguing rather listlessly about going along to the billiard room for a game or two. If they did they would probably include me and I would probably shake my head. Serena Cadence was seated a little apart from everyone—she always was. She always sought the shadowy corner of any room, even in those days. In strong sunlight it was sometimes possible to see that her hands were slightly marked. She covered them with trailing sleeves or those lace mittens ladies sometimes wore for evenings, but every time I saw her hands, it was as if I was seven years old again, standing by the bedside of the nightmare creature that was my mother. It looked as if the disease had gone from my mother to Julius, and then to Serena. If I had been given to biblical thoughts, I might have dwelled on the hoary old lines about the sins of the fathers descending unto the third and fourth generation.

The coffee tray had been brought in, and Colm and old Dr Martlet were considering embarking on a game of chess in the library. But shortly after that Flagg returned, bearing a telegram on a small tray. Most of the country probably heard about the war from neighbours, or in the taproom of their local pub, or even by listening to the wireless—wirelesses were becoming quite common by 1914. Not the Cadences. The information was carried to them by their butler on a silver salver.

It was a long telegram, as those things go. I think it was from someone at the Treasury who was letting all the leading financial houses know what had happened. I do remember it contained parts of the statement made by Herbert Asquith, the Prime Minister, to the Government, and also parts of the King's speech to the armed forces.

Asquith and the King said many things, but the core of the message—the words that I remember so vividly— were these. 'His Majesty's Government has declared to the German Government that a state of war exists between Great Britain and Germany as from 11 p.m. on 4 August.'

The King's statement, in summary, said, 'Germany tried to bribe us with peace to desert our friends and duty. But Great Britain has preferred the path of honour.'

We all listened as Crispian read it out. We were all there, even Saul. He was only a few months old, of course, but I can still remember the bassinet in the corner, and the swathed child lying inside it. They used to place him away from the light, hoping the marks on his face wouldn't be noticed. They were more noticeable as he grew older, but no one ever commented on them.

I remember that old Martlet, stupid old fool, made some crass, sentimental observation about how sad to think an innocent child had been born into a world that was about to see a bloodbath rage across Europe.

Inevitably it was Crispian who said, 'Oh, the war will be all over by Saul's second birthday.'

Cadence Manor, 1914

'I'm not a coward,' said Crispian defiantly.

'I know you're not.' Gil was reading that morning's *Times*, apparently absorbed in the latest news.

'But I find the act of war—of inflicting pain, violence— entirely wrong.' Crispian frowned, trying to sort out his thoughts, aware of Gil watching him. 'They'll all think I'm a coward for not fighting, though,' he said.

'Does that bother you?' said Gil, finally looking up from his newspaper.

'It does, a bit.'

'But not enough to alter things?'

'No. It's because of everything we saw and experienced in Edirne,' said Crispian. 'Not only what was done to Jamie, but the rest of it. All those months of people dying and starving. The sheer bloody waste of human life. It's a—a *deep* feeling. And yet...'

'Yes?'

'And yet I know this is what's called a just war,' he said. 'I know it's one that has to be fought—and it's certainly one that has to be won.'

'And you're having trouble reconciling those two feelings?' said Gil, putting the newspaper aside.

'Yes.'

'Yes, I see that. But if you could fight it in another way,' said Gil, thoughtfully, 'would you do so?'

'I think so. Yes, of course I would.'

'Even if it meant going to France? Belgium? Being in the thick of the actual fighting?'

'Yes,' said Crispian again.

'What about Cadences? Finance is a part of war, isn't it? Wouldn't you be needed there?'

'It runs itself,' said Crispian. 'Well, there's a good Board of Directors. Why?'

'The government needs medical help,' said Gil. 'They're already trying to recruit people through Guy's Hospital. And the Red Cross organization wants volunteers—they're joining forces with the Order of St John. How would you feel about becoming part of that?'

'But I haven't any medical training,' said Crispian.

'If we're being accurate, I've only got three-quarters,' said Gil. 'I never qualified. But I'm going to see if they'll take me in one of the medical corps, although I don't know yet in what capacity.' He leaned forward, his expression for once serious. 'Crispian, if I could get you in with me, would you do it?'

'I don't know,' said Crispian. 'Could it be done? And would I be of any use?'

'God, yes. The Red Cross have already said they need untrained people to man first-aid posts and provide transport. There's talk of motorized ambulances on the actual battlefields—you can drive.'

'Well, after a fashion.'

'Please come with me,' said Gil, and for the first time his voice was stripped of the flippancies and the mocking edge. 'Crispian, please,' he said.

Crispian stared at him. 'Yes,' he said at last. 'Yes, all right.'

❀ ❀ ❀

After Crispian went away, not to fight, but to act as some kind of medical assistant, people jeered at Serena if she went out, and shouted that her son was a coward. She refused to let anyone see how upset and humiliated she · was, but once, on one of her very rare outings through the lanes (Flagg had learned to drive out of sheer necessity), a group of women stood in the road, barring their way.

'Where's your son?' they shouted. 'Not fighting the Hun, is he? Not like the rest of the men.'

'Coward,' yelled another. 'Husband and brother and two sons, I had, and all of them dead save my youngest and he's left a leg in France.'

'We sacrificed our men to the war,' cried the first. 'What have you sacrificed?' She darted forward and thrust a handful of something through the grille of the car.

Serena said, 'Flagg, what...?'

'White feathers,' said Flagg. 'But pay them no attention, madam, for they don't know the truth of it, as we do. Mr Crispian's fully as brave as anyone, going onto the battlefields like he does, bringing the wounded men out.'

'Drive on,' said Serena stiffly. 'Drive round them.' She had been determined to remain seated upright, but as they went around the women she shrank involuntarily into the car's dim safe interior, putting up a hand to shield her face. There was a hot lump of angry misery in her throat but she would not cry—she would *not*—purely because a few ignorant angry village woman had shouted at her. She knew the truth about her son, and that was all that mattered.

As if to balance things out, when she got back, there was a letter from Crispian, which the post had just delivered. Serena was pleased to hear from him, even though the letter was a scrappy one. But it said he was cheerful and well, and that he hoped he might get leave very soon, and he was looking forward to some of Mrs Flagg's cooking after the meagre rations he was getting.

Hetty and Dora thought it ever so romantic that Mr Crispian was coming home, although Hetty thought he ought to be fighting properly. Bandaging people up was not real war, she said, and was told very sharply by Mr Flagg to hold her tongue.

'You don't know what you're talking about,' he said. 'It takes a deal of courage to go onto a battlefield and carry off wounded men.'

Mrs Flagg said she supposed Hetty would have let the poor men lie there like animals, dying in the heathen mud.

'Madam read the letter out to me,' said Flagg. 'I think it was a comfort to her to get it after those stupid women screaming at her in the lane. I'd have to say, though, that the letter didn't tell much, not really.'

'They censor letters from France,' said Hetty, who had walked out with a soldier for a few weeks before he went back to the front.

'Mr Crispian said it was difficult to write clearly because the billet—the place where he was sleeping—wasn't very well lit,' said Flagg. 'Sad that, I thought.'

'We'll light every lamp in the house for him when he comes home,' promised Mrs Flagg.

✿ ✿ ✿

There was never much light inside the small Red Cross post and even on the first day of July only a smeary greyness trickled in. Crispian thought it was as if all the mud and the suffering and the despair had leaked into the whole landscape. At times, struggling to help men who had been shot or wounded from shellfire—helping to carry stretchers, sometimes driving one of the battered motorized ambulances—he had time to think that he had wanted to avoid violence, yet was now in the middle of a violence he could not have imagined.

But the day was starting and it had to be faced, and he thought he would get dressed and go in search of a cup of tea; there was generally a large urn simmering over some-body's fire. He was pulling on his shoes when there was a movement from the bed.

'I thought you were still asleep,' said Crispian.

'No. I was watching you. I like watching you get dressed. You're so neat and graceful. You looked sad, though,' said Gil. 'What were you thinking?'

'Oh, how similar all war is when you get down to it. The stench of gangrenous wounds, the lack of sanitation.'

'Dysentery and overflowing latrines, and stale cooking and cordite,' said Gil. 'Oh, and that awful stuff they use to sluice down the trenches—chloride of lime. And before much longer there'll be the stench of rotting carcasses. They won't be able to bury a quarter of them until all this is over. Do you ever regret accompanying me, Crispian?'

Crispian looked at Gil for a moment. His hair, which needed cutting, was tousled on the pillow like spun floss, and it was probably several weeks since he had been able to shave.

'I don't regret any of it,' he said.

He did not. Nor had he ever regretted what had happened between them on the night they reached the first Red Cross post. They had been in France for only a few weeks—the Red Cross was still setting up first-aid posts near to what would become the ravaged battlefields along the Somme—but Gil had tapped lightly at his door late one night and asked to come in. Crispian had been deeply apprehensive about what the war was going to mean, and when he left England there had been jeers and accusations of cowardice because he had not volunteered for active service. On that night he had been homesick and in a highly emotional state, and it had been the night he stopped fighting Gil, finally and for always.

He had supposed the physical satisfaction with a man would, in the end, be much the same as it was with a woman. What he had not expected—what he did not think he could have achieved with any woman—was the extraordinary mental fusion that took place. He had no idea if this was simply that two masculine bodies were experiencing the same sensations and were both aware of the other's emotions, or if it was because he and Gil had some affinity that went beyond the physical.

And now, almost two years later, he sat at the narrow, grimed window, staring out at the grey morning and tried to think how they would arrange their lives, he and Gil, when this war was over and they were back in England. He could not imagine how they could live, but he could not imagine a world without Gil. He could not, however, really visualize any world other than this grey half-world.

He was about to say he would try to get two mugs of tea to bring back, and that with luck there might be some hot food as well, when a burst of sound from the east reached him.

'They're shelling again,' said Gil, scrambling out of bed and reaching for his clothes to dress with the careless haste that was now part of life. 'You'd think they'd let up for a couple of hours at least, wouldn't you? I think it's back to the main post for me,' he said.

'I'd better come with you,' said Crispian, abandoning all thoughts of breakfast. As Gil opened the door, he said, 'We may as well go together.'

❀ ❀ ❀

Serena was in the drawing room at Cadence Manor when the telegram arrived—the hateful orange envelope that everyone in England feared to receive. She nodded to Flagg to leave her, knowing he would probably wait for news in the hall anyway.

Yes, there it was, as damning and as final as words could be.

'Deeply regret inform you Crispian Cadence killed on the field of battle…Extreme bravery, despite being non-combatant…Outright shot to head, no suffering…Sincerest condolences…'

After what felt like a very long time, Serena became aware of the telephone ringing, and then of Flagg's voice saying it was Dr Martlet, and would her ladyship speak to him. He would switch it through to her, if so. Serena hated the telephone and it was extremely unreliable anyway. But she said yes, she would speak to him.

Dr Martlet's voice said, 'Lady Cadence? I think you've had a telegram?'

'Yes.'

'Crispian.'

It was not quite a question, but Serena said, 'Yes. Crispian's gone. I don't know why one uses that word, except it seems less harsh...' She paused, because to use the word 'dead' about Crispian, who had been so alive, so bright and good and so very strong, might bring the deep and dreadful grief welling up from her heart. She remembered how he had written that his billet was not very well lit, and how Mrs Flagg, loyal to her finger-bones, had vowed they would light all the lamps for him when he came home. They would never light them now because Crispian would never come home.

Gillespie Martlet said, 'Gil's dead as well.'

'Oh, no. I'm so sorry.' The words came out colourlessly, but in Serena's mind was the vivid glowing image of the two young men who had gone out to France, both of them so very brave, despite what people had thought and said of them.

'They were both killed while carrying the wounded away from the battlefield near the Somme, seemingly,' said Dr Martlet. 'And from the date and time, it seems they went together.'

CHAPTER THIRTY-FIVE

The Present

V ERONICA'S DAY HAD started off looking a bit dreary—nothing much to do, no dear old Clem to phone for a gossipy chat, no shopping trip or lunch planned. Then, out of the blue, the phone rang and the voice that by now sent little thrills of delight all over her said, 'Berenice? Are you by any chance free this evening?'

That was like him, flattering her by assuming she had a frantic social life, implying he did not really think someone like her could be free at such short notice.

Veronica pretended to consult a diary. 'I am, as it happens,' she said. 'What exactly had you in mind?'

'I thought I might look in for a drink,' he said. 'Would that be all right?'

Would it be all right? But it was never a good idea to seem too eager, so Veronica said, 'Yes, do call. That would be nice.'

'Half seven? I'll see you then,' he said, and rang off. He never spent much time on the phone.

He arrived punctually as always. He had told her once that punctuality was the politeness of kings. He said it was believed to be a phrase coined by a French king. This was one of the things Veronica found so entrancing:

he was widely read and so cultured. She was toying with the idea of taking some kind of evening class so she could match him. It would make for an evening out and she could buy some smart dark suits to wear to the classes.

He complimented Veronica's new hairstyle; she had been able to get a last-minute appointment at the local salon after he phoned and had had blonde highlights put in, so she was pleased he noticed. She waited, hopefully, to see how the evening would unfold and by way of opening the subject, asked how long he would be staying.

'All evening, if you can put up with me.'

'I think I can manage that.' They smiled at one another. It was wonderful how much in accord they were. Veronica said, 'And the entertainment? Did you have something in mind?'

He smiled, and his whole face lightened. 'I did, as a matter of fact,' he said. 'I've been looking forward to telling you about that.'

Veronica sighed with pleasure and leaned back against the sofa, stretching her legs sensuously. She was wearing expensive black stockings with killer heels. The heels were crippling to walk in but they looked really good, so it was a pity not to show them off a bit.

The entertainment was to be another of their role-playing games. He was endlessly inventive. She marvelled at how inventive he was. He ought to write a book or something. He had laughed when she had said that once.

Tonight he was going to be a house-burglar. Not the rough kind, of course. Not like an inarticulate teenager, high on drugs, smashing a window to get in and grab the DVD-player or the stereo. He would be the old-fashioned kind: the gentlemanly cat burglar—Raffles, perhaps, or Arsène Lupin or even a swashbuckling Scarlet Pimpernel.

'Slinking into the house under cover of darkness,' he said, watching Veronica. 'Initially after the jewels owned by the lady of the house.'

'But ending up in the bed of the lady of the house?' said Veronica, and was delighted when he smiled approvingly. 'You clever girl, Berenice,' he said. 'You have no idea what a delight it is to talk to someone who understands so instinctively. So many ladies don't. But you're different, aren't you? That's exactly what I had in mind. Let's see, it's ten to eight. How about if I stroll down to the wine shop on the corner and collect a nice bottle of something for our sophisticated burglar to enjoy later?' He stood up. 'When he gets back he might find the front door is on the latch so it would be easy for him to get in. He'd come in really quietly, but once he is in he might get all kinds of surprises, mightn't he? Perhaps even a welcome he hasn't bargained for?'

'Oh, *yes!*' said Veronica gleefully.

It meant another of the frantic scrambles around the bedroom while he was gone, setting the scene. She could never prepare ahead because she simply had no idea what he would want, but tonight was fairly easy. She pulled on an ivory silk nightgown he had not seen before and thrust the discarded clothes hastily into the wardrobe. A quick dab of scent, then she turned down the lights leaving only a faint glimmer from the bedside lamp. At this time of year it was not absolutely dark at eight o'clock, but it was dark enough to warrant lights and half-drawn curtains. She got into bed to wait for his return.

Her bedroom was at the front of the house so she would probably hear him coming in, unless he was as mouse-quiet as the burglar he was pretending to be. She had left the bedroom door ajar and there was a low light in the hall downstairs so she would see his shadow on the stair. She glanced at the bedside clock. It was only ten past eight—he would not be back yet. It was a ten-minute walk to the wine shop. Say eight to ten minutes inside the shop getting the wine, then another ten minutes back. He could not be here before twenty past eight at the earliest. She was just thinking up a few suitable lines to use—he would expect her to get into the spirit of the game—but before she could do so, from downstairs came the faint sound of the front door being softly opened and then closed.

Veronica smiled, pleased he had been so quick, and watched the door, waiting to see him come up the stairs. He was taking a long time about it and the house was very quiet. Was this part of the game? Perhaps he was pouring the wine, or even pretending to search the downstairs rooms before coming upstairs, wanting to keep her in this strung-up state of anticipation. If so, she could have done without it because actually the silence was starting to become slightly scary. It would be a really good fantasy once it got going, but lying here in the near-darkness was making her feel a bit vulnerable.

Ah—there was the sound of soft footsteps on the stairs at last. Now they could begin. To start them off (also to dispel the unnerving quietness), she called out.

'Is someone there?' This was what anyone would say, hearing a sound.

There was no response, so she tried again, and this time was annoyed that her voice sounded a bit shrill. 'Who's there? Are you a burglar?'

A shadow moved on the stair. Veronica half sat up in the bed. In another minute he would appear in the doorway and say something and Veronica would stop feeling so unaccountably frightened.

The shadow came nearer and her heart began to race because there was something wrong about it. Too tall for him? Too short or too plump? She pushed back the bedclothes and reached for the dressing gown at the foot of the bed, but even as she did so the shadow became solid; it stepped into the room and Veronica let out a gasp of surprise. But the figure was across the room before she could do anything, pushing her back against the pillows, catching her off guard. Glaring eyes stared down at her and there was the glint of a knife being raised.

The figure said, 'I'm not a burglar. You know who I am, don't you, Veronica?' And then, on a throaty hissing note, 'I'm a murderer.'

There was no time to fight, no time even to cry out. Veronica felt a dreadful tearing pain in her throat that sent a searing agony down to her lungs, and she heard someone in the room give a wet bubbling gasp, then realized it was herself. For the space of two heartbeats she stared up in horror at her killer, then blackness closed down and she slumped across the pillows.

❧ ❧ ❧

Ella had not gone to Veronica's house with the intention of killing her. She had gone to ask her, openly and directly, exactly what she had meant about Clem's diaries having vanished and about Ella being the one to find his body. It would be an entirely normal thing to do and they would have a civilized discussion. Veronica would understand Ella's concern and Ella would find out exactly what Veronica had said to the solicitor and the coroner's official. She did not phone beforehand so as not to give Veronica time to prepare a story. Veronica was a great storyteller. Actually, she was a liar, if you were going to give the thing its proper name.

Circumstances favoured Ella. Amy had gone out— probably to meet that Malik man. Derek, as usual, was at one of his interminable rehearsals. Ella would be glad when that wretched opera had had its week's run at Bramley Town Hall, and life returned to normal. Still, it meant there was no one in the house tonight to ask where she was going.

She drove to Veronica's house—there was no need to be secretive about an innocent call on a friend—and parked in the street a few yards away because she could see a car in Veronica's drive. It was not the little hatchback that Veronica drove and Ella frowned, because it had not occurred to her that Veronica might have a visitor. Might it be this mysterious lover, about whom she had been dropping all those heavy hints? Ella had no wish to meet him, and she had even less wish to ring the doorbell and be greeted by Veronica in a tousled state of undress. She slowed her footsteps, trying to decide what to do. She had got as far as the gate when a wholly different emotion slammed into her mind.

She recognized the car parked in the drive. She stood there for a moment, her mind in chaos, and as she did so the front door opened and a figure came out. It walked quickly down the drive and Ella stepped back into the shadow of the thick hedge, ready to run back to her car. But the figure turned in the other direction. Ella watched it until it turned the corner, then went into the house. Her mind was swirling, and something seemed to be filling up her entire body—something that was furious and scaldingly painful, and something that whispered to her what she should do. Ella nodded slowly, because she could see the whispering voice was right. It was absolutely clear what had to be done.

She went into the house—the front door was not locked—and, still in the same scalding dream-state, went through to the kitchen. What to use? That was the question now. What about a knife? Yes, there was a rack of them on the work surface. Ella took the largest and tested it on an apple lying in a bowl of fruit. The blade was shockingly unsharp, which was typical of Veronica, so Ella gave it a few turns in the sharpener standing nearby. It would be dreadful to bungle this, with Veronica being such a friend all these years. Satisfied the knife was properly sharp, she went upstairs and into the bedroom. Then she stabbed her oldest friend twice through the throat.

❧ ❧ ❧

After it was done, Ella stood looking down at Veronica's body for a long time. The corrosive fury had left her and it was as if she stared into a black gaping void. She had no idea what to do next and the yawning chasm was stopping her from thinking. It was the faint clatter of the knife slipping from her nerveless hands that snapped her back to awareness. The black void dissolved magically and Ella was able to think properly again. She stepped back from the bed, which was all bloodied and messy. Had any of the blood gone onto Ella? Yes, of course it had, it was on her sweater and her hands. But her legs and her shoes were all right.

She went into Veronica's bathroom, took off the sweater and washed it as thoroughly but hastily as she could. Veronica always had nicely scented soap and the towels were a very good quality. Ella dried her hands, then went back downstairs and pushed the sweater into the handbag she had left in the hall. It was a large everyday handbag with a sturdy metal clasp. She had left her jacket on the end of the banister and she put it on, buttoning it up to the neck to hide the fact that she had only her bra underneath. To make sure, she took one of Veronica's scarves from the hallstand and wound it round her neck, draping it over the jacket's fastenings.

What else? She had probably left any number of fingerprints everywhere, but she was a frequent visitor to Veronica's house so that was all right. She was just looking round the kitchen to make sure she had not left anything incriminating, when the front door opened and someone came quietly into the house and went up the stairs.

Ella had expected this, and the plan that had slid neatly into her mind earlier was very clear. She knew exactly what to do.

She went out through the kitchen door and walked quietly along the side of the house. But she stopped under the front bedroom window, which was Veronica's, because she wanted to hear, she wanted to make *sure*...

She made sure all right. The cry that came through the half-open window was unmistakable. Ella smiled to herself, and felt in her handbag for her keys. They were quite heavy keys because she always had Derek's car keys on the ring, as he had her keys on his. She had insisted on that for years, saying they never knew when they might find it useful.

It was very useful now. She stopped by the car parked on Veronica's drive and quietly opened the driver's door. The familiar chamois driving gloves were in the side pocket; Ella pulled them out and wiped the bloodstained knife on them. She was careful to leave enough smears of blood on the handle to be noticeable but she made sure she wiped the handle thoroughly enough to get rid of her own fingerprints. Only when she was satisfied did she drop the knife and the gloves onto the seat next to the driver's.

Then she locked the car again and went back down the street to her own car. In a moment she would make a call to the police. It would be an anxious, slightly distressed call, and it would bring them out to the house of her oldest friend. Once inside the house, they would find Ella's cheating faithless husband standing over the murdered body of Veronica Campion, with whom he had been having an affair.

CHAPTER THIRTY-SIX

AMY HAD CRIED for almost the entire evening, mostly for Gran, who looked as if someone had stripped all the bones out of her body, but also for Gramps, dear, well-meaning Gramps, who had been taken to the police station and locked in a cell, and was going to be charged with murdering Veronica.

Amy simply did not believe he had done it, although she supposed it was just about credible that he had been having it off with Veronica. It was important to remember that because people were old—well, OK, older—it did not mean they were past it. Gramps had clearly not been past it if he had been screwing Veronica. In fact, when Amy thought back, Gramps often had a definite glint in his eye. He was actually quite nice-looking, with that thick silvery hair and dark eyebrows, and his enthusiasm for his beloved opera and his interest in the people he worked with was rather endearing. The more Amy thought about it, the more she thought Gramps might be rather admired at the council offices and in the amateur operatic circles. But this started her crying all over again, because it made her remember how he had loved his rehearsal nights and enjoyed talking about them, and how he had played some of his Gilbert and Sullivan CDs, and how she had planned to talk to him about *The Deserted Village* music.

Whatever the truth of all this, she was not going anywhere until it was put right, even if she had to miss the whole of next term and even if she had to miss her exams. At some point she would have to phone her parents, although she had no idea what she was going to say to either of them, and specially to Dad. It was not a thing that could very easily be told over the phone. Amy was suddenly unreasonably annoyed with Dad for going out to Africa to build bridges for somebody and taking Mum with him, so that neither of them was here.

The really upsetting thing was that the evidence seemed so damning. Two CID men called at the house and explained everything. Amy had not had a great deal to do with the police, but she thought they were being very considerate.

It was almost midnight when they arrived, apologizing for disturbing Mrs Haywood at such a late hour, which Amy thought an unnecessary remark to make, because they must know that if your husband had just been carted off for murder you were not likely to head for bed at the usual time. Gran had been sitting in the chair by the fire since she got back, shivering and staring at nothing. But when the detectives arrived she seemed to make a huge effort, and by the time Amy had made coffee for them, she was talking almost normally.

They questioned her carefully but very thoroughly. She had gone to her friend Veronica Campion's house earlier tonight, that was right, was it?

'I did go to Veronica's,' said Gran in a wobbly voice that Amy hoped would not break. 'There was no particular reason for the visit, except that we've rather clung together since Clem Poulter died. Childhood friends, you see. We were supporting one another through the loss. I just felt I'd like to see her. She would have understood. At least,' said Gran with a brief glint of her old waspishness, 'I thought she would.'

'You didn't phone ahead?'

'No. We hardly ever did. We both knew it was all right to just turn up. Her home was mine, just as mine was hers.'

Amy looked up, startled, because Gran *never* wanted people to call on her out of the blue and she never called on people without arranging it beforehand. She always said it was the height of bad manners. Perhaps she was trying to protect Gramps, though.

'What time would it be when you went to Mrs Campion's?' asked the inspector.

'Eight o'clock, or thereabouts. I can't be any more precise. Amy, what time did you go out?'

'Straight after supper,' said Amy. She had been hoping to see Jan in the Red Lion. He had not been around, but she had stayed for an hour or so, talking to one or two people she'd met at the quiz nights. 'It was probably around quarter past seven,' she said.

'That sounds about right,' said Gran. 'And Derek went out about the same time. He said he had a rehearsal,' she said. 'He's in the Bramley Operatic Society, Inspector.'

'Yes, we know about that. We've been checking up there, Mrs Haywood. I'm afraid it seems Mr Haywood hasn't attended many of those rehearsals for about a month.'

'He was seeing Veronica on those nights,' said Gran, half to herself.

'It's almost certain he was. We've questioned a couple of her neighbours and they saw Mr Haywood's car parked on the drive on three or four occasions.'

'Yes, I see,' said Gran. She frowned, then appeared to make another effort. 'I should think I got to Veronica's house around twenty to eight. I parked a little way down the street because I saw there was a car already on the drive.'

'You recognized it as your husband's car, though?'

'No, I didn't. I'm sorry if that sounds odd, but I just registered that Veronica had a visitor. I probably noticed it was the same make and colour as my husband's, but I'm not even sure about that. I certainly didn't look at the numberplate or anything like that. There was no reason to.'

'There wouldn't be anything to identify it?' asked the sergeant. 'Anything on the back seat or in the windscreen? A sticker for the AA or National Trust or something?'

'Neither my husband nor I stick things on car windscreens,' said Gran, a trifle sharply. 'I like a car to be clean and uncluttered.'

'Of course.'

'But I did hesitate about ringing the bell,' she said.

'Why was that?'

'I'm afraid it was social embarrassment,' said Gran. 'Veronica had been hinting at a new man in her life.' She gave a small laugh and Amy wished she had not because it sounded false and forced. Gran seemed to realize it and said, 'So I didn't want to intrude on anything.'

'Very understandable.'

'I was trying to make up my mind whether to simply come home, when I heard her scream.'

'You heard that from outside?'

'Oh, yes. Her bedroom is at the front. When I looked up the little top window was open. I heard her quite clearly.'

'Was it just a scream or did she actually call something out? A name, for instance?'

Gran hesitated and her eyes slid away from the inspector's sharp regard. Amy had the unwelcome thought that Gran *had* heard Veronica shout a name and the name had been Derek, but she saw Gran was going to be loyal. Even though Gramps had been shagging Veronica, Gran would still be loyal to him.

'It was just a cry,' said Gran, determinedly.

Amy found it so upsetting to see Gran so obviously trying to shield Gramps she thought she might start crying again, so she pretended to go out to the kitchen to reheat the coffee.

When she got back they were still talking about the scream.

'None of the neighbours heard it,' the inspector was saying and Amy thought there was a slightly sharper note in his voice. It was ridiculous to think he was trying to catch Gran out, but for a moment she did think it.

'I don't suppose they would,' Gran said. 'It's a detached house with a fair bit of garden on each side. And at that time of the evening people would have televisions on.'

'Possibly so. What did you do when you heard the scream?'

'There were two screams at least,' said Gran. 'Then a sort of crash, as if something might have been knocked over in a struggle.'

'What did you do then?'

For a moment Amy thought Gran was going to say, in her most acidic voice, 'What would you have done in that situation?' but she said she had run back to her car.

'You didn't think of trying to get into the house?'

'I did not. For all I knew it might simply have been a...a lovers' quarrel.' The expression came out with distaste. 'And if it was a house-breaker, I certainly wasn't going to face him. I did what I should think most people would have done. I went back to my car and used my mobile to call the police.'

'We've got a record of the call,' said the sergeant, who had been making notes at a furious rate. 'It was logged at eight ten.'

'I think I said something about hearing screams from the house and being afraid someone might be in trouble,' said Gran. 'Whoever I spoke to told me to wait in my car with the doors locked, and they would send someone straightaway.' She leaned back in her chair as if saying all this had exhausted her, which made Amy feel anxious for her. But Gran took a deep breath, and went on. 'After about ten minutes a policeman and policewoman arrived. They saw me, and again told me to stay put. They said it was most likely what they called "a domestic", but they would check. And then, after about a quarter of an hour...Her voice wobbled much more now and, to Amy's horror, she began to cry. 'After about a quarter of an hour,' said Gran, weeping in earnest now, 'they came out with my husband and put him into a patrol car. They wouldn't let me speak to him. I don't even think he knew I was there...'

Amy said, 'Inspector, is there anything else, because I think...'

'Not for the moment.' The two men stood up. 'Thank you very much, Mrs Haywood,' the inspector said. 'I'm sorry to have caused you this distress, but you'll understand we have to ask these questions. Your husband hasn't been charged with anything so far, but I'm bound to say things aren't looking good. The knife was in his car, you know. He'd tried to wipe it clean on some driving gloves.'

'But you said you found him actually in the bedroom,' said Amy. 'He wouldn't have done all that—um—stuff with gloves and things, then gone back into the house, would he?'

'We did find him in the bedroom and that's one of the details we've still got to iron out,' said the inspector. 'But there could be any number of reasons for him to go back in. He might have realized he'd forgotten something—left a coat behind or a scarf.'

'Or,' said the sergeant, 'simply gone back to check he hadn't left any clues.'

'But,' said Amy, 'why would he kill Veronica at all?'

'The likeliest explanation is that she was exerting some pressure on him over their affair,' said the inspector. 'Perhaps threatening to make it public—to tell Mr Haywood's wife about it. He could have lost his temper and tried to silence her.'

Amy said incredulously, 'But he wouldn't. He's the gentlest, most unviolent man you'd ever meet,' and caught a quick movement from Gran.

'Yes, madam?' The inspector had seen the movement as well, even though Gran had tried to suppress it. 'Were you going to say something?'

'No, except—no, nothing at all.'

'Mrs Haywood, we will get at the truth of this in the end,' said the inspector. 'So please say whatever you were going to.'

'It's only that Amy isn't right,' said Gran, sounding very reluctant. 'My husband does have a bit of a temper. Quite a hot temper, actually. I don't suppose many people have ever seen it because he keeps it well reined in. But it's there, all right.' She gave a small shudder and hunched her shoulders, wrapping her arms around her body as if for warmth. Amy stared at her in horrified disbelief, but then Gran put up a hand to shade her eyes, and said, in a thready voice, 'And now, if you really have finished your questions, I should like to take one of my pills and go to bed.'

❀ ❀ ❀

Ella was not going to be complacent about what she had done tonight, but she thought she could feel cautiously pleased with herself.

She felt very strange, slightly dizzy and unconnected, as if she had taken some strong drug that was creating a thick glass screen between her and the rest of the world. That would be the shock of seeing Derek go into that slut Veronica's house. When Ella thought about that—when she thought how they had cheated and lied and made a fool of her, probably laughing at her behind her back—a wave of such intense anger swept over her she wanted to scream.

But if they had laughed at her Ella was having the laugh on them now. Veronica was on a mortuary slab and Derek was in a cell at the local police station, waiting to be charged with murder. Ella would make very sure he *was* charged; she had made a start on that by telling the CID inspector that Derek had a temper. In the days ahead there would be other things she could do—small but telling things—that would add to the impression of his guilt. She supposed she ought to feel sick and horrified at finding Derek and Veronica were having an affair, but she did not, although she had given a good performance of it. It had fooled Amy and the CID men, that was for sure.

For the next few days she would continue to appear as a wife devastated but loyal and prepared to forgive. She would visit Derek at the police station—she did not want to, but people would find that admirable. So brave, they would say. My goodness, Ella stood by that rat Derek Haywood when most other women would have turned their backs.

Ella would turn her back in the end, of course. Whether he was found guilty or innocent, quietly and discreetly she would file for divorce as soon as possible. Then she would sell this house and buy a smaller one, a bungalow perhaps. She did not think she would move away from the area. She was liked and admired, and people would be sympathetic and supportive.

She thought back over the last few hours, examining all the details, making sure she had covered all her tracks. There were no flaws, no weaknesses anywhere. But just as she was finally starting to slide into sleep she was horrified to realize she had missed something potentially damning.

The policewoman had insisted on driving her home from Veronica's house, using Ella's own car, saying she was not fit to drive herself after such a shocking experience. Ella had agreed and, once in the house, had come upstairs, leaving the policewoman to make a cup of tea.

She had the handbag containing her bloodstained sweater with her, and automatically put it at the side of the dressing table where she always kept the bag currently in use. There had been plenty of time to discard the jacket and pull on a sweater before going back downstairs, and also time to check her appearance in the bathroom mirror. But the bag, with its damning evidence, was where she had left it. How could she have forgotten it?

She got out of bed and opened it. The sweater was crumpled up, the bloodstains dried to a horrid dark brown, and the blood had marked the bag's lining, which meant the bag would also have to be destroyed. Moving quietly so as not to disturb Amy, she transferred most of the contents to another bag of similar size. The little make-up purse, her address book, her wallet and the mobile phone all went into the other bag.

She would not feel safe until she had got rid of the stained bag and the sweater. Derek said you should always do a thing right away. Seize the day, he said. *Carpe diem.* That had been Derek pretending to be learned. Veronica had probably been impressed by it, although she would not have been impressed if she had had forty years of it, as Ella had.

But she would seize the day now, or rather the night. She pulled on trousers and a sweater, and slipped her feet into flat shoes. Carrying the bag with its damning contents, and without switching on any lights, she went down the stairs and out through the kitchen door. She would bury these things where she had buried Clem's diaries. Later, perhaps at the weekend, as originally planned, she would pretend the hedge clippings over them needed burning. Amy would think she was being absurd, bothering about garden rubbish when Derek was in a police cell, but Ella would be querulous and insistent. It would give her something to do, she would say. Something ordinary to occupy her mind.

She fetched a trowel from the potting shed and went down the path to the end of the garden around the side of the conservatory. As she glanced through the glass sides, she saw the oleander bush, and smiled slightly, remembering Clem.

The end of the garden was where they generally got rid of garden rubbish, and where they occasionally had barbecues. Derek liked barbecues; he usually donned a silly chef's hat to grill sausages and spare ribs. He would not be doing that in the future, and Ella would not have to buy the ingredients for the complicated marinade he insisted on making, messing up the kitchen and splashing soy sauce everywhere.

But it was a part of the garden that was not overlooked, and in any case it was two o'clock in the morning. Amy's bedroom was at the front of the house; she would neither see nor hear anything. Ella bent down, brushing away the few hedge clippings and scooping out a good deep hole for the bag and the sweater, which she put on top of Clem's diaries. She patted the earth back in place, replaced the hedge clippings and, satisfied with what she had done, returned the trowel to the shed. Back in her bedroom, she got into bed again and this time fell asleep almost at once.

❀ ❀ ❀

Amy could not sleep. She supposed nobody would sleep after such extraordinary events. She went over and over it all in her mind, while the bedside clock ticked its way round to half past one, and then two. This was infuriating. If she did not get some sleep she would be like a piece of chewed string in the morning, and she had to be strong and resourceful for Gran. But the more she tried to sleep, the wider awake she became.

She got up to take a paracetamol, then went quietly downstairs, not wanting to wake Gran if she had managed to get to sleep, but thinking she would find something light to read. Gran's taste ran to the milder kind of chick-lit and historical romances—there was a whole shelf of Georgette Heyer in the sitting room—and Gramps liked nineteenth-century sea battles: Alexander Kent and Patrick O'Brian. Amy could not decide between Regency ballrooms and Regency sailors so she took one of each. She was about to go back upstairs when she heard footsteps outside the house. Her heart skipped a beat: surely they were not about to have a break-in on top of everything else? Perhaps it was the police returning with some news. But the police would not creep furtively round the house like that. Amy switched off the table lamp and went cautiously to the window, drawing back the curtains slightly.

A figure was half-kneeling, half-crouching over a patch of ground at the very far end of the garden and after a moment Amy saw with astonishment that it was Gran. She watched, trying to see what on earth Gran was doing. It looked so furtive Amy did not want to call out, and when Gran stood up and turned back to the house Amy scooted back to her bedroom. She heard Gran come in and go quietly into her room, then the house fell into silence. Amy, her mind tumbling with bewildering images and theories, finally drifted into an uneasy half-sleep towards dawn.

She woke at seven thirty feeling exhausted and almost as if she might be about to have flu. The day was leaden, rainclouds gathering overhead. It was unthinkable to ask Gran what she had been doing in the garden last night; Amy could not stop thinking it was something that would incriminate Gramps and had to be got rid of. But then she remembered Gran telling the inspector about Gramps's temper, and the more she thought about that, the more she thought Gran had deliberately tried to plant the idea that Gramps had a violent side.

Trying to appear normal, she made toast and scrambled eggs and persuaded Gran to eat some to keep up her strength. She could not help Gramps unless she stayed strong, said Amy firmly.

The CID sergeant and a policewoman arrived shortly after nine with Gramps's car.

'It's not really material to the case,' said the DS, 'but we had to get forensics to give it the once-over anyway. It's as clean as a whistle. I'll leave it in the drive, shall I?'

The policewoman, who was the one who had brought Ella home last night, asked if a few overnight things could be put together for Mr Haywood.

'You're still keeping him at the station then?' said Gran.

'Well, yes, for the moment.'

'I can see him, can I?' said Gran, surprising Amy.

'Yes, certainly. The inspector wants to see you anyway.'

'Why?' said Gran very sharply.

'Oh, only to check your statement before it's printed for you to sign. Standard procedure. We'll give you a lift if you prefer. I don't expect you feel like driving.'

'Would you like me to come with you?' asked Amy. 'I could drive.'

But Gran seemed to want to do this on her own, which Amy understood.

'In any case I'll probably be there ages, what with going through the statement and so on. You'd be hanging around for hours.'

So instead Amy hunted out a small overnight bag and helped Gran pack it. She waited until the police car had driven Gran away, then fetched a small spade from the garden shed.

It was easy to see where Gran had been. There was a little heap of twigs and bits of hedge at the very end of the garden and it was obvious that the ground had been turned over. The threatened rain had started, huge drops that spattered down on the ground and soaked the thin shirt Amy had on. She shook her hair angrily out of her eyes and tried to persuade herself that whatever Gran had been doing last night was entirely innocent.

But she had only dug out a few spadefuls when she knew it was not innocent at all. The things Gran had buried were quite near the surface. Amy dropped the spade and kneeled down. A bloodstained sweater— Gran's oatmeal cashmere sweater she had been wearing yesterday. The leather handbag she often used, the lining visible, also bloodstained. And beneath it was what looked like a stack of leather-covered books. Amy prodded them. They were damp and the pages were already shredding so it was impossible to know what they were, but she could see they were handwritten.

It was raining even more heavily now and Amy scraped the earth back, replacing the twigs and branches. Then she put the spade away and went back into the house, thinking hard. After a moment she went to the phone and dialled the number of the Red Lion, praying the news about Veronica and Gramps would not have got out yet.

It seemed it had not, but it also seemed Dr Malik had gone out first thing after breakfast. Who was this speaking? Oh, Amy Haywood. Well, in that case, they could tell her Dr Malik had mentioned going out to one of the villages. Something to do with his research, seemingly—a nearby church, the receptionist thought he had said. He was going to check on something he had found a couple of days earlier. Was that any help?

'Yes, it is,' said Amy. 'Thank you very much.'

She put the phone down. It was just on half-past ten and Gran would probably be at the police station for another hour at least. Amy went upstairs to dry her rain-soaked hair and combed it more or less into shape, her mind still going over what she had found.

Back downstairs, on the message pad Gran kept by the phone she scribbled a note saying she had borrowed Gran's car and was going out for an hour or so. She would pick up something for their lunch. After a moment, she added a note to say Gran must of course call her if she needed to. She would leave her mobile on. As she drove off the drive she found she was already feeling better at the thought of talking to Jan.

CHAPTER THIRTY-SEVEN

B Y THE TIME ELLA reached the police station she was already feeling better. She knew how she must play this. The brave wife, determined to help her errant husband through an ordeal, but, just under the surface, a hint of bitterness and anger—the kind of anger that might let an unguarded, potentially damning remark slip.

The duty sergeant took her to see Derek. He unlocked the door and Ella paused before going in, taking in the bleak tiled walls and the squalid lavatory arrangement behind a half-screen.

Derek seemed fairly composed. Ella had wondered if they were going to have embarrassing or emotional scenes, but he was neither embarrassing nor emotional. He thanked her for coming, and said he was very sorry indeed that she had found out about his fling with Veronica. That was all it had been, he said, very seriously. Nothing more, nothing deeper. It had been a lapse, a brief weakness, snatching at his vanishing youth, wanting to feel he was still attractive.

'You do understand that, don't you?'

'I understand everything,' said Ella, sitting primly on the edge of the narrow bunk bed. 'Have they charged you with the murder yet?'

'No, but I'm told they'll have to do so in the next few hours, or let me go. They can't hold anyone for more than about twenty-four hours without making a formal charge. Habeas corpus, you know.'

It was like Derek to show off his stupid pointless knowledge at such a time. But Ella only said, 'I see. Have you got a solicitor? Do we need to arrange that?' This would be the normal thing to ask, although the only solicitor they knew was the man who had done the conveyance of their house fifteen years ago, and he had probably never seen the inside of a magistrates' court, let alone a criminal one.

'The police said they can arrange that if I want,' said Derek. 'There'll be a duty solicitor they can call in.'

'We don't want legal aid,' said Ella sharply. 'I hope you made that clear. We'll pay whatever fees are necessary.'

'Let's not worry about that yet,' said Derek. 'I expect it won't come to it anyway. Clearly some mad house-breaker got in and killed her. It'll all be sorted out quite quickly, I dare say. I'm just glad to think my parents didn't live to see this. You haven't phoned Andrew, have you? Well, don't— not yet, at any rate—and don't let Amy phone him either. There's no sense worrying him unnecessarily.'

Ella agreed she would not tell Andrew and went out. The duty sergeant showed her into CID to go through her statement with the inspector. Ella was not particularly worried about this because the story she had told was so very near the truth it was unlikely she would be caught out.

She was not caught out. The inspector took her through the details once again, then thanked her and said everything seemed clear. The statement would be ready for her to sign later that day. They would bring it out to the house, if that was all right? By then they would know if they had enough of a case to charge Mr Haywood. Would she be all right on her own?

'I'm not on my own,' said Ella. 'My granddaughter's with me. And I have very good friends—although

I'd rather not tell anyone about this until I know what's happening. My husband might be back home tonight and this sorry business over.'

The policewoman drove her home. It was still raining, although not as hard as it had been earlier. Ella went into the house to find the note from Amy, saying she had gone out, taking Ella's car, which Ella found annoying; Amy might at least have waited to hear how her grandfather was.

It was almost twelve o'clock. She went into the kitchen to make a cup of coffee and look at what they might have for lunch, and it was then she saw the tiny pieces of mud on the kitchen doorstep and the small, still-damp footprint next to them.

Ella stood looking at the marks for a long time, all thoughts of lunch gone. Probably the footprints and the mud were not in the least sinister. Most likely Amy had gone into the garden for some perfectly ordinary reason and had not wiped her shoes thoroughly enough on coming back inside. But Ella could not think why Amy would need to go into a rain-sodden garden at all. There was no washing to take in or hang out, and no rubbish to be emptied. Milk was delivered to the front of the house and had been brought in first thing.

She opened the kitchen door and looked out, trying to persuade herself she was being neurotic because she knew what was buried out there. Amy would not know about that, though. Or would she?

Ignoring the rain, Ella went down the paved path to the potting shed, and opened the door. It was dark in here. For years she had asked Derek to fix up some kind of light but he had never got round to it. Too busy, he always said. Now Ella knew what he had been busy with, the cheating adulterer.

Last night she had used a trowel to scoop out the earth and pat it back in place. The trowel was where she had left it, slightly muddied but dry. But alongside it was the small spade Derek used for borders, the spade that was seldom called into service. Somebody had called it into service recently though, because it was wet and smeary, and clumps of soil clung to the edges.

With the feeling that she was moving through a nightmare again, Ella closed the shed and went down to the place where she had buried the sweater, handbag and diaries. She could remember exactly how she had left the ground in the small hours: the ground patted flat and smooth, the hedge clippings so carefully arranged over it.

The ground was no longer flat and smooth. It was churned up, the wet earth scattered around, the hedge clippings in an untidy heap.

Amy. It must be. Somehow Amy had found out what Ella had done—perhaps she had even seen last night—and had investigated. Amy knew. She *knew*. Ella felt sick and dizzy at the realization.

But where was Amy now? Had she gone to that man, that academic she had become so friendly with?

Ella went back to the house, locked the kitchen door, then, glancing at the steadily falling rain, put on her waxed jacket, and wound a scarf round her neck. It was Veronica's scarf, the one Ella had taken to hide the blood-stains after killing her. It was a very nice scarf, silk and cashmere, and she might as well make use of it. She picked up the keys to Derek's car and set off.

She went first to the Red Lion. She had no idea what she would do or say if they seemed to know about Derek and Veronica—news travelled so fast in a small place like Upper Bramley. The receptionist, whom she knew slightly by sight, was not at the desk, but one of the barmen wandered out and asked if he could help. He was ordinary and friendly and Ella was fairly sure he had not heard.

She explained about trying to find Amy, saying there had been a muddle about meeting up and she thought

Amy might be here. 'And her mobile's switched off.' This was untrue, but he would expect her to have tried phoning.

'Nuisance for you,' said the barman sympathetically. 'She isn't here, but as it happens I had to go out about half an hour ago and I saw Amy driving out of Bramley. That'll be why her phone was off. If she was driving, I mean.'

'Are you sure it was Amy?'

'Oh, yes. In fact she waved to me. She's been in a few times so we're on waving terms, you might say.'

'Which way was she going?'

'Oh Lord, where was it? Sparrowfeld Lane, that's it. Down Mordwich Bank,' he said. 'Does that help?'

It did not really, but Ella said, 'Oh yes, thank you.' She hesitated, then said, 'Is Dr Malik in, by any chance?'

'No, he went out first thing. Off on some of his research, I think. He said he wouldn't be back until this evening.'

Then it could not be Malik Amy had gone to meet. Ella was relieved to know that at any rate. She thanked the barman, went out and got back in the car.

Sparrowfeld Lane and Mordwich Bank. Where on earth had Amy been going? Ella drove down Mordwich Bank, going rather slowly because she was not very used to Derek's car, which was bigger and more powerful than her own, looking out for her own car as she went. She absolutely must find Amy before she could talk to anyone about the stuff buried in the garden. She would not phone, because she needed to see Amy's expression and reactions. At least Amy had not gone to the police station, which was just off the High Street. Or had she? She might very well have some misguided idea of helping her grandfather by reporting her findings; she thought a lot of Derek, Ella had often noticed that. Supposing Amy had gone to the station first, asked for the CID inspector from last night and been told he was out at Cadence Manor, working on the unidentified body case? Mightn't she go out there to find him?

Ella glanced to her right, to the shallow dip of Priors Bramley. Dare she go down there? Yes, why not? If she met anyone she would say she was curious to see the place now it was open again. If she met any police, who would know about Derek, she would say she had to get away for an hour or so to clear her head.

There was not much traffic and, as she turned off the main road and went down the last stretch of bank, Priors Bramley looked deserted. There were lengths of blue-printed tape saying 'Police Incident' lying on the ground, but that was all. But however deserted the place might be, one person was certainly here, because parked a bit untidily on a grass verge was Ella's car.

Ella parked nearby, locked the car, and set off. If Amy did know about the sweater and the bag and diaries, Ella had to persuade her they were innocent. If she could not do that, then a way must be found to prevent Amy talking about them.

As she walked along, hoping to see Amy at any minute, her own childhood memories stirred. There was the little shop where her mother liked to buy knitting wool, and further along was the bakery that had sold Clem's currant bread. A thin mist lay everywhere and droplets of moisture clung to the buildings—Ella did not know if this was from the rain earlier or from the decontamination spraying.

As she went round the sharp bend in the High Street the past pressed in more insistently. The grey misty desolation heightened it: she had always remembered the past—her own past—in monochrome, like an old newsreel.

Just around the curve of the road was St Anselm's; at the thought of it Ella's apprehension ratcheted up several notches. But probably she would not need to go as far as the church—she was bound to see Amy at any minute. There was no sign of Amy, however, and, despite her resolve, as Ella reached the church she slowed down and then stopped, staring at what had been the path going up to the main entrance.

The trees that had screened St Anselm's still stood, but they looked dry and diseased, the trunks pitted and the remaining branches grotesquely twisted. Had the Geranos done that? For a moment Ella saw her mother's scarred face, and she shuddered. The lich-gate had partly collapsed, but it was almost as she remembered it. 'Sometimes they rang a lich bell,' Clem had said. 'The death bell, they called it.' How long was it since the lich bell had rung? No one would ring it for the man who had poured out the music and sobbed so painfully that day. And that second body? Would anyone have mourned for that person? Who had it been, anyway? Because I only killed one person that day, thought Ella.

Whoever the dead people had been, their stories were in the past. Today Ella could go inside that church right at this minute if she wanted to and nothing would hurt her. She stepped through the lich-gate and went a little way along the path, thinking she would take a brief look. Amy might even be in there. She had talked about some holiday project or other involving the place, although Ella could not believe Amy would be thinking about work this morning.

The headstones of the graves jutted up like dark teeth against the damp air, and mist clung to the sick-looking trees. Ella glanced up at the clock tower. Would anyone wind the clock again?

The church seemed to have withstood its half-century of desolation well, despite the stories about it crumbling away from dry rot or deathwatch beetle. Ella stood in the porch, trying to see inside. There seemed to be only the grey shadows and the brooding silence, and she turned to go back. She was halfway down what remained of the path when, from inside the church, came a sound that caused an icy hand to clutch her stomach. She spun round in horrified disbelief.

Music. Harsh, difficult music—not quite melody, not even quite chords, but unformed embryo sounds, ugly but recognizable, as if a piece of music was struggling to be born...Or as if music smothered for half a century was trying to make itself heard again.

It was as if huge invisible hands had picked Ella up and flung her back into the dark fear of her childhood. Panic coursed through her. He was still in there. Even though she had killed him fifty years ago—even though she had been sure he was dead!—he was still here. Somehow he had survived and he was trying to play his music again.

The struggling, fragmented sounds came again—deformed, like *he* had been deformed—then died away. The silence closed down, but Ella was scarcely aware of it. She was nine years old again, terrified of the man who had come down the stairs from the organ loft and crept towards her with that shambling walk...The man who had stood in the dim room inside Cadence Manor and looked at her, while the dreadful dead figure of Serena Cadence sat in the shadows, staring at nothing...

From out of the church came a figure, the outline blurred in the leaden light and the face obscured by the shadows the old church cast, but recognizably the figure of a man. Ella's reason spun wildly away from her, and she gasped and stepped back.

As the figure started to walk towards her, she gave a sob of fear and turned to run, not towards the main street and her car, but towards the left, towards Cadence Manor.

The past was still swooping and darting about Ella, but she was remembering the manor as somewhere she could hide, somewhere she had hidden in the past. Sobbing and gasping she went towards it. Here were the gates: the massive stone pillars on each side were cracked and eroded, and one gate lay on the ground while the other hung drunkenly from its hinges. But the lodge was still there, and beyond the ruined gardens she could see the outline of the manor.

Ella stopped, aware of a jabbing tightness in her chest. A stitch, that was all it was. Mum would be quite annoyed with her for running so fast and getting so upset. No—her mother was dead, she had been dead for years, and Ella was grown up. But everything around her seemed to be distorting. The entire landscape was somehow skewed and it was confusing her. But *he* was still here, she had not been confused about that. He had walked out of the church towards her, the reverberations of the distorted music still thrumming faintly on the air. She looked back down the street, then went up to the gates.

At one level of her mind—the level that was still maintaining a fragile hold on the present—she registered the signs of the police investigations. There was a kind of Portakabin parked alongside the lodge with 'Police' on it, but there was no sign of life from within the lodge, and everything was silent and still. Ella looked back down the village street again, then, taking a deep breath, stepped through the stone pillars.

As she did so, the remaining gate moved slightly with a groaning creak that sounded as if a hoarse voice whispered the word 'murder'. The past closed around her.

CHAPTER THIRTY-EIGHT

'YOU SEE THE PROBLEM,' said Amy, sitting on a dusty window ledge of St Anselm's church.

'Yes, certainly.' Jan had prowled round the edges of the ruined church while she talked, but his absorption in what she was saying was unmistakable.

When she stopped he came to join her on the window ledge. He was wearing the herringbone greatcoat again and the hem was dusty where it had trailed on the ground. His hair flopped over his forehead and Amy wanted so much to reach out to smooth it back that she had to sit on her hands.

'Amy, I'm desperately sorry about what's happened,' he said. 'You must be utterly shell-shocked.' He did not proffer meaningless conventionalities; he did not say he was sure it was all a mistake and not to worry because it would all turn out all right. He said, 'It's polite to say I'll do anything to help, isn't it? And I will, of course. But maybe the best help I can give you at the moment is to see if we can find an innocent explanation for the sweater and the handbag you found.'

'And the notebooks.'

'I'm not forgetting the notebooks,' said Jan, 'but let's deal with the bloodstains first. Could your grandmother have cut her hand or had a nosebleed? Then been afraid the bloodstains on the sweater would be misunderstood if the police found them?'

'She hasn't got any signs of a cut,' said Amy. 'And I don't think she suffers from nosebleeds. There were a lot of bloodstains, Jan. Really a *lot*. And I can't think how bloodstains would get on the inside of a handbag.'

'Fair enough. Neither can I, but we'll look at all possibilities. How about the notebooks? They could be old ones she's getting rid of.'

'At two in the morning? When your husband's in jail suspected of murdering your oldest friend? I know I'm sounding negative, but you have to admit it's pretty flaky behaviour.'

'They could be old diaries,' said Jan, frowning as he considered this. 'Again, it might be that she's afraid of something being misinterpreted—something she wrote in the past, or something she didn't want anyone to know. Not necessarily anything criminal.'

'I know,' said Amy. 'And I could accept Gran getting rid of old diaries if they had scandalous stuff in them, though the handwriting didn't look like hers. I could accept the bloodstains as well. But not the two things together on the same night.'

'It is stretching it a bit.' He paused, frowning, then said, 'I think you're going to have to ask your grandmother right out why she buried that stuff, and what it's all about.'

Amy had been hoping he would not say this. 'I'm not sure if I can,' she said.

'You can. Say you found the stuff because you saw her burying it, and you're sure there's nothing wrong— you trust her completely—but with everything that's been going on you'd appreciate a bit of reassurance.'

'I suppose that's a reasonable way of putting it,' said Amy, rather unwillingly. 'That couldn't upset her, could it?'

'No. Do it as soon as you can, before you have a chance to get cold feet. And...' He paused, then said, 'I'd like to say come down to the Red Lion and have dinner with me. But I think you'll have to stay with your gran until this mess is sorted out—until your grandfather is let out. You can't leave her on her own at the moment.'

'I know that.'

'But you could phone to tell me the results,' said Jan, 'because I'd like to stay until—well, until I know you're all right. You've got my number, haven't you?'

'Yes.' Amy glanced at her watch. 'I should get back.'

'If you can give it another five minutes, I'll come back with you.'

'It's not far. And I'm not likely to get lost,' said Amy, looking round for her tote bag.

'No, but the ground's slippery from the spraying and there's rubble everywhere. Please wait for me. If you tripped over or slipped in the mud at least I could pick you up.'

'Is that what you've done anyway?' said Amy, who had not realized she was going to say this. 'Picked me up?'

A sudden smile lightened his face. 'No,' he said. 'Oh, Amy, no.'

'Well, good.'

His hand came out to push a strand of hair back from her face. 'You look,' said Jan softly, 'like a small Victorian ragamuffin, perched on that windowsill amidst all the rubble and dust. Amy, let's have that dinner together when this is all sorted out.'

'I'd like that.'

'Good.' He still did not move away, and the moment lengthened. Amy thought: he's going to kiss me. I'm not sure if I'm ready for that. Oh hell, yes, of course I am.

But he did not. He merely said, 'Give me another five minutes then we'll go. I just want to see if the organ loft is still intact. I should think it's somewhere through those stone arches.'

'Where did you park?'

'On that lay-by on Mordwich Bank. I wanted to walk down the bank and see what the village looks like from above.'

'I parked on the edge of the street at the other end,' said Amy.

He picked up his battered briefcase, which had been lying on a pew, and went towards the stone arch. Amy was wondering if he wanted her to follow, or if he would prefer to be on his own, when she became aware that someone was outside the church. There was the faint sound of footsteps and she turned to look towards the porch, not exactly apprehensively, but certainly a bit startled. The village had seemed deserted, but the police might still be around.

But no one seemed to be there. Amy thought she might have heard a stray dog or an inquisitive cat. What else prowled round ruins? Oh God, don't let it be a rat. She went towards the door and called out, 'Hello? Is anyone there?' But this sounded so ridiculously like the hammy old question people asked at séances that she followed it up at once by saying, 'I'm just having a look round. We were told it was OK to come in.' The 'we' was deliberate, meant to indicate she was not on her own. She was about to call out to Jan when she heard his voice.

'Amy, come and look at this.'

'What is it? Where are you?'

'In the old organ loft. Through the archway near the window and there's a flight of steps. They're a bit battered but perfectly sound.'

Amy abandoned the quest for the footsteps and went over to the arch. There was a smallish alcove beyond it, with half a dozen narrow steps, enclosed by stone walls. She went cautiously up, and as she reached the top, light poured in from a tall glassless window. After the dimness the brightness, even on such a dull morning, was unexpected and Amy blinked, momentarily dazzled, but through the brightness aware of a curious feeling of loneliness. When her eyes adjusted, she made out a towering structure with a bench drawn up to it.

'What—'

'It's the church organ,' said Jan, softly. 'The one donated by the unknown Cadence. We still don't know who he was, and I'm not sure we'll be able to find out, but I think this is where he found his "still, sad music of humanity".'

Amy stared at the remains of the instrument. Parts of it had rotted, and in places had fallen away from the main structure, but a metal frame with what looked like a couple of dozen tubes was still in place. It was inexpressibly sad, like seeing something that was not entirely dead, something that had lain quietly here for half a century, determinedly clinging to its hold on life, hoping all the time that it might be found and rescued. She shivered, and became aware of how desolate and cold the old church was.

Jan was kneeling in front of the frame, the briefcase open, a sheaf of rather untidy notes half spilling out.

Amy said, 'What are those lengths of old drainpipe?'

He smiled. 'They're the organ pipes—the ones that have survived. The wooden ones have almost entirely gone, but these are some kind of alloy and pretty much indestructible.'

'They're all different sizes.'

'Yes, of course they are.' He reached up to tap one of the pipes, and a faint sound thrummed through the small space. Amy had the impression that something within the ruined organ shivered slightly.

'Would they still play properly?'

'If the pump was working, they might,' said Jan. 'They work on the principle of any wind instrument. I can't see the pump anywhere—it was probably one of the old bellows kind, though, and it's most likely rotted away

436 WHAT LIES BENEATH

altogether. But if I took a couple of the pipes down and blew through them they'd produce a musical note. Like a flute or a recorder. Didn't you play a recorder in a school orchestra when you were small?'

'I bashed the drums,' said Amy, and he smiled.

'See these pipes with the wide diameter? If I blew through those they'd produce a flute tone. The narrow ones would sound more like strings. Over there are the reed pipes and...' He looked at her and smiled. 'I'm getting carried away. But in layman's terms, these would sound like the pipes of Pan and those larger ones would be more like the QE2 coming in to dock or the Last Trump on Judgement Day.'

'Well, if you're going to try any of them, don't make it those in case the graves start opening up and disgorging the walking dead.'

'You've been watching too many late-night horror films.'

'I'd rather have the QE2 than the walking dead. They're pretty cobwebby, aren't they?'

'Cobwebs can be cleaned.' He reached for the organ pipes again, and began to wipe them with a handkerchief.

'Jan, they're filthy,' said Amy in horror, as he selected three and peered at them more closely.

A look of unmistakable mischief showed on Jan's face, making him suddenly look much younger. 'I'll risk it,' he said, and before Amy could say anything, he raised the two small pipes and one slightly larger one to his lips and blew softly through them.

The sound that tore through the ruined church was like the wail of a creature in its death throes, but Amy had to admit it was recognizably a musical chord.

Jan lowered the pipes and looked at Amy. 'That wasn't exactly "the still, sad music of humanity", was it?' he said.

'Not even close, in fact it was nearer to the QE2 after all.'

'I'd like to have made it the opening chords of *The Deserted Village*,' he said, rather wistfully. 'That would have been really appropriate, wouldn't it?'

'You're a closet romantic,' said Amy, as Jan tried another set of chords. 'I tell you what, though, I've still got Gramps's camera in my bag. We'll have a shot of this before we go, shall we? Because—' She broke off and they both turned sharply at the cry of unmistakable fear from beyond the church.

'Someone's out there,' said Jan, going to the head of the stair and peering down.

'Oh God, yes, I thought I heard footsteps a few minutes ago, only then you called me up here and I forgot about it. It was probably only a forensic police guy or a curious local, but whoever it was I bet you've spooked him for life.'

'I'd better go out and explain,' said Jan, starting down the stairs.

'OK. I'll go and get the camera from my bag. I left it by the altar. You go ahead and I'll catch you up. After that I really must get back to Gran.'

❀ ❀ ❀

Ella had not paused in her headlong flight to Cadence Manor.

The trees surrounding it had the same diseased look as the trees in the churchyard, and in places the high brick wall had fallen in. Through the gaps the house looked stark and unprotected. Ella glanced across at the lodge and hesitated, wondering if it would be a better place to hide. For a moment, threads of the present came to the surface of her mind and she remembered the police investigations. Were they still working here? They were not in the lodge, that was clear, but might they be at the manor? No, everywhere seemed quiet and still.

He would find her if she hid inside the lodge but he might not do so in the manor. She went down the once-smooth carriageway. This was the way they had come all those years ago, she and Veronica and Clem. Were they with her now? No, of course they were not: they were dead. But people who were murdered walked, everyone said that. Ella glanced nervously over her shoulder, but nothing disturbed the brooding stillness.

Here was the house. She picked her way through the rubble, grateful she was wearing boots, but frowning for a moment, because hadn't she come out in her good sandals? No, that was for school. And it was in the past. She must keep the two things separate. But ever since that painful struggling music had bawled out of the old church she had had the feeling that something had been torn and that the past was spilling out.

She had reached the terrace and saw the opening in the walls of the manor where the big French windows had been. Ella looked over her shoulder again. There was nothing to see, but he was out there, of course. He was stalking her, she knew that. She took a deep breath and stepped inside. Everywhere was cool and dim, and there was a faint sound of water dripping somewhere. One of the marble columns had collapsed, and lay in great splintered sections on the ground. Beyond it, near what was left of the staircase, was what looked like the remnants of a chandelier.

Even though Ella did not believe in ghosts, she knew there were ghosts here. Old Lady Cadence with her ravaged face, dead in the dim, over-scented room. She was here, all right, pointing an accusing finger at Ella. 'Get that bastard out of my house,' she had said. That bastard, *that bastard*...The ugly shameful word still resonated on the air, just out of hearing, and with it the sound of the faint scratchy gramophone with the needle that had stuck and played the same few chords over and over...Someone had played that exact music just now in the church.

Here was the room directly beneath the bedroom where she had hidden with Veronica and Clem, and where she had pushed the man to his death. She stood in the doorway, thinking it was a smaller room than she remembered. The sound of water dripping was louder in this part of the house; it was a desolate sound, but it was also slightly annoying in the way a dripping tap was annoying. After a moment the drips formed into a series of horrid jabbing words: *I'm not dead, Ella...I'm not dead...*

'I know that,' whispered Ella. 'You're still here—I heard your music in the church. I saw you coming towards me.'

He had stayed in the shadows of the church today, just as he had always done, but it did not matter because she knew it was him. His face was etched on her mind like acid. Distorted features, with mad eyes...The terror and fury she had felt all those years ago welled up, and at the same time she heard a faint footstep outside. She turned sharply. *His* footstep? Of course it was.

She would have to hide from him as she had done before. Where? She looked frantically about her. The chimney breast was still there, a tangle of police tape across it, but little different from how it had been all those years ago. The hearth was a gaping hole, full of broken bricks and mud, and Ella darted across to it. A breath of sour dank air met her, but the chimney shaft looked more or less intact. She hesitated; then, as the footsteps came across the cracked terrace she stepped inside the chimney shaft, trying not to breathe in the black bitter-smelling darkness. She stood absolutely still, listening for *his* footsteps, just as she had listened for them in this very house more than fifty years ago, together with Veronica and Clem.

Whoever he was, that man, this time she would kill him properly.

CHAPTER THIRTY-NINE

THE STRANGE THING ABOUT Crispian's death in France was that I hadn't expected him to be killed. I thought he would come home, adorned with any number of medals for bravery, and that he would still stand between me and Cadences.

But he didn't. He died in the Somme, along with Gil Martlet. A few years earlier that would have solved the entire thing and Cadences would have passed to me. But now there was another obstacle in the way. Saul.

No one actually came out and said it, but it was clear to anyone who could count that Saul was conceived shortly before we all left England, at the time when Julius had entered the final stages of his loathsome disease.

'Saul's free of it, though,' said Crispian to me once, on a brief leave from France in 1915. 'Dr Martlet is definite about it.'

Dr Martlet would have sworn away his immortal soul and told every lie known to man if it would inveigle him a little more into Serena Cadence's good graces. I'll acquit those two of ever embarking on anything physical. Serena was the original ice maiden, and Gillespie Martlet was one of those bloodless, sexless men. It was one of nature's quirks that he had fathered a son like Gil. But Martlet's one aim in life was to surround Serena with whatever fictions and fantasies made her feel safe and pampered, so for the first few years of Saul's life the fiction was maintained that he had escaped the taint that had killed his father.

He had not escaped it at all. I knew it, and everyone in Cadence Manor must have known it. By the time he was two his face showed definite signs of lesions—scar tissue radiating around the mouth—and his nose was developing into what I later learned was called saddle-nose. It's as if the bone and gristle have collapsed and apparently it's a classic symptom of congenital syphilis. I don't remember if there was ever any formal arrangement or agreement that I should take over Saul's care, but somehow, with Crispian in France and Serena becoming more of a recluse every month—and Colm already a recluse anyway—it's what happened.

I never had the stomach to kill Saul, though. I'd like that understood. I'd like whoever reads this to know it's the absolute truth. I'm a dying man, for God's sake (twenty-four hours left), and I'm hardly likely to lie in these pages while death's gibbering at me from the shadows. In any case, killing Saul would have been too risky. There were too many people around, constantly watching him: Mrs Flagg, the sour old witch Crossley, who looked after Serena, and the two maids. They all flapped around him constantly. I always thought they were trying, consciously or unconsciously, to make up for Serena's indifference, because it was clear to me that Serena could hardly bear the sight of Saul. So I didn't dare attempt anything. Also, if Crispian came back from the war I would still have to kill him, and the death of the two brothers, no matter how carefully I staged it, would raise everyone's suspicions.

But once Crispian was out of the way for good I took over Saul's upbringing completely. I was subtle about it. I recall I even demurred at one point, suggesting there were people better qualified to undertake the task. But to have control of him was what I intended all along. History's chock-full of wicked uncles and rascally cousins and illegitimate heirs (ha!) scheming to get their hands on the riches of their wards. I promise you, Richard III had nothing on me, and if I could have walled up that child without fear of discovery, I would have done it.

But there are more ways of getting control of a fortune than by committing murder.

❀ ❀ ❀

By the time Saul was four, with the dogs of war still ravaging Europe, Martlet and Serena finally admitted that Saul had inherited the disease my mother had brought into the family. They all agreed it was so tragic. (Tragic was a word used a good deal about my family.) But in Saul's case the illness need not necessarily be fatal, they said firmly. There were things that could be tried. Medicine had made great strides since the war. War was a forcing house for all kinds of discoveries. There was a very good chance that Saul Cadence could beat the disease.

I listened to all this solemn discussion, and thought: he won't beat it if I can help it! I was in touching distance of the Cadence empire by that time. Everything was being held in trust for Saul's twenty-first birthday and I was one of the trustees, along with Colm, who was less than useless, Serena, who hardly ever left the manor, and a couple of doddering old men in London. I could manipulate the whole lot of them easily. Meetings were held at Cadence Manor three or four times a year, but they were a travesty. Colm said very little, Serena was usually too unwell to attend (or said she was), and the two London fossils deferred to me over everything. I used to prepare my proposals in advance and pass neatly written sheets round the table. They were so relieved to have the work done for them, they agreed to anything I put forward.

The concern they all had, of course, was whether the legacy that had sent Julius mad would send Saul mad, too. Mad people certainly could not be allowed to inherit huge banking concerns and estates. And if Saul really did end in being pronounced insane, who was the next in line to inherit? Colm was the nearest, but he could be discounted. He did not want it and he was not capable of dealing with it. So who, but Colm's son, quiet reliable Jamie?

Having read this far, my unknown reader, can you doubt that I manipulated the treatments Saul was given? By that time there were antisyphilitic drugs, in particular one called Neosalvarsan. Small, bullet-shaped tablets. So easy for Saul to swallow. So easy for his unscrupulous guardian to substitute with harmless pills of bismuth or soda, flushing the real pills down the lavatory. I looked solemn and sad when old Dr Martlet or his colleagues shook their heads over the progress of the disease in Saul, and told one another that after all there was no clear cure, that Neosalvarsan was not the cup of life or the elixir of health that had been promised.

They would keep trying, though, and in the mean-time the best thing for Saul was to live quietly in the country, tutored and taught in his own home, all under the care of his widely read and selfless cousin Jamie. They would hope, they said, that the seeds of Madness did not bear fruit.

I nodded in agreement, and scribbled my under-standing and acceptance.

I had no intention of trying to cure Saul. I meant to foster the seeds of his madness to bear an entire orchard of fruit.

As for my own madness...

Any thoughts I might have had of the darkness vanishing after Edirne were soon dispelled. Shortly after we arrived back in England, the familiar pattern reinstated itself. There would be weeks—often even months—when I would dare to hope it had retreated for good, and then would come the familiar wrenching path in my mind, and the sensation of invisible ogre-hands twisting my whole being into a totally different shape.

I always managed to shut myself away in my bedroom until the spasms were over, but I could never be sure that the Crossley woman would not decide to mount a cleaning operation and that Hetty or Dora would not appear with mops and buckets and dusters. Eventually I solved the matter in a rather strange way.

The inhabitants of Priors Bramley had to walk across Mordwich Meadow to St Michael's most Sundays, and St Anselm's was used for a brief service only once a month to comply with some ancient law. The old village church had widespread dry rot, which nobody seemed prepared to tackle, or perhaps nobody could afford to. It needed the kind of restoration Crispian would probably have offered to fund, but I was not going to let Saul's trust (which I intended one day to be mine) be plundered to eliminate dry rot in a crumbling church. I never fathomed the intricacies of the rule about the services—the Church of England can be as twisty as a corkscrew—but I do know they had to hold a service there no fewer than ten times a year or the church would have become deconsecrated or something. That seemed to worry people. I wondered if they visualized Lucifer and his legions forming an impatient queue on Crinoline Bridge, waiting for the moment when this small and obscure village church would step outside the sanctified protection of the English Church and the powers of evil could go pelting down Mordwich Bank and take up gleeful residence.

In practical terms it meant St Anselm's was empty for long periods of time. So, when I felt the darkness start to claw at my mind, I slipped through the gardens, out through the manor's gates and along the road to its shadowy solitude. I seldom met anyone during that brief walk: the shops and houses were further along and the church had gradually become wrapped in its own solitude.

But here's a strange thing. Once inside the church, with the cruel violent Hyde persona tearing at me, I could never stay in sight of the altar and the various religious symbols near to it. I simply couldn't. I always went up the narrow steep stairway to the organ loft, and that's when I was truly safe.

It was an extraordinary feeling to crouch in that small space with the silent shadowy church all round me and the towering shape of the organ at my back, and to fight the ravaging demon in my mind but it's what I always did. And then, one dull grey afternoon, I took more notice of the organ. That was the day I discovered it still had some life in it, although not much, I have to say. Investigating warily, I found I could pump air into the pipes—only a very little that first time, but enough to make it shiver into life. I stood there for a very long time, then, with daylight fading and grey-green shadows stealing into the church, fumbling awkwardly for the notes, I played a chord. As the sound resonated in the enclosed space, I felt as if something huge and invisible had opened up inside my mind and something dark and malevolent had flown out. I promise you it was so vivid an experience I could almost hear the beating of wings on the air. It's not too wild a fancy, is it, to think it was my own inner madness taking flight?

I should explain at this point that I could read music in a modest way. As a child I was taught to play the piano. Crispian was taught as well, but although he banged conscientiously at the keys, he was never much good. I don't know that I was much better, but seated in that deserted church, my mind still bruised, those lessons came back to me. And the next time I went to St Anselm's I played more than a couple of hesitant chords.

As with most things, the more I played, the easier it became. I bought a gramophone for Cadence Manor. I said it was because I thought Saul might respond to music, but of course it was really for me.

Then I discovered a stack of abandoned music in St Anselm's vestry and embarked on several of the pieces—warily at first, and then with growing confidence. Initially I had gone to St Anselm's to hide, but once I began to play, the music engulfed me, and I no longer cared if anyone knew I was there.

There was a good deal of Bach among the music I found, but there were several other composers. Early on I came upon a piece of music called *The Deserted Village*. It had been written by an Irish composer somewhere in the mid-to-late 1800s, and it was actually an opera, but at some time in Priors Bramley's history, some organist or choirmaster had transcribed the overture for organ. The score was handwritten, but perfectly legible. I didn't play it—not then—but I was intrigued by the title, and by the scribbled note at the top stating that the opera had been based on an Oliver Goldsmith poem. So I wrote to one or two of the London stores, asking if a gramophone recording of the opera was available. I didn't expect much, but within a few days one of them replied, saying they had a recording of the overture and part of the entr'acte. It had, they thought, been part of a set of recordings of the whole opera, but sadly the others had been lost. However, if I was interested in purchasing this single record they would be very happy to dispatch it. A relatively modest price was quoted, with an air of suggestion about it, almost as if they expected me to challenge it or even haggle.

I didn't challenge and I didn't haggle. I bought the recording. And as soon as I listened to it, something deep inside me responded. I cannot explain it—I never have been able to explain it—but I understood what the composer had tried to convey: the journey from sunlit tranquillity into darkness. And from that darkness, there's an even deeper descent into a savage loneliness, as the village called Auburn is abandoned and left to its ruined grounds where birds forget to sing. Only one person remains in Auburn— 'The sad historian of the pensive plain'—scraping a meagre living from the few things that still grow there.

❀ ❀ ❀

When Saul was six and the Great War had been over for a year I wrote to the vicar at St Michael's church in Upper Bramley, suggesting the Cadence family would like to install a new church organ at St Anselm's.

We did, I wrote, appreciate that the church itself was in a poor state of repair and in need of some help, but for the moment funds did not permit addressing that. So many investments had been affected by the war. However, as the vicar no doubt knew, the present organ was also in a poor state of repair. Would it be permissible for a new one to be installed, entirely at our expense? Sadly, three members of the family were in frail health and unable to make even the short journey to Upper Bramley for the various services, but the family had a shared love of music and considerable solace and pleasure had been derived from listening to it in the peaceful surroundings of St Anselm's. Would the vicar be so kind as to approach his bishop and seek approval to this proposal?

The vicar did approach his bishop, and from the tone of the reply sent three days later, the entire diocesan board had almost fallen over themselves in their eagerness to accept. Of course they saw the veiled promise that the dry rot might later be dealt with, and of course they were going to accept this initial gift.

The organ was duly commissioned and installed in 1920, and the bishop even agreed to the engraved plaque

I requested for the framework. A Christmas service was held there with a couple of other churches for its dedication. I didn't attend, but Serena and Colm did, taking Saul. The servants went as well, very smart in their Sunday best. Flagg said afterwards that it had all been very tasteful, Mr Jamie sir, very nice indeed.

When the small flurry of excitement died down, I was able to play the new, beautifully pitched organ whenever I wanted. No one ever disturbed me: in a general way the details of what had been done to me had got out, and I think people hearing the music probably thought, Ah, there's poor Mr Jamie from the manor, poor tragic soul. Mutilated by those heathens, but finding comfort and solace in God's music.

None of them could have known there were times when the struggle was so intense I had to break off—times when I would sob with the pain and the sheer bloody strength of the clawing tearing madness…

It wouldn't let go, you see. It simply wouldn't let go. And at times it became too much for me. There were nights when the evil greedy Hyde triumphed and I would slink through the lanes and the villages around Cadence Manor. It wasn't so easy to find victims; it was the depths of the country and people were not so ready to go out and about, particularly after dark. Also, in the years following the war, the country was still recovering and it took time for life to return to a semblance of normality.

But in any society and in any time there are always a few loners—girls, occasionally men—who can be found if you look in the right places. Railway stations are a good source; it's easy enough to wait outside a railway station and watch for a solitary traveller. Bramley Halt was quite a busy line for a good many years and in those days of which I'm speaking—the twenties and then into the early thirties—girls still came to the country to visit or to work. There weren't many 'big houses' left by then; the war

had swept away so much of the class divisions and it had
certainly swept away much of the old feudal system. But
there were some. Girls would come to the area to take up
a position as parlourmaid or housemaid. And if one or
two failed to arrive at their destinations, no one enquired
too deeply. Perhaps there would be an irritable letter sent
to the agency who had engaged them, but other than that
people would simply say how unreliable girls had become
since the war. It was annoying and inconvenient, but the
agency could supply another one.

I generally got rid of my victims' bodies by tumbling
them into the back of a goods wagon. God knows where
they ended up, but wherever it was, it was miles away and
no connection was ever made with Bramley or Cadence
Manor.

But it wasn't until Saul was sixteen that I suddenly
saw how I could use my own darkness to get him out of
the way.

❁ ❁ ❁

I was returning late at night from a very unsatisfactory
expedition. I had spent most of the day fighting the
darkness, but around ten o'clock that night I had given
in and slipped out of the manor by the side door. I found
a girl all right, but she fought me like a tiger and, as the
fishermen say, she was one who got away. But before she
did so, she clawed my neck and hands quite severely.
I slunk back to the lodge, furious with her and myself,
the darkness still biting at the edges of my mind, my
wounds stinging.

I went through the gates as quietly as I always did,
and through the shrubbery. I didn't trouble to be particularly furtive; it was after eleven o'clock and no one was
ever about at that hour.

Except that someone was on that occasion. Colm was walking along the drive, and he saw me at once. His mild eyes peered at me in surprise. He said, 'Jamie? You're covered in blood. And your clothes are torn.'

I was reaching for the slate and charcoal pen I always kept in a pocket—although I had no idea what I would write because what *can* you write about being covered in blood with your clothes torn and muddied at eleven o'clock at night? But he said, in a voice I had never heard him use, 'Jamie—is it Saul? Has he been violent in some way?'

Saul. There it was, you see, all laid out for me, without my having to do a thing. I made a gesture of deep sadness, then nodded.

'I was always afraid of this,' Colm said after a moment. 'That violence would erupt. Can you tell me what happened?'

I did tell him. I scribbled it all out on the slate, and what I wrote was nothing more than the truth—except that I made it appear that Saul had been the attacker, not me. Saul had slipped out of the house, believing himself unnoticed, I wrote. I happened to have seen him and followed at a distance, not wanting to intrude on his privacy, but wanting to make sure all was well.

'That's like you,' Colm said, his weak eyes teary with emotion. 'And you'd try to protect him, I know that. You'd have kept this from us if you could. If I hadn't walked down to the gates tonight, to clear my head after working late...

The doddering old fool! But I kept to the story he had already half-handed me. Writing quickly, I described how I had seen Saul pounce on the girl, but when Colm asked if I knew who she was I shook my head firmly. I had managed to pull Saul off her, I wrote, although he had resisted me fiercely. Here I made a brief gesture, indicating the deep claw marks and the blood.

'And the girl?'

I wrote that she had run into the darkness. 'And Saul?'

That question nearly did floor me. Then I wrote, 'Should be in his room by now,' and Colm nodded as if this was acceptable. I saw that the image of me ushering Saul back to the manor and his room had taken root in his mind.

'This is dreadful,' he said.

I wrote, 'Do we talk to him? Challenge him?'

I saw him flinch, and smiled inwardly. Colm would never seek a confrontation.

'Oh no,' he said. 'I don't think that's necessary. Providing we can be sure—'

'That it doesn't happen again?'

He stared at the words for several moments, then said, 'Exactly. And if we can be sure it won't happen again...

I wrote, 'It won't. I won't let it happen again.' But of course I did.

Later

Earlier I spent half an hour trying to break through the wall at the back of the cupboard I found nearly seven days ago. But it seems to be a solid wall, and there's no means of breaking through. I tried, of course. I tore my nails and chipped my knuckles, and I hardly dare write this, but at the end of that hour I had worked free a small section of wood panelling. I'm too exhausted to do any more now and my fingers are too sore. But I shall return to it soon. Oh God, if only I can get out that way, if only...

Because if not, in eighteen hours' time, I must face my death.

❀ ❀ ❀

If I'm to be honest, I'd have to say it was the years of the 1930s that finally brought the realization that Cadences and all that went with it had slipped away from me.

It wasn't that I failed in my attempts. I intended Saul to be pronounced insane and unfit to inherit Cadences and he wasn't far from that. But over the years, Cadences itself diminished. It didn't go with a bang, but a whimper. By the time Saul was eighteen it was no longer the golden glittering prize; it was a husked-out shell, barely making a profit. I don't think there was one specific cause that killed it. The American Stock Market Crash in 1929—the infamous Wall Street Crash—wiped out billions of dollars in a single day, and the financial markets throughout the entire world suffered as a result—except, I believe, in Japan. People said the Crash put an end to the roaring twenties. It certainly began the end of prosperity for Cadences. And even if Cadences could have rallied from that, the Second World War came and finished the task. And all the things I did—all the lives I took and all the lies I told and deceits I practised—I needn't have bothered.

It's sad and ironic to look back and know all of that.

But for the moment I have returned to my desk and these pages, and it looks as if I have spaced out my story very well indeed, because I see that all I have left to write is the account of what happened with that village slut Brenda Ford.

❀ ❀ ❀

The fact that I went after Brenda Ford surprised me then, and it still surprises me, even ten years afterwards.

At the time of the Brenda Ford incident I was fifty-seven, if anyone wants to know. That's not so ancient by today's standards. People of fifty-seven are capable of all kinds of remarkable things. Politicians and bankers seem to dodder on into their dotages. Look at Winston Churchill. He was getting on for seventy when he rallied Britain to win the Second World War.

There was nothing very special about Brenda Ford, nothing that should have tempted me or stirred up the darkness. She wasn't especially pretty or attractive. She had nice hair, though, I do remember that. I also remember that she looked and moved like a trollop— that's a word you don't often hear used nowadays. But when I was much younger it was a word people did use and Brenda Ford would certainly have been marked out as a trollop. It wasn't so much the way she dressed or used lipstick—she was actually rather modest about that. It was the way she walked, with a kind of swing to the rump, and the way she looked at people with a kind of come-hither expression.

I'd seen her from a distance several times. She worked in one of the village pubs, and I think she probably had a bit of a reputation among the young men of the area. It's not difficult to spot that: the giggling, the deliberately provocative glances. Twice to my knowledge she saw me. I always wore a deep-brimmed hat to shade my face and turned up the collar of whatever coat I was wearing, but she certainly looked at me at least twice. The second time I felt the excitement start to beat in my mind and I felt the darkness stir. I thought: the next time the darkness comes over me properly, I'll have you, my dear!

And so I did. It was a remarkably satisfying experi-ence. When I caught her up in the lane along the side of the manor at first she put up a small show of resistance, saying she wouldn't have any truck with a man who wouldn't tell her who he was.

'I've seen you watching me,' she said. 'Real silent mystery man, aren't you? Just like in the pictures.'

God knows who she was likening me to. There was a bit of a pretence at coyness—a token protest that she didn't usually do this kind of thing. Like hell she didn't. Once down on the grass she writhed against me like a snake, and in the first five seconds it was clear she knew most of the moves in the book. When finally I left her, she giggled and said, 'Good night, silent mystery man. I hope we meet again.'

❀ ❀ ❀

Three months later the stupid little bitch came squealing up to the manor in floods of tears, to tell Serena Cadence she was pregnant.

CHAPTER FORTY

Cadence Manor, Late 1940s

SERENA, LOOKING BACK over the years since Saul's birth, thought they had managed things as well as anyone could have done. The handful of people who knew the truth about him—Dr Martlet and the trustees, and dear Jamie, of course—said how extremely tragic that none of the treatments had done much to alleviate the disease in him. Serena supposed she should have known that the child born from that mad, angry, darkness—the child who had clung on in the womb despite all her attempts to expel it—would eventually succumb to the madness of his father.

None of them said it was even more tragic that the treatments had not alleviated the disease in Serena herself, though.

'But we can be thankful for the periods of remission,' Dr Martlet said.

She had never endured the mercury procedure again. Dr Martlet had suggested it, but Serena shuddered away from it. There had been pills of some kind, which she had swallowed diligently, but little by little the disgusting disease had crept over her. She lived, now, in the same twilit world in which Colm's wife, Fay, had lived all those years ago. She did not go out and no one came to the house except Jamie and Dr Martlet, growing old and grizzled nowadays, but devoted as ever. He gave her draughts for the pains that racked her bones and soothing lotions for the sores on her skin. As he said, there were times when the disease seemed to withdraw its teeth and she was free of it. Neither of them said, but both knew, that these times became progressively shorter.

Serena often wondered what they would have done without Jamie, so patient with Saul, so trustworthy in every way. Jamie had guarded and safeguarded Saul through all the difficulties, acting as tutor and almost as gaoler in equal measures. He would not let Saul sink into the same darkness as his father, wrote Jamie on the slate he always kept with him. Serena could trust him over that.

The years slid by. The Second World War—the war people said was really a continuation of the Great War—was not very troublesome in the depths of the country, although Mrs Flagg, growing cantankerous with the years, said it was not easy to get food, and if Mr Churchill thought a family could eat a proper nourishing meal on the scrimping rations allowed, Mrs Flagg would just like to see him try it.

But despite wars and shortages and the increasingly shrill tone of the modern world, Serena was able to find a degree of contentment. She need not go beyond the manor's grounds if she did not want to—and she seldom wanted. Occasionally she and her small household went to St Anselm's for a service; there had been a very pleasant Christmas service one year, after Jamie arranged for the church to have the new organ. Jamie had become very knowledgeable about music; Serena thought it was something to do with him having been in the East all those years ago with Crispian and Gil Martlet. She knew—she supposed they all knew—that Jamie sometimes went quietly along to St Anselm's to play the organ when the church was deserted. There was no particular secret about it and one was pleased to think of him having such a hobby. Occasionally it occurred to her that Jamie did not have much of a life, but he always seemed content.

And then, in the middle of an ordinary afternoon, came the event that was to knock the placidity of Cadence Manor and Priors Bramley into tumult.

'A person to see you, madam.' Flagg, becoming more tottery with every year but determinedly clinging to the old standards, made the announcement while Serena was sipping a cup of afternoon tea. She enjoyed her afternoon tea; it was so nice to be able to obtain good China tea again, and she generally had the small silver flask to hand so that a judicious measure of brandy could be added if she felt unwell.

'Does this person have a name, Flagg?'

'Ford, madam. A Miss Ford, I believe.'

The name meant nothing to Serena and she did not want to see this person, this Ford, whom Flagg clearly considered beneath her notice. Despite the Lapsang Souchong with its spike of brandy, today her skin felt as if it was on fire, and there was an ache deep in her bones as if they were being pounded to ground glass. But she said, 'I can see her for five minutes, I suppose.'

Ford turned out to be a rather pert-looking girl with cheap shiny stockings and a skirt and coat that tried rather unsuccessfully to imitate the current fashion. Serena took this in at a glance; living quietly in the country did not mean she did not take notice of what people in the wider world wore. Fashion magazines were delivered to the house and the accounts at Harrods and Debenham and Freebody were still used.

She sat up very straight in her chair, ignoring the wrench of pain in her spine, and said, 'Yes, Ford?'

The girl said, 'I'm here because your...' A pause as if she might be trying to sort something out in her mind.

'Your son raped me three months ago,' she said. 'And I've just found out I'm pregnant because of it.'

Serena stared at her. 'Nonsense,' she said crisply.

'You'll excuse me, Lady Cadence, but it's the truth.'

'You may well be pregnant, but my son can't have anything to do with it. He's an invalid. He lives quietly here and seldom goes out.'

'Your son,' said the girl, 'attacked me just outside the walls of this mausoleum one night'—she paused to cast a disparaging glance around her—'and he left me lying on the ground while he scuttled back through the gates.'

Serena said at once, 'If it was night how could you know his identity?'

'Who else would it be? He lived here, in the manor—I saw him come back inside.'

'That proves nothing,' said Serena after a moment.

'It was him all right,' said the girl. 'Your precious family isn't going to wriggle out of the responsibility for this.'

'How dare you speak to me like that?'

'Oh, come out of the Dark Ages, Lady Cadence,' said Ford. 'I can speak how I want. Your sort don't own the world any longer. We're equals nowadays, or hadn't you noticed? Did the Second World War pass you by, like the First did?'

The First World War...Crispian going so courageously into the grey mud of the battlefields, and never returning...

Anger rose in Serena because this girl knew nothing, *nothing*. But she said icily, 'I think you're here purely to get money. This is all lies.' She stood up, indicating the interview was at an end, and saw the girl hesitate.

But she stood her ground. She said, 'I'm telling the truth. And if you don't agree to help me, I'll tell everyone what Saul did to me.'

Saul...The casual familiar use of Saul's name stung Serena but it also set off a small alarm in her mind. Supposing there was some truth in this?

She said, 'I will consider what you have said. But I make no promises.' She thought for a moment. Dr Martlet would be here at the weekend; he, along with Jamie and Colm, would deal with this. 'Return here on Saturday,' said Serena. 'There will be a doctor here who will verify your condition.'

'I'm agreeable to that,' said Ford.

'In the meantime, I shall discuss this with my family, and let you have a decision then.'

After the girl had left, Serena sat for a long time, staring straight ahead of her, the tea forgotten. She would talk to Dr Martlet when he arrived, but before that she would, of course, talk to Jamie. She could not imagine what she would do without Jamie.

Jamie Cadence's Journal

That business with Brenda Ford could so easily have gone disastrously wrong. Quite apart from anything else, Saul, confronted with the problem, would certainly have denied it, even in his increasingly torpid state. The Ford girl herself, faced with Saul, might have withdrawn her charge. Worse than that, she might have identified me.

The charge she made of rape I found interesting. I had most certainly not raped her that night; she had been willing and eager. Avid, almost. 'Good night, silent mystery man,' she had said. 'I hope we meet again.' Would a girl say that to her rapist? So unless there had been a second encounter after the one with me—unlikely, although not impossible— Miss Ford must have concocted the rape story to save her reputation and apply more pressure to the family.

It might be vanity that prompts me to say I handled things with subtlety and skill (they say all murderers are vain), but I do think I dealt with that business well.

The first concern was Saul. He had grown docile and biddable over the years. That was in large part due to the constant sedatives—and to the fact that I doubled and tripled the dose Martlet prescribed—but I think it was also because he lived such a retired life. When you don't see people or talk to them, there's no mental stimulation. Saul had never been mentally stimulated and he had hardly been beyond the confines of the manor. The expression 'cottage mentality' perhaps applied to him.

It was to this cottage mentality that I made my approach. I wrote a careful account for him—not too complex, which would have bewildered him—explaining a silly village girl had accused him of attacking her. I didn't use the word 'rape': he knew, in theory, about sex, but unless he was fooling me to an extraordinary degree, he had no experience of it.

I wrote that there were greedy and wicked people in the world, and the girl who had made the accusation was both those things. Watching him read that, a frown creased his brow, and he looked up, seeking reassurance. A thin shaft of sunlight fell across his face and I saw that the radiating lesions around his mouth and eyes were cruelly clear.

I reached for the slate.

'You don't need to worry about any of it,' I wrote. 'I know you didn't do it.' There was a twinge of irony in writing that. 'And I'll make sure you aren't punished.'

'Thank you, Jamie,' he said, and went back to reading the rest of what I had written. In essence, it was that I would look after him and that he need do nothing at all.

'You'll keep the bad people away?' he said.

I nodded, and took his hand and squeezed it. There was sometimes a curious affinity between us. I could often sense his thoughts, although it's as well that he never sensed mine.

I know all this portrays me as the worst kind of cheating conniving blackguard and villain, but it's what I am. It's what I've always been.

❁ ❁ ❁

The thing that worked in my favour over the Brenda Ford business was that the ground was already prepared. Colm had seen me that night, and he thought I had rescued that long-ago girl from Saul's brutality. So, for once he came out of his scholarly seclusion, and seated himself at the dining table with Serena, old Martlet, and me. That dining room and that long oak table had seen some assemblies in its time, but I'd lay good money it had never played host to four people, one of whom was a murderer and a rapist, discussing how best to pay off a blackmailing village girl. For Brenda Ford was black-mailing us, of course. We all knew it, but none of us could see how to sidestep it. Even I couldn't. But none of us, for different reasons, was going to tell her to speak out and be damned: Serena, because she wanted to protect Saul and also her own fragile seclusion; Martlet because he wanted to protect Serena; and Colm, because he could not bear to think the world might intrude into his ivory tower. As for me, well, I had any number of reasons for not wanting too close scrutiny on the origins of Brenda Ford's unborn child.

Martlet had examined Miss Ford and confirmed her condition, giving it as his opinion that the pregnancy was about three months advanced.

Colm then told the story of how, some time earlier, Saul had apparently attacked a local girl. 'It was only Jamie's intervention that saved her,' he said. 'You remember that night, Jamie? We met unexpectedly and you told me what had happened.'

I nodded reluctantly.

'He tried to protect Saul,' said Colm, and Martlet nodded, as if this was the behaviour he would expect of me.

'So you see,' said Colm, 'in the light of that, it seems likely that Miss Ford is telling the truth.'

'I agree,' said Martlet. 'And all she wants is to bring the child up decently. She wants a degree of financial security.'

'I don't trust her,' said Serena.

'She's fighting to get help for the child,' said Colm, mildly. 'That's understandable. Even admirable.'

I wrote, 'Martlet, what did you make of her?'

'It'd be my guess she's been something of a flirt,' he said. 'But I think she's genuine enough about this.'

'She's a hard-faced little liar, who's out to get money from us at any price,' said Serena tartly. 'You're all far too ready to give in to her.'

'Lady Cadence, if we don't make her an allowance, she will undoubtedly tell people she was raped by Saul and that the family refused to help her.'

'How do we know she won't do that anyway? I don't care for being blackmailed by the likes of *Ford*,' said Serena in her iciest voice.

I wrote, 'I think I have an idea for blocking that.'

'None of us can be sure she won't spread the story anyway,' said Colm. 'But, Serena, are you prepared to risk the secrets of this family being bruited around Bramley and all the villages? I'm certainly not.' He paused, then said, very gently, 'And there are too many secrets, Serena. Julius and Saul. Even Jamie...'

'There's nothing discreditable about Jamie's condition,' said Serena, and I saw Colm start to say something. I could guess it was that I had been accused of being a spy all those years ago in Edirne.

Serena guessed it as well, I think, because she said, impatiently, 'Oh, very well, do what you want. But make sure the money's paid to her regularly. Through a bank, if she possesses a bank account. I don't want the slut coming up here to demand money. I shall deal her very short shrift if she does, I promise you.'

'I'll take care of it,' said Colm, but the look he sent me made it clear that he knew I would be the one who would really take care of it.

'And now,' said Martlet, clearly relieved, 'what should we do about Saul?'

I reached for the slate and wrote quickly. 'I'm afraid we've reached a time when Saul will have to be kept under restraint.'

They read it and looked at each other, and I could see the memories surging up: Old Julius and that shameful locked room at the top of the London house; Crispian and I getting him out of the country, out of the reach of wagging tongues and rumour mills. With that knowledge, I wrote, 'Lock and key?' on my slate and passed it round the table.

'A locked room,' said Martlet at last, 'would need a gaoler.'

There was a long silence. I waited and I enjoyed waiting, all the while knowing they were hoping I would volunteer for the task. None of them had the courage to actually ask me, though, so I let the silence stretch out. Then I wrote, 'Let him live in the lodge. I'll live there with him. I'll be his gaoler.'

It was Martlet who said, warningly, 'It could be for many years, Jamie.'

I wrote, 'I know that. But I feel responsible for what's happened. I should have kept a closer watch on him.'

'That girl,' said Serena, and for the first time there was a sob in her voice. 'Because of her Saul will have to be locked away. Jamie will have to act as gaoler to him.' She beat on the table angrily with her fist. 'Because of Brenda Ford, several lives are being ruined.'

'Saul was always likely to be a risk,' said Martlet gently.

'I can't see it like that,' said Serena. 'I can only see that she's responsible for my son being locked away for the rest of his life.'

'The rest of his life,' said Colm slowly. 'Jamie, are you sure you're prepared to do this?'

I nodded, then wrote, 'I will do it for as long as necessary.'

And as I passed this round I saw the relieved acceptance in all their faces.

❄ ❄ ❄

So there it was yet again: the Cadences closing ranks. Protecting their own, because the might of the law must never, God forbid, touch any of the family. Never mind that the family commits half the crimes in the Newgate Calendar (and let's face it, I've certainly done so), a Cadence must never be subjected to the vulgar rigours and indignities of the judicial system.

My idea for scotching any rumours Brenda Ford might spread worked quite well, I think. I managed to get a story into the local newspaper about her having been attacked, stressing there was no truth in the rumour that her assailant had been a German spy left over from the war. The war had been over for several years, but people were still nervous about Germans, and from time to time there were small panics about spies and fifth columnists. Denying the rumour had the effect of putting it into people's minds. So if Brenda did tell people the child's father was a Cadence, in the light of the article no one was likely to believe her. The child...

I had no particular emotion about the child. I couldn't see that it would make any difference to my life, apart from having to send a cheque or a money order of some kind each month to its mother. I thought about it long and carefully, but I couldn't see that the child would ever have any effect on my life.

CHAPTER FORTY-ONE

Jamie Cadence's Journal, Concluding Pages

OVER THE LAST SEVEN DAYS, writing this, I've sought to put a barricade between myself and the inevitable ending to my story. I've poured out my emotions and my fears and confessed my sins (most of them), to this journal, all the time pushing away what I know is ahead. There was even that brief space when I thought I might escape, but I know now that the wall at the back of the half-concealed cupboard won't provide a way out. There's little more to write now. I've squeezed every drop out of the memories while writing this journal and there's little more to say. And already I can hear the sounds beyond my window. I know what they mean. Oh God, I know only too well...

But before I lay down my pen for what I think will be the last time (and *there's* a splendidly dramatic line to write!), there are perhaps a few loose ends I should tie up.

❀ ❀ ❀

After that venal little slut Brenda Ford succeeded in screwing money out of Serena—including the deeds to a tiny cottage in Bramley—it was agreed that we had to create what would effectively be a prison for Saul.

'As much,' said Colm, 'to protect people from him as to prevent him being taken away to some grim institution.'

'Or worse,' put in Martlet.

'You think he'd be regarded as responsible for his actions?' said Colm, surprised.

'I think it's a risk we don't want to take,' said Martlet drily.

The Cadences may cheat a bit, but they do have social consciences where the rest of the populace is concerned (except for me; I never had a social conscience or anything approaching it). But they agreed that Saul had to be strictly confined, and they looked to me, as always, to deal with the practicalities.

I surprised myself over that, because I rather enjoyed it. I had never thought of myself as very practical, but it was interesting to draw up the plans and arrange for workmen to come down from London, and turn the lodge into a virtual prison house.

There was a big bedroom on the first floor and it was not difficult to create a small bathroom opening directly off it. Bars were fitted to both windows—thick strong iron staves, driven deep into the fabric of the walls at top and bottom. The windows overlooked the main drive leading up to the manor. In fact, one window had a direct view through the trees of the main entrance. Anyone going up to the manor would probably see the bars at the lodge's upstairs windows, but it was a risk that had to be taken. And not many people did come to the manor by then.

While the workmen were there, I got them to build shelves on each side of the fireplace, and I stocked the shelves with books. I bought a second, more up-to-date gramophone, and later, when such things were more easily obtainable, I added a wireless. Saul liked music and by then it was a necessary part of life for me. It drove the darkness back—not every time and not always completely, but it was a powerful defence.

I believe Colm told the various workmen a mixed version of the truth—that an elderly member of the family was given to wandering off and it was necessary to create a degree of security. For safety's sake, he said, there needed to be bars and locks. Very sad, but there it was.

He was believed, of course; no one who ever met Colm would have suspected him of any kind of deceit. And it wasn't so long since the aristocracy hid away their mad relatives, rather than consign them to some bleak asylum.

After the work was finished and the workmen had left Priors Bramley, I managed to fix two stout bolts: one to the outside of the door of Saul's room and another to the main outside door. It meant both doors could easily be secured from outside. I think I did a very good job there.

Serena insisted the lodge should be as comfortable as possible. There were certain standards one should not lose, she said. I looked at her, and I saw how the disease had marked her and how she walked so slowly and painfully around her dim rooms, and for the first time I was aware of an unwilling admiration. I wrote that she had my promise that Saul should be comfortable in his prison.

And so he was, for the next ten years. He really was, I can say that honestly.

Food was sent down from the manor, and either Hetty or Dora—both of them ageing considerably by that time—came each day to cook and clean.

The strange thing is that Saul and I found a degree of companionship during those years. We had our books and our music, and we listened to the wireless in the evenings. There were plays and concerts and discussions. I even taught him to play chess, although he was very slow and I nearly always won. But he thought it a grand, grown-up thing to do and he was fascinated by the carved ivory chessmen, which had been his grandfather's and which were kept in a carved wooden box from Florence.

At times when I thought he was sufficiently sedated we walked in the grounds of the manor, but the walks were as slow as the chess games; the constant sedatives had given him a kind of shambling gait. Or perhaps it wasn't the sedatives, perhaps it was simply that the syphilis was getting hold of his bones by then. If I said I felt guilty about that I would be lying. I didn't feel guilty. I still wanted Cadences and all that went with it as much as ever, and I wasn't going to let this half-demented creature cheat me, not now, not when it was within touching distance.

We weren't entirely isolated. Serena sometimes got Flagg to drive her down to the lodge, where she sat in her son's room and sipped a glass of sherry or a cup of tea. Flagg was far too old to drive by then, but in a place like Priors Bramley no one noticed or probably even cared. Saul sat quietly and obediently in his chair on those occasions, watching Serena speak, occasionally mouthing the words she said, like a child learning to talk. Later, of course, Serena was too infirm to move very much and she stopped coming. Martlet and Colm still came, though, and once Martlet brought down a colleague for a new opinion on Saul's condition. That only confirmed what we already knew.

In the main, Saul's life had not altered so very much from when he lived at the manor. Or had it? There were times when he would look at me very pensively, not saying anything, just looking, as if he was trying to see into my mind.

❄ ❄ ❄

It was Serena who suggested there should be a good stock of provisions inside the lodge. Colm had died the previous year—Flagg found him at his desk, apparently bent over his books but in fact stone dead—and her own health was deteriorating fast. I think she was becoming aware of the frailty, even the mortality, of all humans.

'Supposing,' she said, seated very stiff and upright in her shadowy room in the manor, 'something were to happen to you, Jamie? I don't mean anything dreadful, but what if you were taken ill, or you fell while out walking and broke an ankle, and Saul was locked in that room, unable to reach anyone.'

The words, 'And you couldn't call for help or use a phone,' hung on the air between us.

It was a reasonable concern. Serena, for all her faults, wasn't without intelligence or, indeed, a degree of imagination. Flagg and Mrs Flagg had retired by then, Hetty had left to live with an elderly sister, and there was only the faithful, and somewhat younger, Dora to look after Serena. Dora came to the lodge just twice a week by that time, bringing stews and pies that could be reheated, and bread, which she bought in the village, together with butter, cheese, eggs and milk. She cleaned the rooms while she was there and took washing back to the manor. I used to walk up to the manor to dine or have lunch with Serena two or three times a week.

So we called workmen out again, and a big walk-in store cupboard was made off Saul's room. The shelves were stocked with a variety of tinned food; rationing had recently been withdrawn and most food could be bought easily by then. There were tins of meat and fruit; sardines and herring in tomato sauce, and soup squares. Condensed milk, lunch biscuits and packets of dried egg. And large canisters of tea and sugar, and bottled coffee. I had a couple of cases of wine and several bottles of brandy as well. Saul never drank that, of course—or, if he did, it was at my subtle invitation, when Martlet or one of the others was expected and could see him in a slurred-speech, blurred-eye condition.

Perhaps the lingering memory of the siege in the fort at Edirne, and of Gil going out with the soldiers to shoot the rats, was still with me, because when I saw the shelves of food, I felt surprisingly comfortable and secure.

❀ ❀ ❀

Did I say I never expected Brenda Ford's child to impinge on my life? That statement is another of the ironies about my life.

In fact I never saw the girl until that sultry autumn evening when Brenda brought her to the manor—I think either to complain that the money wasn't reaching her, or perhaps to ask for more. I never knew which.

I didn't see exactly what happened that evening. I was in Colm's library; I had walked up to the manor to see if he had had any books on late eighteenth-century music. I had put a gramophone record on—I remember it was my beloved *Deserted Village* overture—and left the doors open while I searched. Serena never minded my doing that, even though the old gramophone at the manor was a bit unreliable and scratchy. Once or twice she even said the music soothed her.

But even from the library I heard Brenda shrieking that night, saying something about needing money. Then I heard Serena's furious voice, although I didn't hear exactly what she said. But even though she was so fragile you could have snapped her bones in two with your hand, she still had that indomitable spirit. Without it I doubt she'd have lived as long as she did, for the disease that had killed my mother and old Julius had ravaged her very severely. Even so, she was not prepared to be browbeaten by anybody—and she did not like or trust Brenda Ford.

I left them to it. I couldn't risk confronting Brenda, even after so many years. I stayed in the library until I heard her go, then I went downstairs. I remember how I went into the drawing room, not realizing what had happened at first, just seeing her seated in her usual place. I remember, as well, how the gramophone had been restarted. I thought Serena had done that; it wasn't until afterwards I understood it must have been Brenda Ford, trying to put everything back as it had been, trying to cover up what she had done.

I never thought Brenda deliberately killed Serena. I don't think she was capable of killing. Whatever had happened had been an accident. I was just taking in the fact of her death when the child came back. She didn't immediately see me, but I saw her. My daughter. You'd have expected me to feel some rush of emotion, some recognition, but I didn't. I studied her dispassionately, seeing that she was very like Brenda and hardly like me at all. She was staring at Serena with horror and it was only when I reached out to switch off the gramophone that she realized I was there. She stared at me, then ran out almost at once, and even though she couldn't possibly have seen me in any detail in that dark room, I always had the feeling she never forgot me.

Whatever the truth behind Serena's death, as far as I was concerned it was another thing to lay at Saul's door. I didn't have to think twice. I locked the room with Serena's body seated in its chair like a stiff-legged, staring-eyed doll, and got Dora to telephone Martlet. He came that same evening, arriving just before midnight in a hired car.

He said, 'Was it Saul who did it?' and I nodded. Even though Cadences was no longer the beckoning prize it once had been, I still instinctively added this new and useful crime to Saul's account. Because I didn't know what the future might hold. I still had that tiny unquenchable hope that one day Cadences might be rich again, and the deceit and the lies might still be worth it. They might even be worth the agony I suffered in that Turkish courtyard, with the stench of blood and fear tainting the air.

'Ah, well,' said Martlet sadly, and wrote the death certificate out there and then.

That was when Cadence Manor was closed for good. Dora went back to her family's home somewhere in the north and Martlet returned to London. I don't think he had any patients by then; I think the creation of the National Health Service had altered the practice of medicine radically, and he was too old to bother.

It meant Saul and I were on our own and I had to address myself to the practicalities of living. It was unthinkable that I should ever go openly into Priors Bramley, or, indeed, anywhere else. After thought, I wrote and posted an order for provisions to be delivered every two weeks from a big neighbouring town. Anonymous, you see? The account would be settled through the bank each quarter and the order was to be exactly the same each time. The carrier was to leave it at the gates where it would be collected. What they thought of such an arrangement I have no idea. Probably they assumed some eccentric remnant of the family still lived in the decaying old manor. I didn't much care what they thought.

And for the next four or five months everything was perfectly all right. Life went along quietly and peacefully—until that spring afternoon when I found a local newspaper someone had left in St Anselm's church. Blazoned across it were the headlines:

PRIORS BRAMLEY TO BE SUBJECT OF
GOVERNMENT EXPERIMENT. AEROPLANE
TO FLY OVER VILLAGE AND DROP
EXPLOSIVE DEVICE TO DISPERSE VARIOUS
CHEMICAL SUBSTANCES. VILLAGE TO BE
SEALED SO THAT EFFECTS OF 'GERANOS'
CAN BE STUDIED.

Beneath that again was a sub-heading which said, 'Geranos is a compound, believed to contain sulphur mustard.'

I stood in the old church, reading the newspaper article, and panic seized me.

The article described the evacuation of the village. They actually used the word 'evacuation', which must have been dreadfully reminiscent of the war for many people. There was information about how a new road had been planned and then postponed, and details of compensation paid, compulsory purchase orders and rehousing. Several of the older inhabitants had resisted being moved, but had finally yielded and gone to live in one of the neighbouring villages. I hardly took that in, because one single fact was burning deep into my brain.

It was the date of the paper. This was old news. People had known about it for two months, but I, in my island of isolation within the grounds of the manor, had known nothing, heard nothing.

The date when the Geranos would be dropped was given. It was in eight days' time. There was a lot of technical information about the composition of Geranos, and a lot of false-sounding reassurance as to how it was not harmful, but that the village was to be sealed off as a precaution.

I took little notice of these empty reassurances, because I knew—I *knew*—what sulphur mustard did to people. I had heard the screams of the soldiers in Edirne. And in one week, Priors Bramley was to be drenched in the stuff.

I had eight days to get out of the lodge and find somewhere to live.

❊ ❊ ❊

I risked walking a little way along the village street, ready to bolt for the concealment of the church, but I saw no one. Eerily and disturbingly, this had become the deserted village of Goldsmith's poem, but it was not the tyrannical hand of Enclosure that had emptied the village; it was the governmental one of planning and experimentation.

I returned to the lodge because I had nowhere else to go. Once inside, I shut the doors and sat down in the little sitting room, which I had made into my own retreat. My books were there and my gramophone. All the things I had amassed over the past ten years, all the things that were precious to me. Not a single one was of any help now. I had absolutely no idea what to do, or who to ask for help. The lodge had no phone, and even if it had I could not have used it. All my communication with the outside world had been through Serena or Colm or the servants. Since Serena died and the remaining servants left, if I needed to contact someone I simply wrote a letter and posted it in the pillar box in the lane by St Anselm's.

Vague ideas of trying to get to the old London house went through my mind, but the house had been rented to some government department during the war, and had stood empty since. And there was another difficulty: it was forty years since I had travelled with Crispian and Gil to Greece and Turkey; since then I had set foot outside the manor's gates only to go as far as the church. I, who had plotted and schemed to control a once-thriving international private bank, had now developed a cottage mentality akin to Saul's and I was afraid of the world beyond the gates.

I can understand now that when they cleared the village they thought they had cleared all the dwellings. Cadence Manor was empty—it had been empty since Serena's death the previous autumn—and I presume, although I can't know for sure, that some sort of compensation had been paid for it. But I don't know who got it. I don't know to whom any letters about the evacuation of the village would have been sent. Certainly not to the manor, nor, of course, to the lodge, which would be assumed empty. The only person who knew Saul and I were here was old Martlet, miles away in London.

But somehow I would have to find the courage to go out of Priors Bramley and find someone to whom I could explain about Saul and me, living at the lodge. The prospect sent the fear scudding across my skin, but it would have to be faced. I would write it down, explain I was disabled from a long-ago accident and unable to speak. Then I would ask for help in getting the two of us clear of the village.

I sat by myself for a long time, working all this out. It was only when I realized it was dark that I came back to a sense of awareness of the world. Saul would be waiting for his supper. He couldn't tell the time, but he knew when we ate.

I put together a meal and carried the tray up to him. He was waiting for me, but he was not at the table by the window as he usually was at mealtimes. He was standing behind the door. I didn't know that, though, and I drew back the bolt, turned the key and went into the room as usual. He leaped out, lifting one hand high over his head and, too late, I saw he was holding the carved wooden box that contained the chessmen. With a cry of triumph, he brought it smashing down on my head. I dodged instinctively, the tray of food crashing to the ground, but I wasn't quick enough and the blow fell on the side of my head. Pain, shot with jagged crimson lights, exploded in my skull, and through it I was aware of Saul laughing. A child's laughter. The laughter of a child who has tricked a grown-up and is delighted with itself. He was never really much more than a child, you see. There was no viciousness in him. I'd like anyone reading this to know that.

As I tumbled into unconsciousness, I was distantly aware that the laughter had been replaced by a different sound. The sound of the door closing, the key turning in the lock and the bolt being shot across. And Saul's scampering feet going down the stairs and outside.

❀ ❀ ❀

I tried the door at once. Of course I did. I shook it and rattled it hard, and banged at the door knob for all I was worth. But the lock on the outside was a very hefty affair indeed—I had made sure of that. And the bolt was the one I had fastened on myself, a thick stout shaft with steel plates holding it in place.

At first I thought Saul was teasing me. I thought he would be sure to come back. He had never been in the outside world on his own and after he got over the first glee of being free he would be bewildered. He would come running back to the safe familiarity of this house.

So I ran cold water in his little bathroom and bathed my head where the blow had fallen. It ached abominably, but that would have to be ignored for the moment. I went to the bigger of the two windows and looked through the bars. Below was the shrubbery and beyond it were the overgrown gardens of the manor and the drive. I could see the front of the manor—I could even see the crumbling pillars flanking the main entrance. But of Saul there was no sign.

I pulled up a chair and sat by the window, watching, waiting for him to come back. It was half-past four, and on an early spring evening it was starting to grow dark. He would come back when darkness started to descend, of course he would.

But he did not.

The night I spent can probably be partly imagined. Not more than partly, though, because I shouldn't think there are many people who suddenly find themselves locked away by a madman, facing the prospect of contamination from a substance containing sulphur mustard.

Sulphur mustard. The words sent my mind back across the years, to when I had lain in the infirmary in

Edirne and heard the screams of the soldiers. I had never seen them, those poor wretches, but I had seen the nurses shuddering and sickened from tending them.

I ate the remains of the food I had prepared for Saul—I even rinsed the plates in the tiny bathroom. Then I lay on his bed, and tried to sleep. He would be back in the morning, hungry and bewildered and contrite.

But he was not.

The day dragged on. I spent most of it at the window, watching for Saul—watching for anyone.

At intervals I returned to attacking the door, trying to work the bolt or the lock loose. All to no avail.

It was midday when I discovered the electricity supply had failed. I suppose it had been disconnected—in fact it was surprising it hadn't failed sooner. It added to my sense of isolation, but looked at sensibly it did not really make much difference to the situation. I had oil lamps and candles that could be used when it got dark.

Towards evening, I considered what I could do if Saul did not return. Surely someone would walk through the village one last time, to make sure no one was here? Could I attract their attention? How? The only sounds I had been able to make for over thirty years were unformed grunts, so ugly I was careful never to utter them. But I might be able to throw something out of the window.

The bars at the window were thick iron, spaced at two-inch intervals and set well away from the glass panes. I couldn't reach the glass with my hands, but if I had something sufficiently long I could jab it between the bars and smash out the glass, a shard at a time. I surveyed the room, and chose a large photograph frame, solid silver, enclosing a faded portrait photo of Serena and Julius. It was thin enough to slot between the bars and the silver should be hard enough to shatter the glass. I removed the photograph and laid the frame on the narrow sill, ready. Then I wrote a careful note, saying I was trapped inside the lodge and please to come inside and up the stairs to unbolt the door. I wrapped it around a small book, which would go in between the bars. Then I placed it on the window ledge, ready. The instant I saw or heard anyone outside, I would smash the glass and throw the book and note out. All I had to do was wait.

❀ ❀ ❀

Seven days. That's how long I've waited now.

My condemned cell has been relatively comfortable. As condemned cells go. The store of food has lasted—I have Serena to thank for that.

At intervals I've tried to break out. I've hammered against the walls for hours on end, hoping to chip out plaster, and I've tried to prise up floorboards, to see if I can get into the rooms beneath. None of it has been any good. Perhaps if there had been implements in this room— hammers or chisels or saws—I might have managed it, but there's nothing.

At first I thought the supply of drinking water might be a problem, and I wondered if I was fated to die from thirst. Be honest, reader, if you had to choose between dying from thirst and dying from having your lungs and your bones burned by chemicals, which would you pick?

But the taps in the bathroom still ran water, and presently I remembered that when the bathroom was created in this room, the workmen put a large water tank on the roof. I have no idea of its capacity, but I remember seeing it manoeuvred into the loft space with considerable difficulty. It must be about three feet cubed, certainly sufficient to hold several dozen gallons. When the tap is turned on, water comes from that storage tank, which is then automatically topped up from the mains. I had to assume the mains had been turned off, but the stored water remained in the tank. I thought as long as I was sparing with it, it would last the week.

I've been sparing. I've drawn a bucket each day, and drunk only as much as I felt was necessary. I've barely washed. Oh God, it's been so reminiscent of Edirne and the siege...except that in Edirne we knew there was more than a fighting chance that we would get out and get back to England.

I've stood at the window for long hours, watching and hoping someone would appear. But the village is silent and deserted. It really is Goldsmith's ravaged landscape gloomed with sorrows, the matted woods where bats cling...

Several times I've glimpsed Saul through the trees, walking along the village street. Each time I've willed him to come back up to the lodge, but he hasn't. There's still time, of course...

I suppose he's sleeping in one of the abandoned houses—that he's found food there. He'll be seeing it as a grand, grown-up adventure. I'm seeing it differently. To me he's the pitiful solitary inhabitant Goldsmith depicted in his fictional village, Auburn. The houseless one, scraping food from the poisoned fields. What does that make me? 'The sad historian of the pensive plain', I suppose.

❈ ❈ ❈

Yesterday I had a brief moment of hope when I remembered the grocery delivery and I stood at the window for hours, ready to smash the glass and throw out the note. But no one came, and I have to assume the delivery people knew about the Geranos experiment and since they had been paid up to date, they assumed the delivery would no longer be required.

Now it's the seventh day. There's a dreadful biblical ring to that, isn't there? It's deathly still everywhere, as if the village is waiting for its fate.

❧ ❧ ❧

A little while ago—just after eleven o'clock—three children came running into the drive, and my heart leaped with hope. I snatched up the silver frame and began smashing it against the larger of the two windows. They must surely hear and look round.

But they did not. They were running quite fast. There were two girls and a boy—I could see that although I couldn't see their faces. They ran along the drive, occasionally glancing over their shoulders, and hesitated at the entrance of the manor. I had broken a small piece of window away by that time, and I was managing to knock out several more splinters of glass. But it was far more difficult than I had expected; the iron bars got in the way and I constantly banged my knuckles against them. My nails were torn and bleeding from the glass, but nails and knuckles heal. Bones and flesh burned by sulphur mustard do not. I continued the task.

Very faintly I heard one of the children cry out, and the three of them went into the manor. I stared in an agony of apprehension, willing them to come out again, wanting them to come back down the drive. It was then that another figure came loping along the drive, a slightly shuffling, shambling gait that I knew. Saul. Saul was going after the children. And the children, it was safe to assume, were frightened of him and had bolted into hiding in the manor.

They might as well have stood on open ground and called to him to come and get them. Saul had grown up in that house; he knew every corner, every stair, every alcove and chimney of it. He would find them. I didn't think he wanted to harm them, but they wouldn't know that. They would only see the lurching walk, the face misshapen and scarred, and they would be terrified. Too terrified, certainly, to notice the puny attempts of a prisoner in the lodge.

As I stood there, the attempts to break the window abandoned, I heard the church clock chiming from St Anselm's. Midday. As the last chime died away there came a sound from above: a soft purring as if some huge invisible animal was approaching. The plane, with its terrible cargo, was heading towards Priors Bramley.

❈ ❈ ❈

I don't know—and I never will—what took place in the manor between those children and Saul. I do know that after a short time there was a vivid flash of colour from the side of the house as the children ran helter-skelter towards the old garden wall. They vanished from my sight, but it didn't take much intelligence to guess they had climbed over the crumbling wall into the lane, and gone across Mordwich Bank.

Of Saul there was no sign. I never saw him again. I never saw anyone again.

❈ ❈ ❈

And so now my story is told.

The plane has flown away and beyond the windows a misty golden dust is billowing everywhere. Where it touches, it leaves an amber glaze. I know it for what it is, of course. I know what it will do to me. What I don't know is how long it will take me to die.

❈ ❈ ❈

The ticking clock that has marked the passing hours over the last week shows that it's seven o'clock.

Normally I would be preparing a meal now, drinking a glass of wine. But half an hour ago my skin began to prickle and burn, and when I looked in the mirror I saw blisters forming on my neck and along my hands and arms.

CHAPTER FORTY-TWO

The Present

JAN CAME OUT of St Anselm's, stopped by the lich-gate, and looked down the village street. There was no sign of the person he and Amy had heard—the person who had given that unmistakable cry of startled fear at hearing the music a few minutes earlier.

He walked towards the village itself, until he could see round the curve in the road, but everywhere looked deserted and whoever they had heard must have gone in the other direction, towards Cadence Manor. Jan looked back at the church. Amy would be out in a minute; she would see him walking up to the manor.

He had thought the police would still be working in the grounds, particularly since that second body had been found, but there was no one around. There were tapes saying 'Police Crime Scene', as there had been at the other end of the village, but that was all. Jan was about to retrace his steps when he saw a blur of movement within the grounds. Had it been someone whisking out of sight? Or only an animal—an inquisitive cat or even a stray dog? He thought the movement had been too big for an animal, though, and he paused, unsure whether to go up to the house. There had been some peculiar things happening around here—the finding of the two bodies and then the murder of that woman Veronica Campion and the arrest of Amy's grandfather. But that cry of fear they had heard surely could not be connected to that. He stepped through the gates and began to walk along the driveway.

Cadence Manor, when he came into full sight of it, really was the forgotten mansion amidst the poisoned fields. Jan found it sad. It was not even the classic ghost-ridden manor; it was simply a derelict house that had outlived its era—that era of weekend parties with elaborate dinners, and of race meetings and shooting parties. Once, thought Jan, people wandered through these gardens on scented summer evenings, carrying drinks onto a terrace, the younger ones giggling in the shrubbery as kisses were snatched. It was a privileged age, as long as you had money. Presumably in those days the Cadences had plenty of money.

Directly ahead was what must be the original main entrance. Jan thought he would take a quick look inside, call out to see if anyone really was here, then go back to the church. He stepped inside, trying to avoid the worst of the damp and the puddles. There were dozens of muddy footprints, presumably from the police and forensic people, but they had dried out. He wondered how far the police had got with their enquiries. And then he saw that there were recent, wet footprints. Someone had come in here within the last few minutes.

Jan called out. 'Hello? Is someone here?' His voice echoed eerily and the words bounced back at him. He tried again. 'Are you in here? I wanted to say sorry if we spooked you with the music in the church.'

There was absolute silence, but Jan had the impression that someone was very close to him, listening, perhaps even watching. He looked round, but nothing moved. Probably whoever he had glimpsed had gone out again. But the footprints went in and did not seem to come out again. They crossed the big hall, and went into a room on the left. Was that where the person was? Perhaps it was a child, frightened by the music, and hiding.

Jan went towards the doorway and called out again. 'Don't be frightened. I only want to reassure you that I'm not a ghost.'

The room was a large one with the remains of tall windows and a French window at the far end. There was a massive fireplace on the inner wall, with a gaping hole where the hearth had been, full of broken bricks. The feeling of being watched increased, but that would be his imagination. As Amy might say, it was pretty spooky in here. And whoever had come in here could have gone out through that opening. He would go back and tell Amy he had not been able to find anyone.

He paused for a moment by the chimney breast, interested in the carvings, wondering if they might once have depicted a family coat of arms and whether Amy would like to see them. As he stood there, from out of the sour dank blackness of the chimney shaft, arms reached out and hands with fingers like steel closed around his neck. Before he could do anything, something came round his throat like a whiplash—something orange and brown and faintly scented—and was jerked tight.

Jan struggled and clawed at the thing round his throat, but his attacker held on. A dreadful pressure began to build up in his head and his lungs felt as if they were being crushed. Crimson-shot darkness closed down on him.

❈ ❈ ❈

As Ella stood up, looking down at the prone body at her feet, she was aware of a soaring triumph. She had done it. Finally and at last she had killed this man who had haunted her dreams, this man who played the threatening music, and who knew all the secrets. She went on looking at him, wanting to prolong the feeling. He was lying face-down in the rubble, his hair tumbled forward. She could not see his face, but she did not need to. He was the man who had stood in this very house and seen her mother kill Serena Cadence. The knowledge that she was finally free of him made her feel light-headed.

Strangling him had been a strange experience. Two things had been in her favour. One was the element of surprise, and the other was that she was wearing the scarf, which she had been able to twist round his neck from behind. He had clawed frantically at the scarf, trying to loosen it, but he had not been able to, and he had gone down as if pole-axed. This was very good indeed; Ella certainly could not have strangled him with her hands, and Veronica's scarf had worked splendidly.

She bent to retrieve it and the memories swirled forward again, because she had had to retrieve a scarf that other time. She had come running through the French windows into this very room to get it because it had her name on it and Mum had said no one must ever know they had been at Cadence Manor today. But *he* had known, this man. He had stood there watching. That was why he had to die.

Ella put her hand up to her head because it was starting to ache dreadfully and she was beginning to feel confused. But the scarf would not give her away today, any more than it had that other time. She put it back on and went out of the house, using the main door. Now she could go home.

As she drew level with the lodge, a faint doubt came into her mind. There was something else she had to do. Someone else she had to deal with. Who? Ella frowned, but could not think who this person might be. Someone who knew something, was it? Yes, there was someone who knew something—who had seen her do something. She went on thinking about this, hardly noticing where she was going, but aware of the shocking state of the manor's grounds. Mum always said the Cadences were irresponsible, though.

As she went back through the old gates, someone came walking towards her—someone vaguely familiar. A girl—a young woman—with a tumble of dark hair, a bit untidy, and an odd set of features, a bit like a cat. Who...? The throbbing pain in Ella's head suddenly cleared and she felt the world wrench itself back into its correct place. Behind her were the ruins of the old manor, and it was derelict because it had been empty for fifty years, the air all round it diseased from Geranos. How could she have been so confused? She had been thinking about her mother and the scarf, and how they had gone home to watch Ella's television serial.

The girl coming towards her was Amy, and she was the one Ella had to deal with next, because she had found those things Ella had buried: the sweater with Veronica's blood on it, and Clem's diaries. *That* was what she had been trying to remember, only the past had become mixed up with the present. But she knew it all quite clearly now and she knew Amy must not be allowed to tell anyone what Ella had buried in the garden.

❀ ❀ ❀

Amy had seen Gran coming from quite a long way off, but she had not immediately recognized her. At first she thought it was a gypsy or a semi-vagrant, someone who had been scavenging through the ruins. This was deeply sad. Amy had a five-pound note in her bag; when the woman got nearer, if she looked really down and out Amy would give her the money. She was not very good at doing that kind of thing and she could not really afford to give away five pounds, but she would mumble something about having had a windfall and please share it with her.

It was a huge and sickening shock to realize suddenly the woman coming towards her—the woman to whom she had been planning to give money—was Gran. Amy stopped dead in the middle of the road. *Was* it Gran, though? It was certainly Gran's waxed jacket, and that was her leather bag slung over one shoulder. For a wild moment Amy wondered if her first assumption had been right, and this was a vagrant who had mugged Gran and stolen all her things. But as the figure came up to her, she saw it really was Gran, although Amy had never seen her like this. Her hair was all over the place and it was powdered with what looked like brick dust. And there was a dreadful look on her face—a kind of mad, staring-eyed look.

Amy managed to say, 'Hi,' in a rather wobbly voice, and Gran came up to her and stopped. Amy saw her dart a look up and down the deserted street. She said, 'Gran, what on earth are you doing out here? Is anything wrong? It's not Gramps, is it?'

'No. I've just been looking round. Interesting to see the place after so long.'

'How did you know I was here?' said Amy, trying to convince herself that Gran was sounding perfectly normal.

'What? Oh, I thought you might have gone down to the Red Lion to find that man you've been seeing. But they thought you might be out here.' She took Amy's arm. 'Let's walk up to the manor before we go home. You've never seen it, have you? It's an interesting old place. And there's a wonderful view from the lodge.'

Amy did not really want to go up to the manor, but Gran was propelling her along, and it seemed better to humour her. As they went, Gran talked, not in her usual way, but in a half-mumble, almost as if she had forgotten

Amy was there. Most of it was inaudible, but once she said, very clearly, 'You have to silence people, you know. It's not always a very nice thing to do, but sometimes it's necessary.' But before Amy could think how to answer this, she said, 'Here's the manor gates,' and they were inside.

'It's a bit sad here, isn't it?' said Amy as they approached the lodge. 'A bit lonely.'

'Yes, but we'll be able to see the whole village from upstairs. We might even see traces of Geranos. It's like amber, you know. A kind of dirty copper glaze. It smothered everything all those years ago.' She did not quite look at Amy. She slewed her eyes round very slowly, then finally focused on the top of Amy's head.

Amy said, 'But have the police finished here? Is it all right to go in?'

'Oh, yes.' Gran pushed open the door and went in, and after a moment of uncertainty, Amy followed her.

It was dim and chilly inside the lodge, but Amy hardly noticed it, because the minute she stepped through the door a wave of such intense unhappiness hit her she flinched. Whoever lived here had been deeply, *deeply*, unhappy. Or was it simply that she knew a dead body had lain here for a great many years?

Gran seemed to be sensing the atmosphere as well, and Amy said, 'Are you all right? You don't look very well.'

'Of course I'm not all right,' said Gran sharply. 'And I shouldn't think I look well at all, with your grandfather in prison for murdering that bitch Veronica Campion.'

Amy was standing just inside the door, in a narrow hall. She forgot about the aching despair in here, and said, 'But we don't believe he really did it, do we?'

Gran had been looking towards a staircase with carved banisters, but when Amy said this, she turned her head very slowly. 'Why don't you believe it?' she said, and as Amy was trying to frame a reply, Gran said, 'You found the things I buried, didn't you?'

Amy was still not exactly frightened but she suddenly had the uncomfortable feeling that the lodge was very remote and very quiet. No, it wasn't so remote at all—Jan was somewhere nearby.

She said, 'What things? Let's walk back to the car and go home and talk about it. There might be some news from the police station.'

'You found the things I buried,' said Gran, as if Amy had not spoken. 'The sweater with that slut's blood on. And the diaries—Clem's diaries with all the things about the past.' She moved back to the doorway, and stood there, blocking the way out. The light was behind her and Amy could no longer see her expression.

After a moment, she said, 'Yes, I did find them. I absolutely wasn't prying, but I saw you bury them. I couldn't sleep that night, so I got up. I know there'll be an ordinary explanation, of course.'

'People always want an explanation,' said Gran. 'That's always the danger. And people remember things. Things they mustn't be allowed to talk about.'

Clearly Gran was having some kind of breakdown or suffering from a nervous reaction to finding Veronica's body and Gramps being arrested. It was hardly surprising. But there was still the question of that sweater and she had just said something about Clem Poulter's diaries...

'It's important to stop them talking, you see, Amy. But I've always been very careful to be considerate. I was even considerate with Veronica...' She seemed to suddenly recollect herself. 'It's Veronica's blood on that sweater I buried,' she said.

Summoning up her courage, Amy said, 'From when Gramps killed her?'

'It served her right,' said Gran. 'Forty-two years of marriage and he goes to bed with my oldest friend.'

'Shouldn't we get back...?' If Gran would only move, Amy could scoot out through the door.

'Let's go upstairs to see the view. I came in here to see it a little while ago. Oh, the stairs are a bit slippy, though, and they're quite steep. You'll need both hands for the banister—put your bag down here. You've still got Derek's camera, I see. It was a very expensive one, so you hadn't better drop it.'

Amy was starting to feel very uneasy, and the last thing she wanted to do was go up the dark stairway, but Gran was still standing in the doorway, so perhaps it would be better to humour her. She slung her bag over the end of the banister and went up the stairs, Gran following. There was a square landing at the top with several doors opening off it. A smeary light came in through the grimy windows, showing the marks of recent footprints, and debris left by their investigations. A coil of tape with 'Police Investigation' on it lay in a corner.

'It's a lot bigger than it looks, isn't it?' said Amy, hoping to strike a down-to-earth note, willing Gran to snap back to her normal self.

'It is, isn't it?' Gran was holding Amy's arm. 'This is the room I told you about.'

Amy said, 'But there's a bolt on the door.'

'Exactly,' said Gran, and gave Amy a push so hard it sent her stumbling forward. She half fell, knocking over an old gramophone, but before she could scramble to her feet, Gran had pushed her flat to the ground and was twisting her hands behind her back and tying something round them. Amy fought and kicked out, but Gran was frighteningly strong.

'It's the camera strap that's round your wrists, in case you wondered,' said Gran. 'I took it out of your bag before I followed you up here. It's leather, so I don't think you'll be able to break it.' She gave a vicious tug to the strap, jerking Amy against the window wall. Amy's shoulder banged against one of the iron bars, and she gasped at the sudden pain. Before she could recover, Gran said, 'I'm looping the strap round one of the bars. I'm wondering whether I ought to gag you as well so you can't shout for help. I don't think anyone will come out here—the police have finished all their investigations—but I don't think I'd better take the chance. I can use my scarf. It was Veronica's, so it won't matter if it's found.'

Trying to sound as normal and as calm as possible, Amy said, 'You don't need to do any of this. Untie me and we'll talk about it. I'd like to hear about everything.'

'Oh, I can't do that,' said Gran at once. 'I can't risk you talking to anyone ever again. You know too much.'

'But you can't leave me here,' said Amy, incredulously.

'I can,' said Gran. 'I don't want to leave you to die if I can help it. Of course not. And if I can think of another way of keeping you quiet, I will. But for the moment you'll have to be kept out of the way. I made sure you left your bag with the phone downstairs, you notice? And I might decide you need to die. I'm not ruling it out. It'll be quick and clean, if so.' But Amy saw the sudden doubt in her eyes.

'Someone will find me,' she said quickly. 'So we'd be much better to go home and sort this out.' Jan will find me, she thought.

'No one will find you,' said Gran, in eerie echo. 'Not now I've killed *him*.'

'Who?' A lurch of new fear jabbed at Amy.

'The man from the church. All these years and he was there all the time. You wouldn't think it was possible, would you? But it's true. He saw what happened when Mother killed Serena Cadence, you see. That's why I had to get rid of him. He might have talked—told what he saw.'

'Your mother killed Serena Cadence?' I'll keep her talking, thought Amy. And she'll see that she's got to release me. 'Tell me about your mother,' she said. 'I never knew her.'

'She didn't mean to kill Serena Cadence,' said Gran. 'It was an accident. But she sat there in a chair, dead, staring at me with dead eyes. And her skin was…there was some sort of disease on her skin. It was terrible. I never forgot how terrible she looked that day.' Her eyes were glazed and staring, as if she was seeing something terrible. '*He* was there as well—he saw it. He could have thought it was deliberate. I was afraid he would tell people my mother was a murderer. They'd have put her in prison—they might even have hanged her. People were still hanged in those days. I couldn't have that.'

'No, of course not. You couldn't have been very old when that happened.'

'I was nine. If my mother had been hanged they'd have put me in Bramley Gate Orphanage,' said Gran. 'Where they put children nobody wants.'

'Awful for you,' said Amy. 'I do understand. Who was the man who saw you?'

'I never knew. I thought I'd killed him, but he's still here. I found that out today. I saw him inside the church. Imagine it, he's been living in this poisoned village all these years. It's extraordinary. That stuff they dropped burned my mother. It scarred her dreadfully, even after just half an hour in the village. It didn't burn *him*, though. I don't understand it.'

The body they found, thought Amy. Oh God, that's who she's talking about.

'I heard him a while ago, playing his music in the church,' said Gran. 'That's how I knew he was still alive. So I hid in the manor. That's what we did all those years ago, Clem and Veronica and me.' Incredibly and eerily there was a faint childlike note to her voice now. 'We thought we'd be safe in there, but we weren't. He came looking for us that day. He came looking for me today, as well—I saw him come out of the church.'

'Gran, that wasn't your man, that was Jan Malik! I was there with him.'

'No, it couldn't have been. Because of the music, you see. That other time when he came after me, I pushed him and he fell. But I really have killed him this time. I strangled him with Veronica's scarf.'

Amy's mind was tumbling in horrified disbelief. She had not sorted out all the threads of this mad narrative, but one thing stood out starkly and clearly: Gran had heard the music Jan had tried to play on the dead church organ, and somehow linked it to a man she had killed fifty years ago. And so she had killed again, identifying him with the same man—the man who had seen her mother cause Lady Cadence's death. Amy felt a bleak cold despair close over her at the possibility of Jan being dead, and for a dreadful moment she did not care if Gran left her here to die or not.

'And now,' said Gran, 'I think I had better gag you.'

Amy discovered she did care about living after all. She fought for all she was worth, kicking and writhing, but she was hampered by having her hands tied behind her back, and also—she had not bargained for this—she was hampered by it being Gran she was fighting. But in the end the scarf was over her mouth and knotted at the back of her head. It felt soft and light and it had a faint expensive scent in it. But it stopped her from making any sound.

Gran stepped back and considered her handiwork, then nodded to herself, and went across the room. The door slammed shut and Amy heard the bolt slide home. For a moment there was silence, but Amy could sense that Gran was still there. Was she considering whether she was doing the right thing? Would she come back and free Amy?

Then there was the sound of Gran's footsteps crossing the landing and going back down the stairs. Silence closed down over the old lodge.

❀ ❀ ❀

Jan came back to consciousness slowly and painfully. At first he was not sure where he was—it seemed to be somewhere shadowy and dank-smelling—and it felt as if a thick band was clamped around his throat and his chest.

Memory began to trickle back in little threads. He was in Priors Bramley and he had gone into the old manor house, hoping to find the person who had been outside the church so he could explain about the music. There had been muddy footprints, which he had followed, and then hands, impossibly strong, had clutched at his neck and wound something around it, pulling it tight. A scarf? Yes, there had been a glimpse of orange and brown. He remembered struggling and trying to tear it off, then he thought he had passed out, presumably from lack of oxygen. So what had happened to the assailant? Had he panicked, or had he assumed Jan to be dead and run off? Jan got cautiously to his feet, wincing as a jag of pain went through his throat. For a few moments the floor tilted, but he held on to a piece of masonry and waited, and the dizziness passed. Had he been mugged? But when he felt for his wallet it was still there, and so too, when he checked, were his money and credit cards.

A different fear suddenly rushed in. Whoever had attacked him might have run back to the village, and Amy was still there. Would she be in danger? He felt in his pocket for his phone. He had no idea how much time had passed since his attack, but he could call 999 right away and the police would come straight out. He was still feeling light-headed and infuriatingly weak, but he would worry about that when he had made sure help was on the way and Amy was all right.

The phone was not in his pocket. It was not in any of his pockets. Jan checked them all again, then looked around him, hoping it had slid out when he was attacked, but it was nowhere to be seen. He frowned, then another memory came back. His phone was in his briefcase, still in St. Anselm's. Then there was nothing for it but to get back there as quickly as possible, and trust to all the gods at once that he would not meet his attacker a second time, and above all that the attacker would not meet Amy.

Infuriatingly, the dizziness was still with him, and every step he took needed a huge effort. Jan got as far as the hall and paused, gasping for breath, his chest and throat feeling as if they had been scoured. But he managed to get outside, and the fresher air cleared his head slightly. He stood for a moment, considering what to do, then began to walk down the drive to the gates. It took an immense effort. His legs felt as if lead weights hung from them, and his throat was still raw.

He could see the gates, rusted and brown with age, but tiny glints of their original gilt were catching the watery sunlight. To the right was the old lodge house. Jan summoned all his strength and began to walk down the drive. He had no idea which way his attacker had gone, and he had no idea, either, where Amy would be. He reached the gates, paused for a few moments, then forced himself to begin walking down the road to the church.

❀ ❀ ❀

The lodge house was the eeriest place Amy had ever known. Several times she thought she heard soft footsteps approaching and hope bounded up, before she realized it was only the old roof creaking, or the drip of water somewhere after the rainstorm. Once something scrabbled over her head, then there was a light beating of wings beyond the bars of the window. The aching loneliness she had sensed earlier seemed to press in on her, and she had the feeling that invisible hands reached out, begging for help...

And if she was going to let herself start imagining *that* kind of thing, she would end up a gibbering maniac and she would never get out! Gran would come back quite soon, and this would all turn out to be a gigantic mistake. But then Amy remembered how Gran had talked about a woman sitting dead in a chair, staring out of a diseased face, about how Gran had said she killed some man when she was a child. She had said it quite clearly: she had killed him then and she had killed him again today. Oh Jan, thought Amy. Don't be dead. Please don't be dead.

At intervals she pulled against the leather camera strap for all she was worth, but it held firm and all that happened was that she rubbed what felt like yards of skin off her wrists and made her bruised shoulder hurt even more fiercely. Then she tried to shout through the gag, but all that came out were strangled grunts, which sounded so eerie in the silent room she gave up.

After this she tried to dislodge the gag, but it was tied too tightly and after several attempts shreds of silk got between her teeth and made her splutter. Spluttering against the gag made her feel sick so Amy gave that up as well.

She sat down on the ground, her back to the barred window, and looked about her. The room was a large one and it looked as if the police had been in here as well. A modern torch lay on top of a big old-fashioned desk, and in one corner was an open case containing what Amy thought were forensic brushes and tweezers. Hope surged up, because if police equipment had been left behind, surely someone would come back to get it? But when would that be? It might be days.

The room looked as if it had been comfortably furnished. There were pictures and mirrors on the wall, a large deep settee, a bed with cushions, and several easy chairs. Beneath the other window—which was as firmly barred—was a drop-leaf table. On one side of the fireplace were shelves with books, and on the other side was a neat stack of old vinyl records. Amy began to get a picture of someone living here, someone who had liked books and music—yes, there was the old wind-up gramophone—and who had eaten meals at the table, perhaps looking out over the drive. But why the bars and the bolt on the door? Was this where the body had lain all these years? That was a pretty spooky idea. It was even spookier to think Amy's body might soon lie here as well. But it would not happen, of course. Gran was just trying to frighten her into keeping quiet about finding the bloodstained sweater. This last thought sounded so ridiculously like the title of a 1930s crime book, Amy tried to put it out of her mind.

The camera strap stretched far enough for her to stand up, lean over the deep window sill and see down into the ruined grounds. Would she be able to attract the attention of anyone who came along? She was just wondering if she could reach the desk and somehow hurl something through the window, when there was a movement beyond the bushes, and with a massive rush of relief she saw Jan coming out of the manor. For a wild moment she did not think: he'll get me out of here, but: he's not dead.

Shouting was impossible, but she might bang against the bars to attract his attention. She tried to reach the sill with her foot, but it was quite a high sill and she only got her foot partway up. In any case she was wearing trainers, which would not make much sound against the iron bars. But there must be something she could do that he would hear, there *must*...

Her eyes fell on the old gramophone lying near to her feet. Could it possibly be wound up? Could she manage to do it with her hands tied behind her back? Incredibly, there was a record on it. Amy could see the label, and although it was faded and age-spotted, it was still readable: 'The Deserted Village by John William Glover'. John William, thought Amy, I think you might be about to save my life.

❀ ❀ ❀

Jan had gone about thirty yards along the road when, from within the tanglewood grounds of the old manor, he heard a sound so uncanny his skin prickled with horror.

Music. Elusive and blurred, as if it was struggling to make itself heard, or as if it was coming from a very long way off. It was as if cobweb strands of the past were trying to weave themselves into a pattern, and Jan stood very still, an icy finger seeming to trace a pattern down his spine. Somewhere in this sad lonely place, someone was summoning up the echoes of music written more than a hundred years ago—music that was now virtually forgotten and almost lost. *The Deserted Village.*

Then his mind snapped back on track, and he realized the music was coming from the lodge, and that it was cracked and difficult because it was being played on an old gramophone. But by who? His attacker? Jan was still light-headed from being half strangled: he was not sure he was in any shape to cope with those strangler's hands a second time. But supposing the strangler had got Amy in there? How long would it take him to get to the church and his phone, and to summon the police. Ten minutes? Perhaps another ten for the police to get here? Much too long.

He went doggedly back through the gates, and into the lodge. He was starting to feel as if he might have fallen into a nightmare without noticing. The music was louder now, and there was a banging from upstairs, as if somebody might be kicking a piece of furniture. It was then that he saw Amy's tote bag looped over the banister. He forgot about being light-headed and went up the stairs two at a time.

He had no idea what he was going to find in the bolted room, and he was totally unprepared for the sight of Amy in an awkward huddle by an ancient gramophone, her hands tied behind her back, a scarf wound over her mouth. He was even more unprepared for the wave of emotion that swamped him.

The record came to the end and the needle scratched against nothing, maddeningly and rhythmically. Jan did not even notice it. He was tearing the scarf away from Amy's mouth, and dragging at the leather strap binding her wrists.

Gasping explanations showered over him. 'I couldn't think how else to make you hear,' said Amy. 'I think I might have pulled both shoulders out of their sockets, but I managed to wind the thing up. And—'

It was at this point that Jan pulled her into his arms and kissed her. Her shoulders did not appear to be out of their sockets at all, because her arms came round him and she clung to him as if she would never let him go.

CHAPTER FORTY-THREE

'I'M AFRAID,' SAID the CID inspector, facing Amy, Jan and Derek Haywood in the warm, safe sitting room, 'I'm very much afraid that your wife, sir, was responsible for Veronica Campion's death.'

Amy had known someone was going to say this sooner or later, and she thought she was prepared for it. She was not, of course. The words were like blows. But if it was bad for her, it must be agony for Gramps. She looked anxiously at him, and thought that although he had looked pale when he was brought home from the police station, now he looked grey.

But he said, 'I do realize that, Inspector. Was it because...' He glanced at Amy, then said, 'because Veronica and I had been such close friends?'

'Not entirely,' said the inspector, and Amy was deeply grateful to him because Gramps instantly looked better. 'It's difficult to piece it all together,' he said, 'but going on what Miss Haywood told us...He looked across at Amy as if checking she was happy for him to go on. Amy nodded, and he said, 'We think your wife was somehow involved in the death of one—perhaps both— of the bodies at Cadence Manor. And that she was afraid of something coming out about it that would incriminate her.'

'But those bodies had been down there for fifty years, hadn't they?' said Jan. 'She'd only have been a child.'

'She was ten when the village was closed,' said Gramps unexpectedly. 'That's not so very young.'

'Indeed not,' said the inspector. 'And if Mrs Campion knew something—was threatening to talk...They were old schoolfriends, remember.'

'Did you ever find evidence to identify either of the bodies?' asked Amy.

'Nothing to speak of. We did find a watch that looks relatively modern, but there's no means of knowing who it belonged to. Forensics think it was gold-plated but the gold's almost entirely worn away, so any surface marks have gone.'

'Will my wife be charged with any of this?' asked Gramps. 'With Veronica's death or the attack on Amy or Dr Malik?'

'We're still compiling medical reports, psychiatric assessments, but—I'd say it's out of the question.'

'She's not fit—not mentally fit to stand trial?' Again Gramps seemed able to face these dreadful facts.

The inspector said, 'She has no memory of what happened. The psychiatrists don't think she's faking that. They think she's somehow closed off all those acts. I don't pretend to understand their terms of reference, but they've talked about denial of something traumatic—something in her childhood, they think.'

Something in her childhood. I know what it was, thought Amy. Serena Cadence, staring with dead eyes out of a diseased face...She shuddered, then said, 'Gran talked about a man who had seen her mother commit a murder— well, not commit it exactly, but cause a death. She thought her mother might go to prison or even hang, so she killed him to stop him talking about it. But when she heard the music in the old church—'

'That was me,' said Jan.

'Yes, when she heard that, she thought that man wasn't dead after all.'

'And tried to kill him again,' said the inspector, nodding. 'Yes, that's what we've put together. But when I tried to question her, she seemed to shut down.'

'What will happen?' asked Amy.

'I don't know. But it's unlikely she'll be allowed into the world again.'

Broadmoor, thought Amy, in horror. Or a place like Broadmoor. An asylum for the criminally insane. Gramps will never bear it.

But he surprised again. 'Can I see her?' he said.

'Better not, sir. Not for a while, at any rate.'

After the inspector had gone, Jan got up to follow him, but Gramps, glancing at Amy, said, 'Would you like to stay to supper, Dr Malik?'

'I'd be intruding,' said Jan. 'You've got all kinds of family things to cope with and talk about.'

'I don't know about intrude,' said Gramps. 'You seem to have been pulled into most of it already. You'd be very welcome,' he added, and Amy thought he sounded a bit wistful. 'It'll only be something simple, of course.'

'Simple is fine,' said Jan. 'If you're sure it's no trouble I'd like to stay a bit longer. Thank you.'

'No,' said Gramps, leaning forward. 'Thank *you.*'

'For staying to supper?'

'For saving Amy.'

There was a sudden silence. Then Jan reached out to take Amy's hand. 'She's worth saving,' he said.

❀ ❀ ❀

After Jan had gone, Gramps came into the kitchen to help Amy with the washing up. Amy could not ever remember him doing this before.

As they put the plates away, she said, 'I keep thinking I'm going to wake up and it'll have been a nightmare.'

'So do I,' he said. 'Is that everything done now? Good. Let's have a brandy.'

When the brandy was poured, he said, 'Amy, I'm sorry you had to find out about Veronica. I was trying to regain my vanishing youth, I suppose. Silly old fool, aren't I?'

'No,' said Amy at once.

'I've only got a few years to go at the office, you see. I'd been dreading retiring.'

'Did Gran know you were dreading it?'

'Oh, no,' he said at once. 'She thought retirement was something people should look forward to. She didn't understand about the loss of the companionship you get in an office, or the loss of—of purpose and usefulness.' There was a faint rueful smile, a ghost of his usual one. 'To call my work useful is glossing it,' said Gramps. 'A local authority auditor doesn't exactly save the world or make people's lives easier. Not like the kind of work your father does, for instance. But it provides a service, you know. It makes sure things are being run honestly and fairly.'

'I know that,' said Amy. 'And you'll find other things to do when you retire.' She had half expected him to add something like: 'Your grandmother was always a bit odd.' Or, 'I saw the signs of something wrong years ago.' But he did not. He was loyal to her in his way, dear Gramps. Amy thought one day they would be able to talk about Gran properly, but for the moment Gramps seemed to find it easier to focus on the practicalities.

He drank some more of the brandy, then suddenly said, 'I like your academic.'

'He's not mine.'

'I think he'd like to be.'

'He's probably got a wife back in Oxford,' mumbled Amy.

'He hasn't.'

'How d'you know?'

'I asked him.'

Oh God, Gramps had done the Victorian what-are-your-intentions thing with Jan, and Jan would have been hugely embarrassed, just as Amy was now hugely embarrassed, although it did not matter because now she would never see Jan again.

'I was very tactful,' Gramps said. 'I just asked if he would have to go back to Oxford soon, to be with his family.'

'You said that?' This did not sound so bad after all. 'What did he say?'

'That he only had a sister and some nephews. And that he had no intention of going back until he was sure you were all right. That's your Cheshire-cat smile,' he said as a grin broke on Amy's face.

'I shouldn't be smiling at anything at the moment, what with Gran and all. Gramps, about that—she'll be in some kind of—um—institution, won't she?'

He had been staring into his brandy, but he looked up. 'Oh yes,' he said. 'I think we can be sure about that.'

'It's awful,' said Amy.

'Yes, but it's not Ella any longer, you know. Not my Ella, the girl I married.'

This was so unbearably sad that Amy had to fight back tears. She stared into her own brandy, and eventually managed to say, 'But an institution—an asylum...Gramps, it'll be dreadful for her.'

'She killed at least two people,' he said. 'She was probably going to kill you.'

'But it wasn't the real Gran,' said Amy a bit desperately. 'You've just said that. Or didn't you mean it?'

'I did mean it.' He reached out to take her hand. 'Amy, I think she'll cope in a way you and I can't understand,' he said. 'When I look back, I can see all the times when she twisted situations so that they looked how she wanted them to look.'

'Lied to herself about them?'

'No, she doesn't lie, exactly. But she twists things around and forces them into a shape that's satisfactory to her. She'll do that with this place where they've put her. She'll mould it into some form she can accept.'

❀ ❀ ❀

Ella quite understood she had to stay in this hospital place for a while. They had explained it all to her. A sickness, they had said, and she rather had the impression that they regarded her as an unusual case. That meant it was important to give them all the help she could. One heard of case studies being done, research, articles in the *Lancet*.

When they questioned her, she admitted to headaches and some confusion. It was a curious confusion, though; almost as if she lost long spells of time—hours and hours or even as much as a whole day. When she tried to remember what had happened during these lost times, there was only a jumble, a messy darkness threaded with faint echoes of music, and with people who stared out of dead, open eyes...

She told them all this, because if they were studying her case they would need to know everything. They wrote things down and nodded, and occasionally gave her pills.

What she did not say to them—although she might do so later—was that although the staff seemed excellent, she was not overly impressed with the actual hospital. Several times she wondered why Derek had paid all those private-patient-plan subscriptions over the years if it was not to make use of them now. She would ask about that when Derek came to see her.

But she had to say this was a somewhat old-fashioned set-up, what with the faded curtains and old-fashioned bathrooms. A few coats of emulsion would not have hurt the walls, either. Even so, Ella slept very soundly each night, and during the day it was remarkably easy to blot out the bleak rooms and echoing corridors, and the sound of doors being locked.

'We have to lock the doors,' they told her. 'To keep everyone safe.'

Ella said she quite understood that; there were so many wild people about today. It was the parents' fault. Young people were not taught standards, not like she had been.

One of the doctors talked to her about Priors Bramley. He seemed very interested in it. She had been there recently, hadn't she? he said. Ella said, no, she had not been to Priors Bramley since she was ten years old. She had gone there with her friends, Veronica and Clement, and the three of them had walked along the village street on the day it was to be closed.

He was interested in Veronica and Clem, so Ella told him all about them. How they were good friends, all three of them; they had been so from their schooldays, in fact. They would certainly be coming to visit her, she said. Veronica would no doubt try to flirt with the doctors a bit, but that was just her way. She would be very smart, they would all admire her clothes and jewellery. Clem would be interested in the old building and ask about its history. He liked history.

Ella told the doctors and nurses to be sure to let her know the minute Veronica and Clem arrived. And her family, of course. Her son was working abroad, but Derek would come and probably their granddaughter, Amy. They would all like Amy, said Ella proudly. She was a lovely girl, so intelligent. She and Ella were very close.

She took the pills they gave her and looked forward happily to the visits of Derek and Amy, and her dear good friends, Veronica and Clem.

Final Entry in Jamie Cadence's Journal

I don't think I can write much more. There's a dreadful searing pain over most of my body, and I can feel it eating down and down into my flesh. Oh God, this is dreadful...

But I'll manage to finish this last page, I think. I shall sign it, then put the papers in the desk drawer. I don't know if they'll ever be found. I don't know if one day—years ahead in the future—people might walk through Priors Bramley again, and see the ruined old manor house and perhaps wonder about its history and the people who lived here.

The people who lived here...

They're all gone now. Serena and Julius, Crispian and Gil. Colm and old Dr Martlet and the Flaggs. They're all entombed in the urns and sepulchres of mortality. Who wrote or said that? I've forgotten, if I ever knew. I think it must have been somebody who mourned the passing of England's great houses. Cadence Manor wasn't a great house, but in the main it was a good one. Except for that seed of disease that came into the family with my mother and destroyed us all.

I'm finding it more and more difficult to breathe, and my lungs feel as if they're on fire. Moments earlier I heard dreadful formless screams and my heart leaped with hope because I thought someone was at hand—someone who would rescue me. But then I understood that of course it's my own screams I'm hearing.

It's mid-afternoon—the ticking clock tells me that and I think my mind is becoming affected, because a little while ago I thought I heard voices outside, as if someone might have come into the manor grounds and gone across the kitchen garden. I tried to get to the window to see, but I can no longer stand upright. But even if entire armies marched across the old gardens I couldn't call out to them.

Three days ago I found the old wind-up gramophone in the back of a cupboard. It's one I bought in the 1920s, and put away when I got a better, electricity-driven one. But after the power failed I was glad of something to drive back the silence.

I'm trying to do that now. I've played several pieces, but today I've played the music that always meant so much to me, *The Deserted Village*. If ever there was a prophetic piece of music, it's that. It's the music I shall hear as I die.

I believe I'll die soon now—I hope so. The pain is becoming worse now, and I can barely breathe.

I wonder if these pages will ever be found. I hope so. I'd like those people of the future to know my story.

The Present

The young man from the forensics department investigating the Cadence Manor bodies passed the autopsy to his inspector.

'Cause of death for both bodies,' he said. 'The Cadence Manor chap had a broken neck. I'd say a straightforward fall from the upper floor.'

'Ah. Well, that's as we thought. And the one we found inside the lodge?'

'A bit more complicated, sir. As you know, it was found seated at the desk in that upstairs room. We haven't found conclusive proof, but there're indications of chemical burns on the surface of some of the bones.'

'That stuff they dropped on the village in the 1950s?'

'That's the conclusion. It's our guess he was some sort of recluse and had no idea what was happening outside. If he was trapped in that room—'

'Yes, I see. It's a pity,' said the inspector, 'that those papers in the desk were so badly affected by the Geranos.'

'We got the first sentence, sir. But it doesn't tell us anything.'

'What did it say?'

'"The time has come when I will have to do something." That was all that was legible.'

'What a pity,' said the inspector. 'It would have been interesting to know who that man was.'

AUTHOR'S NOTE

England has many 'lost' villages—remote pockets that once were thriving communities, but that, for widely different reasons, now lie dead and silent, as if preserved beneath dusty amber glazes.

In the main, they were lost to the laws of enclosure, to coastal erosion or monastic depopulation. But there are also plague villages, wiped out by the Black Death, villages—sometimes entire towns—drowned by the creation of reservoirs, rural communities and hamlets abandoned for no known or discoverable reason. Sadly, the histories and even the names of many of these have been lost, and all that remain are earthworks and perhaps a lonely church.

But there are also places that have been the subject of strange, even macabre, experiments. Gruinard Island—the 'anthrax isle' in the Scottish Highlands—sealed off from the world for almost half a century. Places such as Porton Down and Sellafield whose sometimes-contentious, occasionally-mysterious, research has become uneasily etched onto the fabric of England's lore.

Priors Bramley is fictional. But its counterpart can be found in more than one village in England.